A LIFETIME WAITING FOR ETERNITY

A LIFETIME WAITING FOR ETERNITY

BY KLEY V

To Dad . . .

. . . say hello to Ely

CHAPTER 1

ELY

That scent . . . the fresh perfume of Dead Sea salts mixed with that particular floral aroma that I loved so much. The glowing natural light of the candles against the glossy walls, the dancing vapor leaving the water's surface, the warm feeling around my body, the weightless sensation of floating in hot water, everything added up to create the perfect setting for my mind to drift away. I was ready for my private spa experience, one of two indulgences that I allowed myself.

I was living the perfect life. A beautiful house, a job I enjoyed, a loving husband, and good health. What else could I ask for? What Rob had been picking up on wasn't anxiety about moving. I was afraid. Afraid that so much perfection couldn't last forever.

But that was nonsense. I was happy, and that was what mattered. I couldn't imagine a better way to start our life in the new house. I realized I'd better keep my mind on the following day's experiment. If I was right, it was going to be a great day.

"Ely, darling. Dinner's ready."

His words echoed far away in the background. I checked my watch. I had slept for almost an hour without realizing it. A delicious aroma was wafting up from downstairs. Dinner was definitely served.

I didn't want to make him wait, so I put on my bathrobe and walked downstairs barefoot, drying my hair with a towel. From the staircase, I noticed a warm light reflected on the dining room wall. I knew that song playing in the background, Michael E's "Precious Jewel."

"What's this?" I asked.

"A special occasion deserves a special celebration," he said with a seductive smile.

He had prepared a Michelin-star truffle mushroom tagliatelle. The wine, an Italian Barolo. I had no idea where he found that wine—it certainly wasn't among the couple of dozen bottles that we'd packed. He must have been planning the dinner for a while. It was a perfect treat for my tastes.

"You shouldn't spoil me like this. I could get used to it."

"Spoil you? If I were Emperor Jahan, the Taj Mahal would have your name on it."

"Well, if that's the case, I suggest you begin collecting as much white marble as you can."

We smiled and kissed each other. It might sound silly, but these little exchanges made every day special.

He removed the cork, cleaned the bottle's throat, and poured the wine.

"To our new home."

"Each object . . ." I looked at the light reflecting on the wine for a moment. "All that stuff we put in boxes, every single item has found its own place in this new house. Everything adds its bit to create that harmonious ambience that I like so much, don't you think?"

"Yes, everything's so perfectly placed that they've become invisible. Look, I never realized we still had our Julia Child. And that coffee machine? I thought we'd gotten rid of that years ago."

I took a sip, ignoring him.

"Look around, Ely. You've put everything exactly where it was in the other house."

He was right. Unconsciously, I had reproduced our old house, right down to the knickknacks on the end tables.

"Well," I said, "it doesn't look bad, does it?"

"I don't know about you, but we're moving house. It should be the start of a new phase in our lives."

"Give me time to get used to it. You know me. I don't like change. If it were up to me, I'd live in the same house forever."

"OK, but you can't deny this house is spacious and much more comfortable. Look at the kitchen, twice the size of our last one."

"It's big and beautiful, but you can't deny that the tiny kitchen was also cute, and it was equipped with everything."

"I know you miss it, but you'll see, Ely. You'll feel at home soon." He poured a bit more wine. "By the way, don't you think we should start giving some of our things away? This could be the perfect time."

"You must be joking," I said, digging into the pasta. "Everything has a meaning for us." A lot of the stuff around us might have seemed useless, but it all represented a bridge to our past.

"In any case," I said, "if you want to get rid of stuff, why don't you start with yours? There's a box of sci-fi novels back there that you haven't opened for a while."

He laughed. "You like your stuff very much, don't you?"

"So now it's *my* stuff! You're the one who remembers how, when, where, and why we got every piece."

"Ely, let's be realistic. We managed to fill the old one-bedroom house in ten years. How long do you think it will take us to fill this new three-bedroom house?"

"Maybe another ten years. No, twelve—we've got an attic now." We smiled at each other.

We kept talking throughout dinner. He picked out different objects to give away. He knew I would never agree to any of them, but it was good mental exercise. It also showed that I was the one who remembered the stories behind each object, even though he was the one who had bought most of them. They were the physi-

9

cal evidence of him spoiling me in every possible way.

After we drank our last glass of wine, we cleared the table. I started washing the dishes, singing my favorite song, "Italian Song" by Vangelis. He sat down again, listening. I knew he loved it when I sang that song. When I finished, I turned around.

"Rob, I have to wake up early tomorrow. Should we go to bed?"

He gave me a playful look. "After you."

That night we made love with a passion that I had never experienced before. We became one soul.

Rob was right. It was an excellent fresh start.

CHAPTER 2

ROB

A distant whispering woke me up.

"Rob, darling."

"What?"

"It's ten past eight. We're late."

Ely's voice snapped me out of my dream. I felt as heavy as a rock. The sunlight slipping through the gaps in the blinds looked like seagulls on the walls. Without looking outside, I knew it was a beautiful day. If it were up to me, I would have remained in bed until midday.

She kissed me and then got up. "Move, move, my sweetie bear."

"I didn't hear the alarm."

"That's because it didn't ring."

She got the bathroom first. She needed to get ready quickly; she had an experiment scheduled for that day. A team from MIT would be there to observe. It was an important day for her.

Still feeling a bit dozy, I went down to the kitchen to make breakfast. It was a slack day for me at the office. I didn't have any important meetings to do, so I left the car for her and planned to take the train.

I was setting the table for breakfast when she entered the kitchen.

"No sweet dreams last night?" I asked.

"I need to get used to the house. And you?"

"Like a bear in its cave. You know me; I can sleep standing up."

"Lucky you. I tossed and turned all night, waking up every single sound. Smells good. Thank you. That's what I need."

She downed a cup of coffee and then prepared to leave.

"What about your toast?" I asked. "Don't tell me you're leaving without breakfast."

"Sorry, darling, but I'm in a hurry. I don't want to be late in front of all these people."

She scooped up her handbag. "I forgot some papers in the studio. Would you mind . . ."

"Sure. I'll get them."

I ran to the studio and looked for them on the table. So much stuff.

"They're on the sofa, in a pink plastic folder!" she said.

Perfect. I found them right where she said. When I returned with the papers, she gave me a kiss, then went to the door and stopped, her hand on the doorknob. "You know, Rob, I have a feeling that today is going to be a long day. I'll call you if I have to stay late."

"No problem. I'll take care of dinner. Good luck."

"I almost forgot, I left a sticky note on the fridge with a list of things we need to buy at the supermarket. Love you."

That was the woman I loved. Always taking care of everything.

"Love you too," I said.

That morning she was happy, very happy. Seeing her like that just a couple of days after we moved in was enough to make me happy too. She was looking forward to this experiment, something to do with a relativistic collider, and I was looking forward to settling into our new house.

I was just finishing my coffee when I heard an explosion outside followed by the sound of shattering glass. I ran to the window.

It took me a moment to recognize the tangled metal strewn across the front yard. I tore out of the house, fast, desperately fast.

CHAPTER 3

ELY

W hat's going on? I was trembling. It felt like a shiver going from my chest to my feet. I had no idea where I was.
I remembered the sound of sirens, voices—Rob's voice among them—but nothing else.

My body was relaxed, calm, placid despite my being unable to move any part of it or feel any sensation on my skin. I couldn't see or hear anything. I thought for a moment that I had been anesthetized, but if that were the case, why was I conscious? Maybe I wasn't, and this was a dream that I wouldn't remember after waking up. Except that I was awake and perfectly aware of what was happening.

"Can anybody hear me?"

I didn't hear anything. I wasn't even sure if I had said anything.

I remained calm, but after a while of being immobilized in

the dark, I became bored. Then impatient. Claustrophobic.

I was just beginning to feel overwhelmed when I felt a strange tickling on my feet, like they were trying to levitate. I noticed my hands doing the same. It was like I had balloons tied to my legs and arms, pulling them up, as if they were trying to lift my body off the bed. I tried to fold my arms, but I had no control over my muscles.

Then, like a rope snapping under tension, I felt released. I could finally move. But it was still like moving in a place without gravity.

My vision returned gradually. I looked around and saw some medical equipment being taken out by a couple of nurses. So, I was definitely in a hospital. I must admit I was frightened when I saw myself beneath . . . myself, levitating off the bed. But I realized immediately what was going on. I was in a deep sleep and having the most bizarre dream of my life.

I was close to the ceiling when I saw the two nurses leaving the room with the medical equipment.

Was this really a dream? If not, then what? Was I experiencing one of those out-of-body experiences that some people talked about? In any case, being aware of what was happening wasn't helping much.

I started spinning, flying out of control, heading straight for a wall. I braced for impact. But then I felt . . . nothing. I opened my eyes, and I was in the corridor outside my room. I had just passed through the wall!

Then the two emergency doors at the end of the corridor opened. It was Rob.

"Ely! Ely! Where are you?" he said, desperately checking several rooms.

He ran toward where I was and then stopped in front of the room door.

"Rob, I'm here!"

He didn't respond.

I followed him with my eyes, which, apparently, I could still move. He fell on his knees. Why had he done that? Why was he crying?

15

"Sir, let me take care of you," one of the nurses said while helping him stand.

I continued moving across the corridor, then through another wall. I was drifting like a feather on a soft breeze, and nothing was getting in my way.

Then something grabbed my hand and stopped me from spinning.

"Who's there?" I shouted.

"OK, sweetheart, your first lesson is going to be control. Otherwise, you're going to fly away like a balloon."

The voice was very familiar . . .

"Grandma?"

"It's strange, isn't it? The first time you experience this weightlessness sensation. But it's no big deal; you'll get used to it."

What kind of conversation was this? I remembered having many dreams that involved my grandparents since Grandma passed away more than ten years ago. I figured this could be one more. I was probably lying on a hospital bed suffering from traumatic shock.

Right?

"Ely, listen carefully. I'm here to help you."

"Help? I just need to wake up from this dream." I was worried about Rob. He seemed so distressed. I had to tell him that I was fine.

"No worries. You'll see him soon. Now, I need you to keep your mind focused on me. Trust your grandma, and come with me."

How did she know I was thinking about Rob? While I was still trying to puzzle that out, she took my hands and slowly pulled me toward the door. I didn't know what to do. Should I push her away? How could I do that? She was my Grandma . . . wasn't she?

"Look at me. Get rid of these thoughts, and keep your sight fixed on me."

I saw Grandma going through the door. Then everything around me faded away.

CHAPTER 4

ELY

We were in a meadow full of wildflowers. It was a quiet place. Not a blade of grass was moving. It felt so peaceful.

Except . . .

"Grandma, where are we? And how did we get here? We were just at the hospital—"

"Hush, child. Isn't it beautiful? This is the place where we receive our family newcomers. It's where we give them our welcome."

"Welcome? Newcomers? Who and what are you talking about?"

"One question at a time, darling. Do you remember the accident?"

I discovered the memory was much clearer than it had been. "I was leaving the house when a car hit me. Why do you ask?"

"Well, sweetheart, that's why you're here with me."

"What are you talking about? Right now I'm at the hospital with Rob."

"And yet here you are, talking to your grandma, who died many years ago."

"I've dreamed of you often enough in the past, you and Grandpa. This must be another of my dreams."

"I wish it were."

"I heard the sirens, cars. Rob was talking to me. Everything was vivid, intense . . . real."

She gestured around her. "And this isn't?"

"No. I told you, it's a dream."

She remained silent with a sorrowful look in her eyes. Could it be possible? No, this was worse than a nightmare. I was getting scared, and the only thing I wanted was to wake up.

"You won't wake up, honey. You're not sleeping."

"Stop reading my mind!"

I looked around, searching desperately for a way to escape. I couldn't conceive of the possibility that it could be true.

"Ely, listen—"

"Stay away from me!"

I tried to run away but instead spun out of control.

Before Grandma could move, two soft hands helped me regain control. A moment later I found myself surrounded by people.

"My little baby."

That sweet voice . . . Mom, Dad! Without a thought, I threw myself into their arms. I hugged them both with all my strength. For a moment I didn't care if it was a dream. I was finally with them.

"I've missed you so much," I whispered.

"Shush. You don't have to say anything, sweetheart." Mom said.

"We've never left you, my little girl," Dad added in a tender voice. "We've always been beside you."

"Elizabeth, it's me."

I turned around, and there they were. The family I had missed for so long.

"Grandpa, I'm so happy to see you. Uncle John, Aunt Mary, you're all here . . . and well."

I was wrong. How could this be a nightmare if I was surrounded by loved ones? I wanted to give myself to them, but I couldn't allow myself to indulge the illusion. No matter how much I wished it was real, I knew it was a dream.

"Mom, Dad, what is this? Why are you all here?"

"That's a little tricky," Dad said. "Sometimes things happen for reasons that we don't understand."

"No, it's all of you who don't understand. Rob and I are happy together. We just moved into a new house. We have plans. Don't you see? I can't be here. It's just not right."

"Sooner or later we all have to come here," Grandma said. "It's the natural order."

"But I have to live my life first. That's the natural order too."

"This is still part of your life," Mom said. "Ely, we have so many things to show you."

I needed to stop this. I had to think logically. I needed to find something that would bring me back to reality. There had to be some kind of inconsistency, incongruence, something that would help me realize this was all just my mind's creation.

"Please wait a second. How is it possible that you look like the photo I have at home? Mom, you died fifteen years ago! You haven't aged at all. You're all dead. It doesn't make sense."

Mom shook her head and smiled sadly. "Darling, you've always been very inquisitive, so difficult to convince."

"Much like your grandmother," my grandpa said proudly.

"I'm a scientist, remember?"

"We know where your love for science comes from," Mom said. "That's why we've chosen your grandma to be your mentor."

"Mentor?" I remembered my tutor when I was a student but now . . .

"That's the way it's been done since the beginning. One generation helping the next," Dad said. "There are many things that don't make sense to you now. Grandma will help you with the transition, make things easier for you to accept. You literally have eternity to understand and get used to things. But right now it's important that you know you're not alone. We're all here with you."

I didn't know what sort of game my mind was playing with me, making me argue with the most important people in my life. But I decided to go with it. What harm was there in that? I felt safe and protected around them. Looking at my family gathered together, I thought it wouldn't be too bad if all of this were real.

"Sweetheart," my father said, "we know how overwhelming this is. But you don't have to do anything now. Just relax and come with us. We'd like you to meet other members of our family, earlier generations who would love to meet you."

Dad took the lead. Grandma came closer and took my hand while smiling at me. As we started moving across the garden, I remembered how Rob looked when he came into the room. That's when I realized I had to stop this crazy but lovely dream.

"Grandma, I can't stay here. I need to see Rob."

"You're right, but first things first. I'm sure you'll feel much better when you see him. Come, I'll take you to him."

As my vision grew blurry, I heard Dad's voice fading away in the background. "I hope he'll help her realize we're not a dream."

CHAPTER 5
ROB

Days, weeks, maybe months had passed since Ely . . . since my life stopped.

It was early in the morning of another dateless day. Every day was the same, with no memory of what I had done the day before. I closed my eyes. Her smooth hair, her almond-shaped eyes, her faint smile and light, ladylike snore. I could sit for hours remembering her, drawing her face in my mind, down to the finest details. It didn't matter how many years we had been together; every day at her side was a gift.

I was tempted to stay in bed all day, but I made an effort to get up. On the way to the bathroom, I looked at a photo on the dressing table that I had always loved. We were so young then. Everything was ahead of us . . .

"Good times, weren't they?"

I thought she was still asleep.

"Yes, they were. Do you remember how old we were when your father took this?"

"Six, maybe seven." She smiled as if remembering something.

"What?"

"Nothing."

"Come on, tell me."

"You know, the only clear memories I have from that time are those with you in them. You definitely impressed that young girl."

"Did I? I thought she was more interested in my handyman skills."

"Handyman? No way. I liked to watch your face every time I decided to add another floor. You never got used to seeing them collapsing, no matter how many times we did it."

It was true. I used to be very disappointed when, after hours of playing with wooden bricks in her house, the structure collapsed because Ely wanted to add another floor. But I thought I had been better at hiding it from her. "So you knew."

"Of course, and let me tell you, I haven't changed a bit. We have to fill another twenty boxes, and this time we're truly going to test your handyman abilities. Let's see how much stuff you can put inside, and I hope this time you won't be disappointed if they break."

I tripped over a couple of boxes still left in the corridor since the day we moved in. I should have taken them to the garage, but I didn't feel like doing anything, worrying about anything. I didn't feel like . . . anything.

I stopped to look at my reflection in the bedroom mirror. What was happening to me?

All my emotions had disappeared, even the most basic ones. My heart was still beating, and my lungs were still breathing, but everything else inside me had dried out. Like a hollow tree, I looked normal from the outside, but inside I was little more than sawdust and rot. And I didn't know how to turn my life around, to do anything except spend the next sixty years waiting for the end.

I swiped my tablet and saw a message on the bottom of the screen. Oh no, more emails, still with messages of condolence.

Everybody kept telling me the same thing: "You have to move on," which was exactly what I had been doing . . . moving from one place to another, from one day to the next, like a boat adrift in the ocean, constantly in motion but without any clear heading.

I didn't want to show my real feelings to them. They would think I was facing my loss with an unbearable pain, grief, and depression. But I wasn't feeling that.

Was it normal?

I guessed every person mourned in a different way. At the beginning I thought I was lucky because I wasn't crying all the time. Now I wasn't so sure. Every day without her was like a single drop of water falling on my forehead, slowly but unstoppably driving me insane. My lifeless existence had become the worst torture I could have ever imagined.

"Why? Why?"

I couldn't understand why she left in that way. All our plans were undone. There was no way I could make sense of what had happened.

I opened the blinds. The sunlight illuminated the room for the first time in days. Since our childhood she had stood there, always shining on the paths I took, giving me the strength and the reason for everything I had done. Now that she was gone, darkness was all around me. How could I have gotten closer to her? How could I have loved her more? How could I have held her longer? How was I going to live without her?

I realized I was in the kitchen. It had to be time to make breakfast. I could smell coffee—I must have already made it. I turned around to pick up a cup.

"Oh ma la oh oh me giova oh,
pe dolae già po va po;
e sha me co oh me gioma ah,
pæ dü le pa tus dac. . ."

"Italian Song," her favorite song to sing while making coffee in the mornings. I enjoyed listening to her voice so much. Unconsciously, I'd put two cups on the table. That was my everyday

23

life, doing things as if she were still with me.

I opened my office email on the tablet while having my coffee. No news on the few projects that I was still following from home.

The TV was on in the background bringing other voices into the house. "This morning, another suicide victim was found dead in the river. The body of a middle-aged woman appeared to . . ."

I didn't have much to do today, so I went upstairs to move the two boxes left in the corridor to the garage. One of them was broken, so I lifted it carefully when I recognized one of Ely's old photo albums inside. I couldn't help myself. I sat on the floor, opened the first one, and let my memories carry me away.

It was incredible how tiny she was when she was born. Her head in one photo was so small compared to her Mom's hand. If I remembered well, she weighed about five pounds. Her parents were still young at that time, and yet they didn't have any more kids. I never understood why.

Ah, her first birthday party. She used to say it as one of the biggest birthday parties she had in her life. She probably spent most of the time sleeping, but it didn't matter. The party wasn't really for her. I looked at her dad. He was so happy showing off his little daughter. Her grandparents were more than willing too. What nice photos.

And there we were—I think it was the first photo of us together. We were about eighteen months old. My parents had just moved from California to the house next to hers. It was a surprise when my parents met hers and realized their babies had been born on the same date. From then on, our families became inseparable.

It was clear that I had taken the next photo—Ely and her parents after the school karate championship. Half of their bodies were out of the frame, and Ely was tilted to the left with the sun over her shoulder. She was a mess, but it was still a good job for a ten-year-old boy. The photo had had a special meaning for her. It was the last photo taken with her Mom and Dad. A few days later, they were killed in an accident on their way to a conference in Montreal. She still missed them.

Her parents took her to my house before they left that weekend. I don't know what I would have done if they would have taken her on that trip.

After the accident, her grandparents moved into her house, partly because they didn't have room for a growing teen but mostly so she could spend more time with my family. By then my parents were like parents to her.

I took special care of her. Since that sad day, I'd never left her alone. I knew we were too young, but I believed deep inside that we were already in love.

The other album covered our high school graduation. Once again, we were together everywhere. Her grandma had arranged a nice celebration, invited all our friends and their families. That period was tough for Ely. Her grandpa had passed away the year before, and her grandma joined him six months after graduation. She was left completely alone, but I was there, always beside her like her personal sun trying to shine on her path through those gloomy years.

The doorbell brought me back. I wasn't feeling like visitors, so I didn't answer.

"I know you're in there! I can hear the TV. Open the door, Robert."

It was Peter, an old friend—he had gone to college with Ely. Now he was working in the same research center but in a different area: fluid dynamics.

I made a huge effort to get up. It felt like I'd been sitting there for ages. I walked downstairs toward the door as if I were dragging a boulder. I opened the door slowly, but he pushed his way into the living room.

"I've been leaving messages, and you haven't been answering them. Where have you been, man?"

I walked to the sofa and fell back onto it. "Here and there."

He glanced around. "The house looks like a war zone. This coffee smells terrible. When was the last time you made yourself a fresh pot?"

That was right. I had made that coffee some days ago, maybe the previous week, I didn't remember.

I tried to say something that would change the subject from

25

my current lifestyle. The last thing I wanted to hear was some-body telling me what to do. "Don't tell me you changed your job," I said, "and now you've become a homme de ménage."

"Rob, look at how you're living. You have to move on."

When would people stop saying that? I could still hear Ely's voice waking me up on weekends. "You can't sleep all day, my sweet little bear. Get up, move, move . . ." Even a single word was enough to open the door to the past. Not that I minded getting lost in memory. It was the only way I could still hear her, see her . . . be with her.

"Hey, hello, are you still there?"

I didn't want Peter to see the world in which I was spending most of my time. "Everything is fine," I said. "As well as can be ex-pected." I wanted to change the subject, but I couldn't hide what I was feeling. My voice was not steady enough.

"It's not, and you know it."

"Listen—"

"No, you listen to me. I've tried to support you, and I'm pre-pared to do whatever I can to help you rebuild your life. But no matter how much I try, you keep pushing me out of your life. I'm not going to sit by and watch you slowly detach from reality until one day I won't be able to reach you anymore."

I couldn't deny anything. It was all true. But how could I open myself to share my feelings and still keep myself together? I knew he wanted to help me, but I was so fragile that even the smallest help would do more harm than good. He wouldn't un-derstand that thought.

"I need time; that's all."

"You don't get it, do you? It's not a question of time. You get worse every day. Just look around you. This isn't you."

Even though I didn't want him to get too close to me, I could tell he was sincere, and it touched me.

"If you really want to help, then just . . . sit quietly next to me. Ely and I have always considered you our best friend. I know I can count on you. Believe me, that's all I need right now."

To my surprise, he cleared space on the couch and sat down.

I'm not sure how long we sat together in silence, but it made me feel better. I think.

"Now tell me," I said finally, "what brings you here?"

"The center called again. They're waiting for you to go and collect Ely's stuff."

He had mentioned it . . . was it two weeks ago? Ely had been very popular among her colleagues, but I was in no condition to see them. Too many condolences would overwhelm me.

"I told you already, I'm not interested in visiting the center."

"I know. But they still need you to go and sign some documents. They're not allowed to get rid of one of their member's things. This is going to be hard for you, but you have to do it. I already arranged for the HR staff to put all of Ely's personal things in one place. You can go in and out and not see anyone."

"Please, Peter, it's just papers."

"Some of them may be important papers. I helped them organize everything into boxes. It won't take much time."

It looked like I couldn't escape from this. And I did owe Peter that much.

"OK, I'll go."

"I'll be there waiting for you."

"Thank you, Peter. I think I'm going to need an extra hand to carry Ely's things." That was not the real reason why I needed him. I knew I would fall apart if I had to walk through Ely's office alone.

"Good! What about tomorrow afternoon?"

"Four o'clock?"

"Great. See you there. And listen, like it or not, I'm hiring a professional cleaning service to help you with the house."

"In your dreams. Bye, Peter, and close the door when you leave."

He was such a practical person. Maybe that was a requirement to be a scientist. I was sure his groundedness would help me a lot the following day.

I stared out the window. I felt better when I concentrated on something in the distance. I imagined Ely coming to me. My thoughts drifted away as my eyes closed . . .

"Ely, do you want cream and sugar?"

No answer. Maybe she hadn't heard me. It didn't matter. I always brought her a cup of coffee with cream and sugar, when she was enjoying the sunshine in the garden. I opened the back door and saw her playing with kids, lots of kids. I turned around and realized our house was in the middle of a school playground. She began to walk toward the swimming pool, waving for me to join her.

"I know I've been away for a while," she said when I got close to her, "but don't worry; I'm fine. It's you who I'm worried about."

Then I heard a big airplane passing just above us. We ran and jumped into the swimming pool, just managing to get underwater as pieces of flaming metal fell into the pool. Ely was smiling beside me. Why wasn't she worried about the airplane? Or about breathing? I started to feel the need for oxygen. As I swam toward the surface, I heard a siren. Ely was no longer beside me. I turned back and realized she was beneath me, waving.

Waving goodbye.

I held out my hand, but she just sank deeper.

"No, no I can't, I can't leave her down here no . . . no . . ."

I rolled off the couch and managed to pull myself up enough to look at the clock. It was 7:33 in the morning. I had slept the whole night.

I stood there, trying to shake off the mix of happiness and despair that came with dreams of Ely. As I began preparing myself for another lifeless day, I couldn't help but wonder where those dreams were taking me.

CHAPTER 6

ELY

I didn't remember how many conferences I had attended, but I did remember the way I could never bear the idea of being away from Rob. I could usually convince him to join me, but when his work made that impossible, I would call him every day, sometimes several times a day. I never thought things could turn around so much that I would find it painfully difficult to be with him.

Several weeks had passed. I'd been at his side all the time, watching him slowly fall apart, incapable of doing anything about it. It was the helplessness that made everything so painful. I was there, right beside him, and still he couldn't see me, couldn't hear me, couldn't feel me.

He went to bed. I laid down beside him until he fell asleep. The movement of his eyes, the rhythm of his breathing, the funny, kitten-like sounds he made when he dreamed . . . I loved it.

Apparently, I no longer needed to sleep, so after he drifted off, I moved up among the clouds, the place of my childhood dreams. When I was a kid, I used to picture myself surrounded happily by clouds made of fluffy white cotton candy. Being able to float around clouds reminded me of those times of innocence, simplicity, and unconditional acceptance, something that I was no longer capable of. Rob was now my only concern. Everything else was simply irrelevant.

Dawn was the sign that it was time to go back to Rob. I missed not waking to the sounds of birds singing or even the alarm clock. I used to love that seductive sensation of warmth just after waking up, when the warm sheets invited me to stay in bed just a bit longer. All gone.

Rob got up early. The previous night he hadn't been able to fall asleep, and that had taken its toll in the morning.

"Good morning, my darling," I said. "It was one of those nights, wasn't it? It doesn't matter though. Today is a beautiful day. Come and see this gorgeous dawn." Talking to him made me feel like we were still together. What a silly idea.

I went to the kitchen and mimicked cooking his breakfast. Even though during the week we were always in a hurry, we still had time to have a nice hot mug of coffee with milk accompanied by toast, butter, and jam. In the meantime, the TV was on, so we could hear the morning news in the background. Those moments together were priceless.

The last few weeks had been very revealing. I had discovered so much about Rob by truly paying attention to him. There was no noise, no pressure, no worries, nothing to distract me from him. Tasks as simple and trivial as making coffee gave me new insights into his feelings. Two spoons of sugar was a sign that he was feeling down. Drinking with closed eyes meant he was remembering something he had dreamt. Two consecutive sips meant he was nervous. A blank stare while mixing the coffee meant he was thinking of me.

After a while Rob came into the kitchen. He didn't make any fresh coffee, just took what was left over from the previous day's breakfast. He walked toward the sofa with his cup half empty.

Work, traffic, meetings, just excuses. I regretted not having pushed those things away and given him the attention he deserved. It would have made my life a hundred times more meaningful and much more enjoyable. Now the only remaining part of our glorious breakfasts was the TV.

I felt somebody was coming—Peter, good old Peter. I was so thankful to him for taking care of Rob. I hoped someday I would be able to tell him personally.

Peter was saying something about the state of the house. I looked around and realized for the first time the squalor in which Rob was living. How could I not have noticed? Rob was worse than I thought, worse than I was prepared to accept.

I sat down and listened to their conversation. I wished there was a way to tell Rob that I was listening to him.

"What? Please don't tell me he has to go to my office," I said to Peter.

"Yes, you're right, my dear," I said to Rob. "It's going to be very difficult. But don't worry. I'll go with you."

It was a short visit. After Peter left, Rob went back to the armchair. He stared out the window. I placed myself in front of his eyes once again with the silly hope that somehow he could see me. It didn't matter how long it took; I'd be him until his last day.

After a while he fell asleep. I sat beside him as I used to do and laid my head on his shoulder. He moved as if he were going to take me in his arms. I wondered if it would have been different if we had family. At least with a child, he would have had a reason to keep his life moving, but after the airplane accident, everything changed.

It was night again when I felt somebody coming. "Grandma! It's good to see you."

"Ely, we need to talk. I want you to come with me."

"Sorry, Grandma, I can't leave Rob."

"He's sleeping; he isn't going anywhere."

"But—"

"I'm not asking."

I had never heard Grandma talk like that. She had a sad ex-

31

pression on her face. It had to be something serious to worry her like that.

She took my hands. The surroundings changed as we started moving. I was still amazed by how easily I moved through walls. It would take me some time to get used to that.

CHAPTER 7

ELY

Moving through walls still made me dizzy, and this time was no exception. It always seemed as if I were going to crash. I guessed practice would take care of that.

We stopped in an old house. The furniture looked hauntingly familiar. It felt like home.

"It's good to be back, isn't it? I miss it so much."

"Where are we, Grandma?"

"We're in my house—well, it was my house."

Of course. I had moved in with my grandparents for a few weeks just after Mom and Dad passed away. It still had that charming atmosphere I loved so much. The furniture was a mix of much-beloved family heirlooms—a polished dining room set from the 1930s, a marble-topped Victorian table—mixed with carefully selected modern pieces. Or they were modern at the time I was there. Everything seemed unchanged, even after so many years.

Before I could ask what was going on, Grandma spoke. "Ely, we're very worried about you."

"Worried? Why?"

"Be honest with me. Don't you think it's . . . unusual that you're still alive after your death? Most people are shocked by that. Making sense of what happened becomes their first priority. But you . . . you haven't shown even the tiniest interest in learning what happened. Since you arrived, your only concern has been Robert."

"Is there a problem with that? I just want to be with him."

"Please, Ely, don't get me wrong. Being with Robert is fine— necessary, actually. What worries us is that you're interested in him to the exclusion of everything else. I might be able to understand that attitude with an ordinary person, but for a scientist like you . . . it's just not normal."

I shrugged. "I'm worried about him. He's taken everything very badly. I couldn't bear the idea that something bad could happen to him."

"I understand, Ely, but you can't stay with him all the time. It's not good for him, and it's not good for you. You have to overcome your fear of leaving him in order to embrace your new life. It might sound harsh, but that's what I think."

"Grandma, don't you see? I caused everything he's going through. I did this to him. I should have looked both ways that day when I left the house."

"Ely . . . one of the easiest ways to handle grief is to blame yourself. In that way, you find a quick answer to why it happened. Believe me, it wasn't your fault. You must be strong to face that."

I didn't argue. I couldn't. She was right. I was afraid to face my own guilt. And I couldn't be sure I had been responsible. The other driver, well, he had been moving so fast that it might have been impossible to get out of his way. Grandma's eyes told me that she understood my feelings.

"I don't want to leave him," I said. "I didn't do it when I came here, and I won't do it now. I'm going to be with him for as long as he needs me."

"It won't help him. It's not helping him. You can't change what happened, but you can still change his future. What will you do if, when the time comes for him, he asks you the questions you're not asking now? Where he is, why he's still alive. What will you say? You'll be the one helping him through his transition."

"Me?"

"Yes. You'll be his mentor."

I hadn't expected that.

"It's been decided," Grandma said. "There's no other person here as close to him as you, so you have to be prepared. And the sooner you get ready, the better."

"Grandma, please, don't you see? How can I help Rob if it's been so difficult for me?"

"That's exactly why you've been chosen. He has to learn to live without you, just as you have to learn to live without him. At least for the time being."

Grandma's words shocked me but not for the reason she thought. She was right about how my attention was devoted only to him. But above all, she spotted how little I understood my new . . . situation. I was afraid of losing him, as if I were still with him. But I had already lost him—or, rather, he had lost me.

Being ready for him meant only one thing though: we were going to be together again. That meant that, in some sense, I had never left him. Our separation was just momentary, and he would be with me soon. A selfish thought, I suppose. I was essentially wishing for his death. But I wasn't ashamed. I couldn't live without him, and there was nothing I could do about it.

"You're giving me a big responsibility," I said.

"Don't worry; you'll do fine. We've all been there, sweetheart, as students and teachers. Nobody can go through the transition without help, and by accepting that help, we also receive training. Mentoring the future mentors. The way I'm here for you, you'll be there for him. No worries; you'll be ready."

"One generation helping the next."

She nodded.

Her words worked. There was no time for self-pity. If it was my job to prepare everything for Rob's arrival, I had some work to do.

Now that I thought back on it, what had happened to me? I used to think there was nothing more exciting than understanding the unknown. Now everything around me was unknown, and I had people happy to explain it. The curiosity and wonder that had inspired me to become a scientist was starting to wake up. I wanted to know . . . everything.

Grandma smiled. Of course, she had been reading my thoughts.

"All right," I said. "Where do we start?"

"Slow down; we've still got time. First, you need to master the basics."

"The basics?"

"When you were born, you spent years learning to control your body. You had to wait two years to begin to walk and three years to articulate your first sentence. Now you have a different body, no longer moved by bones and muscles but by your mind. You can't control your new body unless you have a disciplined mind. So, your first lesson will be to control your thoughts."

"Like a rebirth?"

"Exactly. You've noticed how I always take your hand to move from place to place, haven't you?"

"Now that you mention it, why do you do that?"

"Because you still haven't learned to walk in this world. You remember the first time at the clinic when you spun around, out of control? Again, lack of mind control and focus. We move at light speed, and if you don't have good concentration, you can end up far away in a hurry."

"Wait, wait, wait. Light speed?"

"Naturally. We don't have mass."

"OK, sorry, Grandma, I . . . I don't think I can control something that I don't understand. You said I have to start with the basics. Well, tell me first, how can I still see you without eyes? Am I sensing light somehow?"

"Well, I hope you have an open mind." She sat down on the sofa and gestured for me to sit next to her. "Your eyes were designed to capture light. If you saw a red box, it was because the red wavelength was reflected while the other wavelengths were absorbed."

"Grandma, I studied this at secondary school. Please . . ." Sometimes I forgot that I was twelve years old when she left me.

"OK, but don't ask me to repeat myself." She still had that tough way of dealing with students, which had made her such a good teacher. "Your eyes were the only part of the body sensitive to light. Now your entire body senses light."

"Like the way I used to sense hot and cold through my skin?"

"Exactly. The molecules in your skin were reacting to increased vibration of the molecules around you. Now your body reacts to different wavelengths."

A body that could see through the skin? I held onto the sofa, which felt surprisingly solid. "So what happened with my other senses? Can I still taste or smell?"

"Not really. But you're not going to need those senses anymore. You don't have to eat here. Your body is its own perpetual source of energy. Isn't that amazing, darling?"

Or depressing. Not only would I miss food, having a body that was a perpetual motion machine meant I could toss out the conservation of energy and the law of entropy. It looked like everything I had studied was useless.

"OK, Grandma, no food, fine. No fragrances, also fine. All logical things for a massless body. But how can I still talk, think, move . . . it doesn't make sense. Please tell me what happened."

She slid closer to me on the sofa and took my hand with such sweetness that it made the question irrelevant. "Nothing out of ordinary, sweetheart. You still have your body. It's just . . . different. It takes some time to get used to it. We're all like you."

"Yes, but how does it work? How does it cohere? What rules does it work by?"

"Darling, I thought I could help you understand this world, but I can see now that as a scientist you need different explanations than I can give. Come on; it's time to meet a friend of mine."

She stood up and extended her hand. As soon as I took it,

37

we started moving. As we got closer to the wall, I couldn't help thinking about what she had just said: I still had a body.

We passed through the wall as if it weren't there. And in some sense, I suppose it wasn't.

CHAPTER 8

ELY

In the blink of an eye, I found myself in the main hall of a library—dizzy, of course. The building was deserted. We walked through the reading room and into the stacks, packed with books behind gorgeous, glass-fronted bookcases. Suddenly, I realized I couldn't smell the much-beloved old library smell—leather, dust, furniture polish, and accumulated wisdom. I was in a different world, and I was suddenly more curious than ever.

All the corridors were alike, empty. Grandma was in front of me, silent, concentrated on her own thoughts. Maybe I'd been too harsh, expecting too much from her. I should have been more considerate and gone somewhere else to find the answers. Except that I couldn't move on my own.

"Grandma, what do people do inside libraries?" I asked, trying to make conversation.

"Ely, do you think people's natures change when they pass

away? People who were interested in how the world behaves are now interested in how the afterlife world behaves."

"Are you saying that people still do research on the afterlife?"

"Sort of." She laughed. "We're nearly to someone who can explain everything you want to know. When you meet him, feel free to ask him anything you want."

We entered into the cosmology section. I saw two people on small chairs wearing wool suits with a cut that looked about a century old. They were discussing some strange hyper thing. Like my grandmother's home, they were very familiar. It couldn't be!

"Hi, gentlemen," Grandma said. "I hope I'm not interrupting anything important."

One of the men, with slicked-back hair, a long face, and thick lips, rose and gave her a hug. "Dear Beth, it's a real pleasure to see you again." Then he looked me up and down. "Tell me, who is this young lady?"

"Allow me to introduce my granddaughter, Elizabeth. Ely this is—"

"Niels Bohr. I know. You're . . . you're the father of atomic theory. You figured out how it all worked." It was him! One of the most prominent minds of the twentieth century.

He gestured around him. "Perhaps less so than you think. Certainly less so than I thought."

"It's a tremendous pleasure to meet you," I said.

"No, the pleasure is mine." But he shook his head as if that weren't true. "If you'll forgive me, you're very young. Too young to be here, I think."

"Well, Niels, that's why we came to see you," my grandmother said. "It was an accident that brought Ely to us."

Mr. Bohr's face sagged. "I'm so sorry to hear that."

"I'm her tutor. I've been trying to explain her new situation, but she's a scientist —"

"A scientist?" For the first time, Mr. Bohr put a soft smile on his face. "Explaining the afterlife to a scientist. A tough task, isn't it?"

Grandma nodded. "She keeps asking questions that go beyond my knowledge. I need your help."

40

"Of course. It will be an honor to help your granddaughter."
He turned to me. "Young lady, you can stay with us for as long as you want." With a smooth movement of his hand, he invited me to sit in one of the chairs. I was not used to this formal politeness, but I loved it. It reminded me of a BBC costume drama—like something out of Jane Austen.

"Thank you." I turned around to ask Grandma to join us, but she was already gone. The other person to whom Mr. Bohr had been talking had also disappeared.

"So, young lady, here we are," he said. "Tell me exactly where you'd like to start."

Since my first day at university, I had fantasized about meeting famous scientists of the past. I used to imagine myself in the classroom listening to their lectures. Now that I was in front of one of them though, I was speechless.

"Don't be shy," he said. "I'm a good friend of your grandmother's. I'm here to help you. Tell me what you'd like to know."

"Well, Mr. Bohr – Dr. Bohr--"

"Please, call me Niels."

"Dr. Niels . . ."

He smiled.

"Sorry, Niels." I took what felt like a deep breath and managed to get some control over my nervousness. "I'm . . . dead, it seems. So how can I still see you, hear you, talk to you?" The more I talked, the more I found my confidence. "No eyes, no ears, no mouth . . . and yet, here we are."

"Elizabeth—"

"Please, call me Ely."

"OK, Ely. You're not asking the right questions. I'll never forget what my good friend Dorothea said: a problem clearly stated is a problem half solved."

Dorothea? Dorothea Brande? No way. That would be impossible. Or maybe not.

"Anyway, you need to start with more basic issues that underlie your apparent access to senses that you no longer have."

"So, which basic questions am I supposed to ask first?"

"Calm down, Ely. There won't be a quiz."

Wow. I had just met him, and I was already snapping at him. I hoped we could write it off to nervousness. Anyway, it looked like people there could read my feelings. I'd have to be more careful how I chose my words. "I'm sorry."

"No worries. Come, let's take a walk."

We strolled around the library, which was dotted with comfortable-looking overstuffed chairs—which I realized must not exist in some sense.

"What if we start talking about . . ." He looked straight into my eyes. It was like he was looking inside me. And maybe he was. "Well . . . where we are, and let's leave what you've become for later."

Apparently, once he had decided on the best way forward, he didn't look back. His voice became steady and strong, as if he'd explained this many times before. "We're used to our three-dimensional world, and some physicists manage to think in terms of four dimensions. However, the space we know is only part of a much larger whole expanding over many more dimensions."

"How is that possible? We've never detected these extra dimensions before."

"Haven't we? Have you ever seen what attracts two magnets to each other?"

"Magnetism?" We'd known how magnetism worked since Maxwell. Why was he mentioning it now?

"Yes, and we thought we knew how gravity worked after Newton, until Einstein came along and rewrote our understanding of it. So, have you ever seen a magnetic field?"

I had no idea what point he was trying to make. Under normal circumstances, I would have walked away. But these weren't normal circumstances, and he wasn't a normal person—that is, meeting him was far from normal.

"I guess no, I haven't held a magnetic field in my hands," I said, "if that's what you mean."

"That's right. That's because what we call a magnetic field exists in one of these extra dimensions. You can see the effect of the magnetic field, but you can't see the field itself because it's tangential to our reality." He paused for a moment. I couldn't hide my incredulity. "We interpret a higher-dimension phenomenon as if it were happening in four-dimensional space, but Ely, don't feel shocked. It's understandable."

"Understandable? Fine, but there's no scientific evidence that proves what you're saying is true."

"And yet, here you are."

"I . . . all right, good point."

"Imagine an iceberg moving in the ocean. Now let's assume that the only thing you can see is the tip of the iceberg. The ocean and the space below its surface are completely undetectable. How could you explain the tip's movement? Well, you would develop the concept of the ocean field. You would argue that the interaction of this ocean field with the tip of the iceberg generates a force that moves the tip along the field lines—the ocean currents."

"But what you call the ocean field is just the underwater currents pushing the bottom of the iceberg. They exist."

"Of course they do, just as magnetic fields exist. My point is that we locate them in the wrong place. Because we only see the tip of the iceberg moving around, we interpret the ocean currents as a force field located above the surface, but in reality, it lies below the surface. We think the magnetic field exists in the usual three-dimensional space, but it actually exists in another dimension, the Magnetic Dimension."

"I guess the electric field is in the same dimension?"

He nodded. "The evidence has always been around us, but we didn't want to see these extra-dimensional manifestations."

I remained silent. What kind of question could I ask when nothing made sense?

"And that takes us to your question about how you can still see," he said. "That question drives you mad, doesn't it?"

"See, feel, hear. I like my senses, but I'd like to know I can trust them."

"Well, first of all, you have to break with the old conception that dimensions only define empty spaces in which objects exist, like the 3D world that essentially defines an empty space containing energy and matter. There are dimensions full of stillness and vibration, movement, and repose."

43

"This is starting to sound like the luminous ether."

"You can call it that if you want. The fact is, non-empty dimensions exist, and the Magnetic Dimension is one of them. You can see because you are now sensitive to the trace formed by light moving through the Magnetic Dimension. Think about light or photons as a boat. When a boat moves, it pushes the water aside, forming characteristic V-shaped waves. What you see is not the photon—as in the case of your physical eyes—but the trace it leaves behind when it passes through the Magnetic Dimension's quantum vacuum. The bigger the trace, the greater the light's intensity. The faster the trace moves, the higher the light's frequency."

"OK . . ."

"How is it going so far? Are you following me?"

"Not exactly." In fact, I was desolate. How could I accept his explanation? It seemed that my understanding of the world, which I'd invested most of my life developing, was wrong in just about every major respect.

"Ely," Neils said gently, "most people don't care much about the reason behind things. They just move on with their lives in the last world and in this one. But you, you're different. You're looking for explanations that you will not find unless you try to break with your past understanding. It's full of assumptions that are not entirely true. I know it may sound contradictory, but if you want to understand what's going on with your new life, you have to believe first. Explanations come later."

"It's not a question of believing. Everything you say is so . . . strange. It turns everything I know—everything I thought I knew—upside down."

"I had the same problem. I think Albert put it best: no problem can be solved from the same level of consciousness that created it. You have to literally forget the references you learned and move to a new level of consciousness."

"Excuse me, do you mean Albert Einstein?"

He nodded. "You can meet him later. For now, let's try a different, more experimental approach. Let me show you something."

Without warning, he disappeared and then reappeared on

my right side.

"You see?" he said. "If you want to move in this world, you simply think it, and it happens. Or . . ."

He disappeared entirely. I spun around, looking for him.

"And yet," he said, his voice seeming to come from everywhere—or perhaps somewhere inside of me, "I'm still here."

He reappeared. "Voila. You see what a trained mind can do in this world?"

"That's so cool!" I said. "Can you teach me how to make whatever I think of?"

"Ely, you must listen more carefully. I didn't say 'make,' I said 'do.' You can't create things just by thinking about them, even in this world. But you can do things with your mind that you weren't able to do before."

"Sorry . . . you're right."

"Don't be sorry. This isn't easy. It was difficult for me to get used to the idea that almost everything I had worked for, the important things in my life . . . well, I may as well have been studying phlogiston."

He paused as if remembering something. "Anyway, the next lesson is matter. You have to accept the idea that matter is no longer important."

"Not important? How could you say that? Everything is made of matter."

"You're not, and neither am I."

I looked down at my body. I couldn't get past the thought that if I wasn't made of matter, I didn't exist.

"Think about it as a train," Niels said. "A train can only move on rails, right? Well, that's exactly what happened to us and our massy bodies. When we're tied to our bodies with inertial mass, we're tied to three-dimensional space just like a train is constrained to move only on rails. During your transition to this world, you leave your body behind in the material world the way a passenger leaves the train behind when he arrives at his or her destination."

At least we were talking about something familiar, trains. "Why is that?" I asked. "What prevents us from moving beyond three-dimensional space? If you changed the train's wheels, it could move anywhere, like a car. So, what is it? A force?"

His expression told me that I was asking the right questions. "Your grandmother was right; nothing escapes your sight. No, it's not a force. It's the nature of matter itself. We have discovered that matter, specifically the Higgs boson, is a property of three-dimensional space, just as magnetism is a property of the Magnetic Dimension. In other words, objects with mass can only exist in the space that we know because mass is an intrinsic aspect of that space."

His calmness and serenity scared me. He was assuming—wrongly, of course—that because I was a scientist, these things wouldn't shock me. "OK, I get it, at least the 3D part. But please, Dr. Bohr—I mean Niels—you talk as if this situation were normal, but it's not. I'm dead and—"

"Stop!" He stood up and walked around the library room. "We need to clear up that misconception. No, Ely, you're not dead. We're having this conversation because you're still alive."

He calmed a bit and took my hands in his. "You have to expand your concept of life. When you study living organisms within these extra dimensions, life takes on a completely different meaning. We have discovered that living organisms have a kind of special energy associated with being alive: soul energy. Rocks, water, gasses, they don't have it. This energy is what makes up you, me, us. It exists in a particular dimension, the Soul Dimension."

"Back to the iceberg analogy."

"Exactly. You can imagine the tip of the iceberg as our three-dimensional bodies and the underwater part as our soul energy. The same object made of two different parts, each one extending into different dimensions."

"What happens when we . . . for want of a better word, die?"

"Dying is the process of separating ourselves into two parts. Your body remains in the 3D world while your soul energy remains here."

"But why am I still—"

"The principle of conservation of energy. You remember it, don't you?"

"Yes, energy can be transformed but never destroyed, but—"

"Well, that's a universal principle. It extends beyond the material world. The energy associated with your material body is transformed and returned to earth when you die. 'Dust to dust,' as some people put it. The rest, that living soul energy of yours, remains untouched. In other words, you can't die without breaking the principle of conservation of energy."

I was speechless, not because of the weirdness of the explanation but because of the science behind it. I had expected more mysticism. Now it looked like the afterlife could be described, studied, and analyzed. Fascinating!

"But if we don't die, then what's life? Why is a rock not alive? We're made of the same elements found in rocks—oxygen, hydrogen, carbon, phosphorus, nitrogen."

"It's a matter of organization. Our DNA arranges the physical elements in a way that creates special conditions for a permanent, self-reinforcing, localized soul energy disturbance to be formed, and, therefore, for the living organisms to exist. We have already seen matter under certain configurations and conditions showing behaviors that run against common sense. Think of superfluidity—matter behaving like a fluid with zero viscosity at very low temperatures—or superconductivity, special conducting materials showing zero electrical resistance when two electrons couple together within the lattice structure."

"Are you suggesting we're the result of some kind of super-behavior of matter?"

"Close. When the male and female strands of a chromosome combine together, something amazing happens. As the new DNA twists in the form of a double helix, a bridge, a tunnel into a fourth dimension, is created. The soul energy arranges itself around this tunnel, forming an exact copy of the new double-helix DNA. Like the crystal lattice that creates the conditions for two electrons to couple together into Cooper pairs, producing superconductivity never seen in individual electrons, the organic cell creates the conditions for the two chromosome strands to couple, producing that unique behavior never seen in two individual chromosome strands: life. From that moment on, the

DNA provides the blueprint, and its soul energy counterpart provides the building materials. And like any well-constructed building, the energy structure outlasts its blueprints. This unique event is what defines life and ultimately creates a living organism. It's the most incredible and beautiful proof that the whole is much, much greater than the sum of its parts."

"Soul energy? That's why I'm still alive?"

"That's right. Your physical body provides the mold to create the mirrored living entity in the Soul Dimension. The channel between dimensions remains open until one day, after it's fulfilled its purpose, the tunnel weakens and breaks. That's the moment when you detach from your material body."

"The wormhole breaks . . . unbelievable." What else could I say?

I was so concentrated on what Niels was teaching me that I didn't realize someone was behind me, watching us. It was Grandma. I didn't know how long she'd been there, but it had been long enough to generate a look of satisfaction.

"Is the lesson going well?" she asked.

"She's still here," Niels said, "so I guess it hasn't been too boring."

"Maybe it's time for a break. I'll take her from here. I can bring her back later."

I turned quickly to him. "Thank you, Neils."

"My pleasure," he said. "See you soon, Ely."

Grandma and I walked—apparently—out of the library. I didn't feel the floating, disjointed sensation anymore, but she still held my hand, and I was grateful for it. The day was sunny and calm, and the roads were empty.

"Do you think this is normal?" she asked.

"What?"

"That there's nobody in the area."

"I guess not." I didn't know where we were.

"Believe it or not, we're in the same city you used to live in. We're not in a parallel universe. We're in the center of New York."

"New York?" I turned around. "That's not possible!" The building we had been in was the New York Public Library.

"Where is everyone? It should be crowded, people walking everywhere."

"They're here, in this place, just not at this time."

"What do you mean? Is it too late? Is the library closed?"

"Not exactly. Did Neils mention the iceberg analogy? He loves that one."

"Yes, he did."

"Perfect. Then I can assume you're already familiar with the concept of multi-dimensional space, right?"

"I am now."

"Well, time is another concept that carries its own surprises." I prepared myself for my second class of the day. "Unlike in the physical dimensions, where you were constrained to move forward in time at a fixed rate, here you can move across the time dimension the same way you can move any way you want in the three spatial dimensions. Like I said, we're all here but at different times."

"Are you telling me that I can go to the past?" That had only one meaning to me. Could I be so lucky that I might have a second chance?

"Not exactly, sweetheart. You can't go back to the material-dimension past—causality still applies there—but you can move back in time. Let me show you. Take my hand."

People started to appear and disappear as I stood in the same place. I was not moving at all, or at least I thought I wasn't. Suddenly, I found myself surrounded by people dressed like it was the 1950s.

"What happened? Where are we?"

"At the moment, September 24, 1954."

"What?"

"All these people died in the 1950s. They chose this point in time for gathering together." Despite having these people in front of me, it was still incredible.

"You mean they stay in a particular time in the same way people stay in a particular location? Looping through this moment over and over, like Groundhog Day?"

"No, not quite. It's not too difficult to understand, once you

49

see time as a dimension, just like the spatial dimensions. The present is the point where the time dimension intersects perpendicularly with the space dimensions, and that present moment continually moves forward. We used to be tied to the present because our physical bodies confined us there. Like a surfer riding a wave, we move together with the present until we die. At that moment we free ourselves to carry the present with us, and we become capable of moving, or I should say 'swimming,' back and forward in time."

"So, we all share the same location but at different and effectively endless moments."

"Yes. In the same way different people can be in many places at the same time, we can be in many times at the same place."

Crazy! We were all there. Just not now. Or not at the same now.

"What about the future? Can I go and see the future?"

"You're familiar with the concept of the expansion of the universe, aren't you?"

"Of course. The distance between two galaxies becomes larger over time because the space between expands." Space expansion was discovered while scientists were trying to explain the observed high speed of faraway galaxies. I didn't see its relationship to us. Maybe I could find Edwin Hubble to explain it to me.

"Well, there is indeed one, and we can find Edwin if you'd like."

I kept forgetting that people there could read one another's thoughts.

"You'll get used to it," Grandma said. "Anyway, what really expands is not space but the space-time continuum. As space expands in size, time expands in length. The expansion rate is what we measure with a clock. With every second, the Time Dimension expands one second in length. It's like being in a room with one of the walls constantly moving outwards. The room becomes bigger with every second. This simple behavior makes time a unique dimension. It's the only dimension that has a beginning: the present."

"So I can't move into the future because it doesn't exist yet."

50

"I'm afraid so."

I was attending the most fascinating lessons of my entire life, although sadly, I realized I didn't have a second chance.

We walked through the people. They were calm, serene, in complete harmony with one another. They looked at us with dazzling smiles.

"They seem so happy. What do they do, Grandma? How do they spend their lives here?"

"Well, we must think first about how we used to spend most of our time before we came here. Society is based on people working their entire lives to make things that ultimately help us do other things. We make cars to move us, houses to protect us from the weather, phones to communicate. Everything we build is to help us do something."

I was silent. Everything was starting to make sense.

"Now, imagine that if you need to move, all you have to do is think about the place you want to be. Storms, snow, rain, they don't affect you anymore. Want to communicate? Piece of cake. Just open your mind to the person you want to talk to. This is the kind of world we're in now."

"But we still have other needs," I said. "It's in our nature as humans."

"Of course we still have needs, but they're more about self-fulfillment. This is the place when we free ourselves from our basic instincts and material desires and begin to walk the path of learning, developing our pure, divine essence."

"Our spirit?"

"As good a name as any. Ely, you remember the sci-fi stories about space travelers getting in contact with other advanced civilizations—Star Trek and its advanced energy entities? Well, those stories are reality here. What you see around you is the next step in humankind's evolution."

That was astonishing. We were proud of our technological and social advances. Our capacity to understand and achieve extraordinary things had never been greater. We saw ourselves on the pinnacle of our civilization, a place so high that we didn't dare to think of evolution beyond our material needs. Spiritual advancement was something done only by unique individuals like the Dalai Lama and Tibetan monks. But here, spiritual advancement was part of everyone's life. It was a different way to look at the meaning of human existence.

"Grandma, can people change so dramatically? Can they just give up the search for money, possessions, and power? Can we really change our basic emotions—fear, anger, envy?"

"Well, it's not easy for everyone. Every person defines his or her own path. Come here."

In an instant we were in Central Park. The place was much greener than it used to be.

"The park looks different. Where do all these plants come from?"

"DNA is in all living forms, my darling. Animals, plants, they're also here with us, sharing the Soul Dimension. Now look at those people."

"Those over by the lake?" Five people were gathered on the jogging track, sitting in a circle with their eyes closed. "What are they doing?"

"They're purifying their feelings. They're learning to eradicate envy and hate. You see those under that tree?"

I nodded. Another group, this one with their eyes open, was staring at a small blue ball. As I watched, one or another of them seemed to fade away, then come back.

"They're working on controlling their minds. They want to reach levels of meditation never obtained during their previous lives."

"Nirvana?"

"A state of pure consciousness."

"What's he up to?" I pointed to a man stroking a pigeon. It leaned into his fingers, clearly enjoying itself.

"He's working on his relationship with animals. He used to be a hunter." With a sparkle of light in her eyes she took my hand. "I'd like to take you to a particular place."

We moved further back in time. Then we moved in space to a location I didn't recognize—in the middle of a cobblestone street with tall, plain, tan brick houses towering five or six stories above us on either side. Judging by the small, diamond-shaped windows, it could have been any European town from the Middle Ages until the Victorian Age. We walked into a courtyard surrounding a more formal, somewhat more ornate building. I heard music coming from inside, a lovely song. How could I not recognize such a sublime melody? We moved into a large salon.

"Grandma . . ."

"Shush, listen."

A man in the center of the room looked like he could have been from the sixteenth century, judging from how he was dressed. He was seated on a delicate satin-covered chair, his eyes closed and a beatific smile on his face. The room was full of people from different times. It was like a fancy dress party. Everybody was concentrated on his music.

I listened as, from somewhere I couldn't see, a piano, violin, and cello passed a hauntingly beautiful melody back and forth, each instrument supported by the others when it carried the solo line. So much intimacy; it felt like it was my own. It was . . . simply divine.

When the music finished, there was no clapping. Instead, the whole room was flooded with a feeling of gratitude and appreciation.

"Did you like it?"

"Beautiful." I nodded to the man, who was still seated placidly in the middle of the stage. "Who is he?"

"Wolfgang Amadeus Mozart."

"What?"

"Yes, darling. He's still composing music. He has these sessions in which he opens his mind to the audience."

"So . . . what I heard were his thoughts?"

"That's right; the same way he conceives music in his mind."

I realized I wasn't just listening to Mozart's music. I was in direct contact with Mozart's source of inspiration. We remained in the salon looking at him until he stood, gave a shallow bow, and then left.

As we went out of the building, Grandma continued with my lesson.

"It's the same as in our previous life. Some people are more advanced than others, and some have more work to do than others. The lesser are still attached to things. The more spiritually pure a person is, the smoother his or her transition. In any case, there's no hurry. People have all the time to advance and develop at their own speed."

We wandered the streets of what I recognized as eighteenth-century Vienna. My thoughts were racing. For thousands of years, people had feared death. Were our images of demons and dark entities just the product of our fear of the unknown? Was our civilization expanding beyond death? Was this . . . well, heaven?

And how could I have been so wrong?

My mind was still flooded with questions when Grandpa appeared before us. "Beth, I'm afraid I have to interrupt your lesson." He looked stressed. "Ely, I need you to come with me, now. You can continue later."

He was in such a hurry that I immediately thought about Rob. "Grandpa—"

"Yes, I know, my darling. We have to leave now." He took my hand, and we were gone.

CHAPTER 9
ROB

I knew it was going to be a difficult day. I took what had become my usual breakfast—two quick slices of toast eaten over the kitchen sink washed down with a cup of black coffee. Just the idea of visiting Ely's workplace had me trembling. I wanted to get through the experience as quickly as possible. I grabbed my jacket and walked to the garage.

I haven't driven for weeks. The insurance company had given me another car, and I'd used it only two or three times. I got in and started the engine, released the brake, and crept out of the garage and past the point . . . I could still hear the crushing glass when Ely had . . .

The sound of a horn brought me back to the present. I slammed on the brakes as a yellow convertible zipped past within inches of me.

"Hey, go sleep on your bed, idiot!" the driver yelled.

I made an effort to keep focused on the traffic for the rest of the journey.

Peter was waiting for me when I turned into the parking area. He approached as I parked the car.

"Hi, Rob, is everything OK?"

"As well as you might expect. Thanks for being here."

"It's the least I can do. I already spoke with the head of the physics department, and he has all the paperwork ready for you."

That was the Peter I knew, a very organized man.

We went to the head office, and I quickly signed the documents. I didn't want to stay long. People feeling sorry for me made me feel even worse.

It was my first time in that building. We walked through a long corridor that led to Ely's former office. Many offices had their doors open. People looked at me as we passed.

Peter broke the silence. "She was well known in the center, always caring for everyone. All her colleagues loved her."

I didn't say anything.

We finally arrived at Ely's office. Peter opened the door. He explained that the office was occupied by a visiting professor from MIT. I spotted a pile of boxes in a corner.

"I took the liberty of collecting all of Ely's things and putting them in boxes. I organized them—books, papers and publications, her thesis. You know, Rob, I didn't want you to—"

"I know. Thank you very much."

I didn't know what to do with all those boxes. There were so many. He showed me the things inside each box, so I wouldn't have to go through them alone. At a certain point I realized the material was incomprehensible and useless to me.

"Listen, Peter, you know I'm not a scientist. I have no clue what Ely was working on. I think we can find a better use for all this stuff than dragging it back to my house."

"What do you have in mind?"

"I'd like you to donate the books to the library. I'm sure that's what she would have wanted. As for the rest of the papers, have a look and see if there's anything interesting. Take what you want, and recycle the rest. I'll only take Ely's personal items."

"What about Ely's thesis work? I know you wouldn't do anything with it, but it was the last thing she was doing."

I couldn't argue with that. "OK, I'll take that with me as well."

In the end, it boiled down to only one box. It was heavy, but with Peter's help, I managed to put it in the car. I couldn't stand being at the center one more minute, everyone staring at me with an expression of sorrow.

I couldn't tear my thoughts away from the box during the journey home. What had Ely had in her office? Should I go through her things? Would that make me feel happy or sad? I was so absorbed in my thoughts that I was surprised to find myself in front of the house.

"What's that?"

An ambulance and two police cars were parked a couple of houses down the road. Many people were on the sidewalk, watching, talking. I parked the car and approached one of them.

"Why are they here?" I asked.

"It looks like there was a multiple suicide in the Robinsons' house."

I was new in the neighbourhood, so I didn't know them.

"Were they in trouble? I mean, did they have family troubles?"

"Not at all. Very nice couple. Married for more than thirty years. That's why it's so strange. There must be another explanation."

"Like what?"

"I don't know. You only need to listen to the news. There are so many murders lately. We'd better watch our backs."

Not surprisingly, I fell back into depression. The whole scene reminded me of Ely's day.

I went back to the car and managed to carry the box inside. By the time I put it on the dining table, I had already made up my mind. I was going to seal the box and leave it in the garage for as long as I needed before I looked at it.

I felt the need to stay away from the flashing blue-and-amber lights, so I decided to go out for a drink, my first drink in weeks. I drove without a definite place in mind. After a while I found myself in a dark street that looked as if there was a blackout in the area.

I stopped the car a couple of blocks from a bar. The night was so dark that I could hardly see the sidewalk. I didn't know if it was cloudy or if there was a new moon. Honestly, I couldn't have cared less. As I walked to the bar, my eyes never left the sidewalk. A cat darted out in front of me, but that's all I saw.

I was about one block from the bar when, for an instant, I lost consciousness. I fell to my knees. From nowhere, a person stumbled over me and fell. Something metal bounced off his hand.

A knife!

I leapt up, and we started grappling. He was strong, but I managed to drag him off balance, disengage as he recovered, then tag him hard enough to make him fall back. He hit his head on a wall and collapsed. There was a lot of blood.

My depression had disappeared, replaced by panic. I didn't want to have another person's death on my conscience, even if that person had been trying to kill me.

I dropped next to him and checked for a pulse—he was still alive. I pulled out my phone and called 911. The operator told me that the ambulance would take a few minutes to get there. I tried to stand up but felt a strong pain in my right leg.

Shit! Some of that blood was mine.

At that moment a police car roared up, its lights illuminating the scene. Two police officers ran over.

"Are you OK, sir?" the taller one asked.

"I'm fine. Just my right leg."

"Try not to move. The ambulance will be here soon. The paramedics will take care of your leg."

The other officer checked the man who had attacked me. "He's breathing."

"You're very lucky to be alive," the taller officer said.

I managed to make out his name in the strange light. "Why's that, Officer Jackson?"

"There's been a wave of attacks in the city. It might be gangs taking care of business or some coordinated terrorist thing. So far there have been no survivors. Except you."

A couple of minutes later, the ambulance arrived. The paramedic checked my leg. "Not much to worry about, but we have

58

to take you to the hospital."

When they got me into the ambulance, the memories of Ely were inevitable.

I must have fainted during the journey because when I woke up, it was morning, and I was in a room with two beds, both occupied by injured people.

A nurse floated into the room. "Good morning, Mr. Kline. How do you feel?"

"Where am I? I don't remember anything past the ambulance."

"You're in the hospital."

I tried to move my leg. It hurt.

"It's fine," she said. "You've got some stitches. However, you've lost a lot of blood, so you have to stay until the doctor sees you. If you're lucky, you'll be able to go home soon."

Great. Yesterday was my lucky night. Maybe today would be my lucky day. I'd have to remember that after I got back to my empty house.

A few hours later, I received a visit from a police officer.

"Mr. Kline, my name is Detective Sullivan. I'm with Homicide."

"Homicide? Did I kill that guy?"

"No, he's alive and well. I would like to ask you a few routine questions though, if you don't mind."

I breathed once again. "Of course. How can I help you?"

"In the last few months, the number of violent criminal acts in the city has increased to an unexpected level. We don't know how to explain most of them. There've been no survivors. You're the first."

"What do you want to know, Detective?"

"Do you know the guy who attacked you?"

"Never saw him before."

He started walking around the bed. It made me nervous. "Do you know why a total stranger would want to kill you?"

I didn't like the way he was asking the question. It looked like he thought I was part of a gang. "How do you know he wanted to kill me? He might have just wanted to rob me."

"So you don't think he was after you?"

"Detective, I don't know that guy. I have no idea who he is or what he does or, more importantly, why he attacked me. Why don't you ask him?"

"I would, but it looks like he has temporary memory loss."

"I see. Well, I think you'll have to wait until he gets his memory back to get answers to your questions. I'm sorry, but I really can't help you."

With a look of disappointment, he nodded and then walked to the door. "Ah, well, thanks anyway."

He left the room with his mind apparently already on something else. It was disturbing to see the police think of me as a delinquent.

At about five in the afternoon, the nurse told me I could leave. The taxi I had called was waiting for me when I walked out. I hadn't told anybody what had happened. I didn't want to bother anyone. Actually, I didn't want to be bothered by anyone.

When I arrived home, I found the house cold and empty. Nothing had changed. I felt the same as I had the day before when I returned from Ely's office. It didn't matter what I did; I always felt the same way.

I went to the kitchen to fix something to eat and ended up preparing the same ham-and-cheese sandwich as I had eaten the day before. I opened a beer and then went to my studio, the only place in the house where I still felt comfortable. It was a small workshop with an architect's drawing table and an Apple computer with all the 3D design software I could buy. I loved modern art, particularly neo-surrealism and digital realism. Ever since I was a teenager, I'd been drawing surreal worlds where I could free my imagination. Unconstrained worlds where everything was possible.

The walls were covered with many posters of surreal worlds, where the main subject was the sky. I used to imagine the view from a planet at the center of the Milky Way—all the stars and planets so close that darkness was banished. I kept all my finished works and sketches, some still placed carefully into special tubs and flat boxes. This was my passion. There was a time when

60

I hoped I could make my living from it. Now I was hoping it would help me lose myself in one of those surreal worlds.

I sat down on a small sofa and switched on the TV.

"In another day of violence, three people have been found dead in different parts of the city. The police are trying to crack down on the gangs responsible for the latest crime wave. Since last October, ninety people have been murdered. Neighbouring counties also report an increase in crime . . ."

I didn't realize the crime spree had been going on for the last few months. I had been too caught up in my own problems. Now I understood all the police attention to my case and realized how lucky I had been. I still didn't feel it though.

I surfed the channels, looking for something a little easier to watch and settled on a rerun of a mindless sitcom. I ate half of the sandwich and realized I wasn't very hungry. I fell asleep almost immediately. It must have been the blood I had lost.

Just before I drifted off, a thought occurred to me. Why had I survived? What exactly had happened in that alley?

CHAPTER 10

ELY

In the blink of an eye, we were in a dark street with no people and no cars. Grandpa and Grandma were beside me, silent. I looked around; nothing was moving.

"Grandpa, why did you bring me here? What's the emergency?"

"Shhh. Keep your eyes open. Something's going to happen, and we've got to stop it, but I don't know how."

Happen? What was he talking about? From his tone, it didn't sound good.

We kept watching the street. A cat ran out of a house, scared. Then a man appeared and felt his way down the street in the darkness. He stopped at the corner and slipped into an entranceway. Why was trying to hide? From what? From whom? Then I saw something in his hand: a knife. Was it to defend himself?

The sound of footsteps drew my attention. I looked around, and the silhouette of a man appeared on the other side of the corner.

Rob!

Instinctively, I ran toward him and threw myself against him, trying to push him, but I went right through him.

Damn, no mass.

I turned around and saw him on the ground. The man was also down, but he recovered quickly and lunged at Rob. They started fighting.

I tried to hit the man with my hands. I jumped on his shoulders, scratched his face, but I had no effect.

Then the man fell and didn't get up.

"We did it! We stopped him!" I said to Rob. With my arms open, I threw myself at him—and through him—as he took out his phone and called 911.

He didn't even know I was there. And in most important ways, I wasn't. How could I stand it? How could I protect my love like this? He was all I had left.

A soft hand touched my shoulder.

"Grandma," I said. I couldn't hide my feelings, so no words were necessary.

I turned to Grandpa. Watching Rob being killed was not the kind of scene I would have liked to have seen. He knew I couldn't do anything to prevent it, he had still brought me there. There had to be a reason, and I wanted to know what it was.

"How did you know this attack was going to happen?"

"I didn't. The visit to your office depressed him to the point that, for the first time, he decided to go out. A dangerous neighborhood, dark, empty streets. What I can say is I was worried about him."

How could I have missed it? I was supposed to be with him during that visit. Damn. I got lost on Niels' teachings without realizing I had left Rob alone, unprotected.

"Ely, there's more going on here than just Rob. You have to come with me."

"Grandpa, please. I can't leave Rob alone. I want to make sure he's going to be fine. His wound . . ."

Without letting me finish, Grandpa grabbed my arms. Suddenly, we were in a different place.

It was a room decorated with eighteenth-century furniture and a couple of wax mannequins. I realized we were in a museum. I felt people around me, but I couldn't see them.

Grandma appeared beside me. "Gentlemen, you have to project yourselves. She hasn't gone through the whole training yet."

Three points of light began to shine close to us. The light was very bright, a color I had never seen before. Then three men appeared. I didn't recognize any of them. They were tall with athletic bodies, and they were dressed in armor. Definitely some kind of warriors.

"Did you all see what happened?" Grandma asked.

"Yes, we did," one of them replied.

"Do you believe now?"

I looked at the strangers and then at her, utterly confused. "Grandma, who are these people?"

"There's a group of unique people who, throughout time, have looked after every one of us. They are known as the Gli Custodi. These men are part of that group."

"I don't need anyone to look after me."

"Sooner or later everyone needs to be reminded of the right path, in particular when one is young in this world. It's difficult to walk the path without giving in to the temptation to go back. They're always there, helping us to go through, enlightening our path."

I didn't understand what she was talking about, and that made me uneasy. "In any case, we're not walking any path right now. Why are they here?"

"You didn't notice, did you?" she said.

"What?"

"You stopped Rob from being killed."

"What? That's impossible. Rob and the other guy weren't even aware of my presence."

"Think again. What happened when you saw Rob?"

"Well, I ran to him. But I couldn't—"

"Oh yes you could. He fell because of you, and that's a remarkable event. No one has ever had the ability to communicate physically with people like you did today."

The implications were beginning to sink in. I presumably had no mass, but I'd run into Rob and made him fall. "Is that possible? I mean, given what Neils said about how things work here?"

"We were told that you have a special gift, but we never imagined it would be so powerful." Grandpa looked at the Gli Custodi people. "Now, gentlemen, give the message to the rest of the covenant. It's critical that we implement our plan as soon as possible. Rob could be in danger again, and next time we might not be so lucky. We could lose our only chance to fix the situation."

"Wait, wait, wait," I said. "You guys have to tell me what's going on. Grandma, please, could Rob be in danger again? What problem are you trying to fix?"

As the three strangers disappeared, I heard the thoughts of one of them. "It's true . . . they're our last hope."

CHAPTER 11

ELY

The three guardians were definitely hiding something, and Grandpa and Grandma were looking at each other secretly. I remained silent, watching them and waiting for an explanation.

Grandpa spoke first. "Ely, we're facing a critical situation that is threatening the life of the loved ones left behind. Some people in our world have found a way to influence people in the physical world."

"What do you mean? Communicate with them?"

"Not exactly, my darling." Grandma said. "They can change the way people think and behave."

"Sorry, I don't follow you."

"They can make people kill themselves."

"What? But why?"

"You remember what I told you when we were at the library? About how the nature of people doesn't change, even after death?"

I nodded.

"Well, history is full of people who hated their fellow human beings. They tortured and killed innocent people for . . . the sake of doing it. Now that they're here, they still have that same hatred against humanity."

"Grandma, I—"

"Shhh. Listen. It's a force that comes from within, controlling what they do and feel."

"But we're in a totally different world. They can't hurt us, can they?"

"They don't want us. They want the ones we left behind."

"I don't understand, Grandma. You told me that we're the next step in human evolution. How can such people still exist?"

"I also told you that some people were more advanced than others, and some of them could choose different paths."

"But how? How could they choose such a different path? And why now?

"For most of history," grandpa said, "people who died accepted unconditionally what they found here. Their minds were unaccustomed to scrutinizing what was happening to them. Faith helped them to accept everything. But a few centuries ago, people started seeing the world with a scientific eye, investigating and challenging everything around them. In the same way it brought about advances in technology, psychology, sociology, biology, it's a wonderful thing that brought us a deeper understanding of what we are and the world we live in. But it had some unintended consequences."

"You mean these people are using science to find a way to . . . influence living people?"

"Yes. To unbalance the subconscious of the living."

"Unbalance?" Grandma said.

"The subconscious normally maintains an equilibrium between survival emotions. The constant interaction between happiness, anger, jealousy, fear, shame, disgust, love, envy, and guilt dictates the way we behave. A little push in one direction can make us stronger people. A little shove in the opposite direction and . . ."

"So they've found a way to mess with people's basic feelings."

"Exactly. We believe they've discovered how to use the DNA bridge to indirectly interact at the subatomic level with the neurons of the limbic area of the brain. We don't know how they do it, but we do know that they trigger a guilt and shame so profound that frustration and depression take control, making people unable to fight and searching for a way out of this nightmare, leaving them with only one option."

"Suicide."

"Indeed."

"But if it's as bad as it sounds, why don't you just go and . . . get them."

"Because we can't. We don't know where they are. As you know, our world is bounded by the universal principles of quantum mechanics. When we move at light speed, there's no way we can identify an individual soul energy and simultaneously locate its position in the time dimension."

I nodded in understanding. "The uncertainty principle."

"That's right. As long as they move, they're everywhere and nowhere. We can't do anything to follow them."

"But what about when they don't move? Look at us now, easy to locate."

"Niels told you that space is bigger than we thought, right? Well, they move in space and in time. With no means of tracking them down, they can be literally anywhere at any time. It's like trying to find a person in billions and billions of universes."

"So . . ." I stopped. This was madness. "If we can't locate them, how do we expect to catch them?"

"There is one moment we can get them, when they enter the symbiotic stage. Once a person is chosen, they develop a temporary bond through the soul energy, turning the victim into a host. They can't leave the person while this link exists. Only when the host dies and the link breaks."

"But what if the person doesn't die?" I had a vision of someone saddled with an evil influence in their very DNA for the rest of their lives. "Can they still leave the host? Can the symbiosis be broken?"

"Yes, but it's not instantaneous," Grandpa said. "The process of undoing the link takes some time, and that's precisely what gives us the opportunity we have to catch them. If the host is kept alive long enough, we can identify their locations and get them while they're still attached."

"Then we wait until they undo the symbiosis, and we catch them."

"We don't have to wait until they leave the symbiosis. We can cut the link as soon as we locate them."

"Great! Then you've got the solution," I said.

"I'm afraid it's not that simple," Grandpa said. "The host has to be kept alive long enough for us to find them. When they notice that we're searching for them, they push the host to kill himself immediately. They're gone by the time we arrive. We can't do it from our world. It has to be done from the other side."

I started connecting the dots. "So . . . you want me to contact the people of the material world, so they can help us keep the hosts alive."

"Not all people. Just Robert," Grandma said.

"Rob? Why him? You said my contact with Rob was unique. How can I do it again?"

"Apparently, you have a gift that we can't explain." Grandma said. "It's unimaginably powerful, but it's concentrated only on one person, Robert. Call it chemistry, a sixth sense, spiritual development, or just . . . love, but you two have a connection that transcends worlds. We've never seen anything like it before."

That made sense. Rob and I used to have a strong intuition about each other. Sometimes it was so strong that we joked about a supernatural source.

"Of the two, you're the strongest." Grandma added. "We've known about your gift since you were born and have followed your development. Robert is different. He developed his ability to listen after he met you."

"So I'm the transmitter, and Rob's the receiver?"

"Sort of," Grandma said.

I felt like Neo. The chosen one.

"Ely, please, this is a serious situation. We need your help," Grandpa said.

"Sorry." I shouldn't have joked about it, not even in my mind. "How much time do we have?"

"Every minute counts," Grandma added.

"Tell me what I have to do."

"First, establish communication with Robert. We have to let him know that you're here. Unfortunately, that's not going to be easy."

Grandma was right. Rob thought I was dead, and he was not prepared to change that.

I knew what Grandma and Grandpa said was important, but I was really doing it for myself. To be able to talk again to Rob meant everything to me. I never thought it would be such a torture to be beside him without being able to talk to him, touch him . . . kiss him. I was prepared to do whatever it took to be with him again.

Grandma and I began practicing my ability to get inside Rob's mind. This was new for both of us, so trial and error was our only option. After several attempts it was clear that I could only communicate with him while he was asleep. When he was awake, his mind was under the influence of so many external stimuli that it made it virtually impossible to get to him.

We tested different sleep stages. In the end, we determined that the REM stage was the best moment to establish communication with him. This was when his brain activity was high—similar to when he was awake—but his sensory input was minimal. In short, I had to learn to enter Rob's dreams.

In the end, it turned out to be unexpectedly easy. The key was to learn to synchronize the frequency of my thoughts with those of his dreams. We needed to be thinking in resonance, so one fed the other through the DNA wormhole. But that was not all. Once inside, finding my way through was the difficult part. His subconscious was in control of the dream, not him. His thoughts were erratic, and incoherent. What made things even harder was that he was unaware of what was happening in each dream. He was simply an actor, directed by his subconscious. His mind was not free; it was manipulated by the scripts presented to him.

I tried to appear in different ways. Once or twice, I managed to draw his attention, but it was like talking to a bird. He looked at me and heard my words, and yet he continued on as if nothing had happened. I didn't know how to stop him from performing his role in the dream. For him, I was simply part of the background.

After a few more attempts, I realized I needed to find a different approach, but what? I was running out of options.

Then one night he dreamed that we were walking alongside a busy road, and a truck whizzed by right at our side. It shocked him and woke him up in the middle of the dream. I was expelled almost instantaneously, then got inside again just after he fell asleep. To my surprise, it was the same dream, as if his subconscious were trying to finish it.

That was it!

If I could stop the same dream over and over before it finished, I could create a sequence of the same dream happening again and again. At least in principle, a recurring dream could attract his attention.

I started analyzing each dream. That was where being a scientist was a real advantage. I studied all the different options. One thing came out of this analysis: it was useless to try to stop the dream by doing something directly to Rob. I needed to wake him up through something else. One option was to influence something happening in his dream, but what? How?

Each dream was different, so I couldn't prepare anything in advance. I would have to improvise. Grandma kept telling me that my connection with Rob was unique. Well, this was the moment to test it.

"Very interesting, Ely. A recurring dream. Yes, it might work." Grandma said when I explained it to her. I was entering unfamiliar territory, so her feedback was vital. "However, you're overlooking something important. What are you going to say to him? What do you want him to remember? Don't forget that he sees you as part of his dream, so when he wakes up, he might not remember a thing about you."

She had a point. A recurring dream could make him try to decode the whole dream, and that wasn't what I wanted. He needed to only remember me.

"Any suggestions?" I said.

"Well, what about your thesis? If I remember right, you were working on something that might help open his mind to the possibility."

I had completely forgotten it. Since I had arrived there and learned the universe was nothing like I'd imagined, my PhD work had lost its relevance. But she was right. My research could be the key to help Rob understand what was happening in his dreams. Would it work? Would he believe it?

Once again, the only way to find out was to try.

CHAPTER 12

ROB

Ely and I were walking through the hallways of my old high school, which was somehow also in Renaissance Florence.

"Isn't this great?" I said. "I remember a year ago when you saw that picture of Firenze. You fell in love with that church—Santa Maria del Fiore, wasn't it?"

"Robert," Ely said, "listen to me. We have to talk."

Why was she talking like this? She never called me "Robert." And she sounded so formal, so serious. I looked at her. She was wearing a red tunic. A few seconds earlier, it had been a bright yellow T-shirt.

"What happened to your clothes?" I asked.

"Listen, the killings are not what they look like. We have to stop them—you've got to stop them. The notebook. Read my notebook."

Just then a truck burst through the gym doors, bearing down on us. I grabbed Ely and dove out of the way.

Once again, the same dream. When were they going to stop?

I had been having these dreams since I was attacked three days earlier. They were always the same. Ely was there, wearing bright, outlandish clothes. And then the truck appeared and ran us down.

Damn. I thought I was getting over Ely's death, but instead I was getting worse.

The TV was still on. It was already late, so I stood up to go to bed. The telephone rang. I didn't pick it up. It rang again, and the answering machine switched on.

"Rob. Answer the phone, I know you're there. Come on. I need to talk with you."

I picked up the phone. "What do you want? It's late."

"Rob! Open the door. I'm in front of your house."

The phone went dead, and Peter started knocking at the same time. I opened the door.

"Thank goodness you're alive. I heard about the attack. Why didn't you call me?"

"How did you find out about it?" I hadn't told anybody about it just to save me from this kind of situation.

"It's been three days, plenty of time for the gossip to reach my brother's office. Remember him? He's a doctor at the hospital. Now tell me, what happened?"

"It was nothing. I was attacked by a man. He was trying to rob me. But I'm OK. No worries."

"What do you mean 'no worries'? I've already lost one best friend. I don't want to lose my second."

He went to the fridge and got a couple of beers. He threw one of them to me. "You look like you haven't slept for ages. Are you sure everything is fine?"

That was the problem with having people around; I could never hide things from them. "Yeah. It's just these nightmares. I can't get rid of them."

"Have you been taking any sleeping pills?"

"It's not that. I fall asleep fine. But then I have this recurring dream that always ends with an accident. And Ely, well, she's always there."

"Rob, listen, my friend, what happened to you was very hard, but there's no going back. You have to learn to live with it."

"No, I've had plenty of difficult nights since Ely's accident; you know that. These dreams . . . well, they're different. They only started after the attack. I always wake up having the feeling that it was real, that I was with Ely. Then when I fall asleep again, the same dream."

"You still miss her a lot, don't you?"

"Yes, I do, to the point of obsession. I see people on the street who remind me of her, I smell her perfume in the lobbies of buildings." As I heard my own words, I realized he might have a point. But it wasn't the time for discussing anything. "You know, maybe you're right. It must be my inability to accept that she's gone."

"Come, let's go out for a drink. You need some fresh air."

On my way to get my jacket, I thought of something. It was a crazy thought, but a lot of crazy things had been happening lately.

"Peter," I said, "do you have any books that belonged to Ely?"

"Sorry. Books?"

"Yes, the boxes that you took to the library. Do you know if Ely was reading or writing any books?"

"I don't know. The boxes I took to the library were all textbooks used in the center's lectures. Nothing special. Unless there's something with her research work. She was working almost day and night. Why do you ask?"

"In my dreams she keeps telling me something about a book. Actually, a notebook that I have to read."

"Well, you've got her thesis work. Remember the box you took home? You've got everything inside that box."

Of course. A notebook was used to take notes. What better reason to have a notebook than her thesis.

"Peter, on second thought, I don't feel like going out right now. I'd rather stay here and try to rest."

"What? But you just agreed to go."

"Sorry. Let's do it tomorrow afternoon." I walked him to the door. "I'll call you tomorrow. And, Peter, thank you for coming, really."

I closed the door behind him. I knew it was not the most polite way to end his visit, but he would understand.

I went to the garage without wasting a second. There it was, the box containing Ely's stuff. We never talked much about her research. She used to spend a lot of time in the laboratory, so much that when we were at home, she preferred to talk about my job, not hers. In any case, I wouldn't have understood a word.

I hoisted the box on the workshop table. When I opened it, her perfume hit me. I stopped for a moment and took a deep breath. Eternity, the perfect name for a perfume.

I made an effort to keep my mind focused and started going through the contents. There were several notebooks. I opened one of them. It was full of formulas. I opened a second. A third. Lots and lots of formulas and equations.

What I was doing, following a dream? What a fool I was.

I was about to give up when I noticed a pink notebook with rounded corners at the bottom of the box. I knew Ely's favorite color was pink. I slid it out from under the rest of the papers. That's when I realized it wasn't a notebook; it was a diary.

On the first page was a note.

If you find this notebook, please return it to Elizabeth Trebor . . .

That was so her. Always thinking about the unexpected. She kept telling me about precautions that she had to take while doing dangerous experiments in the lab. I turned the page and found an introductory note.

I've never written a diary before. I'm not the kind of person who writes her thoughts on paper. But this is different, and I have no idea why. I have this force deep inside me that keeps pushing me to write. Maybe it's a waste of time. Maybe not. I suppose I'll find out when I finish.

This was weird. Ely never told me she was writing a diary. I looked inside. January, February . . . then nothing. I turned the pages until I got to July. Then I found the first day that she started writing, July 13. Exactly three months before she died. Why then? I had a feeling that I would find out soon.

July 13
I'm a scientist, so by definition I should only believe in whatever I can measure. The scientific method, my guiding doctrine: observation, understanding, hypothesis, experiment. I have recited these words so many times, and yet I find myself writing about something that goes against all these scientific principles.
I don't remember when it started. I must have been 10 or 11 years old when I had the first dream. One day I woke up with a feeling that there should be more to the world than what I could see. I thought I was crazy, but that sense has been with me ever since. I realize now it's why I became a scientist, why I chose atomic physics. This sense that the world is larger than I knew has defined almost everything I have worked for, including this writing.
I have to go now. Rob is here.

July 14
I have to be more careful—Rob really shouldn't see these notes. I'm sure he would consider them childish, and I'm not sure he'd be wrong.
Today was my first day in the lab. For the last year, I've been preparing myself for this day. I've done a lot of theoretical research, working out the details of my chosen topic. At least that's what I've told everybody. Of course, I wanted to know more about the investi-

gation subject but not for that purpose. I have managed so far to hide the real objective of my research from everyone. I need to prove that what I have been dreaming about, what I have sensed for so long, is real. Why do I feel this way? I don't know, but I have to find evidence that a bridge to that world exists.

July 30

Today I finished the first set of tests at the Relativistic Heavy Ion Collider. It hasn't been easy, but at least I'm ready now to validate my theory. I need to get into the quantum world, to find the connection between our world and the rest.

I know string theory predicts a multiverse and multiple dimensions. Everybody talks about it. But I've never been interested in describing it. What lies beyond this world is irrelevant to me. However, if it exists, there must be a bridge between the two worlds. As long as I can find that bridge, I know there's something on the other side, and that's all the evidence I need to believe that my parents are alive. That Grandpa and Grandma are with them. I wish I could share this with Rob, but how? They're dead. At the very least, he'd worry about my sanity. Sometimes it sounds crazy even to me. And I'm not sure he'd be wrong.

August 21

Another day and another failure. I don't know what I can do differently. Maybe it's because I don't know where to look. Almost a month in the lab and I'm already running out of options. I should have never taken this subject.

September 22

I think I'm going to abandon my thesis

October 13

I think I found something. Maybe the problem is energy. I'm using particles that aren't moving fast enough to overcome the energy barrier between dimensions. Let's see the results of today's experiment. If this is the case, I won't be able to do here what I need. Maybe in Europe.

I'll look into it tomorrow . . . Rob is waking up.

CHAPTER 13

ROB

I couldn't believe it. All those years, and Ely hadn't said a word about her dreams. Why keep them to herself? I had thought we were close to each other, but she was trying to get evidence that her parents were still alive. Energy? Particles? I had no clue what it was about, but it all started with a dream.

What about my nightmares? Were they connected? Were they really dreams or was she . . .

No, it couldn't be.

It was cold. I spent several hours in the garage reading Ely's diary. Then I went inside to the kitchen to get a drink. It was 3:23 a.m. I sat on the sofa with a beer in one hand and the diary in the other. I couldn't help but think about how I had missed it. My thoughts took me far away from this world . . .

We were walking through the back alleys in our hometown, which was somehow also in Renaissance Florence. "Wow," I said, "our first holiday in Italy. I remember a year ago when you saw that picture of Firenze. You fell in love with that church. What was it called? Santa Maria del Fiore?"

"Rob, listen to me. How many times do we have to go through the same dream? Wake up! Follow the notebook."

Just then, a diesel locomotive came bearing down on us from behind. I grabbed Ely and dove to one side.

Holy shit!

I was sweating, my mouth dry, my hands shaking, and my heart beating like crazy. Was that really Ely? Was she trying to talk to me? But how could . . . She was dead, wasn't she? My dream . . . her dream. What if . . . what if it really was her? In her diary, she said she was trying to get evidence of the afterlife. Was she trying to do it again?

No, it was only a dream.

I clutched my forehead. I was getting a pounding headache. What was happening to me? All these doubts were driving me crazy. Was this what a mental breakdown felt like? I was about to cross the line over to insanity, and I knew that once I did it, there would be no way back.

Did I have anything to lose? Even if I was leaving everything behind, life didn't have any meaning without Ely. I couldn't just let this go. I had to try.

It took me about thirty minutes to get to Peter's house. Once there, I knocked on the door several times. It took a while before Peter answered.

"Hi Peter." I walked inside the house without an invitation.

"Robert! Do you have any idea what time it is? Are you alright?"

"I'm not sure. I need to talk to you."

"It's five in the morning."

"I think maybe Ely is still alive."

81

He didn't say a word. He didn't have to. His face was a poem.

"Listen, just listen," I said. "I found Ely's notebook—in fact, it's her personal diary. She was working in the lab trying to contact her parents and grandparents. They've been dead for more than ten years."

"What are you talking about? I've been with her many years. She was working on—"

"That's exactly what she wanted you and everyone else to think. She was hiding the real reason for her research. Read it."

I showed him the notebook. He read Ely's pages.

"Can you see it? She was seeking a bridge, a way to communicate with them. I think she's trying to do the same with me now but from the other side."

"Robert, please."

"I'm having these dreams. Ely's always in them, and she always says the same thing: the notebook. Follow the notebook. Does that sound like me processing grief?"

"Well, no . . ."

"Peter, you've got to help me."

"Help you? How?"

"In the notebook she mentioned that she needs faster particles." I searched for the page where she mentioned it. "Look. What does that mean?"

Peter read it and then looked up at me. "She was experimenting with heavy ion particles colliding at relativistic speed—you know, atomic particles accelerated at an incredible speed and then crashed into each other."

"I get it, but why more speed?"

"The energy of an atomic particle is associated with its speed—the faster it goes, the more energy it has. She wanted more speed because she wanted to increase the energy of the collisions."

"But why?"

"The only way we can study the internal structure of the most basic subatomic particles is by crashing them at speeds close to light speed."

"Can it be done here?"

"No. We don't have machines powerful enough to do it."

"What about somewhere else? Europe? Can it be done there?"

"Yes, the Large Hadron Collider."

"What is it?"

"The world's largest highest-energy particle accelerator. It's managed by the European Organization for Nuclear Research or CERN and is located in—wait a moment. How do you know that?"

"Know what?"

"As we speak, CERN is preparing to test a revolutionary design that will push particle energy well above the previous record of 14 Tev."

"In plain English please."

"With this new design, scientists expect to push their collisions closer to light speed than ever before. This will create atomic particles that are so small that some people believe it's—"

"We have to go there," I said.

"No way."

"Peter, it's in the notebook."

"It's just Ely's ideas, hopes, dreams."

"Maybe, just maybe, she is trying right now to prove it. Think about the recognition you'd receive, the first scientist to prove the existence of the afterlife. What about that?"

"And what about my reputation as the first scientist turning mad on behalf of a friend."

"But what if she was right?"

"Rob, my dear friend. She's gone."

I was desperate to bring her back, and I might have been deluding myself. Peter knew it too. In fact, I could count on that.

"I promise you something."

"What?"

"If nothing happens, I'll make every effort to get my life back again."

"But . . ."

"I promise you, my friend. By the way, you don't have to make the reason behind our visit public, do you?"

"I'll think about it."

"Peter, please."

"OK, but you've better keep up with your promise. Let me

83

make some calls. I know some people in Genève who may be able to help us."

CHAPTER 14
ELY

G randma, it's working! He read the notebook!"

"Yes, my darling. Though he hasn't made it easy."

For the first time I was experiencing the connection with Rob that Grandma had talked so much about. It was easily the best thing that had happened to me since I died.

"Let's not claim victory just yet," she said. "We've only attracted his attention. He's not ready to listen yet, let alone believe."

"But he's going to Genève."

"Looking for evidence that you're real. He still doesn't believe in his dreams. He wants to believe, but he needs proof." She hesitated for a moment. "You know what? We have turned a relatively safe and manageable dream into a big problem."

Suddenly, I could see it. "He's looking for physical evidence, isn't he?"

"That's right. We're in very deep shit."

But Rob was going to the Large Hadron Collider, where they spent all their time looking at matter at a very small scale. I still hadn't wrapped my head around the physics of this new world, but I knew it was separate from the material world—they existed in different dimensions. It was impossible from my world to do anything with matter. They only intersected each other at the tiniest scale. At least that was my theory . . . just a theory.

"Wait Ely, that might be a possibility." Grandma said, reading my thoughts once again. I didn't know how long I could put up with this lack of mental privacy. "This level of communication hasn't been done before, but it might work. You were trying to do the same thing, weren't you?"

"Yes, while I was working at the center."

"Then maybe you can continue your work from this world. We don't have much time. We have to figure out how."

"Grandma, we don't have a particle accelerator here."

"I know, darling, but there could be another way. Come on, we've got to talk with Niels. I know he's been working on something related to this."

In an instant, we were back at the library. We found him in the history section. This time he was alone.

"Niels, we need your help." Grandma said.

"My dear Beth, always in a hurry. Tell me how I can help your sweet grandchild."

She didn't say a word. They both closed their eyes. That was all.

"I see," he said a moment later. "It's very risky. That's why it's never been tried before."

"What hasn't been tried before?" I asked.

"Go to the center of everything," he said, "the singularity where all dimensions converge and merge into one single master dimension."

The bridge between worlds! That place existed! It was indeed real. I had been right all along. But if this communication was possible, why—

"Yes, of course you were right," Niels said, "but it's more complicated than you realize. And it's never been tried because no-body from the other side has been ready to listen. Let's put it this way: if we look at the macro-space instead of the micro-space, this would be equivalent to sending a man to a planet ten billion times the distance to the farthest-known galaxy in the universe. Do you think your people would be able to see that man cutting a sunflower on that planet? That's the scale we're talking about. Billions and billions and billions and billions of times smaller than where we are now. No one from the other side has been able to see so deep into the micro world . . . until now."

"The Large Hadron Collider."

"That's right. For the first time people can access the micro world well beyond the atom and particle level. That's one of the two things we need in order to make first contact."

"What's the other?"

"We need to be able to send someone down to that point to do something that alters a particle's basic behavior in such a way that it can be detected and recognized from the other side."

"Send the man to cut the sunflower," I said.

"Exactly."

"I guess that's the easy part."

"Not really. At that scale, time, space, and all other dimen-sions merge together into a singularity. Not even the laws of quantum mechanics work in that place. Nobody knows what to expect, neither they nor us."

"But how can you get to such a small scale?" I asked with a bit of skepticism.

"You're learning to travel in multiple space and time dimen-sions. Well, there's also a path to the smaller-scale dimensions. We call it the In-Out dimension."

"Another dimension?"

"I told you before; space is much bigger than we thought."

This was unbelievable.

"In the same way you move right-left, up-down, or back-ward-forward in our 3D space, you can also move inward-out-ward. It's a weird dimension. We don't know much about how it originated except that it exists. Think of it as being perpendicular

87

to all other dimensions. But the most intriguing aspect of this dimension is that it shows statistical self-similarity."

"You mean like fractals?"

"Exactly."

A dimension with fractal properties? What an amazing thing. It was easy to see the self-similarity in a cauliflower, where a branch, a small piece, looked like the whole thing, but for a dimension?

"Self-similarity means that one small part of an object is a reduced-size copy of the whole object," he said. "Now imagine what happens when you move down in a dimension with these characteristics. Can you picture it?"

I could only think of a Mandelbrot set being zoomed down, revealing further variations of the same fractal patterns. "What I see on a small scale is a copy of what I see on a bigger scale."

"Well, a statistical copy, to be accurate. The thing is, there's no way to tell one scale from another because every scale looks similar. When you move through the In-Out dimension you lose any reference that will tell you where you are. You can easily get lost in the scales. A few daring people have tried to travel into this dimension. None of them have returned."

"Wait, you want to send somebody on a journey to a place completely unknown and without a return ticket? That's suicide!"

"Not for everyone." They remained silent, looking at me.

I backed away. "No. No way."

"Ely, I know there are many things we don't understand. Your connection with Robert . . . well, it's unique. It extends beyond the limits of both worlds. There's plenty of speculation but no scientific explanation. But the important thing is that connection could be your pole star, your compass that will lead you safely back to us."

"Rob? But he's still alive. How can he help me?"

"You sense each other's presence. At the very small scale, you won't feel anything; space and time will be too compressed. But as you move up, you'll begin to sense his presence. You'll know when you're at his side."

"How do you know it will work?"

He remained silent. At that point it was clear. This was my decision and mine alone. But with Rob at my side, I was confident that it could be done.

CHAPTER 15
ELY

I remember some scientists talking about the fractal properties of the universe," I said, "but never something like this. I can't believe we've never detected it before."

"How could you? There's no way to access the In-Out dimension from the material world. People can see small scales with powerful microscopes or big scales with huge telescopes but never actually move to a different scale."

I was doing groundbreaking research in two worlds at once. It was thrilling. And a little frightening.

"To change scale in the material world," Neils said, "you need to be able to compress or expand an object. You can't compress an apple to the infinitesimal scale. You'd get a fusion explosion long before then. But we're not in 3D space, and we're not made of matter anymore, so there's nothing to compress."

"I see."

Fractal theory was always applied to objects. Fractal space was new! I couldn't wait to know more. "Tell me, where should we begin?"

"Well, first of all, you have to learn to replicate yourself at smaller scales."

"Wait, wait. I can reduce my body and become smaller at will?"

"Stop right there. I didn't use the word 'reduce.' I said 'replicate.' Think about snowflakes and how if you magnify any particular piece, it looks exactly like the original."

"Replicate . . . OK. Um, no, not OK. I don't get it."

He approached me and took my hands. We started walking backwards, but this time was different. The speed of everything slowed down. I watched the room as if I were looking through a window. I was inside the room but looking at it from outside!

Still holding my hand, he looked at me. "Impressed? Just wait."

He gave me a pull. It felt like jumping down a step on a staircase. In the blink of an eye, we were looking at the whole city. Another jump, and we were looking at the entire planet.

I gazed around, fascinated. "How is it possible?"

"We've only changed a few scales. If we keep moving, we could get lost."

"Can you show me how to do it?"

"Well, that's the point, isn't it? If you're ready, we can start right now."

"Let's do it."

"OK. Come with me."

He took my hands again, and we jumped back to our normal scale. Suddenly, we were in a white room. I looked around. There was no floor, no ceiling. Actually, I wasn't sure if it was a room at all.

"This is the place where we experiment with the In-Out Dimension. It's our lab, closed and isolated from everything outside. Here, we can't get lost."

"What is it?" I asked.

91

"It's a time-space anomaly, a natural phenomenon. An empty bubble created in the In-Out Dimension."

"Cool. Are there a lot of these?"

"Not now, Ely. We have to keep focused. We don't have much time, so let's start."

Niels was not considering that everything was still new and amazing to me. But above all, he should have considered my mental privacy. No wonder there weren't many crowded places there.

"Come on, Ely, focus," he said. "You have to learn to reduce your mental activity to only one thought. The change in volume between scales is so big that it can deform your soul. It will break apart your mind unless you're able to focus all your power on a single idea."

We began the training to help focus my thoughts through meditation. Not an easy thing for someone with so many questions in her mind. In a world where my thoughts were actions, I had to learn to get my mind under control and soon.

After what seemed an eternity, I got familiar with the process. Clean thoughts, visualize, and so on.

In my first attempts, I managed to change one or two scales down and up. Then three, four, and six scales. The white room gave me a reference point when I went back to my scale.

It felt like a freefall but having everything under control—like a flying dream. It didn't matter which direction; inward and outward felt the same. I learned to maneuver with precision, to accelerate, decelerate, and stop. It was the closest feeling to having a body that I had had since my arrival.

"You're doing well," Niels said. "Actually, much better than I expected. Robert will be watching the experiment very soon, so we don't have much time. Practice as much as you can."

I practiced without rest, always a few scales smaller than my scale. I was careful never to move too far down. I recalled a little book that I read about fractal geometry during my first year at university, particularly a basic concept in fractal theory: the length of a fractal shape depends on the size of the meter used for measurement.

It was amazing to read that Britain's coastline got longer as the measuring stick decreased in size. So, for an infinitely small stick, the length of the coast would approach infinity. This was exactly what had happened here, only to the dimension itself! The In-Out Dimension became bigger as I moved to smaller scales.

Niels was right when he told me to believe first, understand later. These concepts were beyond understanding, even for a scientist like me. I needed to accept them first. Why and how could be investigated later.

These ins and outs became a teaching lesson for me. So much to learn . . .

Grandma appeared next to me. "Ely, the time has come." Then she looked at Niels.

He nodded. "She's ready, Beth."

"Good. Rob is already in Genève. We have to join him."

She took my hand. For the first time I felt confident enough to move by myself without her help. But I didn't want to show her how much I had learned with Niels. She was my tutor, so I let her lead me.

93

CHAPTER 16
ELY

Suddenly, we were at CERN. Rob was already in the control room, waiting for the collision to begin. Niels was there with us too.

"Ely, you know you don't have to do this," Grandma said.

"Actually, I kind of do. Don't worry. Niels showed me everything I need to know." I turned to him. "Didn't you?"

"You know everything I know," he said. "Let's hope it's enough."

We moved inside the particle accelerator to the chamber where the collision was supposed to happen.

"Ely, be careful." Grandma said.

"Don't forget, follow your feelings on your way back," Neils said.

"I will."

I eased into the In-Out Dimension. It was like standing on top of a skyscraper, ready to jump into space. I couldn't help feeling scared. Niels believed that, if there was any chance anyone could come back, it was me. But what was the likelihood that it would really happen? What would I find down at the smallest scale? Even without a material body, could I survive there? I didn't know why I was puzzling myself with such questions then and not before.

In any case, it didn't matter. I made a last effort to pull myself together, and then I jumped.

I was familiar with the first few scales. Everything became bigger, but this time the scale kept growing so that I lost perspective of the objects around me. Then everything went pitch black.

I stopped for a moment to get my bearings. Incredible! I saw points of light shaping what looked like the Grand Canyon, not that I had ever seen it in person. I must have been at the micrometer scale; things looked like what I'd seen through optical microscopes. It was so amazing. I could grasp the infinite possibilities available for a scientist. It was a chance to study cells, viruses, or similar objects directly. I could simply drop down to whatever scale I needed and do my analysis in person.

I had the chance to study nature in a way that it had never been done before, but at the same time, all this knowledge couldn't have been more useless. I wasn't living in the material world anymore. What incredible possibilities, and yet they weren't worth pursuing! Niels had been right, again. I definitely needed to redefine the purpose of my life if I was going to live it happily. And my first purpose was to communicate with Rob.

I continued dropping to smaller and smaller scales. I stopped a couple more times, the last one down around the scale of atoms, I guessed. Huge, empty space between illuminated points scattered all around. They could be the lights of stars shaping a galaxy. The different scales really did repeat in a fractal pattern!

I spotted something moving around the closest light on my left. It looked like a ball with a fluid surface. Waves? Particle-wave duality? I could actually observe it firsthand—

I had to focus.

I began dropping through the scales again. From that moment on, there was no more to see. The material world I knew was left behind.

I didn't know where I was or how much I had scaled inward. I was considering the possibility that this was a bottomless abyss when suddenly the sensation of being in a free-fall started to diminish. My speed slowly reduced to a point that I ended up floating —disembodied with no points of reference. Thanks to my training, I was still able to think coherently.

What an alien world. There was nothing around me that I could relate to my world. No knowledge or previous experience could help me to understand it. As the first and perhaps the last person to reach such a small scale. I thought that I should take some time to look around.

I tried to move forward, but it was virtually impossible to follow a straight path. All around me, space itself was waving so slowly that it seemed like I was watching it with a slow-motion camera. That was strange. Particles at subatomic levels had lifespans of millionths of a second! How could everything move so slowly?

I couldn't help but think like a scientist. Motion was related to speed and speed to distance and time. So, slow speed might be due either to time being expanded or distances being compressed. With each change of scale, I was decreasing my size, so the same distance would be perceived as larger, but the time . . .

Time invariance, of course! Time invariance with the scale could explain why everything was moving so slowly. Clocks ticked at the same speed at all scales, therefore measuring the same time for a single event no matter the scale at which was happening. If it took one second to walk one step in one scale, it would take the same amount of time to walk one step at all scales, even though the real walking distance was smaller at smaller scales. It would take ten times longer to walk a mile in a scale ten times smaller.

This was amazing. I wanted to see more—wait! If my theory was right, one minute there was equivalent to one minute at the scale of the collider's control center. I had one hour before the experiment began!

I was trying to make sense of what was happening when I felt a tickling in my legs. I looked at my feet. I was melting! Something on this scale was affecting me—as if I needed more problems. So I had less than one hour. I had to find where the collisions were going to occur, and I had to do it quickly.

I tried to move faster, but I sensed something preventing me from doing so, like the resistance of water when walking out into the surf. I noticed some undulations forming around me. Unbelievable; I was creating some kind of waves with my movement.

I had to think quickly! Did this mean I could feel a force? Waves in . . . wait. Could it be possible? There was only one logical explanation: I was effectively feeling the material world. I was at the scale where all dimensions converged. Time, Magnetic, Soul, And Space—all the dimensions were right there. The center of everything. So, sensing matter and fields meant I could interact with it and, therefore, do something with it. Something that might send a message to Rob.

Was I right? I didn't know, and I didn't have time to test the theory. It was my only chance. It had to be right.

I still hadn't found the exact location of the collisions. The experiment was designed to reach this scale, so if the collisions were strong enough, they would produce a particular kind of vibration. Although everything was waving, that vibration should have stood out from the background. I concentrated on feeling my surroundings, let my mind blend with it, entering into perfect harmony with the waving space around me.

I sensed something at my back. Strange vibrations were coming from one particular location not far from where I was. It had to be the collider; they must have started the experiment. Now the only thing left was to hope that all my hypotheses were right.

I started moving in circles around the area the vibrations were coming from. Small circles . . . large circles. If I was right, I would be able to create enough waves to alter the vibrations produced by the collisions. The vibrations and the waves would superpose, showing a circular resonance pattern when detected back at the accelerator. As crazy as it sounded, it was the only thing I could do.

After several circles, my arms began to fade as well.

Time was running out. I had to leave immediately, or I would never make it back.

I started moving up through the In-Out Dimension, still not sure if I had done enough.

After moving up a ways, I had to stop. I was in those intermediate dimensions where there were no reference points—where I wasn't sure if I had just moved up, down, or sideways. I was scared that I would get lost in one of those infinite scales. I concentrated even harder on a single thought that could calm me down: Rob, his face, his voice . . . and how much I missed him. Then I moved again.

At some point I felt him. That made me smile. I was going to be with Rob again. I gave myself up to my feelings and I followed him, slowing down until I felt him right beside me. I was so lucky. Neils was right.

Then I felt people around me, many people. Then I heard a voice . . .

"Ely, you did it! You came back!"

CHAPTER 17
ROB

The airplane was about to land in Genève. It had been a long flight, almost eleven hours, with one short stop in Montreal. I was tired, even though I slept most of the way. It was probably jet lag. Peter was sitting beside me, Ely's book in his hands. It had been one of the few nights I hadn't dreamed of Ely.

"Peter, what time is it?" I asked.

"Finally. It's 9:15 a.m., local time."

"Sorry about that." I couldn't imagine how boring it had been for Peter to sit almost the whole flight with a sleeping guy at his side.

"It's alright. I've had a lot to read. You're right, Rob. I can't believe how Ely was able to hide her real intentions for so long."

"Tell me about it. It doesn't say much about our relationship, does it?"

He remained silent. We were both feeling the same way: confused.

A flight attendant walked down the aisle to check that everybody was ready for landing. We fastened our seatbelts.

"What do you think she's doing?" I asked.

"I have no idea."

The airplane touched down smoothly at Genève Aéroport, only fifteen minutes away from CERN. A taxi took us through the town center. The city was relatively calm with no big traffic jams. Soon, we arrived at the complex. It was a beautiful dome-shaped structure. We went inside and approached the reception desk.

"Good morning. We have a meeting with Dr. Anderson," Peter said to the receptionist.

She checked her computer. "Welcome to CERN, Dr. O'Brien. Please have a seat while I let Dr. Anderson know you've arrived."

After a few minutes, a man approached us. "Hi, Peter."

"Steve, good to see you.

"How was the flight?"

"Not bad for a New York-Genève flight." Peter said. "This is Robert Kline. Robert, this is Dr. Anderson."

"Nice to meet you, Dr. Anderson."

We shook hands. "Please call me Steve," he said.

After a string of security and ID checks, Dr. Anderson accompanied us to a meeting room. He pulled Peter away to talk about something privately. Luckily, the room had excellent acoustics, and I managed to hear their conversation.

"So, Peter, you want me to take your friend to the LHC control center. You know that's a highly restricted area."

"I know, but this experiment has massive implications for the scientific community."

"Just because of that we can't allow external people wandering around the main control room."

"We don't need much attention. We only want to be present during the experiment, so Robert can collect the information for his article. Two chairs in a corner would be enough."

"Fine. But we've known each other for a long time, so please come clean. That thing about writing an article; he doesn't look like a journalist. What's up?"

"Steve, I didn't want to tell you by phone. He's my best friend's husband. She died a few months ago. He can't accept she's gone. He believes she's talking to him in his dreams. He thinks she's going to try to contact him today through some kind of subatomic bridge. He's getting worse every day, and I don't know what to do. Please, this is a personal favor. I need to help him get his life back again."

"Not an easy request. You know that."

"You were my supervisor on my PhD research. You know me well. I wouldn't ask for it under normal circumstances."

"Well, sure."

"I hope that when nothing happens today, he'll begin to accept the truth about his situation."

Dr. Anderson turned toward me, unable to hide the sadness in his eyes. "OK, gentlemen, we have a test in about two hours. In the meantime, my assistant, Sarah, will show you around the center. Robert, I hope this tour will give you some background for your article."

"Thank you." Prior to our arrival at CERN, I had thought Peter was with me on this, but I was wrong.

Sarah took us through the different areas of the main building—offices, libraries, laboratories, and so on. It was interesting, but I wasn't really present. I was thinking about what was going to happen in the collider room. I was so sure that Ely was there, but how did I know? Maybe Peter was right, and I was obsessed to the point of losing touch with reality.

We finished the tour in a waiting room.

"Gentlemen, do you have any questions about what you've seen?" Sarah asked.

"No thank you." Peter said.

She turned to me. "Mr. Kline, would you like to see any particular section of the center?"

"Thank you, but I've seen enough for today. You've been very helpful."

At that moment her beeper sounded. "It's Dr. Anderson," she said. "The test is almost ready. He wants me to take you to the control room. Please follow me, gentlemen."

I tried to keep from trembling. I was either going to discover that Ely was still with me or that I was going insane. The trembling grew worse as we stopped at a set of double doors.

"I'm going to leave you here," Sarah said. "Dr. Anderson is waiting for you inside." I tried to hold myself together as she opened the door for us.

We entered a huge room full of screens, cables, and keyboards. It was like a cross between the NASA control room and a big electronic retail store.

"Here you are, gentlemen." Dr. Anderson walked toward us and gestured toward a couple of chairs close to a big window. As I got closer, I saw a huge room, a cave a should say. A pipe surrounded by lots of cables and devices ran through the middle.

"Welcome to the control center," Dr. Anderson said. Then he began to talk with Peter as if I wasn't there. Well, I was a mad widower, after all, not a journalist. Besides, they were discussing electron volts, and tesla . . . something. I didn't have any clue about what these things meant.

"Yes, Peter. The discovery of tachyonic particles opened the door to a new world for us."

"Faster-than-light particles, the dream of all scientists."

Dr. Anderson shook his head. "It's not a dream anymore."

"How do you create these particles in the lab without breaking the relativity theory?" Peter asked.

"The secret is to jump over instead of going through the v equals c singularity. The theory establishes that no particle can be accelerated to speeds faster than light. We don't accelerate particles; we create them with already faster-than-light velocities from the collision of highly concentrated neutrino beams. Obviously, these particles behave weirdly, but we're getting there."

"What scale are you planning to reach with today's collision?"

"The Planck dimension, around 10-35 meters."

"But that requires energies of about 1028 eV, which is impossible to generate with today's technology."

"That's right—if you want to accelerate particles. We get this level of energy from the other side of the singularity. Once tachyons are created, increasing energy is a matter of reducing their speed, and that's something we can do."

"That's incredible."

"It is. Well, that's what we're going to do today, smash a few neutrinos and see what happens."

Dr. Anderson asked Peter to take a seat while the test was being performed. He pointed to a particular computer screen where we were supposed to see the test's results.

"So, Rob, how does it feel to be in one of the biggest laboratories on earth?" Peter asked.

"Impressive. What are those . . . things?" I pointed to the huge, tube-shaped amalgam of pipes and cables in the tunnel below.

"The two largest detectors in this complex, Atlas and CMS."

"I see." Apparently, he could tell from my face that I didn't really.

"Steve explained the details of the experiment to me," Peter continued. "They're going to test the latest upgrade. It's a great day for them."

"What kind of upgrade?"

"For this experiment the detectors have been upgraded with new Cherenkov radiation detectors. They're responsible for gathering the data generated by the collisions of new particles that. Sorry, Rob, in simple terms, we're going to witness the most powerful atomic particle collision that humans have ever made."

That was exactly what I wanted to hear. If Ely was right, this was the moment to prove her theory.

I sat down, still shaking, and tried deep breathing, but it didn't work. Peter sat beside me. People were running from a screen to another, the room filled with a climate of excitement.

After a while, I heard a cheer. Everybody started shouting, hugging, applauding, shaking hands. "It worked! It worked!" It looked like Peter and I had missed the best part. I had to admit, I should have listened to Peter when he told me that nothing was going to happen. I'd been a fool.

Before I had the chance to apologize to Peter, a tense silence invaded the room.

103

"What the hell is that?" someone asked.

I stood up, but I couldn't see the screen through the crowd. I walked slowly through the people. Peter was right behind me.

I could only see part of the screen through the shoulders of a couple of scientists: white spirals on a black background. Someone leaned toward the screen with a napkin and tried to clean what looked like a dusty spot stuck to it.

I recognized that spot. "That's not possible."

Peter heard my voice. Pushing two men aside, he managed to see the screen. He saw the spot, and then he stared at me. Dr. Anderson was looking at me as well.

I couldn't believe my eyes. It was there.

I left the room running. "Rob, Rob, wait. What happened?" Peter said.

I pulled a piece of paper from my wallet and showed it to Rob. "Look at this."

"What is it?"

"The day Ely died, she left this note stuck on the fridge."

And then he saw it. "No way . . ."

It said "le, Love ely," and it looked exactly like the mark on the screen.

His silence was all I needed.

CHAPTER 18

ELY

I felt a sense of rejoicing around me. There were a lot of people, some of them I didn't recognize, and yet I could feel they were all happy for me. Grandma was among them.

"Sweetheart, you did it! You came back! I thought I was never going to see you again."

"I was so scared, Grandma, but Neils was right. Rob led me back. I can't explain how, but I've never felt so close to him."

I wanted to talk to Niels. I was sure he was more than interested in what I had seen at the lowest levels and what it meant about reality. I looked around, searching for him, and my head began to spin. It felt like I lost consciousness for a microsecond.

Grandma looked at me with concern. "Are you alright, darling?"

I shook my head slowly. "I don't know. For a moment it felt

like I was going to faint."

"Do you want me to—"

"No, Grandma, I'm fine."

"You're a very brave girl. I'm so proud of you."

I smiled. "Where's Grandpa? Neils? I saw things down there. It's really amazing. I have to tell them everything."

"Later. Going to faint is not normal. You need to rest."

She took me to a quiet garden that I didn't recognize. The feeling of dizziness continued for a while. She kept an eye on me as we watched time pass by.

Then, Grandpa appeared. "Ely, I want you to come with me," he said before I had the chance to explain how happy I was.

"Grandpa, it's amazing. Even at the lowest scales, time is—"

"Later, Ely. Now there's something I need you to see."

He took my hand, and we made a jump to . . . Peter's house? Why had Grandpa brought me there? We entered through the main door and moved to the kitchen. Then I saw him.

It didn't make any sense. Peter was on the floor with a knife in his hand, mumbling something about not being able to see the light, about having nothing left. Why was Peter saying those things? I'd known him since high school, and he had always been such a happy person.

Wait a moment. . . . what was that?

A black shadow oozed out of Peter's body. It was big, at least two meters tall. Seamless and smooth, it flowed out of him and wrapped itself around him like a dark, translucent robe, as if it wanted to protect him, but from what?

We were far enough away that it didn't notice our presence. It had human features—legs, arms, and a head—or at least I thought it did. But its eyes caught me unprepared. They were deeply, serenely calm. I was expecting something more evil or diabolic, but instead it projected a natural, caring symbiosis with Peter.

How was that possible? That thing was trying to kill him! Yet its calm revealed a creepy lack of guilt, remorse, or empathy. I had only seen that kind of behavior once before, in psychopaths.

The thing started struggling, like it was trying to pull away. Something was holding it back, something inside Peter's body.

106

That thing had hijacked not his body but his mind.

I saw a movement in the garden. It was Rob. What is he doing there? He walked into the kitchen, then rushed at Peter and tried to take the knife from his hand. I was desperate to stop them, the two people I cared about most in the world.

"Wait," Grandpa said.

Suddenly, at the bottom of the kitchen, two bright lights began to shine. Two figures stepped from the lights and dashed toward Peter.

The shadow fought even harder to pull away.

Peter began to convulse, as if he were having an epileptic attack. Rob seized the opportunity to get control of the knife.

The bright figures unveiled bright swords and sliced at the shadow. The shadow began to scream, a sound of absolute, unimaginable terror. It was still screaming when one of the bright men pulled out a glowing string and wrapped it around the dark figure. Then the two of them disappeared as quickly as they had come, taking the figure with them.

I realized I was gripping Grandpa as tightly as I could. He ran a comforting hand up and down my back.

"Ely, that man would have died if it weren't for Robert's intervention. He prevented him from taking his own life."

"But it doesn't make any sense. He's my best friend. He wouldn't . . ."

"I know."

"What was that thing? It looked horrifying."

"Not what. Who."

"What do you mean?"

"That thing was once a woman. She's what we're fighting against."

"A woman? How? Grandma told me they were people who had chosen a different path of development. But that thing can't be human."

"I don't think it is now, but it was once. We call them the Antiscians. They're people who follow the opposite path. They live on the opposite side of the world."

"But she looked so different from us."

"Don't forget, we only see each other by what we project. What you saw was her projection. The terrifying image tells you how much wickedness exists inside her."

"And those two men, who were they?"

"Do you remember when Robert was attacked on the street?"

I nodded.

"Well, they're members of the same group that appeared beside him, the Gli Custodi."

"Where did they take her?"

"All captured people are taken to an isolated place where they are helped to reestablish their internal equilibrium—to bring back what they were before. It's a secret place; just a few people know where it is."

"And if they don't change?"

"They have to stay there indefinitely." Grandpa released me from his embrace and took me by the shoulders. "Ely, the pressure on us is building. The number of killings has increased over the last several weeks. We have to fight back, and we need Robert's help. You must contact him."

"Do you want me to go back into the In-Out Dimension? I don't think I could survive another trip."

"No, no, no. We only allowed you to go there because we desperately needed to convince Robert. Without his trust there's no possibility of any communication. He has to believe it's you who is talking to him, that you're still alive."

"Talk? Do you mean I can talk to him?"

"We think so," he said. "When you get in touch with him while he sleeps. We discovered that he enters a semi-detached state of mind where his conscious and unconscious minds separate from each other, creating a temporary mental gap that allows both of you to interact. We believe you'll be able to talk to him while his unconscious mind is in charge of his dreams."

So far, I had been able to enter his dreams and alter some background conditions, but there hadn't exactly been an interaction between us. If what Grandpas was saying was true, it would be unbelievable. "How can I do that?"

"He believes in you now, and that should make a difference.

No worries; your Grandma will help you. Now please go; we don't have much time."

CHAPTER 19
ROB

We talked for most of the trip back from Genève. After what had happened, I was so excited that I didn't think I'd ever sleep again.

Peter was more skeptical. "Rob, I'll admit, there are clear similarities between Ely's signature and the trace on the screen. But just for argument's sake, what if it was only an anomaly, a single conjunction of elements that happens once in a lifetime? Please think about that possibility."

"OK, Peter, let's follow that through. It's a rare, once-in-a-life-time anomaly, but I was able to predict it in advance. Months of planning, countless tests, and thousands of people working on this project, and then one guy on the other side of the Atlantic with no clue whatsoever about the experiment knows this rare random anomaly is coming."

"Don't close your mind. It's similar to the lottery. You choose a number today, and later you win. How could you have predicted the winning number?"

"In the lottery, for every winner there are tens of thousands of losers. If you're one of them, you play again next week. This is like one guy buying one ticket, one chance to play, and hitting the jackpot. I'm sorry, but I know what I saw, and I know what it means."

We broke off when the captain announced we were landing.

Our plane landed at JFK airport at 10:35 p.m., three hours late. We shared a taxi into the city and talked about our plans for the rest of the week during the drive. The taxi dropped Peter off first. I heard real pity in his voice when he said goodbye. He was clearly convinced that I had lost my mind.

I got home half an hour later and went straight to bed. After crossing the Atlantic twice in less than forty-eight hours, my internal clock had no idea what time it was. So, I slept for hours and hours.

I woke up early the next morning. I didn't remember any of my dreams. In fact, I may not have dreamed at all. For the first time in months, I felt calm. It was a deep relief to know that Ely was . . . how I should put it . . . still there.

But now that I knew she was trying to contact me, why? Everyone hoped, deep inside, that there was life after death. Was that what she was trying to do? Comfort me? But in my dreams, she kept mentioning her notebook, and now there was the "CERN anomaly," as Peter called it. Was she trying to show the world that she had been correct about the afterlife? And what did she want me to do, if anything?

I switched the TV on and then started making my breakfast with the news on in the background.

Terror at a luxury hotel in Boston. Several guests had been killed by a gunman who held them hostage during a two-hour siege and then committed suicide. Police were concerned by the trend of killings across the state . . .

I changed the channel. I wasn't in the mood for bad news. No matter how much relief they provided, Peter's words echoed in my head. What if . . .? I needed to do something about it.

For centuries, people have been trying to contact their deceased loved ones. Why not? I could call a medium.

No, I couldn't. Ely wouldn't have approved from this side, and I doubted her opinion had changed. As a scientist, she would have taken a more pragmatic approach—hypothesis, data, analysis, and so on. Yes, maybe that's what I had to do.

I needed to ask Peter if we could analyze the records of the experiment, in particular the image with the anomaly. I had only glimpsed it from a distance. Maybe I had seen what I wanted to see. I had to see it again and compare it with Ely's signature, this time using a more scientific approach.

I called Peter's office. Nobody answered. I called the laboratory where he was supposed to be working. A colleague told me that he hadn't shown up that day. That was strange. On our way back from the airport, he had mentioned that he would be at the center for a couple of important meetings.

His cell phone was off. I decided to call him at home. Maybe the trip had taken its toll on him too. Again, nobody picked up. No answering machine. He used to keep the answering machine disconnected only when he was at home, so he was probably still there. But why he wasn't answering?

The morning show I'd switched to picked up the news about the wave of killings. I started worrying seriously about Peter. Maybe I was letting the news influence me, but it didn't matter. I decided that I needed to check on him.

It took me almost an hour, fighting traffic, to get there. His car was parked in front of his house.

I rang the doorbell. No answer. By that point I knew something was wrong. I walked around the house and looked through the windows. Nothing. The back door was open, so I let myself into the living room. A half-full bottle of whisky was sitting on the table.

"Peter?" I heard a noise in the kitchen and ran to the door. He was lying on the floor, a knife in his hand, mumbling something about darkness.

He rolled upright and pointed the knife at me. "I can't take it anymore."

"Come on, Peter, you're drunk," I said, reaching for the knife.

"Stop! Life's not worth it anymore!"

I lunged for the knife before he slit his wrist. He fought back, trying to force it toward his neck. Then he began to tremble and convulse like he was having an epileptic attack. I pried the knife out of his hand and tossed it into the next room.

This was insane. He was not the Peter who I had known for so many years, the person who had flown with me to Genève. It had to be something he had taken by mistake.

A few seconds later, the shaking stopped, and he was calm. It was like someone had thrown a switch. He looked at me. "What happened? Why do I feel so . . . hopeless?"

"Peter, did you take any pills? Tell me the truth."

"No. You know me. I'm clean. And what are you doing here?"

I helped him sit in one of the chairs around the kitchen table. "Peter, when I came in, you had a knife and were ready to slash your wrists. What happened?"

"I was? I . . . remember . . . I was, wasn't I? Honestly, Rob, I don't know. I went to bed, and I slept like a baby. Then this morning I woke up feeling like the whole world had fallen apart. I heard a voice, a strange voice inside my head telling me to take my life." He put his head in his hands. "I can't understand what happened."

"How are you now? Are you feeling better?"

"Well, I'm not about to end it all. Thank you, Rob. Thank you very much. I'd be dead if it weren't for you. By the way, how did you know I was . . ."

"I didn't. Actually, I came here to ask you . . . never mind. I'm happy you're feeling better. Come, let's go out. You need some fresh air."

We spend the rest of the morning in a café at the bottom of the road. I didn't ask him about getting a copy of the CERN results—it didn't seem the right time. My own problems could wait. Once I was sure he was OK, I left for my office.

CHAPTER 20

ROB

It was 7:00 p.m. when I arrived home after an almost normal day at the office. I went straight to the kitchen and found a few ingredients in the fridge—enough to put together a ham-and-cheese omelet. I cooked without paying too much attention to what I was doing. I was starving, and it was my first proper meal that day.

While I ate, I went over what had happened that morning. For a moment, it was like Peter had been possessed by something . . . something evil. But that only happened in the movies. Of course, people only talked to their dead loved ones in movies too, so . . .

I sat on the sofa, turned the TV on, and fell asleep before I could even find a good film to watch.

"Hi Rob."

I stopped immediately. The voice was familiar.

I had been walking on a busy road. It was like waking up after being asleep for a long time. I didn't know where I was. The place reminded me of New York City during rush hour, but there were fields of corn on the other side of the guardrail. And there were no cars on the road, just people, thousands of people, marching in lockstep like an army.

I was one of them. I had a suitcase in my hand. I wondered where I was going.

"Rob."

I turned round. My legs were shaking, my heart racing. I recognized her curly, golden hair through the black-suited crowd. There she was, as beautiful as always.

We looked at each other without saying a word. Unable to keep myself together, I fell to my knees. Tears flooded my eyes. She kneeled and hugged me. I wanted only to stay still, quiet, to feel her warm arms around me. I surrendered to that feeling.

"Why did you leave me?" I whispered.

"I didn't. I've always been beside you."

I looked at her again. My heart was so happy to see her, but as much as I wanted to be true, I couldn't accept it.

"This can't be real." I got up and stepped back. "Where am I? Who are all these people?" The crowd kept marching, shoving us back and forth as we stood in the middle of the road.

"I don't know. This is your dream, the creation of your subconscious."

"My dream? That's impossible. I have to be asleep to dream. And this conversation, these people . . ."

"Rob, listen to me. We're in your dream, but we're not part of it. Everything around us is the stage created by your subconscious. Your body is asleep, and so is your brain, but your mind is not."

"You mean I'm awake inside my own dream?"

"I know it's difficult to understand, but you've got to believe me."

"Ely, you're gone. My love isn't here anymore. This can't be real."

"And yet . . ." She spread her arms. It was such a typical Ely

115

move that I had to smile.

"Rob," she said, "please listen to me. Do you remember the notebook?"

"Sure, your diary."

"It was me trying to talk to you."

"Talk to me? But you're—"

"I tried several times to make contact with you, but I couldn't pull you out of your dreams. You were so immersed that you didn't even notice my presence. I had to create a recurring dream as a last resort. Sorry about running you down all those times. I imprinted the word 'notebook' in your mind, hoping that when you woke up after many times you would remember it."

"You never said anything about your diary when you were alive. And your research, all our years together, and you told me nothing about it. Why?"

"I was afraid you wouldn't believe me. I hardly believed it myself until I got here. And, be fair, you didn't really believe me when you read it, did you?"

"I believed you enough to go to Genève."

"Yes, after all those dreams. Be realistic, Rob. You wouldn't have believed it. You went to Genève because you doubted, not because you believed. You wanted it to be true, but you went there in search of evidence."

"But you know I wanted to believe more than anything. I put myself in your shoes, and I did what I thought you'd have done in the same situation."

"And it worked. The experiment at the collider, our secret code, it was me giving the evidence you needed."

I just looked at her. I didn't know what to think. That was more than I could cope with.

"Rob, I know it must be a disturbing idea to be talking to me, but death isn't what we've imagined it to be." She paused for a few seconds. "Let's do this step by step. Today is our first contact. When you wake up, you'll remember this conversation; you'll feel as if it were real. And it is. I hope you can accept it. The world around you, the future of everybody, depends on your willingness to believe what I'm going to tell you. Now go, fall asleep, my beloved husband."

CHAPTER 21

ROB

I woke up early in the morning after a long and rather pleasant sleep. And that dream . . .

I sat bolt upright, the conversation with Ely coming back to me in incredible detail.

Was I going crazy? That was definitely a possibility, but it felt very unlikely. I had no doubt in my heart that Ely had appeared to me in person, but I also had a heart full of desire, grief, and pain that was very easy to deceive. And what about my mind? That was the scary thing. I could consciously and precisely go over every element of the conversation—her voice, her skin, her smell . . . damn, it felt exactly as if we'd had the conversation before I fell asleep. I knew it sounded incredible, and I should have felt lucky, but I didn't. Whatever was happening to me was not normal.

OK, so if I was really in contact with Ely, then there had to be a reason. I didn't have any particular psychic gifts. I wasn't special

117

in any way, so why me? And why now months after her death? What should I do now? Keep it to myself? The experiment had been witnessed by many. Should I share it?

I couldn't imagine going public with such a story. Sure, it would get some attention. Unbelievers would think I was crazy, and the believers would consider me illuminated, psychic, or something similar.

I was immersed in my own philosophical reasoning when the doorbell rang. I opened the door, and, to my surprise, it was Peter.

"Hey, how are you doing?" I asked.

"I didn't sleep well last night. You're the only person I can talk to about it. I brought breakfast." He raised his hands, balancing a box of doughnuts with a couple of coffee cups on top.

"Well, in that case, please come in."

We settled onto the couch, which was still warm from my spending the night there, and sipped our coffee. I picked up a French cruller. "So, Peter, how are you feeling?"

"I couldn't sleep the whole night. It was like . . . I was outside of myself. I'm going around and around what happened, and still I can't explain it. It was—"

"Supernatural."

"Well, yeah."

Something in his voice sounded like he might be open to listening to my experience. He was right; he was the only person I trusted to share it with. But to what extent was he ready to know the whole truth?

"You know, Peter, my dreams about the notebook, the experiment in Genève, what happened to you . . . if you put it all together, don't you think they're connected?"

"You mean with Ely?"

"Yeah . . . or something related to her."

"Please don't come again with that."

"If Ely was right, life after death is as real as life before death. Do you think people would be prepared to handle that truth?"

"Are you?"

"I might be able to get used to it."

118

"Rob, you're going through very hard times, which makes you an easy candidate to become a believer, but we live in a time where science runs the world. Extraordinary claims require extraordinary evidence and all that."

He was right. I needed evidence, and it was my own wife in my dreams. But if it was real . . .

"But we have evidence," I said.

"One anomaly in a single experiment? Remember, in science the result of an experiment is only considered true if it can be reproduced. You know that's not possible, and even if we could use that single experiment as evidence, are they really willing to believe it? I saw it with my own eyes, and I still don't."

"It is a start though, isn't it? It would open an entire new world to study."

"Yes, but that's not the point."

"For argument's sake, you can't deny that you would be very happy as a scientist if you could."

"I don't deny it. I can imagine my colleagues trying to unify both worlds into one single theory. Maybe we could even find where all the dark matter and dark energy are. That would be fun."

His attitude changed over the course of the conversation. He was more . . . enthusiastic. Now was time to go deeper into the subject.

"You know, Peter, something that has always been hard for me to understand is why most scientific discoveries provide a person, a company, or even a country some kind of privilege over its peers. I know most discoveries ultimately help humanity, but it's also true that most of the time, organizations and countries are the first to profit from them."

"Welcome to the world of intellectual property. We all know the rules. If you discover something, it's yours. But that may only apply to material discoveries. I'm not sure if it works with whole new worlds. They'd be available to everyone."

"That's exactly what I'm afraid of." I looked directly into his eyes. "Peter, if this is true, we're talking about something that could have the potential to change our societies, our way of life, everything around us, even our conception of life itself."

"Well, we won't be afraid of death anymore if that's what you're talking about. There will be less grieving. Maybe science and religion will finally converge into a single school of thought. These are all good things, right?" He sounded optimistic, something I wasn't.

"And how will things change if people aren't afraid of death anymore? Think of all the people already willing to kill to get what they want. This will make it even easier for them."

"Kill?"

"If we aren't afraid of death, then we won't be afraid to kill. In fact, technically speaking, we wouldn't be killing anyone. We'd be just sending them to the next world."

He stared at the floor. Maybe I'd pushed him too far.

"You know the good side of this?" I said, smiling. "Police work will get a lot easier. Just bring in a medium to ask the victim who the killer was."

That brought back a smile. We ate quietly for a while. Then he broke the silence. "Do you think it was an attack?"

"An attack?"

"Why not? If killing someone we would be just sending him to the other world, then maybe something from the other world could be trying to bring people there or, even worse, bring people here."

This time, his idea disturbed both of us. We remained silent for the rest of breakfast.

CHAPTER 22

ROB

Peter left at about 11:00 a.m. I was already running late for the day. I wanted to learn more about mediums and contacting the dead. If what had occurred the night before was more than a dream, I needed to understand why. I had never been particularly spiritual, and I had never had a supernatural experience in my life. So, why now? Was this a gift that I always had, or had I developed it by chance? I needed answers.

I began with Wikipedia, then moved on to sites that specialized in psychics and spiritual gifts. It was a huge industry, and I spent hours, in fact the rest of the day, searching, reading, downloading . . . looking for an answer.

In the end, I didn't find anything that looked remotely like what I had experienced.

By the time I gave up, it was already dark. Frustrated and tired, I ate the first two things I found in the fridge: a sandwich and a hard-boiled egg. I just couldn't make up my mind. I had become so obsessed with what happened that I didn't want to waste any time.

Then I realized I didn't have to do this research alone.

I left everything unwashed in the kitchen and went to the bedroom. I brought the articles and web pages that I had printed that afternoon. I lay down on the bed with all the material spread around me. Then I read until I started getting sleepy. I had a feeling that I would find answers to my questions that night. Whether they were true or not, it didn't matter. I was prepared to let my dream take me to the unknown.

"Hi, Rob."

This time I found myself walking on a long sandy beach, which was empty except for Ely. It reminded me of the coast of California because of the little sandpipers following the movement of the waves. Well, except for the two suns and a big planet so close that it occupied more than a quarter of the sky. I was wearing Bermuda shorts and a T-shirt. She was wearing a white cotton dress. I could see her shape through the translucent fabric. Her hair was waving in the wind. Her eyes had a bit of makeup. Deep inside, I was afraid it was all an illusion, my mind's creation.

It didn't matter. I missed her every single day.

"Why are you looking at me like that?" she asked.

"Because I miss everything about you. You can't imagine how hard it's been without you. Everything I do, everywhere I go, it reminds me of you."

She took my hand. "I know. I've missed you too. It doesn't matter how much time I spend at your side. It's still difficult . . . for both of us."

"At my side?"

"I've been with you every second since I left. All those nights when you sat on the sofa staring out the window, I was there with you. The first few days were unbearable. I blamed myself for your pain, your depression, everything you were going through. I talked to you—I even shouted sometimes—but you didn't notice."

I had never thought about the consequences of feeling that

way. It never crossed my mind that my attitude could cause such pain to her. All those days of crying and feeling frustrated, upset, and depressed. What a selfish, stupid man I had been. How could I have been so blind?

"I . . . think I felt you, but I didn't. I'm so sorry, Ely. I never meant to hurt you."

"No, don't. It wasn't your fault." She looked away from me. "How could you have known that I was still . . . with you?"

"I saw you die."

"Well, sort of. Rob, I'm alive."

She was right, I was talking nonsense. She was walking beside me, holding my hand. We were having a conversation. How could she be dead?

So far, I had accepted, even believed, everything that had happened. But with the line between dead and alive breaking down and whatever had happened to Peter, it was time to ask for an explanation.

"Ely, it's difficult for me to accept that we're together, walking, having this conversation . . . here in my dream. Can't you see how mad everything looks?"

"Absolutely. It's a shock for me too, and I understand the situation. I can't imagine how difficult it is for you not knowing what's going on."

"So what is going on? How is it possible that you're here with me? You must agree that this isn't normal. It's not, right?"

"I don't understand why we have this level of communication either. Nobody has been able to explain it. They think it's a—"

"They? There are others?"

"They . . . everybody . . . they're all with us."

"You mean everyone?"

She gave me a reassuring smile. "Don't worry. They're not going to come crowding in on us, I promise."

"Just who are we talking about?"

"Mom, Dad, and Grandma and Grandpa are with me. They welcomed me when I arrived, and since then they've been supporting, guiding, tutoring me."

"Tutoring you?"

123

"Things are different here. It's not easy to get used to. The transition is like being born again. You have to learn everything afresh, even the most basic things like walking and talking. You can't do it alone."

"Born again?" I realized I must have sounded childish, asking two-word questions, but I wasn't able to articulate anything more coherent than that.

"Rob, the world we experience is only a fraction of what's really there. Every one of us has to rediscover the world and, most importantly, ourselves."

Some rocks were in front of us. I wanted to turn back, but she climbed one of the rocks and then sat down, staring at the sea. The sunlight created a halo around her perfect face. She was so beautiful. She looked at me, inviting me to sit beside her.

"Ely, if our loved ones are really still among us, why do they let us grieve? Wouldn't it be less painful for everyone if we knew everything?"

"Everything? The time and space we live in is more diverse than we thought, and life within is a lot more . . . complex. It's all around us, and still you can't see it. It defines what we do but you still can't feel it. How could people consider something real if it's not measurable or verifiable with experiments? Science interprets reality as an extension of what's already known. This goes so much against what our senses tell us that it's impossible to imagine."

"Ely, please. Enough science for the moment."

"Sorry, it's just that . . . I understand it all now. But it's impossible to explain. Our definition of reality limits what we consider real and blinds us from seeing everything that's before our eyes. I know it doesn't sound like science, but it's still true."

"Genève was science. What happened was pretty much measurable. Tell me, how did you do it?"

"It's too hard to explain. What I can tell you is that I put everything at risk, so you would believe in me. I needed to open your mind to the possibility that I was still alive, that the conversation we're having right now is real."

"I don't understand. Do you want me to show the world that your theories about life after death are right?"

124

"Rob, I'd never ask you to do that. Both worlds have been separated since the beginning of time. This is the way it is, and we're not going to change that."

"Then why are you here now, talking to me? To make me feel better?"

"I couldn't be happier than if this made you feel better. But there's something else, something that goes beyond what we feel about each other." The next few seconds of silence nearly drove me mad. "Rob, we need your help."

"My help?"

"I need you to listen very carefully to every word I'm going to say. This is not your mind playing tricks on you. You must trust me. We don't have much time. Have you heard anything about a wave of killings?"

I thought back to the news that morning—and the last few mornings, come to think of it. "There does seem to have been a rash of murders lately."

"Well, they're not murders. They're suicides, and they're only going to get worse. They come from my world."

"A paranormal origin? I thought you risked everything just to move a subatomic particle around. How is it that . . .?"

I was willing to believe this crazy dream of mine was real, but this was asking a little too much.

"Do you remember what happened to Peter?" I'd never seen Ely talking so seriously before.

"Wait, you mean his . . ."

"He was nearly driven to suicide because he was . . . well, possessed by an entity that filled him with despair. We call them Antiscians."

"But you said that what we have, you know . . . this thing between you and me, is unique. How are they able to talk to people?"

"They don't talk. They indirectly influence the way people think and feel about themselves. People aren't aware of what's happening; it all takes place at the subatomic level, unconsciously. What we've got is different. You're aware of what's going on. We recognize each other's presence."

"So I saved Peter from being possessed."

125

"You gave us time to get there before the entity forced him to commit suicide, and that's exactly what we want your help for."

"Wait, are you trying to say that you want me to keep all victims alive long enough for your people to catch the . . ."

"Antiscians."

"The bad guys."

"Bad guys . . . yes." I saw a tiny smile on her face.

"Don't you think you're asking a little much? You know me, Ely, I'm a simple citizen.

"We're desperate. We have to do something, and this is our only hope."

Just a word from her was enough for me to go to the end of the world.

"OK, so how would this work? How do I know when and where these Antiscians will strike again?"

"We don't know. We're still trying to figure it out."

"Then where should I start?"

"These attacks seem to be limited by the time-space interface between our worlds. There must be something that constrains their movement. So, we need data. Look at the records of the past killings. Search for any trend or pattern. And ask Peter to help you. He knows statistics, which might come in handy."

She caressed my face with her warm hand. "I have to go now. I love you, Rob."

Without giving me the chance to say goodbye, she just disappeared. I heard a familiar sound in the background . . .

CHAPTER 23

ROB

The alarm clock rang. It was 7:00 a.m. I woke up feeling absolutely relaxed, even though I had apparently spent the night in conversation with my wife.

Antiscians? Trying to kill Peter? What nonsense.

Wait, Peter had said something about someone taking people into the other world. What if he got the idea from a subconscious awareness of what was happening to him? No, the whole thing must have come from my own subconscious, right?

But Peter had really been on the verge of killing himself. How had the urge simply gone away? Could I afford to ignore the possibility? I was afraid, afraid it might be true and that something really bad was about to happen to all of us. It could be the start of a war between worlds.

Ely had told me to analyze the information about the killings. Apply the scientific approach to prove a hunch. What madness.

The line between my dreams and reality was definitely getting blurred . . . something that was making me profoundly happy and at the same time so confused and insecure. There was only one thing I could do from all of this: get Peter on board.

I called him immediately and asked him to have lunch together. He accepted without question. He was so grateful for what I had done that he was ready to do anything for me. I was counting on that. I still didn't know how I would approach the situation with him. I decided I would just have to give it a try.

I left home early. I didn't want to be late. I knew how busy that area of the city was at lunchtime. Today was no exception.

I parked behind the restaurant. Peter was already inside waiting for me.

"How are you doing?" I asked as I approached his table.

"I'm fine. No hint of a relapse. What about you?"

"Not bad."

I sat down. The restaurant was busy. With only one hour for lunch, people didn't have much time to waste.

He ordered a club sandwich with chips and a coke. I took a healthier option with a Caesar salad and orange juice.

We started talking about normal things: traffic, weather, work. I was looking for an opportunity to broach the subject, but the opportunity never presented itself. Finally, I just jumped in.

"You know, Peter, you might be right about the attack."

"Attack?"

"Yes. As you said yesterday, maybe somebody was trying to take you to the other world."

"What? I was just tossing that out for something to say."

"I don't think so. Look, out of the blue, you were hit with a depression so profound that you nearly killed yourself. Is it really ridiculous to think something else was at work?"

His hands balled into fists. He deliberately unclenched them, then rubbed the back of his neck. "Look, Peter, this isn't the easiest thing to talk about. I'm . . . I'm still scared that it could happen again, that there's something wrong with me."

I didn't want to mention Ely too quickly. I wanted him to be the first to bring her into the conversation. "Take it easy. You don't have to worry. It's over. I just spent a great deal of time yesterday night thinking about what happened. All possible explanations. Did you feel anything before the attack?"

"Like what?"

"You know, fever, stomach pain, maybe you ate something that poisoned you. Maybe it made you hallucinate."

"I got takeout from a Thai place a few blocks from . . . wait . . . wait a moment . . . now that you mention it, yeah I remember feeling some fatigue, a strong headache, maybe some fever."

"Migraine? Flu-like symptoms?

"Yes!" He quickly changed the tone of his voice. "Yes, you're right. For a moment it was as if I had the flu."

I knew how to approach the subject now. "A virus, my dear friend. You might have been exposed to a virus . . ."

I hadn't realized how worried he was about it until relief spread over his features. "That explains everything! Oh, Rob, thank you."

Without being aware of it, my dear friend had provided me with the perfect way to talk with other people about the attack—to describe it as a virus.

During the rest of the meal, Peter talked about hallucinations and how a virus could have caused them. I had forgotten that one of his brothers was a doctor. He talked about virus symptoms linked to hallucinations, depression, emotional instability . . .

It was time to take Ely's advice and look at the data. "Well, Peter, we have to prepare our case before we go to the police."

"The police? We? What for?"

"Come on, Peter, do you think you're the only one who has gotten this thing? At the very least, we've got to report that Thai takeout place."

I waved to the waiter to ask for the bill.

"And say what? That I had suicidal hallucinations after eating some infected pad Thai?"

He was right; it sounded silly. I didn't know exactly how I was going to do it—how I could show the link between what happened to Peter and the killings. How would I explain that I knew so much about the killings? Who should I talk to? I had to prepare a much better case before I made my next move.

As we walked out of the restaurant, I realized I still hadn't asked Peter to help me.

CHAPTER 24

ROB

It wasn't until I got outside the restaurant that I realized how gorgeous the day was. Bright sunshine, cool breeze, blue sky, the perfect autumn afternoon. Peter was silent, staring at his shoes while waiting for the valet service to bring our cars. It was obvious he wanted to slip away. That's why Ely always felt so comfortable with him—he couldn't hide his feelings worth a damn.

"Look, Peter, you're right. We can't go right now. But before we leave, I need to ask you for your help. I believe what happened to you might be happening to a lot of other people. And spreading."

"I'm sorry, Rob," he said flatly. "I can't stay. I have a lot to do at the center today. Let's leave it for tomorrow."

The valet arrived and opened the door of Peter's car. "You can tell me later what I can do for you."

"I'll give you a call." My car arrived just after Peter pulled out. I watched him looking at me through the sideview mirror as he drove away.

I went back to the office. Not that I found much to do there. The rest of the crew were gathered inside the glass conference room for the monthly review meeting. One of them left the room.

"Hi Robert. How're you today?" It was the financial director.

"Up and down, Jack. What about you?"

"Trying to fill the gaps. This morning I received a phone call from IBN International and DHL. Both asking where their marketing guru was."

"I'll call them."

"Today?"

"Promise."

"Come and join us."

I shook my head with a smile. I wasn't ready to get involved with office matters. I spent a couple of hours doing some solitary paperwork. Speaking with the two clients lifted my spirits a little, but it was not enough to clear my mind of Ely.

I left the office before the internal meeting finished. It was nearly rush hour, so I decided to take a shortcut through an unpopulated area—an alternative route that Ely had shown me one day when the main roads were blocked. It had been almost a year since I used it, so I drove slowly.

Suddenly, a woman ran into the road. I braked as hard as I could, and the car drifted into a skid. When my car finally stopped, I looked in the rearview mirror.

The woman was on her knees in the middle of the road. Shit! I had hit her.

I got out of the car and ran toward her. "Are you OK, ma'am?"

She was crying and holding her leg—I must have clipped her. I kneeled down and tried to get her to show it to me.

"Why didn't you just run over me?" she said. "I can't live like this anymore."

"What are you talking about?" But then I knew. What had happened to Peter was happening to her!

I glanced in both directions. No traffic yet, but it was only a matter of time. "We need to get you off the road."

I took her by her arms. She tried to pull away and run, but

her leg gave way. I held her tight and half walked, half dragged her to the sidewalk.

Then she started shaking violently. I hugged her tightly, so she couldn't hurt herself.

Then, as with Peter, she came back to herself. It was like she was just waking up. "Who are you? Where am I?"

"You walked onto the road and stepped in front of my car. I almost ran you over." She seemed like a good person, so I decided not to tell her what she had really been trying to do.

"That's ridiculous. I was at home, asleep. Oh, my head!" She gripped her temples with both hands. "How did I—what happened?"

I thought the best I could do at the moment was to help her to get safely to her house. She was barefoot, and her feet weren't bleeding or anything, so I figured she lived nearby. "Where's home?"

She released one of her temples long enough to point to a house a few yards away.

"Please let me help you."

She stood up slowly—her leg was apparently only bruised, I hoped—and let me hold her arm and walk her slowly to the door. Without a word, she went inside and closed the door behind her.

I drove the rest of the way home faster than before. This was the second induced suicide I'd run into. Was it a coincidence or another attack? Or were there hundreds or thousands of such people all over the country killing themselves in this way? It was a perturbing possibility.

I found the house cold and empty. It didn't matter if I could still communicate with Ely; it was going to take a long time to get used to living without her.

I threw together a couple of sandwiches and then went to my studio. I wouldn't get anywhere with the police without knowing a thing or two about the killings, so I grabbed my iPad and started Googling.

The first page was filled with news stories about the wave of killings. I couldn't believe how disconnected I had been from what was going on around me.

Police Reviewing Security in New York City Following a Wave of Murders.

A Wave of Murders Terrorizes Women of Atlanta.

Gangs may be behind the wave of killings in Vancouver.

Neo-Nazis Suspected in Rash of Murders in Boston.

The killings were there, but all the references were to murders. Then I realized if the police came across someone stabbed or shot in their own home, someone with no suicidal tendencies or recent depression, wouldn't they assume it was murder? Interestingly, no one was reporting a national crisis. It looked like no one was connecting the dots.

So how could I convince people that there was a supernatural cause behind the suicides if people didn't realize they were suicides?

Despite my excitement, I started to nod off. I looked at the clock. It was 1:00 a.m. Whatever I was going to do, I'd have to plan it carefully, or I'd end up in a psychiatric hospital.

I went to bed with the hope that I could talk to Ely again that night. Now I needed her help more than ever.

CHAPTER 25

ROB

The following day was completely different from the previous one—grey, cold, and wet. Yet I felt better than I had in weeks, waking up completely refreshed two hours earlier than normal. It was like dreaming while awake, although as unnatural as it might sound, it was helping me sleep better.

I didn't remember having any dreams, though I suppose that didn't mean I didn't have one. Maybe something would come back to me later.

I rushed through my morning routine and then sat down with my iPad, cup of coffee in hand, and went back to searching the Internet for more information.

I found an article from Suffolk county local news portal Long Island Press. There had been a few dozen victims in our area. It sounded crazy when I suggested it to Peter, but going to the local police about these cases would be a lot easier than tackling the

FBI or the State Police. I decided to stop by the police station on my way to the office.

I realized it might be tricky to ask about the killings without raising suspicion. I thought of introducing myself as a journalist, but I didn't have any ID that said as much. A student doing a thesis on criminology? Too old to be a student. A family member of one of the victims? I didn't actually know any of the victims. I was already in the police station parking area, and I still didn't have an answer, so I did a couple of extra turns in the visitor area to find an open spot.

By the time I got out of the car, I knew exactly what to do. Maybe I had dreamed of Ely after all.

The receptionist was an old lady who didn't seem too willing to make new friends that day.

"Good morning," I said.

"Yes?" She continued typing without taking her eyes off her screen.

"Two weeks ago I was attacked on the street by a man. I'd like to know the status of my case."

"Name?"

"Robert Kline."

She typed my name into the computer, then made a call. "Detective Sullivan, I have a person named Robert Kline in reception who wants to know about his case."

She hung up without saying another word. At least it wasn't me. Apparently, she was unfriendly to everyone.

"Take the elevator to the second floor. Detective Sullivan will be waiting for you."

"Thank you." That was a good sign. I was going to see the same person who I had met at the hospital. It would save me from having to explain it all over again.

When the elevator doors opened, he was there waiting for me. "Mr. Kline."

"Hello, Detective."

"What brings you here? I thought you didn't care much about whether we identified your attacker."

"Actually, I do."

He walked me to his desk. Although it was an open-concept office, nobody took notice of my arrival. He invited me to sit down.

"So, what can I do for you?" he said.

"I want to know what happened to him. Is he in jail?"

"With no one pressing charges, we couldn't hold him for more than forty-eight hours."

"So he's back on the street?"

"I'm afraid so." He looked at me without blinking. "So, Mr. Kline, why don't you tell me exactly why you're here?"

I wasn't prepared for such a direct question. Police! They smelled when something wasn't right. Should I just tell him? If so, how? I was sure he would kick me out of the station if I told him the truth, and where would I go then? I needed more time to think.

"I'm worried that guy will come after me again to get revenge for what I did to him."

"You know, Mr. Klein, after more than twenty years on the job, I can tell when somebody is hiding something."

Damn. It looked like there was no other option than to go straight to the point.

"Detective Sullivan, I wanted to know if he was still in jail because I need to talk to him. I believe the wave of killings happening across the country isn't caused by gangs."

He pushed back his chair and cleared his throat. I had his attention.

"We might be facing some kind of outbreak, and I suspect he has something to say about it."

"An outbreak? You mean like a virus?"

"Detective, I guess during the past twenty years you've seen people come here with all sorts of stories. And, yes, I know it sounds incredible. But if it's true, we don't have much time."

"I'm guessing this is more than a hunch."

"It's based on two cases. One, a close friend of mine, was trying to cut his own throat. The other was a woman who threw herself in front of my car."

He was still looking at me, no change in his expression, but he hadn't thrown me out yet.

"Both were in the throes of severe depression, to the point that they were unable to cope with their lives anymore."

"Mr. Kline, if that's the case—"

"But in both cases, with my help, they came back to their normal selves a few minutes later. They couldn't remember what had just happened and had no idea why they might have wanted to kill themselves. The despair went away as if someone had thrown a switch. Both times."

"And what's the relation between these two people and your aggressor?"

"I think he attacked me as an act of despair because he wanted me to kill him. I mean, I'm not a fighter, and I was able to take away his knife easily."

"Mr. Kline, you seem like a good person. You want to help people going through difficult times, and that's a good thing. Don't get me wrong, but two people doesn't add up to an outbreak."

"Detective Sullivan, these are two people that I've run into personally. There are tens of thousands out there. Just look at the news." He blinked slightly. "I suspect that, whatever it is, it's affecting people's hormonal levels, changing them in a way that makes them temporarily insane."

I had no idea where the hormonal stuff was coming from. Maybe it was something Ely and I had talked about the night before. My mind was working fast. The image of my university lectures in biology flashed through my mind like they had taken place yesterday. Something was happening to me, and whatever it was, it was working!

"Interesting," he said. "And how did you reach that conclusion?"

"I have no evidence. Yet. I just wanted to ask the man if he had any recollection of how he felt before he attacked me. He could be the third case."

"As you may know, I can't give you his whereabouts. But I can promise you that we'll deal with your request." He opened one of his desk drawers, pulled out a form, and passed it to me. "Just write out the details of what you want to know. The department will process your request and contact you as soon as it produces any results."

With little other choice, I filled out the form. Then he walked me to the elevator. He didn't say a word and was heading back to his desk even before the doors slid shut. What did he have to do that was suddenly so urgent? With any luck, it was something to do with my case.

CHAPTER 26

ELY

Grandma's help was critical in my learning to dream-talk with Rob. She had been beside me the entire time, advising me, tutoring me, encouraging me. The most difficult thing we had to do was attract Rob's attention while he was still asleep. His subconscious was the master of his dreams, directing the actors on stage. In most of his dreams, he was submerged in his role, unable to think for himself until that crucial instant, that moment of enlightenment, when for the first time he stopped following the crowd and turned back to look at me.

Since then, we had talked a couple of times with no trouble at all. I had been given a second chance to be with him, and it was pure joy. But above all, I was happy for him. I didn't know how long I could have stood by watching him fall apart.

"I think I've established a clear line of communication with Rob," I said. "Don't you agree, Grandma?"

"Absolutely, but it wasn't easy. That journey scared everyone."

"It was frightening indeed. But thanks to Rob, I managed to find my way back."

She fell silent, a silence that communicated a deep fear.

"Is there something you want to say?" I asked. She didn't speak. Although I still wasn't able to read other peoples' minds, I was sensitive to Grandma's feelings. "I know something is bothering you. You can't hide it from me."

"We're afraid for your well-being."

Her words didn't make any sense. "But nothing can happen to us. We live forever, don't we?"

"We don't die in the traditional way, but we can still . . . disappear."

"Grandma, don't scare me." Once again, I was overtaken by the fear of not being able to be with Rob.

"We're made of soul energy and, like any other energy, entropy applies. We can dissipate. We maintain our coherence because we're confined to the Soul Dimension. But at the scale you traveled to, things are different. All dimensions converge into a single scale, and your soul energy could have easily leaked to a different dimension, the way a cup of hot water loses its heat in a cool room. More time down there, and you could have disappeared."

"That's why my legs and arms started disappearing."

She nodded. "You lost part of your soul energy. That's the reason for your lack of focus and dizziness."

Was I sick? Could I have been close to dying again?

"It isn't what you think, sweetheart. You'll never leave us. But you hurt yourself, and now you need time to heal, to regain your normal level."

"Why didn't you tell me that before?"

"We didn't know it. Remember, this is the first time someone has ever come back from those scales."

While we were talking, a person with a tough expression on his face appeared in the room. He was one of the Gli Custodi.

"Elizabeth, we require your presence. Please come with me." His voice carried such authority that the "please" sounded irrelevant.

"Grandma, please, I need you to come with me." I didn't want to go alone. I was intimidated by the Gli Custodi, even though I knew there was no reason to be.

She looked at the messenger, waiting for his confirmation. Then she took my hand, and we moved along with him.

We arrived at an old chamber illuminated by electric lamps. There were no windows, and the walls were made of bricks worn by time with patches of crumbling plaster and some frescos that looked like medieval icons. A white marble statue of a woman lay in a niche in a wall, curled on her side, and a gorgeous mosaic was on one of the columns. It looked like some sort of ancient burial place. Why had they brought me there?

A voice came out of the darkness. "Elizabeth, we finally meet. I've heard so much about you."

A man entered the room. He was dressed in a white tunic that looked vaguely ancient Greek and at the same time very modern, even futuristic.

I stepped back cautiously. I knew I was being rude, but I wasn't able to control myself.

"My apologies. I should have introduced myself. I'm Michael, a member of the Gli Custodi. We are honored to have you here."

He was different from the others. He didn't seem to be a warrior, although he talked like one. Given the way the other warrior treated him, I assumed he was a leader, though he seemed no different from the others. Somehow, I didn't feel comfortable with him.

I stared at the statue. "What is this place?"

"Rome. This is the burial place of Saint Cecilia in the Catacomb of San Callisto."

"Why did you want me to come here?" I asked.

"We have to be cautious. We can't publicly expose your gift. You are unique, but this is not the time to praise your virtues." He turned to Grandma. "Beth, you've briefed her about the situation, right?"

"Yes, Michael. She's also seen them."

"Good." He turned back to me. "Then you know why you're here. The material world is being attacked by the Antiscians, and not for the first time. For centuries we have clashed, and we have stopped them every time, even if we had to hunt them down one by one. This time the situation has changed dramatically. We think they're ready to scale their attacks up to the next phase."

"The next phase?" I couldn't believe it. Since I'd arrived, I'd had nothing but increasingly bad news, one thing after the other.

"A self-sustaining chain reaction of death."

"What? What do you mean by chain reaction?" In my mind, a chain reaction was associated with only one thing: atomic bombs and destruction.

"Some weeks ago we noticed that the Antiscians were doing short raids, a handful of them expending a terrific amount of energy to kill a single person. We didn't understand the reason behind such small waves until we noticed the numbers of victims—thirty-two, sixty-four, one hundred and twenty-eight, two hundred and fifty-six, and so on."

"A geometric progression."

He nodded. "But we couldn't figure out how they were doing it. We captured some shadows, but we still never got any conclusive information about what was going on. Then, two days ago, we managed for the first time to capture three shadows, young enough in this world that we were able to turn them back to normal. What we discovered left us shocked. I want you to hear it directly from one of them. Linda?"

A woman accompanied by a Gli Custodi warrior appeared beside Michael. She was young, maybe even younger than me.

"Linda is a newcomer. She's just made the transition." Michael turned to her. "Please, Linda, tell us what happened to you."

When I heard her scared voice, I realized she was a teenager, much younger than I thought. "I'm not sure when it happened, but one day I woke up with this feeling of frustration about myself and my life. Completely out of control, it quickly degenerated into an unbearable depression. I remember walking out of the shower, then hearing my mother's voice begging me to open the bathroom door. I found myself standing in front of the sink, afraid to clean the foggy mirror."

She stopped for a moment. Michael got closer to her. "Sorry," she said.

143

"Take your time."

She nodded. "Without even thinking about it, I . . . opened the mirror and took a bottle of my father's pills. I don't remember much after I swallowed all the pills at once, but I do remember waking up next to this strange man. I was still depressed, but I was confused as well. I couldn't understand why there was a lifeless body lying beside me. He took my hands and told me to stay calm, that he would explain everything. Before I could reply, he tugged at me, and in the blink of an eye, I found myself in a place I didn't recognize, beautiful but alien. I was surrounded by at least a dozen people."

"Did you recognize any of them?" Grandma asked.

"No, but some of them were like me, just arriving. I was afraid; we all were. The man started talking about what had happened to us, but above all, why it happened and who was responsible."

I wanted to know who that man was, but, with a gesture of his eyes, Michael asked me to let her finish.

"I could see what he was saying. It was like being inside his mind, or maybe he was inside mine. I can't explain it, but we were both somehow unified in one single mind. He shared his bitterness and rage with me, with all of us. It felt like mine. My fear turned into fury. A frenzy for revenge invaded me; revenge for what had been stolen from me, my family . . . my life."

She started crying. I tried to get closer to comfort her, but Michael stepped in first.

"It's OK, Linda. I think that's enough. Go, I'll join you in a moment."

She left without saying a word.

As soon as the girl faded, Michael turned to me, though he said nothing.

"Poor girl," I said. "She was so fragile, so hurt."

"First, they crack the person's mind and destroy his or her will. Then, after the victims have made the transition, they take advantage of the fragility of their souls to invade their minds and force them to feel the same way. We don't know how they get inside their minds, but that's the way they do it."

"Do what? The conversion?"

"What happened to Linda suggests that they have found a way to convert all newcomers almost immediately."

"Turn a person into a shadow."

"That's right, and when they do it in a consistent way, their shadow army doubles in size with each wave."

He was right. If 128 shadows killed 128 people, and they were converted immediately, they became 256 shadows for the next wave. There wasn't any need to be a mathematician to calculate the final outcome.

"Eventually, they will become unstoppable."

"Now you get the picture."

"Why would anyone want to do something like that? Grandma told me that they wanted to control people, not kill them."

"They have tried for millennia to get control of people. The material world has been our battlefield."

"But this isn't just a battle. It's genocide."

"Remember, Elizabeth, death has a completely different meaning in this world. It's just a transition, and that's why we think they might have decided for a lose-lose strategy."

"Lose-lose?"

"Yes. We've stopped them from taking control of people, so they want to fix it so that nobody has control over them. If they can't have them, then we shouldn't have them either."

"Still, it doesn't explain why they hate us so much."

"They can't accept that we're them. Brothers and sisters who once decided to ignore the enlightenment that all human beings have inside and lose themselves in the dark side of human emotions. It's a path that leads to the bottomless abyss dominated by uncontrolled hatred, anger, and envy. A path that, once taken, is hard to return from. We can acknowledge that we're the opposite sides of the same coin—we can understand both sides of the equation—but they can see only themselves and view us as totally other. And completely dangerous."

"But if they're like us, we're like them."

"Absolutely. That's why our people don't take for granted what's been given to them. So many of us become tutors to help others work their way up to a much higher evolutionary level, away from what the Antiscians represent."

"Except that they've found a way to destroy all of it."

"Elizabeth, everything isn't lost yet. As you know, we can stop them while they're in symbiosis with the host. When we first learned about these waves, we thought that each killing was independent, the result of an isolated attack. With your help, we could have had enough time to hunt them one at the time."

He paused, watching, calculating my reaction to what he was going to say. "But now that the attacks are part of a wider chain re-action, dealing with them individually is useless. We've managed to capture a few of the shadows involved in the waves. However, those left behind continue multiplying, doubling in number after each successive wave. We will never stop them, unless—"

"We get them all at once."

"Exactly! Like a virus. You have to remove the whole infec-tion at once. Otherwise, the disease keeps coming back until it spreads throughout the body. We have to stop them before they spread beyond our control."

He sounded confident, something I didn't feel. It was hard to maintain my composure.

"For this new approach to work," he continued, "we need to be able to anticipate their moves and be prepared before they attack again. We have to understand their patterns of attack, lo-cations, timing, everything that can help us predict their future behavior. The problem is, we don't know how to predict an attack of that magnitude."

"Which is where I come in," I said. What was predictable was what they expected from me.

"Actually, where both of you come in. We need you and your husband to work together to identify where and when the next waves will take place."

"Michael, I'm just a woman who loves her husband and doesn't want to leave him. That's all there is to me. I'm sorry, but you're asking for help from the wrong person."

"You're wrong, Elizabeth. Your gift makes it possible for the first time for both worlds to work together. We need you and Robert. When the chain reaction starts, we won't have much time to respond. We have to stop the waves before they reach the tipping point when they become too big to stop."

He took me by the shoulders and stared into my eyes. The energy behind his eyes was . . . disturbing. "I know it's hard to accept," he said, "but I think this time the future of the human race is truly at stake, and you're our last chance to save it."

CHAPTER 27

ROB

I went to the office after visiting the police station. I needed to wrap up a couple of things, more for something to do that would help me to calm down. I wasn't used to dealing with the police, and Detective Sullivan hadn't made it easy for me. Tough, arrogant, suspicious of everything. Just the way he looked at me made me feel like a suspect. I left the police station with no sign that he would help me.

It was already lunchtime when I arrived at the office. A few people were at their desks, those willing to wolf down a sandwich while working. It was the perfect workplace, not only because they let me take time to deal with my loss but also because my colleagues were understanding enough to give me the space to grieve for my wife at my own pace.

I went to my desk. Everything was untouched, unchanged, just like in my house. They were both a reflection of my life, frozen in time since Ely passed away.

I managed to make some progress on one of the projects and replied to a pack of emails, most of them from people asking for things that were already overdue. My life was a mess, but I couldn't—didn't—want to change.

By the time I finished the last email, it was late in the afternoon. While driving back home, I couldn't help but think about what had happened in the last few days. Ely's notebook, the CERN experiment, my dreams, Peter's crisis, Detective Sullivan, it all seemed to be leading me . . . somewhere. It was scary, but I would follow my love wherever she wanted to go.

I wasn't hungry. I sat on the sofa with a beer and a pack of chips. As I looked out the window, my mind drifted away.

"You shouldn't drive so fast."

I was driving a convertible along a road overlooking the sea. Maybe the coast of California, though maybe it was Cannes. The road was empty.

"Please, Rob, slow down."

Her soft voice broke my concentration. There she was. The wind was blowing her hair . . . she was so beautiful. "Keep your eyes on the road." I couldn't. I was happy. Very, very happy.

"Rob, we need to talk. Things have changed. Please pull over."

I had no clue what she was talking about, but I didn't really care. I had my own agenda for this dream, or at least I thought I did. But she looked so full of despair that I forgot anything I might have wanted.

I saw an overlook ahead, and I pulled over.

"What's going on, Ely?" I asked.

"The situation is getting worse. The killings are about to get out of control. The Antiscians have discovered a way to create a self-sustained chain reaction of death."

She was looking at me with such intensity that I could feel her tension all over my body, holding me, preventing me from moving.

She finally broke eye contact and got out of the car. When I'd regained control of my thoughts, I followed her.

"I'm sorry, Ely. I don't really understand. Don't forget, I'm not a scientist. Why don't you start again? Take a deep breath."

"We don't have time. You've got to do something."

"OK, Ely, tell me what's happening."

"The waves of killings . . . they've found a way to double the number of victims with each wave."

"How is that possible?"

"They're able to turn the victims of one wave into the killers of the next."

She was getting closer to a breakdown with each word. "Ely, please calm down. Whatever it is, we'll deal with it."

"You don't get it. A few more waves will wipe out the entire country."

I didn't believe her. Two, four, eight, sixteen, thirty-two, sixty-four . . .

"Rob, don't waste your time. Only twenty-eight waves are needed to wipe out our country's population, and thirty-three will take out the world."

Was I hearing this right? The country's entire population? The world? This dream had gone well beyond my control.

"Stop thinking nonsense. This is a real threat. We have days, maybe weeks. We have to stop them now."

"Ely, I don't have a clue what you're saying. You're talking like we're standing on the verge of our imminent annihilation." This dream couldn't be real.

She spun toward me. "We are! You've got to believe me. Our only chance is to stop them while the waves are still small. After that, everything will be lost."

"Can you see what you're asking?" I shook my head. "How on earth am I going to convince people of something like this? Something that can't be seen but can still kill us all? How do I get people to believe in that?"

She stared at the ocean. "I don't know."

"What about Genève?" I said. "You used the particle accelerator to convince me that you were there, that you were real." She looked at me, not surprised at all. "You reached this world once, and it worked. You did it in a laboratory surrounded by scientists. If you could do it again, I might show them—"

"Rob, the experiment was meant for you and you alone. You were the only person who could read our secret symbol. I hoped that your desperation to have me back would make you believe."

"All right, they don't have a reason to believe. But they thought it was an anomaly, a random event, because it happened once. If you could—"

"Rob, please, it can't. I was lucky to emerge alive from that journey."

"But you did it."

"Yes, but only because of you. Our connection helped me to . . . never mind. Even if I could try again, we'd have to wait until they were prepared to repeat the experiment. It could take weeks. It would be too late by then."

"What if they have plans to do it soon?" I was a little desperate.

"My world isn't part of people's reality. You know how people deal with the unknown. They'd just say it was another random effect. Don't forget that I can influence only one sub-atomic particle. That's not much of an effect. They'd work out an ingenious way to explain it, an equipment malfunction, you name it. It's human nature."

"Ely, I don't know what to do. I had a hard enough time convincing Peter to help me. How do you expect me to convince the world?"

"It's not going to be easy, but we have to try. We need to understand how the Antiscians plan their waves, to find a pattern in the attacks. That's the only way we can be prepared for the next one." She walked close to the edge of the cliff. "The first thing I would do is analyze the last wave."

We both remained silent, looking down at the serenity of the ocean. "What the hell is that?" she said.

She was staring out at the sea. I followed her eyes but couldn't see anything.

"Sorry, Rob, but I have to go now." Then she disappeared. I still wasn't used to that.

151

I found myself alone, fully conscious but still dreaming. It was an amazing feeling. Everything was so real, the wind blowing on my face, the sound of the waves smashing on the rocks, the sunshine warming my skin. I wouldn't have noticed a difference between that place and the real world if it wasn't for the huge planet in the sky that had replaced our moon. Nothing was stopping me from giving myself up to a future with Ely in this imaginary world.

I still held the feeling even after a noise jolted me awake.

CHAPTER 28

ROB

Damn! I had forgotten to turn off the alarm clock. It was Saturday, and there was no reason to wake up early. When I opened my eyes though, I realized the sound wasn't coming from the alarm clock; it was my cell phone. I looked at the time: 9:33 a.m.

"Hello?"

"Can I speak to Mr. Kline?"

"Who's this?"

"Mr. Kline, it's Detective Sullivan."

It was way too early for a routine call. Something had happened. I sat up, still half-asleep. "Yes, Detective. How can I help you?"

"I need to talk to you in person. I have something I want to show you."

"Of course."

"There's a pizza place at Main Street and Yaphank Avenue. It opens at eleven."

I had eaten there with Ely one day on the way back from her lab. "I know the place."

"Good. See you there."

I couldn't believe it. He'd found something. Had he contacted my attacker? I didn't know, but for once I had somebody willing to do something, and I wasn't going to let the opportunity slip.

On my way to the restaurant, I thought about my conversation with Ely. A chain reaction of death. As difficult as it was to believe, it might already be happening.

As I reached the parking area, I saw Detective Sullivan at a table close to the window. The back doorbell announced my arrival.

"Good morning, Detective."

"Mr. Kline." He invited me to sit across from him. The waitress approached us.

"Two black coffees." He ordered them without asking me. If he wanted to be that direct, I had to try to be the same.

"So, Detective, did you talk to my attacker?"

"He left the state. We think he's in Florida. But that's not what I want to talk to you about."

"I'm listening."

"I went through the forensic reports of all local deaths we've had in the last couple of months. Three quarters of the victims were found with a higher than expected level of a cortisol hormone."

He was telling me exactly what I needed, something that might make him believe. "Cortisol?"

"One of the hormones produced by the adrenal glands, one that's linked to depression. However, we couldn't find any trace of infection in the victims. I'm afraid only half of your story can be verified."

Half was better than nothing. "Well, Detective, I think this shows we can't ignore the possibility of an outbreak. If the victims have something in common, the possibility of a common cause of death shouldn't be discarded. No matter how small it is, it suggests that they're connected, right?"

"If so, it's the only connection. The victims were found in

completely unrelated locations. There's nothing pointing to a common source of contagion. I don't see how they could have been infected with the same virus."

So he was thinking about viruses. This was better than I'd hoped. I tried to think quickly. "Unless the whole country is already contaminated," I said. "We have no idea what the incubation time could be. It could've come from neighboring states."

He thought about that for a moment. "All right, that's possible."

"And if it's true?"

He fixed his eyes on me. "That would be . . . bad."

"So, our next step should be to validate our theory." I used the word "our" deliberately. "We need to look for more evidence."

"And how do you suggest we do that?"

"We have to look at the death records for the whole country."

"The entire country? But how do we know what to look for?"

"Suspicious deaths, apparent suicides of people who weren't at risk, high levels of this cortisol thing. I can't promise anything, but I'm ready to search for it."

"The FBI has a database, but I need permission to access it. I'd need to involve my captain . . ."

I could tell from his voice that he intended to leave it for Monday. "Detective, think. If we're right, the whole country is infected by something that could lead to massive waves of deaths at any time. What if, by acting now, could save some people's lives? Even if we could save the life of one person, isn't it worth trying?"

He stared at me for a moment, then took out his cell phone and dialed. "Hi, David, it's me. I know it's Saturday, but I need your help at the station."

I tried not to sag with relief. I had managed to bring Detective Sullivan on board. I was sure that with his help I would be able to find answers to Ely's questions.

"I know, and I appreciate it," he continued. "It won't take long. Besides, you own me one." He put the phone in his jacket. "We need to get back to the station. Our IT expert should be getting there in about ten minutes."

We stood up, and he left a few dollars on the table.

"Why don't you come with me to the station? It'll be quicker if we both go there in a police car."

"Of course."

Suffolk County Police Department was less than two miles south.

"So, Detective, how are the police explaining the rash of deaths?" I asked as we drove.

"They're here and there with no clear connection. Best guess is gangs and other groups taking care of their own business, but most of the deaths don't fit that profile. After talking to you, I made some calls to a few guys I've dealt with in other major cities. They're stumped. I mentioned your virus theory when I talked to them," he added.

"You mean drug dealers?"

"Drugs, prostitution, mafia. Some people think we're going back to the forties with an Al Capone-style of business."

"What about the FBI?"

"I don't know. I don't even know if they're tracking them. Deaths are treated as local matters."

"But how is it possible that the huge increase of deaths is not being seen by the administration?"

He glanced at me. "What do you mean by 'huge increase'?"

"Detective, we're talking about hundreds of deaths!"

He stopped in front of the station door.

"Mr. Kline, do you have an idea how many suicides occur in our country every year?"

"No."

"More than thirty-six thousand. We have more than 2.4 million deaths every year. Some are natural, some are due to accidents, and others are violent. A few hundred unexplained deaths isn't a major deviation from the norm. It's worth paying attention to, but it's not a red flag."

At that moment I understood. The Antiscians were experimenting with a number of deaths small enough to go unnoticed. Waves of hundreds or even thousands of people wouldn't make much of a difference in the total number of deaths as long they happen across the country. It would be almost impossible to pull one wave of killings from the background.

"Mr. Kline, are you OK?"

"Sorry, I never thought there were so many." I had hoped that the FBI database would tell us something. But finding hundreds of deaths among millions . . . the task suddenly looked a lot harder than I thought it would be.

The station was almost empty. A sergeant was behind a counter at the entrance, and another officer was at a desk nearby. Detective Sullivan waved at the sergeant and then led me through without stopping.

We took the elevator two floors down. A narrow corridor led us to a rectangular room surrounded by glass walls, except for the back wall, which consisted of huge TV screens. Computers were scattered at various desks, but only one was occupied. The sign at the entrance said, "Incident Room. Authorized Personnel Only."

Sullivan slid the door open. "Hi, David."

"Detective Sullivan." David looked at me with suspicion. "Don't tell me you've found a new partner."

"This is Mr. Kline. I met him a few weeks ago when he was jumped in an alley"

"I guess you have a good reason to spoil my weekend?"

"Yesterday, Mr. Kline came to me with an idea that, if it's true, could help us solve some of the latest deaths. I need your help to check it out."

"If you're here on a weekend, it's got to be important. So, what do you need?"

"We need to access the federal criminal database."

"But it's—"

"Yeah, restricted for everyone but you. You still keep good contacts with the National Crime Information Center, your former employer, right?"

David looked at him in surprise. "How did you know that?"

"You forget you're surrounded by policemen. We investigate people; that's what we do for a living."

Investigate people? Would it be possible that he knew about my personal life? Ely? My trip to Genève? Was that why he was helping me?

157

David cleared his throat nervously.

"I wouldn't change my mind if I were you." Sullivan said. "I don't know how the NCIC would react after hearing that one of its ex-employees still has access to their database."

Without saying a word, David opened a browser window, then hit a few keys. The screen on the wall lit up with a window for the federal database. He entered a password, and we were in.

He turned to Sullivan. "OK, what are we looking for?"

The detective turned to me. "Mr. Kline, here you have what you asked for."

I thought for a moment, wishing I had better statistics skills. "We need to get access to the police reports of all deaths that have happened in the country during the last two months."

David started typing on the keyboard. Up on the screen, the words "397,411 cases found" appeared.

He glanced at me. "And . . .?"

"Connections, any kind of connections between these cases."

He stopped typing. "OK, this is a relational database with reports stored in tables with specific entry fields. You've got to give me something more specific than 'connections.'"

"All right. First, filter for unexplained natural deaths." It sounded like a good starting point.

He hit a few keys. The figure dropped to 39,794.

"Try those that happened when the victim was alone." I guessed victims of the phenomenon had to be alone; otherwise, the person with the victim would have done what I did with Peter.

That brought us down to 16,217 cases.

OK, patterns, patterns . . . "Can you plot those versus time?"

A line graph appeared with blips at regular intervals.

"That's . . . odd," David said. "Do you want to add murders?"

"No, I want to add recognized suicides."

Without taking his eyes off the screen—or, apparently, blinking—David tapped some keys. A new curve appeared. The sharp peaks were more pronounced.

"What the hell?" he said.

"I don't know."

"Now add deaths related to overdosing."

"Drug overdoses." David said.

"All of them: street drugs, alcohol, prescription medicine . . . whatever can kill someone, including deaths ruled to be accidental."

The peaks changed shape some—a few grew larger, others smaller. Then I remembered what Detective Sullivan had told me that morning.

"Can you access their autopsy records?" I asked.

"Well, autopsies are performed only on specific cases."

"It doesn't matter. Search for a high level of hormones, any kind of hormones."

Once again, more peaks, though these were much smaller. "Detective, I think we have something."

Sullivan approached slowly and leaned forward to see the details. "Oh well, we tried."

"What are you talking about?" I walked up to the screen and pointed to some of the regular peaks. "Can't you see them?"

"David," Sullivan said, "can we see this plot over the last few years?"

David expanded the graphic to cover three years. He was right. The ones in recent weeks didn't particularly stand out.

"I guess you don't expect people to die at a constant rate with mathematical precision in an equally spaced period of time," Sullivan said. "They're normal variations. And it's very easy to see patterns in random data."

He stepped back, looking at the screen as if there would be nothing else to see. "We die when we have to die." Sullivan said. "For the lucky ones, we find their bodies immediately. For the others it takes some time, but we go when we have to go."

"Wait, Detective. What do you mean by 'it takes some time?'"

"In some cases people are found days, weeks, even months after they die. Maybe the housekeeper or a member of the family gets worried; you name it."

"So, we aren't looking at the real date of death?"

"That's right." David said. "But the system has the estimated time of death."

He made some adjustments to the data. Pushing his chair back, he shook his head. "I don't know; I think there's something there. How long ago do you think this pattern started?"

"I don't know exactly. Maybe two months?"

He began typing. "What we need is called a fast Fourier transform. It takes a data set and breaks it down into individual frequencies. If there's a pattern here, the transform will find it, and it can't be fooled."

It took a minute for the computer to work on the data. What we saw on the screen left the three of us speechless.

"There it is," David said, breaking the silence. "Peaks of unexplained deaths every three weeks. Let me use that as a filter."

He tapped in a few more keys, and the original plot against time reappeared. After a second, the line filled in. Now the peaks were clear.

And they were getting larger.

"Well, I'll be a son of a bitch," Sullivan said.

CHAPTER 29

ROB

There we were, three guys staring at each other. It was clear that we had found something, but what exactly? Sullivan pointed to the last peak on the graph. "David, how many are we talking about, here?"

"About nine thousand."

"Against a baseline of . . ." I prodded.

David did some quick calculations. "About six thousand eight hundred and fifty deaths that day."

So, there were about 2,150 cases. Given that some of them may have been real suicides, and that we had doubtless missed some, that was about right for the eleventh wave.

I turned to Detective Sullivan. "Do you believe now?"

"There's definitely something there," he said. "That your theory is true, well, I wouldn't go that far. We need to understand the causes behind the increase. Why and where they happened, the profile of the victims . . . everything that will help us to explain those peaks."

At that point I really wished Ely were there. She was an expert in analyzing numerical problems. I remembered the day when she arrived home with a problem to be solved for the next day—something related to finding trends and patterns in an eleven-dimensional data space. She didn't talk to me the whole night, but she spent hours and hours on the phone with Peter trying to find—

Peter!

"Detective, I think we're dealing with a very complex problem, and we need help from an expert. No offense, David."

"None taken. I'm not a mathematician."

I looked at Sullivan for any sign of concern with bringing someone else to the police station. "If you don't mind," I said, "I'd like to call a friend of mine. He's an expert in statistical analysis. He might help us."

"If you think so. Use the staircase."

"Pardon me?"

"It's the only place here where you can get a signal to call outside."

"Thank you, Detective." I took my phone and walked to the staircase.

"Peter, it's me, Rob."

"Rob! Are you alright? When we left, you seemed—"

"I'm fine. Listen, I need you to come to the police station, right now."

"What? What have you done?"

"No, it's not what you think. You remember what I told you in the restaurant? Well, I'm here with a detective, and we think we've found some evidence. But we need your help to make sense of it."

"I don't . . . Of course. I'm at the lab, but I'll be there as soon as I can."

"OK. I'll wait for you."

I hung up and went back inside. "Peter will be here in about half an hour. He's a theoretical physicist with serious statistical

162

chops. If anyone can help us, it's him." Now that the initial excitement was over, I realized how exhausted I was. "Anyone else here need a coffee?"

"Yes," they replied in unison,

"Come with me," Sullivan said. "There's a coffee machine on the ground floor."

We went upstairs, this time using the staircase. Detective Sullivan and David started talking about police things. I followed behind them.

It was incredible. I was still wrapping my head around the thought that humanity was being attacked by dark spiritual beings. But I had seen it with my own eyes. So far, everything Ely had said was there.

Which meant I really was talking to my dead wife at night in my dreams, which was something else to get my head around.

"What would you like, Robert?"

I snapped back to the present. "Just black coffee, thank you."

While Sullivan fed coins into the machine, David approached me. "Detective Sullivan was telling me your theory. A virus that can't be detected and yet causes suicidal levels of depression. That's pretty damned strange, isn't it?"

I nodded. "The operative word being 'damned.'"

"Yeah. What makes you think it really exists?"

"I happened to be there when it attacked two people. Both of them went from suicidal despair to normal in seconds with no memory of what had happened." I thought for a moment and realized that being as honest as possible was the best way to get through this. "I'm not sure it's a virus, but it seems to be acting that way."

"You know, it's really hard to spot a trend from two cases."

"That's why we're here, to see if we can find something more."

We waited in the nearly empty lobby, sipping our coffees and thinking our own thoughts. After a while, Peter came through the front door.

"Peter, over here!"

"What's going on, Rob? Why are you in the police station?"

"It's OK, Peter. This is Detective Sullivan. Detective, this is

163

Peter, the expert I was talking about."

As expected, Sullivan didn't say a word.

"Peter, I asked you to come here because we need your help."

"We who? The police?"

"Yes, the police." Detective Sullivan said, breaking his silence. "According to Mr. Kline, we need your mathematical skills to verify something. Let's go downstairs."

As we walked down to the Incident Room, I wondered if the fact we were together—a policeman, an IT specialist, a physicist and a . . . well, medium—was just a matter of chance or if it was the result of a carefully developed plan. Maybe Ely or someone was working behind the scenes.

David opened the door, and we filed inside. Peter walked up to the wall screen, which still showed the steady blips. "There's a signal there, I think."

"Show him the Fournier thing," I said.

David clicked on his trackpad a couple of times, and the scatterplot came back up.

Peter stared at it. "A Fourier transform?"

David nodded.

"Well, that looks clearer."

"We've been looking at the number of deaths that have occurred in the last two months across the country," Sullivan explained. "We don't know what these peaks mean, but we think there's a pattern there, and we need your help to understand it."

"You know I'm not a criminologist, right?"

"No, but Robert says you're a statistician," David said. "There are key events buried in this data, and we need to tease them out—isolate them—in order to understand them."

It was time to start working for Ely. "If we can do that," I said, "we might be able predict where and when the next peak will happen."

Sullivan gave a start, then took on a subtle new intensity. I don't think he'd thought that far ahead.

"But they aren't events," Peter said. "They're real people." He was scared, which was understandable. He had been one of the people in these statistics, and I couldn't forget that.

"I know, but trust me," I said. "There's something behind the way the deaths occur. If we manage to identify it, we might be able to stop more deaths from happening."

I'm not sure he believed what I had just said, but our friendship helped to fill any holes of doubt in his mind. He sat down at a computer beside David, stared at the graphs on the screen, then started typing.

Detective Sullivan stood on the other side of the room, staring through the glass at the plain, unadorned corridor. Something personal was happening with him. I wanted to talk to him about it, but he didn't seem like the kind of person to share with strangers.

"There we go," Peter said.

I looked back. The peaks were still there, and it was clearer that they were getting bigger over time, but they were rounder, and the whole thing was lower.

"I did a running mean and corrected for the overall mean. That isolates a lot of the background noise. And what's this hormone thing you were searching for?"

Detective Sullivan explained about the hormone anomalies, which sent Peter back to the keyboard. A few minutes later, another graph appeared, this one with narrow, precise peaks that were much lower.

"OK, I filtered for autopsies with odd hormonal imbalances. I'm sure that filtered out a lot of positive hits, but it isolates one factor."

"Meaning?" Detective Sullivan said.

"There are lots of cases that are part of the pattern that don't show the hormonal thing. But every case that shows the hormonal imbalance fits the pattern." He continued to stare at the pattern. "OK, I think we've got a handle on the core data, at least in terms of timing. Let me try something."

He resumed typing. This time equations and numbers scrolled across the big screen. Then he stopped dead, staring at one number in particular.

"Peter, what happened?" I asked

"This can't be possible."

"What? What can't be possible?"

"That's the Feigenbaum constant! This parameter defines the scaling factor between values at bifurcations. Its value is 2.5092."

"Peter! English?"

He shook his head. "We call it the alpha constant. It's a number that appears in fractal theory and relates the width of successive bifurcations. I think in our case it gives us a clue to the frequency with which the peaks are occurring."

I still didn't understand a word, but he looked like he knew what he was talking about.

"Let me try grouping the peaks separated by a distance equal to the inverse of alpha." He typed in a couple of equations, and a new graph appeared that didn't make much sense to me. "Oh, interesting. It looks like there are many small sequences of peaks. David, pick up that one. Now extract the group of victims located in our state . . ."

A second window appeared on the screen, showing a long list of names. I was waiting to see what other kind of analysis David was going to do when two names jumped out at me—Jane Sullivan and Tom Sullivan. I looked around. Detective Sullivan was behind me looking at the screen, tears in his eyes.

"My wife and son," he said quietly.

"I'm so sorry, Detective." There wasn't anything else to say. I could only imagine what he must be going through. All my doubts about his unconditional help disappeared.

Peter was still massaging the data. "Now we divide the values of each consecutive peak. I want to see how much each peak increases its value from its predecessor."

The incomprehensible graph changed shape again.

"OK, it's faster than a linear progression. Let's try plotting the values in a semi-logarithmic scale and find the average linear line, which is . . ."

"Two," David said.

"Holy shit . . ."

"Peter," I said.

"Well, there's a fair amount of noise in the data, but when

you select one sequence and filter it out, it's pretty clear that the peaks aren't independent. Deaths occur in waves that repeat with a period inversely proportional to alpha. Depending on the sequence, it ranges from a few days to about three weeks. The older the sequence, the longer the period. But for all sequences, the number of deaths roughly doubles with each successive wave. Rob, whatever's going on, it behaves like a fractal."

"A fractal?" Sullivan asked.

"The concept behind them is simple," Peter said. "A small part looks like the whole thing. Take a cauliflower and break off one of its branches. How does it look? Similar to the whole cauliflower."

"But isn't it too simplistic an explanation for the complexity of nature?" David asked.

"That's exactly the point. Complex phenomena don't necessarily need complex explanations. Fractal theory gives simple rules to explain highly complicated behaviors. That's the beauty of it."

For a moment the conversation drifted away from the waves of killings. Although we were all together, our minds were on different things. David was upset about being blackmailed. Peter was intrigued with this fractal thing. Detective Sullivan was trying to come to terms with the loss of his family. I tried to register surprise, but there really wasn't any. After all, it was exactly as Ely had told me in my dream.

"So, we're surrounded by fractal things." David said.

"Everywhere, from our circulatory system, lungs, and brain to trees, clouds . . ."

"And now in a massive outbreak," I said.

A moment later, the elevator slid open, and a team of black-coated men with guns poured out. "Freeze! Nobody move!"

CHAPTER 30

ROB

Sullivan glanced at a point under his shoulder where he doubtless kept a weapon then slowly raised his hands.

A team of ten soldiers poured into the incident room. "You, stop typing." One of them wearing a helmet, body armor, and a large assault rifle pulled Peter off the computer.

"I'm a detective," Sullivan said, "and these people are here under my supervision." His hand went slowly toward his inside pocket. "I'm going to pull out my ID, so—"

"Don't move!" The soldier pointed his gun at him. "Your weapon first."

Using two fingers, Sullivan slowly drew a compact, mean-looking handgun from his shoulder holster and set it on the floor.

"On your knees, hands on your head," one of the men said.

"What's going on?" Sullivan asked as he knelt down.

A couple of agents wearing black suits entered the room.

"I don't think you're in a position to ask questions," one of them said.

I struggled as a soldier tried to grab me, but he blocked my legs with his and pushed me. I fell on my knees with the cold feeling of his gun on the back of my neck. Moments later, we were all in handcuffs with two agents holding our arms.

"Who are you people? Why are you arresting us?" I said. "We aren't doing anything illegal."

Sullivan gave me a quick glance. It dawned on me that he didn't recognize these people. They weren't local cops. Something seriously bad was happening, and none of us had a clue what it was.

They took us upstairs. Two other agents were in the reception area. Outside were four black SUVs and a large military vehicle with no departmental markings on it. I had never felt so scared in my life. Whatever they thought we were up to, I knew we were innocent.

They put each one of us in a different car, sandwiched between two soldiers. The military car escorted us.

We drove for at least an hour to a building outside the city. It looked like a military installation. Soldiers were everywhere.

They took us out of the cars one at the time. I didn't have the opportunity to talk to Peter. I was worried about him. He knew even less than I did about what was happening. Well, maybe not. Still, I felt guilty for having called him.

I was the last one out. They escorted me into a small room on the first floor. I didn't see any of the others. I guessed they put each of us in different rooms.

I remained alone in the room for maybe three or four hours. I couldn't sit still for more than five minutes. I walked around the room, nervous, anxious . . . worried. What was happening? Where were we?

Then the door opened. "Sir, come with me." Two young agents took me to a windowless room full of people sitting around an oval conference table. Neither Peter, David, nor Sullivan were there. A woman was standing at the front of the room.

She was clearly in charge.

"Mr. Kline, as you might expect, we've interrogated your friends, and guess what? They all pointed at you as the mastermind. Detective Sullivan was following your direction, David was doing what you asked on the computer, and Peter, well, you called him to join the party. So you'd better have a good explanation."

"First, why don't you tell me what law I've broken?" I said. "As far I can see, we weren't doing anything illegal."

"Except accessing highly classified information. Only authorized people have access to the federal criminal database, and, of course, you're not one of them."

So they had been tracking what we were doing in the police station. The question was, who were they? And who were they working for? It was clear she knew more than I thought, so I realized I had better cooperate.

"So, Ms. . . . ?"

She didn't say her name, so I continued anyway. "Well, I assume Detective Sullivan told you my theory about the deaths and how they occur in waves. So you know what we were doing with the database."

She pulled out a folder with some papers inside. "A professional man with an engineering and marketing background, a steady job, well liked, no kids, and, unfortunately, a widower as of a few months ago. So can you explain to me how such a simple, upstanding citizen can have a theory about a national crisis that hasn't been made public yet?"

Damn. They knew about it after all. I had no idea what to do. Tell the truth and get myself committed? But I suspected she would be able to see through any obvious lies. She wouldn't let me go without good reason. Whatever I was going to say, it had better be consistent with what the other guys had said. So, I decided to tell as much truth as I could.

"I'm an ordinary citizen who happened to experience two and maybe three attacks similar to those happening across the country. I guess that makes me a bit special, doesn't it?"

"Three attacks that could have been perpetrated by you."

"Nonsense. You've got one of the victims here—Peter. Check

with him. I helped pull him through it!"

"Peter's your friend. He could be working with you. We haven't been able to find the woman yet. The man who attacked you, well, we don't know. He might be dead."

"What are you implying? That this is a conspiracy?"

"You said it, not me."

I was against the wall. Maybe I should have asked for a lawyer, though I wasn't sure the law actually applied where we were.

"Look," I said, "you've got this backwards. I'm not involved in anything."

"Please, Mr. Kline, stop lying to us," the woman said with a soft smile. "We've been following the situation for a while, and we know there's an organized group behind it."

"I'm not . . . I believe we've had an outbreak of . . . something, and I was trying to prove it; that's all."

One of the other people in the room spoke for the first time. "Mr. Kline, outbreaks are due to viral contagions. So far there is no sign of any virus in the victims' bodies."

"I'm not a biologist, but I can tell you, whatever it is, it grows and attacks in waves that show fractal behavior. And I can prove it."

"Some viruses and bacteria show fractal-like growth structures," another person said. "E. coli, for instance. But it's the first time I've heard about the possibility that they spread following a fractal-like pattern."

That apparently reignited a longstanding debate amongst the group.

"Nonsense. Any virus can be detected," one person said. "They always leave a trace."

"Not all of them are detected immediately," another man said. "Look at AIDS. For more than a decade the disease spread silently and undetectably across the population. Even after the illness was detected in 1981, it took us several years before the HIV virus was isolated."

"Yeah, but we also knew people were sick. In this case, there's no evidence of any illness. How could it be a virus?"

The woman's voice cut across the debate. "You said you can

prove it. How?"

"If I'm right, we should be able to predict the next wave. But I need Peter and David and access to the database."

"Access to restricted information?"

"I'm already under arrest. You know I can't leave this building. Who am I going to tell?"

The woman signaled to an agent standing beside the door. He left the room.

"We'll be watching you, Mr. Kline." She called a couple more agents who escorted me to another room with several computer screens. This time the room had a window and an internal wall made of glass. Peter and David arrived a few seconds later.

"Rob, what's going on?" Peter asked. "Who are these people? What do they want from us?"

"Take it easy, Peter. They're trying to stop this thing too. Right now I need both of you to do whatever necessary to predict when the next wave of deaths will come and how big it will be. There are a lot of lives at stake. That's the only way they'll let us go."

"They can't do that to me," David said. "I'll call my lawyer."

"Have you seen Detective Sullivan?"

"They sent him back to the police station," David said.

"Trust me, David. They're above the law." After a couple of deep breaths, Peter and David sat down in front of the computers. As they typed, Peter kept up a steady dialogue with David.

"Take that wave sequence, divide the value of two successive peaks, and plot the results. What's the slope of the line?"

"2.00123."

"Now do the same with the distance between two consecutive peaks."

"1.00562."

"Peter, what do we know so far?" I asked.

"The peaks are, on average, doubling every . . . iteration."

"Wave."

"Fine, wave. But the timing of the waves varies. We've just established that the period of the wave is a function of its size, though it's not a direct linear relationship as we thought. That proportional factor multiplying the inverse of alpha in reality is a function of the sequence and the wave size."

"So?" I was still lost.

"We have identified one particular sequence of waves that has lasted longer than the others. If our calculations are correct, the next peak should be happening . . . right now."

"What? How big is it?"

Peter turned to David. "How current is the information in this database?"

He shrugged. "It depends. The system has around twenty files updated at different times. It's difficult to say, but it must be about two weeks. Why?"

"We're not projecting the next wave but the sequence of killings two weeks into the future." Then he stared at the screen, speechless.

"Peter?"

"Sixty-three thousand three hundred and fifty-six."

I ran to the door, where two agents were guarding the room. I needed to warn people. Before I could speak, the door opened. It was the woman.

"It's now!" I screamed. "The next wave is happening right now!"

"I see. Thank you, Mr. Kline. We've already given instructions to our agents to look for unexplained deaths that occurred yesterday and today. It takes time to update the database, so we will have the results in a few days. I suggest all of you go and get some rest. Today has been . . . interesting."

I couldn't comprehend her coldness. We were talking about tens of thousands of people dying, and she was telling us to relax and get some rest.

"You know, there are people dying right now. How could you be—"

"Mr. Kline, we're going—"

"You don't get it, do you? You won't be able to identify them; not all of them. We're not dealing with murders. It could be a poisoning, a car accident, a drug overdose. It's a massive suicide outbreak."

"We know what we're looking for; I promise you. We've asked

for help from the Centers for Disease Control. Their epidemiologists are the best in the world, bar none."

"But—"

"You'll be escorted to your rooms where you'll be kept until we clarify your intentions."

Once again, the agents took us to separate rooms.

CHAPTER 31

ELY

I had a strange feeling when I left Rob's dream. When I emerged, I found Grandpa in the room, standing beside Rob.

"Grandpa, I was with Rob when I saw—"

"I know. Come with me. We need to go to a safe place."

"What's happening?" I followed him while we moved in time—I had finally gotten the hang of moving by myself through space and time. We stopped in Rob's room, three weeks earlier.

"A new wave of killings has just started. I've been ordered to keep you safe. We don't want anything to happen to you."

"Grandpa, I'm a big girl."

"Ely, you and Rob are the link between the worlds. If something happens to either of you, it would be the end."

"I know, but you can't hide me from what's happening out there. I can't stay quiet knowing that I could be saving someone's life. This isn't right, and you know it."

"It's not a question of saving one or two lives, it's all about your safety. That's the only thing that matters."

"Maybe you're right, but still I can't stay. Sorry, Grandpa, I have to go." I left him behind and returned to the present.

Rob was still sleeping. Everything seemed to be fine. I moved to Patchogue Village. What I saw was the most terrifying thing that I had ever seen.

Cars were abandoned on the streets. Across from me, a delivery truck had crashed into a restaurant. People were curled up and crying everywhere. A man was lying with his supermarket bag beside a woman covered in a white sheet. Another man was taking off his jacket to put it over the head of a person who had been run over by a taxi. Close to them were several black shadows like the one that had attacked Peter. They were scattered all over on the street, in houses, and in cars. Many people across the village were being attacked and converted into Antiscians.

There had to be something I could do. I identified a few places where a bright silhouette was present—Gli Custodi warriors fighting back. But they were outnumbered at least ten to one. People were being killed without knowing by whom or why. They were completely vulnerable, defenseless.

Without a second thought, I moved to the top of a house to try to help. An Antiscian shadow was attached to a woman. She was standing in the window, ready to throw herself out. A Gli Custodi warrior was trying to immobilize the shadow. I rushed straight to the shadow, catching it by surprise. I managed to hold it from behind while the warrior took a blade and cut the link between it and the host. A terrifying sound emanated from that thing.

The warrior put a bright string around the black shadow. Before he disappeared with the shadow, the warrior nodded at me with a soft smile.

"You're welcome," I said.

If I helped one, I could help many more. I moved to another person being attacked. Then to the next.

I helped quite a few warriors, maybe ten or more. It was relatively easy because the shadows weren't expecting to be attacked from behind by a non-Gli Custodi fighter. I was making the difference to all these people, and I didn't want to stop.

Then I moved inside a shop without checking if there was a warrior there first. Unexpectedly, I found myself on my own, face to face with the enemy.

As I got close, the shadow looked back at me. I didn't have the advantage of surprise this time. It followed me as I moved around the host. Although the shadow was in the symbiotic stage with the shop assistant, it was prepared to respond to my efforts to free the host.

I didn't know the extent of its powers, but it was fast and strong. Anyone in a situation like that would have asked for help. My common sense was telling me to leave, but the person that the Antiscian had attached to was a woman in her early twenties, just starting out on a good career and a promising life, if her job was any indication. And she was struggling to bring a pair of scissors to her throat. How could I leave her to death and worse? Call it courage or silliness, but I rushed the shadow.

The image of my last fight with Eleanor Donnally in the third grade sneaked up on me, two girls pulling their hairs. I had never been an aggressive person, but this time I had to get use of all my resources. Although I had stopped practicing it a long time ago, judo had taught me how to prepare for the fight. I hoped I could still apply what I had learned.

I was trying to figure out my first move when the shadow fixed his eyes on me. Find your advantages over the opponent, the words of my sensei were still with me. I knew it was attached to the host, so it couldn't attack me. I had probably a fraction of a second of advantage. That first-mover advantage didn't sound like much, but moving at light speed, I could do a lot in that time.

We looked each other in the eyes for an instant. I still hadn't found a way to break his defense when the woman brought the scissors to her throat. I thought I was in trouble when the shadow leaned against her hand. That's it! A large part of judo involved used an opponent's weight against him.

But we didn't have physical bodies. The shadow had to have other strengths that I could turn against it. This particular shadow was more aggressive than the previous ones, angrier. I couldn't explain it, but I could use it. Anger made people lose control and do foolish things. That was exactly what I needed.

I moved to within a few inches of the shadow but still out of reach. Like an aggressive dog tied with a chain, the shadow lunged at me. That was the moment I was waiting for. I ducked around it and gripped it from behind.

Now what? I had the shadow under control, but I didn't know what to do next. I didn't have any sword to cut the links or any strings to tie it up. A typical misjudgment of a first-time fighter.

While I was waiting for help, that thing did something completely unexpected.

"Do you think that capturing some of us will make you safe? Not this time. We'll be coming after you soon."

"What?"

It thrashed in my grip, but I managed to hold it even tighter.

Fortunately, I didn't have long to wait. Michael appeared with another Gli Custodi warrior and took care of the shadow. The host dropped her scissors and collapsed on the floor.

Michael stayed behind after the warrior left with the shadow. I was ready to keep fighting, but his voice stopped me.

"It's over. They're all gone."

"Did we win?"

He smiled at me like a father responding to a child who had asked a naïve question. "There was no winner, Elizabeth. We just stopped them from taking everyone. The next wave, well, we'll do it again."

For the first time I felt like I could make the difference. I had helped a few warriors, and that was important, at least for me. I knew I had better be prepared for the next wave. We had a lot to fight for.

"Are you alright?" Grandpa was there in front of me. Alone.

"Where's Michael?" I asked.

"He left while you're immersed in your thoughts."

Michael didn't say a word about my first encounter. I was expecting some kind of . . . I don't know, acknowledgement, recognition of a job well done. I still didn't understand these Gli Custodi people.

"Grandpa, this is terrible. We have to stop it. So many people have just . . . gone."

"We're doing as much as we can," he said.

"It's not enough. Every wave makes their army bigger. We need to understand their modus operandi, and we need to do it quickly."

"Robert is making some progress. He's already discovered some basic elements that have given us the first glimpse of their behavior."

Rob! I had forgotten I had left him behind while he was sleeping. "Tell me."

"The waves show fractal properties, which tell us that there may be a pattern behind their attacks. If there's a pattern, then—"

"There's a trend that can be predicted."

"Exactly. And prediction means we can be prepared before they attack."

"Great! So let's get them."

"Not so fast, Ely. It's too early to draw any conclusions."

"Why? What else do we need to know?"

"We need more details about the kind of fractal. If their attacks follow a random fractal, prediction is a bit difficult. But if they follow a self-similar fractal, prediction is simple. You know this better than I do."

I was about to reply when a light appeared in the room. Another Gli Custodi warrior.

"Luke, Elizabeth, Michael requires your presence. Please come with me."

Without any hesitation, we followed him to a room where Michael and others were seated around a rough wooden table. Again, I didn't know where I was. A quick look at the place reminded me of one of the old Scottish castles—rock walls, tapestries, old, blackened woodwork.

"It's becoming clear," Michael said. "It's getting out of our hands. There are too many for us. We can't confront them alone anymore."

The other people were staring at me, making me uncomfortable.

"What do you expect from me?" I asked. "As I've said before, I've done as much as I can. Rob is getting results. We just have to give him time."

"We may not have time," Michael said.

"I'm open to suggestions."

He paused for a moment. I didn't understand what was going through his mind. They could read my mind, but I couldn't read theirs. When this was over, I was definitely going to get more training on mind reading.

"Don't get me wrong," Michael said, "but your husband is about to stop believing in you."

"What?"

"The situation is pushing him to the limit, and we're afraid he could give up."

"Give up?"

"He's been isolated for too long. He's under so much pressure that he's beginning to lose hope."

No, that wasn't possible. I knew my Rob. He wasn't the kind of person to give up. Something else had to be happening.

"Sorry, but I have to go," I said. Nobody said anything, and nobody tried to stop me. I was doing what I was supposed to do.

CHAPTER 32
ROB

Two days had passed since we arrived at the station. They were still keeping us isolated for no apparent reason. They let us work on the system the first day. Everything seemed to go well. We were getting closer to finding the evidence I needed to show them that we were under attack, at the dawn of an outbreak. Then everything stopped.

What was happening outside? Why were they still keeping us separated? What could we possibly say that they didn't know already? I thought I'd made them understand we didn't have time. David and Peter's findings showed everybody that the deaths came in waves. But after two days, it was obvious they were not taking us seriously.

Nevertheless, it was also clear that they didn't want us to feel mistreated. In fact, the place where I was staying was very comfortable. It was like a studio apartment, equipped with everything

I needed—a kitchen full of snacks, a bedroom with a wardrobe packed with brand-new clothes, and a fully equipped bathroom. It even had windows overlooking a nice garden, though it was placed strategically, so I couldn't see anything but trees. My door was locked, as expected, with a soldier outside. He had been my only human contact for the last two days when he brought me food, though I didn't know his name.

But what was really making me crazy wasn't my five-star prison. It was Ely. I had slept two nights in that place with not even a word from her. I went to bed asking her for help, for her advice about what I should do, but I'd gotten no answer.

Could I have been imagining everything? Even the Genève anomaly? Was I missing my wife so desperately that my unconscious had created the entire story? Maybe. Maybe I had created a horror tale about the end of the world because her death was indeed the end of my world.

If so, then being insane wasn't too bad after all. It kept me going. And it was better than being sane in the middle of the end of the world.

The lock snapped open. Dinnertime. The door opened, and the nameless soldier reached through and set the tray on the table.

"Thank you," I said.

For the first time he turned around and looked at me. It seemed as if he wanted to say something. That had never happened before.

"How long are they going to keep me here?" I asked quickly. "My friends, why don't you let me talk to them?"

"You're in the custody of the FBI. They'll come for you when the time is right." Then he left the room, locking the door behind.

Finally, I knew who these people were. That explained why they all dressed alike. Not that it made much difference now.

Everything was calm, so they didn't need us anymore. Probably we would be allowed to walk out soon. All of this would end up as it happened with Ely's dreams.

I relaxed and sat down to eat my dinner, but I found I wasn't hungry. I hadn't done much exercise in my comfy cell. I ate a few potatoes and some vegetables and then left the rest of the food on the tray. I sat down on the sofa. Luckily, there were a few books to keep me busy.

I picked up a book about military strategy in the Vietnam War. I hadn't been good at reading in high school. I always considered it boring, and that night was no exception. I ended up falling asleep.

"Move, move! Run! Faster!"

I was in the middle of an empty country road. It was night, a moon ten times bigger than ours filling the sky. There was nothing around but trees. I was running away from something that I couldn't see.

"Stop, Rob."

I stopped and turned around. "Ely! You're here!"

"Of course I'm here. Why are you surprised?"

"We need to get away soon . . . it doesn't matter. I've been looking for you in the last couple of nights. I'm under arrest in a military facility. The FBI is interrogating me. I don't know about Peter and David. Where have you been? Why the hell didn't you talk to me?" I realized how harsh that sounded. I'd never treated her like that before. "Sorry, I didn't mean it."

"It's OK, Rob. Just calm down."

She looked very real, but why hadn't she been by my side when I needed her?

I stepped back, and she stepped forward. "What's the matter, Rob? Why won't you get close to me?"

"Why didn't you show up during my last dreams?"

"I—"

"Don't say anything. You, this . . . dream . . . tell me once and for all that you're not real!"

"Rob, listen, we've gone through this before. Don't let your doubts blind you again. Let them go. I'm real, and I'm here with you." She got closer to me and caressed my cheek. I closed my eyes to feel her warm hand. It had been too long. When I felt her lips touching mine, I knew I had the real Ely in my arms.

"I just wanted—"

"Shush." She placed a finger on my lips. "Don't say anything," she whispered. "No matter how hard it is, you must believe."

I remained stock still, wanting only to feel the moment.

"We're very lucky to be together after what happened to me. People have to live in pain for the loss of their loved ones. But you, you can live knowing that I'm fine, and I, well, I'm happy we'll be together again when the time is right. We're lucky, really lucky."

I started sobbing quietly, ashamed of myself.

"But this gift comes with responsibilities," she said, regaining her composure. "We have to focus on the most important thing, the killings."

I took her hand. Keep focused? How? She was everything to me.

"I did as much as I could," I said. "Now they have to realize the truth for themselves."

"I was once a scientist, and I know what evidence means to such people. It's something they can touch, something they can see. What they don't know is that, by the time they see an outbreak that's large enough to be unambiguous, it will be too late."

She had a vacant, empty stare. I had never known her to lie, but there was something she clearly didn't want to say. "Ely, tell me."

"You can't imagine how bad the situation is."

"I saw people die, and I saved two who were about to die, one of them being Peter. You don't have to shield me from the truth."

"Sorry, I didn't mean to hurt your feelings. But you sounded like you were ready to give up."

"Give up? You don't get it, do you? I'm fighting to hold onto my sanity. You in my dreams, a cataclysm about to destroy the world—it's a lot more sensible to think I'm in a padded room somewhere. And yet everything I'm doing is because of you. Then you disappear for two nights just when I need you the most . . ."

She stared at the floor.

"Ely, please, stop talking nonsense, and tell me exactly what's going on."

"The last wave . . . was big, really big. I joined those trying to stop it, but there were too many, and they were too unpredictable. We're close to losing any chance of stopping them. If your people don't join us for the next wave, it will be out of control."

Now it was me who was silent.

"Rob, you've got to get out of this room. Find Peter and the other guy. Go back to the computer room. You must find when and where the next attacks will take place."

"What if they stop us?"

"Then you'll join me sooner than expected."

I heard the sound of an approaching bus. We stepped apart with the road between us.

When the bus passed, Ely was gone.

I woke up feeling like I hadn't slept the entire night. But according to the wall clock, it was 7:32 a.m., and I had been out for nine hours. It was time to get up.

I knew that from then on, I would have to fight my way out of this situation. I hoped Ely was right.

I hadn't finished putting my T-shirt on when I heard someone unlocking my door. I grabbed a flower vase from the sitting room table and hid behind the kitchen door. When the soldier came in with my breakfast tray, I smacked him with the vase. He fell over, unconscious.

I broke for the door. No one was in the corridor. I saw other doors—apartments, I guessed. I knocked at some of them to see if I could locate Peter. The third time was the charm.

"Peter, are you there?" I whispered.

"Yes, I'm here. The door's locked."

The soldier in the room! I realized he would have the keys. "Wait, I'll come back."

I ran back and grabbed the guard's keys, then went to go release Peter. A thought struck me, and I went back again. After a quick search, I pocketed the guard's cell phone and then left, locking the door behind me. That would buy us some time.

After trying a couple of keys on Peter's door, I got it open.

"Peter, I'm so happy to see you," I said.

"Rob, where—"

"Later. Where's David?"

"I don't know, but he must be close. I heard his voice yesterday. But Rob, if they catch us—"

"Which direction, right or left?"

"Um . . . left. I think."

I unlocked the next door. "David?"

He showed up carrying a glass of milk. There was no need to ask how he was.

"David, good to see you're OK. Now listen, guys, I don't know why they kept us here, but I can tell you something is going on."

"And what's it has to do with us?" David asked.

"I don't know exactly. It must be something related to what we showed them. In any case, we have to finish what we started. We have to find where and when the next wave of killings will occur."

He cleared his voice, drank a bit of milk, then sat down. "Look around us. We're in a military facility full of soldiers with guns, and we're likely under surveillance. How exactly do you plan to leave? You can get us killed!"

"When have you seen prisoners being treated like us?" I asked. "For some reason, they only want to keep an eye on us, to have us under their control. That's all. I'm sure they won't hurt us if we try to escape."

Peter nodded, pursing his lips. I needed to get to the point quickly.

"Peter, David, I know you blame me for what happened to us, and you're right. But I have a feeling that something really bad is about to happen. More than ever before, I need your trust."

Peter remained silent for a few seconds and then nodded. "OK, Rob, what's the plan?"

I looked at David. He also nodded. "I'm not waiting alone for the soldiers to come."

Excellent, I had my team back.

"First, we need to get access to the system again." I went to the kitchenette. This time I found what I was looking for.

Peter stared when he saw me return carrying the kitchen knife. "What are you doing?"

"Just in case." I checked the corridor. Empty. "Let's go."

We slipped down the hall and up the nearest staircase. I

186

heard the sound of a TV coming from the next floor. Too risky. We continued moving up. Everything was clear this time.

One door at the end of the corridor had a small window. It was some kind of training room, with TVs and computer screens. Two people were inside dressed in civilian clothes. Damn it!

"They have computers inside," I whispered, "but first we need to deal with the two guys. Peter, David, you get the one in the white shirt. I'll get the one in the blue shirt."

"Attacking government employees?" Peter said. "Is this wise?"

"Ask me again later."

I threw the door open, and we rushed in.

"Don't move!" I reached the guy in the blue shirt and put the knife to his throat. "Don't do anything you'll regret."

Peter and David tackled the other guy. The men didn't offer any resistance, which was lucky for us. My hands were shaking.

"What's your name?" I asked my captive.

"Elliot."

"OK, Elliot, stay calm, and we won't hurt you. We'll leave as soon as we get what we want."

"Robert, take this." David tossed me a package of cable ties that he'd found in a toolbox on one of the tables.

"Turn around, and put your hands behind your back," I said to both of them. It took a moment to figure out how the cops did it, but we bound their hands and feet.

"Go ahead, guys," I said to David and Peter once the men were secure.

I remained with Elliot and his friend while Peter and David got on the computer.

After the longest thirty minutes in my life, they were still working on the analysis. I didn't know how long my guard would stay unconscious or how much noise he might make, but I expected company at any moment. "Come on, guys, we don't have much time."

After a while, Peter called me. "Rob, you'd better come here."

On his screen was a map of the country covered with dots of different colors. "What is it?"

"Each color represents a different wave. The most prominent color is the most recent wave."

"And the dots . . . they're deaths?"

"Yes."

"That's a hell of a lot of dots. How big was the last wave?"

"There's a lot of noise that tends to obscure the actual trend . . ."

"Best guess, David, please!"

"Close to sixteen million."

"No . . . no . . ." That couldn't be possible. So many people just . . . gone. "But if we had a wave of just sixty-four thousand a few days ago . . ."

"I don't understand what's going on." Peter said. "A few weeks ago, they were following specific patterns. Now they look completely out of control. There are waves with only hours between them."

We heard a crash, and the door collapsed inward. "On the ground! Now!"

I dropped the knife and lay down with my hands in plain sight. Seconds later, we were surrounded by ten soldiers, their weapons pointing at us. Then the special agent in charge walked in.

"Mr. Kline," she said. "I hope this time you have a better explanation."

What was going on must have been obvious, and yet she was still treating me as if I was the problem. Her attitude made me forget about the guns.

"I don't have one; I have sixteen million explanations."

She didn't even blink an eye. "I think these matters are best discussed in private. Bring him."

"They come with me," I said quickly, indicating David and Peter.

She nodded.

With a couple of soldiers on either side, we were led through a maze of corridors to a big square room with a circular glass table in the middle. It looked more like a meeting room than an interrogation room. A big mirror was hanging on one of the walls. CCTV cameras were mounted in the corners.

"Have a seat, gentlemen."

None of us sat down.

"So, Mr. Kline, sixteen million . . . those are a lot of reasons to hit a soldier and threaten a couple of civilians with a knife."

"Cut the shit!" I said. "You know what I'm talking about. And you know we could've done something to stop this massacre."

"Like what?"

"Anything would have been better than doing nothing. We might have figured something out if we weren't kept in rooms like criminals."

"Sorry for making you feel like that way." There was no hint of a true apology behind her words. "Before we take any action, we need to understand what we're facing."

"Well, you'd better understand fast, or you'll have thirty-two million reasons on your conscience."

"Don't be so cynical."

"I'm not—"

"Enough!" The voice seemed to come from nowhere. Seconds later, the mirror split in two and slid open, revealing six screens, with the images of five men and one woman on them. They were all in uniform.

"Mr. Kline," the same voice as before said, "we're members of the joint federal task force dealing with the recent . . . situation. We've been studying these waves for some time. With all our resources working on it, we still don't know exactly what causes them, and yet you seem to be very confident that you can stop them. What makes you think it's an outbreak?"

I didn't know who I was talking to, but he was certainly further up the food chain that Ms. FBI. "Sir, I was with two . . . three people who I think were infected."

"You think?" Ms. FBI said.

"I was there, and I know what I saw. They were infected with something. They all had the same symptoms."

"We've analyzed a number of bodies, and none of them showed evidence of any virus."

I wanted to tell the truth, but not after he mentioned the word "evidence." So, I decided to be an honest liar. "I can't tell you the answer for that, but we all know, whatever it is, it's been exterminating our people."

"Sir," Ms. FBI said, "I don't think we can decide a course of action based on three supposedly infected people."

"It's not a supposition." Peter said, speaking for the first time. "They were truly infected. I know. I was one of them."

The woman stepped back.

"What happened to me was like the flu. I slowly lost all my energy, except that it was more in my mind than my body. I started losing control of my feelings until I got unbearably depressed. I was about to kill myself when Rob came by and stopped me. Then, almost instantaneously, the depression disappeared."

The people on the screen remained silent.

When I saw Peter's reaction, I couldn't help thinking about being at the right place at the right moment with the right people. I would have lost the argument if not for Peter's testimony. Did Ely have something to do with it?

Now it was my turn. "Sir, I know we don't have much evidence to support our statement, but I also know we don't have much time to look for it. If you have a better option, now is the time to try it. If you don't, at least listen to us."

All screens went off. A minute later only the man's screen turned on again. "Bring them here. We have decided to have an extraordinary meeting of the council. And Mr. Kline, you'd better be right."

The screen went off. For a few moments, the room was silent. Peter and David looked at me, scared. What they didn't know was that I was sure I was right; I just couldn't tell them why.

Ms. FBI broke the silence. "OK, gentlemen, we have a long flight."

I didn't know where they were taking us, but something had changed. We were no longer prisoners.

CHAPTER 33
ELY

I was trying to look at Peter's findings when the FBI strike team burst into the room and pointed their guns at Rob and the others. I was scared at the beginning, but my worries vanished when I saw the woman enter the room. I was still intrigued as to who she was. She forced Rob to leave the room with two soldiers at his side. I should have followed him, but her attitude toward Rob wasn't aggressive, so I decided to stay behind and do my best to understand what Peter and David had left on the computer screen.

It didn't take me long to figure out what those images meant. The attacks were spreading through space and time in a fractal pattern! Finally, we had something useful. With the pattern behind the attacks known, we had, in principle, all the elements we needed to stop the Antiscians. Now I just needed to share the information with the others.

I moved to the castle where I'd met with the Gli Custodi. Only Grandpa was there waiting for me.

"Ely, good to see you," he said.

"Grandpa, good news! Rob and his friends have managed to understand the pattern behind the attacks. It's a four-dimensional fractal!"

I opened my mind, so he could read my thoughts. That was one of the coolest things about being . . . wherever I was. I didn't need to explain, just open my mind, and that was it. The problem was when people read my mind without my consent. That was something I still had to work on.

"I see. Very good. Let's hope it's not too late." If he wasn't optimistic, how could I be?

"Grandpa, of course we have time. We need to go and talk to the Gli Custodi."

"Don't worry. They'll be here in—"

They started to arrive before he finished speaking. I hadn't seen so many lights before. There were dozens, maybe hundreds.

"Good job, Ely." Michael's words were a relief. Finally, some kind of recognition, but it was going to the wrong person.

"Thank Rob and his friends."

"I know. Anyway, thank you all." He opened his mind to all of us. "The situation is clear now. A fractal pattern means they're using the In-Out Dimension to spread. That's why it's been so difficult to find them. They must be hiding the newcomers in a particular combination of space, time, and scale, which means it's absurd to look for them."

He paused for a moment, looking at the floor. If I were him, I wouldn't know how to say the next words, either.

"Let's talk about our real problem," he said. "The waves have increased to such a level that it's almost impossible to stop them."

For the first time I saw an aura around Michael, a reddish halo. I had been told that when people were hyperactive, they couldn't help emitting such a light. He was very worried, just like everyone else.

"The size of the last wave was close to sixteen million. The next one will be thirty-two million. At this point, our chances of success come down to people's ability to assemble an army of that size in a very short time. Currently, America has a military, including reserves, of about four million. And even if they find the rest, they won't be able to prepare for the next wave. They need time, a lot of time."

I heard other voices in my head. Despite speaking quickly, each thought was clear and distinct.

"If they don't have the numbers or the time to assemble their army, we're alone in this fight."

"Yes, we might be alone, but now we know where they're going to strike, so we can prepare our troops."

"We have an advantage," Michael said, "but we still need them. Let's not forget, hosts have to be kept alive long enough for us to find and free them."

"And what about us?" an authoritative voice asked. "We need thirty-two million fighters, not just individuals. Soldiers with the training to get the shadows out of the host's body, and that number doubles with every wave."

"Yes, you're right, Gabriel." Michael said. "But for now that's not a problem. We can build our army relatively quickly. We need to go to the beginning of the century and bring back to the present those people who fought during the two world wars. We have twenty million already with the Russian army alone. The problem isn't on our end."

I couldn't believe what I was hearing. They were talking about a single battle between millions of people. And it was just a minor planning detail.

Nobody said anything for a while. It was clear that there was no direct answer.

Finally, a voice in the background spoke up. "How many waves do we have left?"

I was good at mathematics, so it was easy for me to answer. "Two more." I didn't realize the seriousness of what I had just said until everybody turned their eyes on me. Their silence was clear; we were all thinking the same thing. That could not be possible. I looked at Michael, hoping he would ask me to shut up. His soft smile said the opposite.

"The total population of the country is about three hundred million," I explained. "If we take out the thirty-two million who are already gone because of the previous waves, we're left with about two hundred and sixty-eight million. We need at least one person to look after another one, so we can't afford more than half to be attacked. That's one hundred and thirty-four million. So, thirty-two million the next wave, sixty-four million the wave after that, and we won't have enough people left to fight the third wave."

"But the world population is in the billions," one of the previous voices said. "We have more than two chances to defeat them, don't we?"

This time we all looked at Michael. His response showed me why he was the leader of the Gli Custodi. "It's a matter of global organization. The United States is the only country with the scientific capability to discover what's happening and the resources to coordinate a global response. By undermining America first, the Antiscians expect that, by the time the attacks grow to visible proportions throughout the world, the chaos and panic will make it impossible to mount a response. We know how difficult it is for a country to establish a coordinated defense. I can't imagine how other less-developed countries would react to the attacks. But that's the main weakness of the Anticians' plan. As long as they concentrate on a single country, we have a chance. Or, as Elizabeth said, two chances."

"But I thought they wanted to control, not exterminate," I said.

"We thought the same, Elizabeth, at least at the beginning, but we were wrong. Then we thought they were following a lose-lose approach. However, during your last encounter with that shadow, the one you fought alone, I heard something that changed everything. You remember what he said, don't you?"

"We'll be after you soon."

"Exactly. That can only mean we're wrong again! They don't want to control people anymore. They want us, and they're preparing the army to take us on directly."

Exclamations sounded throughout the room.

"What?"

194

"They can't do that!"

"Impossible!"

"But how?"

"My fellows," Michael intervened. "They want to convert all living people into an army big enough to attack us. They want to bring the war here. They want to control our world."

I hadn't considered the possibility of attacks throughout the world, even less to have the war at our doorstep. If that happened, it would be the end of us.

Despite the threat, Michael remained calm and measured. "Remember, as long their attacks are concentrated, we have a chance. Our strategy must be based on a single, decisive strike. If we try to fight the next wave, and Robert's people aren't ready, we won't stop them, and we'll lose our element of surprise. From now on we have to prepare ourselves for the second wave. That's our line in the sand. We must stop them before they get into our world."

"So, are we going to leave them alone in the next wave?" Gabriel asked.

"No," Michael replied. "We'll deploy part of our forces but only to deceive them. We have to show them that we're still fighting as if we don't realize what they're up to. They must not be aware that for the second wave, we will be waiting for them. But most of all, they must not know about our alliance with the people. That is our ultimate advantage." He turned toward me. "Elizabeth, your safety is paramount for what we're planning to do. Your grandpa will look after you." Then he looked at him. "Take her to a safe time. I'll contact you."

Grandpa looked at me, trying to calm me down. It was too late.

"I'm sorry, but I can't." My voice reverberated as if in an empty cavern.

"I'm not asking," Michael said.

"I won't stand still doing nothing. People who are important to me are still out there. I can't leave them alone."

He stared at me. It was clear he was listening to my thoughts. And I was counting on that. He'd know I wasn't joking.

"One condition," he said. "Stay away from the next wave.

Don't worry about Robert. We'll look after him. We need you, both of you, for our last stand."

I nodded. That was fair.

"What about us?" a voice from the crowd asked. "If we wait for the next wave, they'll outnumber us as well. More than sixty million. We're not enough to stop them."

Where was Michael going to get that many warriors? Maybe he was thinking about going back to the eighteenth century. No. He wanted to look a lot further back.

"We might be tight in numbers, but we're never outnumbered. We'll get the help of our friends, wherever they are. We have to assemble an army of at least sixty-four million of the top fighters from the last couple of millennia."

"Who do you have in mind?" Gabriel asked.

"The knights of the crusades, the Spanish Armada, the French Foreign Legion, the Grande Armée, the Northern Virginia Army, the Confederate Army . . . If we need more, we'll go back to the beginning—the Sumerians and Babylonians, Egyptians, Roman legions, and the Spartans. We'll split into groups. Each one will have a century assigned. Each team will be responsible for bringing back to the present the best soldiers who fought during the assigned century."

His words were terrifying and reassuring at the same time. Terrifying because of the magnitude of the task ahead but reassuring because of the confidence and control with which he spoke. In any case, at least now we were all aware of the size of the problem.

"We don't have much time left," he said. "Everyone has your instructions. Go, my friends."

As everyone started to disappear, Grandpa approached me. "Ely, are you ready? We've been assigned to the twelfth century."

I wasn't very good at history, so I didn't know who we would be talking to.

When we were about to leave, Michael approached us. "Ely, I need you to do something else before you leave."

"Yes, Michael."

"We have to tell Robert that there will be a final attack, and it's

196

not the next wave. They need to be ready at the same time as us."

"Any advice on how they will create an army of sixty-four million people?"

"Remember, Ely, they don't need to be fighters. They just need to look after the victims, to keep them alive long enough for the fighters to get there."

"Understood." I realized that for this part, Rob was on his own once again.

When Michael left, Grandpa took my hand. "Don't worry," he said, "he's a smart person. He'll find the way. Come, I know where Rob is."

CHAPTER 34

ELY

Grandpa left me in an airplane. Rob was there, together with other civilians and military personnel. I didn't know where he was traveling to, but the important thing was that Peter and David were there as well. Someone was taking them seriously.

Rob was asleep. Looking at him, I couldn't help but think how fragile life was. He seemed so peaceful, and yet the world he was living in was about to disappear. I knew it was an unfair, selfish thought, but I was only worried that we could never be together again. In a normal situation, he'd live his own life and meet new people, but now the threat of being converted into a shadow overrode our future. If that happened, I would never forgive myself.

I had always seen eternity as an unrealistic but seductive concept. Now that it was in front of me though, it was meaningless.

I was ready to give up everything and fight for the companion I needed to live through it.

I sat on his legs and hugged him, as I used to do. This time his dream was beautiful.

It was about me.

He was walking on a busy road, full of small shops—the Rue Cler in Paris, more or less. I was watching him from the opposite side of the street. He was very animated, talking to me—or I should say the image he had created of me. Seeing them—us—so happy made me regret all those days that ended with spirited discussions or small fights. If I could go back, I wouldn't have given any importance to whatever it was we were fighting about.

I crossed the street. "Hi, Rob."

He stopped walking, looking at me in surprise. He turned to the other me, but she had vanished.

"But . . ."

"I know, it was me . . . too. I had to wake you up while you were dreaming about me. Sorry."

He smiled. That was my Rob. A tiny expression on his face said everything. He took my hand, and we started walking together as if the dream hadn't changed at all.

"You know, Ely, I could easily get used to this double life. Normal life when I'm awake and with you when I'm sleeping."

I was already used to it. "It doesn't sound bad, does it?"

"Like a coffee?"

"Sure."

We stopped at a café. He held the door open for me.

"Table for two, please," he said to the café manager. He helped with my seat. I knew they were just details, but they were the little things that had made me fall in love with him.

"Please could you bring us a macchiato and an espresso?" he asked the waitress.

"Double or single?"

"Single, please. Thank you."

He noticed I was staring at him. "What?"

"Nothing." I knew it was not the right moment to get down to

199

business, but I didn't really have a choice. "Well, something, yes. Rob, there are important things I need to tell you."

"I was surprised it took you so long to bring it up."

I smiled apologetically. "We've worked out a plan for the last stand. We need your help to coordinate your people with us."

"Coordinate?"

"It's not what you think, Rob. We won't do anything in your world." The weight of what I was about to say was beginning to hit me. "Rob . . . what I'm going to say won't be easy for you or the people around you. I need you to understand that it's not because we don't care but because we—"

"Ely, you're scaring me. What is it?"

"There are only two waves left before everything ends."

"Only two?"

"There are good reasons for that, but I don't have time to explain them now. The thing is . . . we have to put everything into the second wave. Thanks to your efforts, we know exactly where they're going to appear. We need to prepare your people to—"

"Wait, wait, wait. Why don't you tell me about the next wave?"

"We won't be prepared. Neither will you. It has to be the second wave."

"Ely, thirty-two million people . . ."

"I know. If we could save them, we would. But it's literally impossible to be ready."

"No, I'm sure there's something we can do. We can save some lives at least."

"We can, and we will. But a partial result isn't an option. If you let some shadows live, they'll only come back later. We have to stop them all at once."

"But people's lives are important too. That's the reason we're doing this. We can't just let them go."

"Rob, if we attack during the next wave, they'll know we've discovered their attack pattern. They'll change it, and then we'll be back to square one for the next wave. The worst would be if they discovered our two worlds are communicating. They're not expecting your people to be involved in this fight. I promise you, if we launch a full-scale attack on the coming wave, everything will be lost."

We remained silent for the next minute or so, the weight of thirty-two million suicides and our inability to stop them weighing us down.

The waitress brought our coffees. Rob didn't move or say a word. I thanked her with a timid smile.

"One sugar?" I broke the cold silence.

He continued staring at nothing.

"Rob, we're going through a difficult situation," I said while stirring his coffee. "We're trying to save the people living not just now but the next generations too, our future. We need you, and so do they. I need you." I took his hand and kissed it, then put it on my cheek.

He looked at me. "Ely, you're talking about mobilizing sixty-four million people!"

I'd forgotten that he didn't have a Michael—or instant communication across space and time—to get things organized. "Well, you won't have to do it alone."

"Any suggestions?"

I took a sip of my coffee before answering.

"Sorry, Ely," he said, standing up abruptly, "but I need to wake up. I have to talk to Peter and David. Every minute could make the difference."

I watched him go with a mixture of grief and surprise. It was the first time that Rob had left me alone in his dream.

CHAPTER 35
ROB

Peter and David were still sleeping. So were about half the other passengers. The rest were working on their laptops. I was still reeling from my conversation with Ely. I needed to stretch my legs, so I went to the toilet to wash my hands and face.

Thirty-two million sacrificed to save the rest of the population. Could there be a more difficult decision?

I didn't know what was more painful, the helplessness of not being able to save those people or the unbearable weight of knowing it was coming and having to keep silent about it. At least if I could talk openly, I'd be able to share the burden. But there was no way I could convince these agents and the army that we were about to be attacked by our own ancestors.

Shit!

The seatbelt signal turned on, and the captain's voice made

the usual announcements. We were approaching the airport.

I returned to my seat. Peter and David were still sleeping. How could they do that?

A soldier came and woke them up, then asked us to tighten our seatbelts. Through the window, I recognized John Hancock Tower. We were in Chicago.

The landing was soft, and the plane parked at a gate far from the civilian terminal. When we exited the plane, a fleet of black vans was there to pick us up. Each one of us got into a different vehicle. It was like something from a Hollywood film.

We took a highway just after we left the airport. I wasn't familiar with Chicago, so I had no idea where we were heading. The FBI woman and the agents in the van were quiet, which was not a big deal. The silence gave me a chance to think about what I was going to do.

The situation was clear. I was about to meet important people from the government. I had to tell them that 32 million were about to die, and 64 million more would die soon unless they believed a theory cooked up by an ordinary citizen with no scientific training. And I was going to have to convince them without telling them the truth, or they'd think I was nuts (or lying). If divine intervention existed, it had better be prepared to act. Shit! If that was my last hope, we were in trouble.

The cars pulled into an underground parking area beneath a modern office building. I was surprised the FBI woman hadn't spoken to me since we left the military complex in New York. It was difficult to believe there were people in this world who were that cold.

From the parking garage, an elevator took us down to the sixth floor. Yes, down! Peter and David looked at me. "Cool." David said.

When the doors opened, two soldiers were waiting to escort us. On the way we passed by a room with some TV screens. One of them was on the news.

"The population of West Virginia is in a state of panic after the recent wave of deaths . . ." I tried to stop to listen, but one of the soldiers pushed me to keep walking.

We arrived at a big meeting room. I recognized some of the faces from the screens I had seen . . . was it yesterday? Questions raced through my mind. What attitude should I take with them? Assertive about making my point? Passive and polite, waiting my turn? Or should I take a team player role and try to convince each one until we reach a consensus?

"Welcome, Mr. Kline, we've been expecting you." The general turned to David and Peter. "Please, gentlemen, have a seat. We were just discussing your theory about . . ."

"It's not a theory, sir." I had nothing to lose by taking the lead, especially since these people didn't look like they'd be impressed by good manners.

"We know you firmly believe in it." He turned to the others in the room. "Well, as I was saying, so far we've found no evidence of a virus, bacteria, or any other kind of microorganism that could cause this wave of deaths. On the other hand, we suspect it could be a kind of toxic gas that influences people's behavior."

"Is there any evidence of this gas?" I asked.

"Not yet."

"Then it's no better established than a virus, is it?

"That's beside the point," he said. "A virus always leaves a trace."

"No, sir, that's precisely the point. No matter which one we prefer, we don't have evidence for any of the theories. All we really know are the symptoms: a massive, deadly pandemic that comes in waves, doubling in size with each wave. We don't know what's causing it, but we don't have to in order to stop it."

"Sir," one of the others said, "I'm Dr. Thomson, Director of the Centers for Disease Control and Prevention. As we speak, our researchers are working on several options that will lead to the development of an antidote."

"Doctor, you're looking for a vaccine, right?"

"Yes"

"That approach works on standard outbreaks. I'm afraid this is not a classic outbreak."

For a moment, a tense silence invaded the room. Then a woman sitting across the table spoke. "Are you suggesting there's no cure?"

"Not exactly."

"Mr. Kline," the general said, "if you have something to say, say it now!"

I had their full attention. Now was the moment to test it. "Whatever it is, it stops spreading by itself."

"What?" the doctor said.

"I'm speaking from experience. When Peter was infected, he tried to kill himself. I stopped him, and a minute later, he regained control of himself. Since then he's been fine." I looked at Peter to back me up.

"Yes, it's true," he said.

"You didn't give him anything?" the general asked.

I shook my head. "Just a second chance. I took the knife from him and held him tight enough for him to react. The same happened to the woman. She wanted to die, so she threw herself in front of my car. I almost ran her over, but I managed to stop the car and help her. A few minutes later, she started behaving normally."

"But viruses have a natural growth pattern that drops only when the host dies."

"So maybe you're right. This isn't a virus. I can't tell you the causes, but I know how to treat the symptoms."

"So, Mr. Kline," the general said, "you want me to believe that we only have to keep people alive, and they'll get better spontaneously? As simple as that?"

"I think so."

The general turned toward the rest in the room. "I think the best course of action is to continue with the council's previous decision and keep investigating the gas option."

Damn, damn, damn! I had to stop them from making that decision right now.

"Excuse me, sir. With all due respect, you can't do that."

The silence in the room became even thicker.

"You haven't given us any reasonable evidence," he said.

"Right now you don't have any evidence that there's a gas behind these deaths either. You can't throw away an option just because it sounds incredible. Not if we're right about the timing of the waves."

One member of the council who I hadn't identified jumped in. "He's right, General. Right now we don't have time to track down the underlying causes. Maybe betting on all options is the best choice—our only choice. Despite everything, if treating the symptoms works, that's what we should do."

"Mr. Kline, what do you need in order to test your option?"

Then I saw it. I had to use the next wave for preparation too—as a test case to show that my approach could produce results. "Peter, David, based on your analysis, can you identify the locations with the highest probability of infected people?"

Peter nodded. "I hope so."

"General, we need to send your troops to a hundred of these locations. If I'm right, your soldiers will be able to prevent most or all deaths in these locations."

The general looked at the members of the council. There was no objection. He turned back to me. "OK, we'll test all possibilities, including Mr. Kline's. We have to keep working on the virus, toxic gas, and the other options." The general looked at me. "I hope one of them is right. Let's get to work, gentlemen." He stood up and left the room with the other council members.

For the first time, I saw a glimpse of hope in the darkness. They were listening to me. They would save lives. But at what price? Millions of people were about to die, and they didn't realize it.

"Ely . . ." I whispered her name unconsciously,

"Pardon me?" the FBI woman asked.

"Nothing."

"Right. We need you to brief the army on what they should expect to face and the steps they have to take to help the victims. I'll let you know when they're ready. And your friends need to pinpoint the locations of the next attacks."

I nodded and then turned quickly to Peter. "Peter, David, let's go, we've got work to do." Four soldiers escorted us to a computer room on the upper floor. As soon as we got in, they started crunching the numbers, looking for patterns that would tell them where the next attacks would come from. I couldn't stop thinking how the situation had turned quickly from begging to be heard to deploying an army.

Everything depended on getting the soldiers to those locations on time.

CHAPTER 36

ELY

The way Rob left the dream showed a determination that I hadn't seen in him before. Had his desperation prepared him to do anything to stop the waves? I was afraid I might have pushed him too much.

I decided to stay with him in the airplane at least for a while. I knew I couldn't do much, but now would be the worst moment for him to break down.

I followed him into the car after landing. I was at his side for the entire trip. When we arrived at that building, the military personnel outside worried me.

They took him directly to a meeting room deep underground. A spirited discussion had been taking place before Rob arrived. Clearly, they were struggling to find answers. I hoped they were desperate enough to give Rob's answer a chance. The man with the most medals—a general, I guessed—talked to him.

He was a tough person, skeptical of what Rob was saying. The doctor's interventions were incredibly frustrating. He was talking about studies, where on earth I had no idea. Didn't he realize there was no time? And the woman, she was scared. How she . . .

I had to step outside the room for a moment. My worries about Rob were blocking me from being able to assess what was going on.

I went back to the room when I saw Rob—yes, my Rob—arguing with the general. Rationally, honestly—as much as he was able—and passionately. I was so proud of him. I finally understood what he was trying to do: bring about the basic human emotion of fear of making the wrong decision. I wasn't sure if that would work with a general.

But Rob surprised me. A hundred locations? The attack was going to be a lot bigger. Then I understood what he wanted to do. A test. What a brilliant idea! If Rob was right, no one would die at the one hundred locations, and they would believe him enough to mobilize for the larger operation.

His lips, he whispered my name! I moved next to him. "Yes, my darling, I'm with you."

The test meant I had to make sure the Gli Custodi would be at Rob's locations. But that meant I needed to know those locations. I moved with them to a room with computer screens.

It took them a while to identify the locations. Rob had left a while earlier when Peter marked each location on a map and left it open on the table. My loving Rob. That was the kind of communication we always had.

I took off once I learned the locations. Being able to memorize a hundred locations in an instant was one of the cool things about being there. No more problems with memorizing and forgetting things.

I moved back again to the Scottish castle, where Michael met me in the main reception room. He was standing beside the fireplace, as if he knew I was coming. That was one of the less-cool things—no more privacy, in particular from a Gli Custodi like Michael. I wondered where his strength came from. Maybe it was due to his age.

"I see Robert is back on board," he said.

"He's close to getting their trust, but we need to give him a hand."

"A hundred locations, I see."

"He told them that if they followed his advice, no one would die in those locations. We have to make sure that happens. Besides, this is going to be a good synchronization exercise between them and us."

He smiled. "It's trickier than that," he said. "Our intervention will have to go unnoticed by the Antiscians." He paused. "We'll aim at intervening in one thousand locations, including, of course, Robert's one hundred locations."

"A random selection around the country?"

"Not exactly. We'll select them so that, for each test location, there'll be approximately nine other locations within one hundred miles. In this way, the Antiscians will see the success in a test location not as a random event but as a result of the concentration of efforts in a particular area. And there will be enough areas where we fail, of course."

"I want to be there."

"As I told you before, your security is paramount. We can't afford to put you at risk."

"I know, but I wouldn't forgive myself if something happened to him."

"Has anyone ever won an argument with you?" he asked, smiling. I couldn't help but smile back. "Now it's your turn, Elizabeth. Listen to me. Go with your grandpa. We can deal with Robert and his one hundred locations."

It was a very polite dismissal, but it was a dismissal all the same. I left without saying a word.

CHAPTER 37

ELY

Before moving to where my grandpa was, I decided to visit my house—or what had been my house. I needed some time to myself, and although I'd only lived there for a couple of days, it was the closest thing to home. I knew it was illogical to feel that way, but I couldn't help myself. Maybe it was because I was not used to this world or because I was still too attached to Rob. In any case, being there made me feel . . . alive.

I arrived at the entrance. A quick glance was enough to see the condition of the house hadn't changed—messy and untidy but nevertheless untouched. It was incredible; all that time together with him, and yet I didn't notice it.

I walked around the house. It was like time had stopped. A few boxes had been left unpacked from the day we moved in. We'd never agreed on where to hang two portraits. They were still on the dining table.

The kitchen was no different. Our pictures were stuck to the refrigerator with magnets. We had taken them at the park a couple of weeks before I left. What lovely moments.

Then I moved upstairs. All the doors were closed except our bedroom. I stopped in the doorway. Half of the bed was still untidy. The other half was as if nobody had ever slept there. The closet was open. I approached it. I couldn't believe it; Rob hadn't removed my clothes.

I sat on the bed. I saw my slippers beneath the claw-foot bathtub in the bathroom. That depressed me even more. Everybody knew how difficult it was to live after losing a loved one. But seeing it from my side was unbearable. I wanted to be there, and at the same time it felt like I was going back to the day I left.

Being surrounded by my stuff made me wonder . . . Was Rob so deeply hooked into the past that he might never be able to move ahead with his life? What could I have done to make my departure less damaging? What could I do now to stop him from living in the past?

Why did we keep these two worlds separated? If the shadows had found a way to cross them, why didn't we do the same? It would help people accept the departure of their loved ones.

"That's a little simplistic, don't you think?"

My dad's voice reverberated in my mind. "Where have you been, Dad? Where's mum? I've missed you."

He smiled. He had caught me unguarded, so I assumed he had heard all my thoughts. But I was beyond making a big deal out of it.

"Dad, I don't think it's too much to ask for the chance to say goodbye," I said.

"And you believe it's as simple as that? Just a goodbye and then you're gone? People don't leave their previous lives as easily as that. Our dependence on the material world is much stronger than our wills. Our experiences, emotions, thoughts, feelings, they're all grounded in the deep roots of our human nature. They're too strong to break with a simple goodbye."

"But what's wrong with staying with what makes us happy, being with the people we love?"

"You mean our comfort zone? Remember, no one ever grows by staying in their comfort zone."

"What if I don't want to grow? What if I want to keep things as they are?"

"It's not an option. We die to evolve. Death is part of the evolution process. Tell me something, sweetheart. Have you seen anyone suffering or grieving in this world?"

"Not . . . yet."

"Well, you won't see one. People feel that way only during the transition period. Once they see and understand the light ahead, all pain disappears."

"For them. I still can't forgive myself for the devastation and pain that I've caused for Rob."

"My little girl, you've got to stop feeling guilty for what happened."

"You may be right, Dad, but that's the way I feel, and it will be like that for a long time."

"I know, but time is the cure for all pains. However, right now, time is the only thing we don't have. Grandpa should arrive any time. Wait, there he is."

"Ready to go, Ely?" Grandpa said.

"Where?"

He took my hand. "To the twelfth century. We need to find the Templars."

Are you coming with us, Dad?

"It's critical that you remain focused on what you're doing. I don't want to be any distraction."

I said goodbye with a smile. He smiled back.

We arrived in a beautiful garden with spreading fruit trees, fountains, and manicured flowerbeds. The day was bright and the air clear. A few people were walking along a quiet stone path that led to an old building at the end. Well, old by my standards. I didn't recognize the place.

"Where are we, Grandpa?"

"You don't know much about the Templars' history, do you?"

"Not much. Knights, crusades . . ."

"We're at the Convent of Christ in the City of Tomar, Portugal.

213

One of the few places where the Templar Knights found peace."

"Why are they still here?" I assumed they were there, although I hadn't seen them.

"This was one of the few places in Europe that the knights were not hunted down and prosecuted. You know, Ely, people don't like to be in places where they weren't welcome during life. Now imagine how they must have felt after being persecuted all around Europe by the same people they were protecting. A betrayal that deep leaves scars."

We moved alongside the road. As the old building got closer, I realized what it reminded me of. "It's a church, isn't it?"

"Yes, the church of the convent."

"A circular church?"

"Its design was influenced by the mosques that the Templars saw during their battles in the Middle East."

We walked through the church to an internal garden, the Cloister of the Cemetery, as Grandpa continued his lesson. "For hundreds of years, they've been gathering in this convent, a place that they associate with honor, recognition, and trust."

"So, where are they?"

Once again, he took my hand, and we moved back in the time. "Here we are, January 16, 1120."

It was the same building, the same landscape I had seen a few moments ago, but now it was teeming with people. They all looked like warriors, and they all wore white tunics printed with a red cross. The way they dressed reminded me of the film El Cid. That time-space thing, where people shared the same location at different times, was going to take a while to get used to.

"Why did they choose 1120?"

"To remember the Council of Nablus, when King Baldwin the Second presented the earliest knights with the gift of the Al-Aqsa Mosque or the Temple of Solomon, sealing the birth of the Pauperes commilitones Christi Templique Salomonis or, as we know it, the Templar Order. This is the date that unifies all Templar Knights throughout their existence."

"Are all the Templars here? I mean here in this time?"

"No. Only those who have chosen this time location as their

home. There are other times and places where they congregate as well: Scotland, England, Germany, Italy, Switzerland."

"Does each knight have the freedom to choose the place where he stays?"

"Absolutely. They all have different reasons; it's each knight's decision. Take for instance, Switzerland. They never fought in Switzerland, but it was one of the few places outside the church influence in which many Templars found a home after the dissolution of the order."

I was fascinated by Grandpa's explanation. This wasn't just dusty history. I was about to meet these people. As we moved through the crowd of knights, I was surprised to sense a deep calm around me. These people were really happy there.

"Grandpa, why do they look so calm? So happy?"

"They've found their place in this world."

"You mean this place, Tomar?"

"No, my child. They've found a reason to exist in this eternal world."

"A reason to exist?" I hadn't thought about it before, but he was right. Eternity without a sense of purpose was inconceivable, at least for me.

"They're warriors, men who fought their entire lives. Can you imagine how difficult it is for them to be here where there's no more war? But they have a unique element that helped them define themselves even in the absence of war—their order's values and goals. Ideals and values that unify people survive the test of time. The Templars are still here, committed to their original aims: charity and honor through the support of the poor, the sick, the unjustly accused, and the oppressed. Of course, they're not defending holy sites anymore, but their values give them a sense of unity and mission, a reason for their existence even after death."

"But how can they do that? There are no sick or poor people here. Nobody is accused, let alone falsely accused."

"You're quite right. However, there are still people who need help. Some come into this world alone or with families who aren't ready to receive them. Other people with a poor spirit need help to understand this world and to find their developmental path. The Templars help them with the transition. Some become tutors, like Grandma is for you."

"So, in modern terms, they've become a charity organization."

"Sort of."

We approached a particular group of knights.

"Dear Jack," Grandpa said to one. "It's been a long time."

"You know very well that time does not mean much in this part of the world, mon bon ami Luke."

They knew each other? How? Jack had an accent that I couldn't identify—it probably hadn't been heard for centuries before my time. They put their hands on each other's shoulders. There was a moment of silence in which they exchanged some kind of greeting. I couldn't hear what they were saying to each other. Then they started talking.

"Jack, I come in the name of Michael. We need all of you to go back to the present, and I mean every knight in the order. We're facing a situation without precedent. We're searching for all warriors of goodwill from the last two millennia to join us."

"I guess when you say we you mean you and this young lady—who, by the way, shouldn't be here with us."

"Sorry, I should have introduced her. She's my granddaughter, Elizabeth."

"Too young . . . too young," Jack said and then turned back to my Grandpa as if I wasn't there. "So, Luke, what's so big that requires the presence of all of us?"

Grandpa opened his mind to Jack, so he could understand the situation. A few moments later, everything was explained.

"I never thought we were going to face an enemy again," Jack said, "much less the Antiscians."

"Knowledge can be harmless, but when it's in the wrong hands, it becomes lethal."

Jack nodded. He remained silent for a few seconds, like he was assessing something. "A situation like this, so out of control so quickly. How was it possible?"

While they talked, a dark silhouette outside the garden drew my attention. Something moved in the back, but I couldn't identify it. My first thought was that we had been followed by a shadow. There were many big trees planted close together.

Something Grandpa was saying brought me back into the conversation. "The population has grown so much in the last hundred years that it's almost impossible to keep track of every person arriving here."

"I see what you mean," Jack said. "Well, if it's Michael who asks for us, nothing more need be said. I'll go and gather my people. We don't have much time."

Without a word of goodbye, he turned around and moved to where the other knights were gathered. Grandpa left in the opposite direction. I followed him in silence, wondering how he had become buddies with an eight-hundred-year-old Templar.

I was looking at the trees when Grandpa stopped outside the circular church.

"You must be wondering how I know him."

Again with the mind reading. "A person of few words. I guess this is the way people from the past address women."

"Don't judge him. He lived a celibate and secluded life. Besides, he's always been like this. He was my tutor. When I arrived here, like you, I was shocked. My family didn't know enough to help me understand and assimilate what had happened to me. He came and spent his time showing me this world, teaching me, helping me with everything. I owe him."

I was still adjusting to this world myself—my grandfather's tutor was a Knight Templar? "Who was he?"

"Jacques de Molay, the twenty-third and last grandmaster of the Knights Templar."

We continued walking through the garden. I was still drawn to the silhouette. I tried to hide it from Grandpa, but I was too transparent for him. I was looking for it among the trees when I saw a deer appear among the trunks. No, not just a deer; a stag, with huge, beautiful antlers. A few seconds later, an entire herd of deer emerged not far from us. I stopped to watch them. They were so beautiful. The stag looked at me, and then we found ourselves surrounded by ten deer. That was unexpected. They were supposed to be afraid of humans.

"They're so friendly," I said. "Are they from a zoo?"

"No. They're wild."

I stroked a velvety nose. "They behave like pets."

"Animals are our companions in this world. They're not afraid of us because they can see within us, feel our feelings. It's easy for them to recognize a good heart . . . like yours. But that's a subject for another day. Your Grandma will explain everything about animals later. Now we still have other orders to visit. Let's go, Ely." He took my hand, and we were off again.

During that next day or so, we contacted the Order of St. John of Jerusalem, the Teutonic Knights, the Order of the Holy Sepulcher, and a group of others who I didn't know until now. More than twenty in all. Some were more difficult to convince than others, but for all of them, Michael's name was more than enough.

Personally, the journey helped me grasp the real significance of being there and the possibilities ahead. Something I never thought would be possible was happening. I felt hope.

CHAPTER 38

ROB

I walked into the computer room with hope, something I hadn't felt for some time. Although it was a last resort, I finally had people ready to test my theory, a theory created in my dreams that would save the world. A surreal option that needed to be correct at all costs.

Peter and David had the difficult task of identifying a hundred locations where the next wave would strike. They had to be accurate, with a precision reaching the street and maybe the house level. I didn't know how they were going to do it. They sat down and started working immediately.

"Excuse me, we need a board and paper—a lot of paper," Peter said to one of the soldiers.

With a plan already in process, I could do nothing but wait. They were going to be busy for a while, so I decided to go back to the room with the TVs that I had passed when we arrived on the first day. I had the impression that something was being hidden from us. I didn't know the building, so I asked one of the soldiers to take me there.

As we approached, I heard the voice of a female reporter coming from the end of the corridor. Three TVs were in the room, all of them on. What I saw I hadn't considered possible even in my worst nightmares.

The three local news channels were talking about the situation in Chicago. People on the streets were wearing medical face masks. Hospitals had the doors closed; there was no room for anyone else. Streets were in chaos—windows broken, looting everywhere. Tanks and Humvees patrolled. Martial law had been declared and the National Guard called in. The roads out of the city were parking lots, packed with people trying to escape to the countryside.

At that point I realized how isolated from the outside world I had been in the last week. Since they arrested us at the police station, we had been confined to buildings in government complexes, non-commercial airplanes, and protected convoys. I had not noticed how much chaos the sixteen million suicides had caused.

I rushed back to the computer room, my sense of hope gone. The soldier was beside me. Peter and David were still concentrating on their calculations. They didn't acknowledge my arrival. I didn't want to scare them, so I composed myself before they spotted me.

"Guys, any progress?"

"We're working on the mathematical model, but it's not easy," David replied, not taking his eyes off the computer screen. "There's this random noise that obscures the real pattern. It makes each successive wave not exactly double in size but something less. Anyway, we hope the model will describe the waves' fractal behavior. We're almost there."

After a couple of hours, they were still working. A military man with captain's bars entered the room. "Mr. Kline, people are waiting for you."

"What people?"

"They're waiting for your briefing. Please come with me." I had forgotten the briefing that the FBI woman had asked me to give.

On my way out, I thought about Ely and how she would find out the locations. I wasn't sure how long I was going to be at the briefing, so I needed to leave the information where she could see it. There was only one way. I returned to the room for a moment.

"Peter, I don't know how much time the briefing will take. Can you leave a map with the locations displayed on the computer screen? Also, please print me a copy, and leave it on the table. I'll take a look when I'm finished."

"No problem," Peter said without looking up.

I followed the captain. As we walked through different corridors, I couldn't decide what I was going to say. I was already surprised by how little time it took to assemble the group of military men to lead the rescue teams. I only knew that I had to be precise in describing the attacks. If they were off by even a little, many would die quietly in their own homes, only to be found later. If at all.

The meeting room was at the end of a long corridor. Inside were at least fifty officials, all of them high brass. They sat in five perfectly aligned rows of chairs, all of them looking at me. I wished I had the luxury of stage fright, but I didn't. Everything depended on these men.

One official introduced me. He didn't know my name. Showtime!

"Gentlemen," I said, "my name is Robert Kline. I don't know what information you have, but it's surely more than I possess. There are several theories that attempt to explain what's happening out there. Which one is true? Which one should we follow? It doesn't matter. Whatever is going on outside, it must be stopped immediately, whether we understand it or not. So, if someone expects me to explain in detail what's going on, I'm going to disappoint. But I've had two encounters with infected people, and what I did helped them survive. That's what I'm going to tell you about. Let's hope it will be enough to save the rest."

I went on to describe my two experiences in as much detail

as I could remember. "And that's it," I said when I was finished. "If you do it properly, they'll recover within a minute or two. The symptoms just disappear."

"You expect that by preventing them from committing suicide, the disease will just disappear? Like a trick out of a magician's hat?" someone asked.

The comment was met by laughter.

"Do you have a better option?" I asked. "Does anyone in this room have a better option?" My inquiring gaze was met with silence. "What I'm trying to tell you is that it has a threshold, a point after which the infection stops reproducing, stops its development."

"Peak of contagion," someone in the back of the room said. "Contagion" was a word that I was hoping not to hear there.

"Sure, if 'contagion' is the right word. It may not be. After being exposed to two encounters, I can tell you it doesn't look like it spreads equally to everyone."

I didn't like the tone of these questions. "Gentlemen, listen, we could sit here asking all sorts of questions, and in the end, we would still have to live with uncertainty. If you have doubts, keep them to yourselves. The success of this effort depends on everyone being fully committed. So, I ask you to think about this test as the true cure for the disease."

The silence in the room was interrupted by the sound of the door opening. Peter and David entered with two soldiers. They were carrying some papers in their hands.

"We have the coordinates." David said.

One official stepped up, took the papers, and began handing them out. "Each one of you will be responsible for two of these locations. Detailed instructions will be forwarded soon. The personnel and equipment will be available at 14:00 hours. You all know what to do. Dismissed."

Everyone stood up and filed out of the room. For a moment I thought we might be left out of their plans once again.

"Colonel, what am I supposed to do now?" I asked.

"You? We're following your instructions, so be sure you're ready at 14:00 hours."

222

From that moment on, I stopped worrying whether we were in or out. Evidently, it was our show.

CHAPTER 39

ROB

At 14:00 hours, everything was ready. We'd been moved to a building not far from where we had arrived that morning. The officers who attended the briefing already had their instructions. Addresses, equipment, transport, everything was planned in advance. I knew I might be biased, but the efficiency of the army was something to admire.

We were assigned to Colonel Highsmith. As expected from an army official, he was a man of few words. "Gentlemen, your orders are to stay with my troops during this mission. An escort will be assigned to each one of you. He'll look after everything you need, including your security. We have a helicopter waiting to take us to the assigned location. If you have any questions, you'll have time to ask them in transit." Simple, clear, and without much flexibility. Welcome to the army.

A few minutes later, a convoy of six cars arrived. Once again, they split us into different vehicles. I was assigned to the same car as Colonel Highsmith.

"Is this all the people involved in this operation?" I asked. "I was expecting a bigger movement of troops."

"Troops were already sent to each location," he replied. "They're waiting for our arrival."

"Do they know what to do?"

"They have been briefed." I was about to say that this lack of information was unfair, but the colonel continued. "You don't have to worry," he said. "We've already taken care of everything."

I knew he was telling me as much as he was allowed. Anyway, the operation was only part of my concern. It was Ely who was really making me nervous. Had she seen the locations on the computer screen? Would they be ready at her end? Could we actually coordinate? And if we could, would it work? My head was flooded with questions. For the first time I was scared to death. I was responsible for a massive military operation, and if it failed . . . well, civilization wouldn't last long enough for them to arrest me. But behind all that was a dream, a simple dream.

The colonel must have seen my concern. He took a deep breath. "Mr. Kline, may I speak openly?"

"Please."

"The population is more terrified than at any time since . . . I don't know, since the Black Death, I suppose. They haven't been given any explanation of what's happening. People don't know what to do, and, honestly, I don't think we do either. We've been told that it might be a virus, and that's why we have to follow your plan." He wasn't talking as a military man. His watery eyes showed a deeper pain, a pain he could not hide.

"Forgive me, Colonel, but . . . who have you lost?"

"My son and a cousin."

"I'm so sorry."

"I'm not alone. Everybody has lost someone in their family or a close friend. It's terrible."

"Is there any official number of victims?"

"Too many to count. The figure released to the media is hundreds of thousands. The government thinks it's several million.

Personally, I believe we've already reached the tens of millions. Most simply haven't been found." He paused. "You see, sir, why we have so much riding on this operation. If we don't succeed, I don't think there will be much left to do. It has to work . . ."

I was deeply shocked. And impressed. Like Detective Sullivan, Colonel Highsmith had lost part of his family, and yet he was still standing, performing his duties. How many more people were in the same situation? For the first time I realized how far-reaching the idea of an infection was within the population. Although there was no evidence for its existence, a deadly virus gave people an enemy to visualize, to name. Epidemics were horrifying but familiar. There had been many outbreaks in the past with devastating results, but in the end, things went back to normal. Maybe that was what we all needed, something to cling to in order to find the strength to overcome the unknown.

"So do I, Colonel . . . it has to work."

We remained silent for the rest of the trip to the airport, each submerged in our own thoughts.

When we arrived, two helicopters were waiting for us. Everything had been planned in advance, and for the first time, Paul, David, and I were traveling together. The colonel also got in with us.

"Peter, David, great job!" I said. "You guys identified the locations in record time."

"We got lucky," David replied. "Once we hit the right fractal dimension, everything fit together like a puzzle."

"That's nature," Peter said. "Perfect in every sense."

"Colonel, where exactly are we heading?" David asked.

"Milwaukee."

The noise of the helicopter's engine ramped up until we could no longer hear one another. Peter was silent, staring at the lakes below as if he were feeling out of place.

I leaned over and shouted into his ear. "Peter, I'm going to need your help. You're the only person in this operation who has actually experienced it."

He nodded. "Yes, but I was the victim. You're the one who helped me while I was depressed. Remember?"

"You know the symptoms though. I don't."

He smiled as if it were a waste of time arguing with me. I was worried that David felt the same way.

"David, you know where they're going to attack. We need your help now more than ever."

"They?" the colonel yelled. "Attack?"

Oh, damn. My subconscious had betrayed me.

"They, the viruses."

The colonel seemed to calm down again. I had to be more careful.

"We're relying on both of you to identify the victims," I said.

Peter and David were not convinced, but they weren't in the mood to argue. We all stayed silent for the remainder of the journey.

The flight wasn't too long, or at least that was my impression. We landed in a small square. The area was filled with soldiers. Military trucks were parked around the square, and knots of soldiers patrolled the adjacent streets. A cathedral was on one side of the square.

"Where are we?" I asked one of the soldiers.

"Cathedral Square Park."

Of course, I should have guessed.

Colonel Highsmith led us into a tent in the center of the square. It was the operations center. Inside, three soldiers were standing around a table with a map.

"Colonel," one of them said, "the units have been sent to the specified locations. As instructed, people were advised to remain inside their homes. Soldiers are also equipped with body cameras. We'll be able to record every encounter."

"Good. What area do we cover?"

"A nine-by-nine-block grid, total of eighty-one blocks. We will wait for your orders, sir."

"We're ready. I guess now we just have to wait." He looked at me. I nodded.

I walked out of the tent and checked the surroundings. The army was in the streets, and citizens were in their houses or offices.

I went back inside. "Colonel, we can't just wait. Most people are inside. We won't be able to identify those infected unless we see them. We have to let them know why we're here, what's going to happen."

"We could create panic if we do," he replied. "The situation could easily get out of hand."

"Colonel, look around us. Do you think people are going to panic any more than they already are?"

"Point taken. What do you suggest?"

"Send your soldiers with speakers around the area. We have to ask everyone to get outside, to gather in the streets. In high buildings, send your men door to door. Tell the people it's . . . I don't know, a training exercise, nothing to worry about. In this way, we'll be able to identify any changes in their behavior."

"How much time do we have?"

I looked at Peter and David.

"Not much." David said.

Without hesitation, Colonel Highsmith turned to one of his subordinates. "You heard the man. Go."

There was movement and noise outside the tent. Everybody was taking part in the operation except us. How could I wait calmly for the wave to pass, ignoring what was happening outside?

"Colonel, I'd like to join your men," I said.

"We have orders to restrict your movement."

"You know very well how critical this operation is. We can help your men identify the infected people. Besides, at this moment, every person counts, no matter if it's a soldier or civilian. Yes?"

He stood up and walked to the door. "Well, come on, then." Once outside, Colonel Highsmith called three soldiers and ordered them to go with us. He took one street and joined some soldiers. The three of us took the next one.

"What if I get infected?" David asked, looking around as if he was waiting for a lion to attack.

"Then we'll help you. Don't worry, David. Stay focused. Many people need our help."

We went into a three-story building. I suggested splitting up, so each one of us could cover a different floor. Peter agreed. "OK," I said. "See you at the entrance in ten minutes."

I went to the third floor, Peter to the second, and David to the first. Our escorts trailed behind us. I started knocking on doors in one direction, and my escort started in the opposite direction.

"Sir, we're doing a training operation with the army, and we need everyone living in this apartment to get down to the street," I said. "It's not going to be for long. You'll be able to return home as soon as we finish the exercise."

After talking to two tenants, I heard a gunshot from one of the apartments at the end of the corridor. I ran and knocked on the door. Nobody answered.

My escort was at my shoulder. "Sir, clear the door," he said.

He shot the lock. A cat bolted out as soon as the door opened.

We found a man on the floor in the kitchen. The blood pooling beside him was a clear signal that the wave had begun.

"Call the colonel. Let him know that it's started," I said to the soldier, but he was already on his comm unit.

The remaining doors opened as a result of the gunshot. Some of the people were already starting to act oddly. One woman had a knife in her hand.

"Soldier, tell him we need support here."

I dove at her and removed the knife just as she laid it across her wrist. Then I held her tight in my arms. She started shaking.

"Stay calm," I said. "It will pass soon."

I heard screams. I turned to the window. They were coming from outside the building. The bitter cry was enough to describe the scene.

"You're hurting me!" the woman said. I hadn't noticed how tightly I was holding her.

"Are you alright?"

"Who are you? Leave me alone."

She was definitely back to normal. I released her and then ran out into the corridor. At least a dozen people were on the floor being helped by soldiers. I was relieved. The support had arrived.

I glanced at my watch—almost half an hour into it. David and Peter would already be waiting for me at the building entrance. I took the staircase to the ground floor. On my way out, I

229

saw a man leaning out of his apartment door.

"Do you need help?" I asked.

He stepped inside the apartment without saying a word. I didn't like his look, so I followed.

Sure enough, I found him standing in a small living room with a long knife at his throat. He looked at me. His eyes conveyed a hatred that I had never seen before.

"Your efforts are futile," he said. "There's only one way this will end. Our way."

"Don't—"

Before I could lift a finger, he jammed the knife home. There was nothing I could do.

What the hell did he mean? Our way? He looked at me as if he recognized me, but who was he?

I was still trying to make sense of it when I heard Peter's voice. "Rob! Hurry!"

I left the apartment and ran into the lobby, where the others were waiting for me. Without stopping, I walked toward the entrance of the building. Peter and David followed me.

"What happened upstairs?" Peter asked as we walked through the door. "We heard shots."

What I saw outside was a hell beyond any nightmare. Cars were crashed in the middle of the road, dead bodies lay on the sidewalk, a woman was crying beside a man she had run over, a soldier was helping an old man on the floor beside his dead wife, and another was holding a woman on the terrace of an apartment to prevent her from jumping.

I had never been a strong person, and now I could hardly process what was happening. But I realized standing there doing nothing wasn't helping.

I made an effort to focus on the people in need of my help. "I'll explain it later, Peter. Now we should go to the next building. Hurry up, guys." I hoped Ely was here, helping them from her side.

It was another three-story apartment building. This time we decided to stay together. We were alone—our escorts were still helping some of the previous building's residents. We took the lift to the third floor. We heard people yelling and crying and the sound of breaking glass at the end of the corridor. We found a few doors open. Unfortunately, we were already too late for some of the residents.

We began checking for people who were still alive. It looked like there wasn't much we could do. Peter and David entered the first apartment. I decided to go in the opposite direction, where I thought I heard a woman's voice.

After a few apartments, I found an unlocked door. I threw it open.

Nothing. Just an empty room.

When I turned around to leave the apartment, I heard an object hit the floor. I ran toward a door located at the end of the dining room.

There she was, lying on the bathroom floor, whimpering.

And there was blood. Shit! She'd opened her left wrist. I grabbed a towel to wrap it around the wound.

She hadn't noticed my presence, so she got scared when I touched her hand. She pulled away before I could do anything.

"Ma'am, don't be afraid. I'm not going to hurt you. We need to stop the bleeding."

"Leave me alone. I want to die."

She was at the low point. I needed to act quickly. "Of course you'll die . . . but not today."

While I forced her to let me wrap the towel around her wrist, she fainted. At that moment I realized I didn't have much time. She had lost too much blood. "Peter! Peter!"

The sight of blood always made me feel woozy. When I was young, wounds scared me to death. That was a big issue for a kid who enjoyed climbing trees. As an adult, one time Ely cut herself with a kitchen knife. I froze; I didn't know what to do. "Rob, come on, it's nothing," she said. "Go to the first-aid box, and bring me some alcohol and cotton."

Now I found myself fighting for the life of a wounded woman covered in blood. How far was a person prepared to go in a desperate situation? Everybody thought they knew, but no one did until they had lived it.

"Where are you?" I heard Peter's voice.

"Here in the bathroom. Hurry up!"

"What happened?" he asked, running in.

"She slit her wrist. She needs medical help; she's lost a lot of blood. Give me a hand." Peter helped me carry her to the elevator. A minute later we were outside the building. I spotted a soldier on the other side of the road.

"Soldier, call the paramedics."

We laid her gently on the ground. She looked like she was sleeping, but I knew the battle being fought inside to keep her soul. Appearances were deceiving.

Please, Ely, give her another chance. An insane hope—not a good sign. What a nightmare!

The sound of a siren approaching broke my concentration. I looked around when I realized I hadn't seen David since we entered the building.

"Peter, have you seen David?" I asked.

"No. He was in the apartment next to me when you called me."

He had to be still inside the building. Alone.

"Go look for him; he may need help. I'll stay here with her."

He ran into the building.

The ambulance stopped in front of us. I explained what had happened to the woman. The paramedics began taking care of her immediately.

I walked down the street, looking for people in need of help. I didn't know how, but I had a feeling that everything was finally over, that the worst of the wave had passed.

How many people had gone this time? Many for sure. If such chaos had happened there, what about the other ninety-nine locations? Looking at the chilling scene around me, I couldn't help feeling distressed. Had we managed to keep enough people alive?

Whatever the results, I sensed the end was close, very close.

CHAPTER 40

ELY

I was with Grandpa in a city called Uclés, Spain. We were contacting the Order of Santiago, and, once again, we were in a monastery. I was getting used to traveling across space and time—we were in 1174 at the moment. Grandpa was talking to a knight named Pedro Fernando de Fuente Encalado, the order's first grandmaster of the order.

History was no longer the boring subject of books and museums that I hated so much at school. If I wanted to know something about a specific event of the past, I only needed to visit the person involved in it and talk to him. Of course, finding that person could be tricky sometimes.

I was close to a window. The view was superb – gentle pine-covered hillside down to the meseta. I decided to go outside while Grandpa was talking with that knight. I needed a break.

In the last day or so, I had learned more about Medieval military orders than most historians learned during their entire lives. It was incredible, overwhelming and very difficult to assimilate. I could meet the great people that defined the history and who knows, it was possible I could go even further back in time to the origins of the human species, the dinosaur age, and maybe to the origin of life itself.

I was beginning to enjoy the view when I started feeling uneasy. I went back inside. Grandpa was still talking to the knight. It wasn't him. Rob?

Yes! Something was happening.

I was about to leave when Grandpa turned toward me. "What's going on, Ely?"

"Sorry, Grandpa, but I have to go. Something is happening to Rob."

"But we're not done."

"I know. I'll come back. I promise."

"I see . . . Go."

Go, but where? The last time he was in Chicago at the military complex. Was he still there?

The wave! Yes, that's why I was feeling that way. The shadows. Shit!

I moved first in space at the speed of light to the room where Rob and Peter had been working on the computers. Then I moved in time to the present. I was expecting the worst.

When I arrived, Michael and a band of Gli Custodi warriors filled the room. I recognized some of them from the previous meeting.

"Ely? What are you doing here?" Michael asked.

"I need to see Rob. Where is he?"

"Don't worry! He's fine. He's just gone through a difficult experience with the last wave. He's upset but well."

When he mentioned the wave, I got even more scared. It didn't matter what he said; I needed to see Rob.

"We're following him all the time. Like I said, no worries."

Without making a big deal, Michael continued talking to the other warriors. "Everything went as planned. The shadows left with the idea that they were still in control of the situation. We managed to help more than one million people, enough to convince them that we were still fighting but without much hope."

"Michael, one million out of how many?"

"Ely, we know you're very concerned about people, and that's—"

"How many?"

"About thirty million."

"And what about the people in the testing locations? Did they survive?"

"Not all of them."

"How many?"

"We managed to save a third."

"And this is things going according to plan?"

No one said a word. If Rob didn't succeed in his attempt, he wouldn't be able to convince the army, and everything would be lost. I knew I didn't have a heart anymore, but I felt like I was going to have a heart attack.

"What can we do now?" I asked.

"We knew this test was important." Michael said. "However, Ely, its failure was the result of another problem . . . an even bigger problem."

"Bigger than the triumph of the Antiscians?"

"The last wave tested people's ability to get prepared on time. Sadly, they failed. They couldn't keep tens of thousands of people alive, and that was in only a hundred locations. Imagine the challenge of doing it across the country."

Would that be possible? How on earth did Rob not help those people? He had enough time to work with the army to assemble the soldiers needed to look after everyone in those locations. No conclusive results and now big deployment capability issues. What a shit show!

"Do you know what happened?" I asked. "Was it a personnel issue? I mean, not enough soldiers? Was it the locations? Not well defined enough? There must be a reason behind the results."

"Since the wave began, I've been watching them, following them through their preparations, and I can tell you, they have big coordination problems. They weren't able to be at the right spot at the right moment. It's as simple as that."

But I didn't think so. I knew Rob. He would have done the impossible to make the test successful. Something else must have happened, but what?

Anyway, Michael was right. It didn't really matter what the cause was. We had only one more chance, and it was not looking good.

Gabriel arrived. "Michael, we have to move fast. We need to contact Ely."

"It's not necessary. She's right here."

He turned to me. "Ely, you were supposed to be with your grandfather."

"I had a bad feeling about Rob."

"Sometimes I forget the connection you two have. Anyway, did Michael tell you our concern about people's coordination problems?"

"It looks like more than a concern to me."

"I was present in many of the testing locations, and I saw how they couldn't cope with the volume of cases. We won't succeed if people don't do their part of the plan, and so far they don't look like they can."

He was talking to me as if I knew what to do. "Don't look at me like that," I said. "You think I have the answer to this situation? I'm afraid I don't."

"We know, Ely, but you're the only access we have to them. People have to understand the consequences if they're not ready for the next attack."

"Rob knows that. I can't go to him with the same speech again. Give me something useful to tell him."

Once again, no one had a word to say.

"OK, there must be something," I said. "Michael, tell me one thing. You're going to organize an army of sixty-four million people. How do you do that?"

"Well, it's not exactly an organized army. We don't have the usual top-down chain of command. It's more like sixty-four million free agents, fighters who decided to come here by themselves; nobody forced them. They do it because they believe in what this world represents. They trust me, and that trust aligns them with the Gli Custodi and makes them follow my instructions."

The collective belief and trust in one person. Could that apply to Rob? I needed more details. "And how do you do that? I mean, how do you tell them what to do."

"You should know by now. We're all connected. When I open my mind, they hear and see my thoughts. There's no hidden agenda; everybody knows the truth and understands the situation and its consequences."

It was about transparency, visibility. That didn't seem too difficult to replicate on the other side . . . at least in theory. But the trust thing, that's not likely to happen in a world where people are used to distrusting one another.

"Okay, I'll speak with Rob . . . once again."

The test may not have worked out as planned, but now I knew what I needed to look for. I left the room with the echo of those two words in my mind: believe and trust.

CHAPTER 41
ROB

I was walking down the street when I heard a vehicle racing toward me. It was a Humvee, and it skidded to a stop right next to me.

"Sir, Colonel Highsmith requires your presence."

Like a good soldier, I got into the vehicle without asking questions. We turned around and headed back to the main camp in front of the church. I saw Peter in the distance leaving the building with David. Good, one less weight on my shoulders.

The extent of the chaos produced by the wave was appalling. Bodies were everywhere. It was supposed to be one of the key locations identified by Peter and David. There should have been no deaths.

As we approached the main square, I saw the colonel waiting for me outside the tent.

"We have to go to Washington," he said as soon as I got out

of the Humvee. "There's an emergency meeting at 18:00 hours tomorrow."

"Washington? Who wants me there?" I was expecting to return to Chicago.

"I don't know, but I have orders to take you there as soon as possible."

"What about Peter and David?"

"They're going too."

Just then, I heard another car approaching. Peter and David were inside.

Ten minutes later, we were in a helicopter on our way back to O'Hare International, where a Gulfstream C-37A jet was waiting to take us to Washington.

Once in the air, the stress of the last few days caught up to me. I was exhausted. I wanted so badly to sleep, but those images, those people on the street, were engraved in my mind.

Even so, I drifted off as soon as the jet leveled out.

"Hi Rob."

There she was, splendid as always.

"Why don't you just say hello and stop looking at me like that?"

What else could I do? I couldn't hide my feelings from her. "Sorry. Hi."

"What's wrong?"

"This last day has been . . . I witnessed the end of everything. I never thought a wave could carry so much destruction."

She nodded. "It's horrible, I know."

"Since the first time we talked, I've been isolated from what was happening outside. I wasn't aware how serious it was. Then I was dropped into the middle of it."

She took my hand. Her hand was so cold that it felt like a static electric shock. I yanked mine away involuntarily.

It was only then that I realized where we were. We were inside a white room with a few pieces of furniture—a table, two chairs, and a framed picture of our wedding day on the wall. It had no door and no windows. Everything was white.

I got up and walked around. "What's this? Where are we?"

"I don't know. Your subconscious created it."

"No doors, no windows, and all white. Is it some kind of prison?"

"It looks that way."

"Why put myself in a place without an exit?"

"For protection maybe? If you can't get out, nothing can get in."

"Protection from what?"

"From the outside world. You just told me how horrendous it is, so I wouldn't blame your subconscious for creating a defense mechanism to protect you from what's happening out there. I'm so sorry for what you've had to go through."

"It was . . . we were there, helping as many people as we could, and still so many died."

"It's not easy for anyone. I can't wait to see the day when everything is back to normal . . . again. Come."

We sat on the two white chairs.

"I'm on my way to Washington to attend a meeting," I said. "I don't know why they want me there, but I guess it has to do with the test. I really hope we saved the people that we promised. I know it didn't happen where I was, but there were another ninety-nine locations. I need it to work so desperately. They have to believe me."

"So do I, but it won't be easy. You're going to have a tough time convincing them."

That comment didn't sound very encouraging. She must have known something. I gave her the space to tell me in her own way.

"The results," she began. "Well, I don't know how to say it. They weren't good enough."

"What do you mean?"

"We didn't save enough people."

"I knew it. I had a feeling that something was wrong. Did we save at least most of them? How many?"

"Between a quarter and half, depending on the location."

That was bad, very bad. Without a convincing result, the

people I was meeting with would find reasons to explain why it didn't work. The FBI woman in particular.

"What should I do?" I asked.

"Better results would have helped us, no doubt about it, but that's not the crucial point anymore. These results showed something we hadn't considered: the lack of capacity to deal with an operation of that magnitude. Even if you manage to convince them, to engage them in this effort, I don't know how they're going to assemble and deploy the army needed to stop the next wave."

Damn. I hadn't thought that far ahead. Why wasn't anything working in our favor?

"I know it may sound fatalistic," she continued, "but if we can't save people in a hundred locations, how can we expect to save millions across the country?"

"So is this it? Is it over?"

"Sorry for always bringing bad news. You know it's just as bad on our side."

I nodded. "I don't know exactly what I'm going to do, but I'm sure about one thing: I'll do the impossible to make them believe. They'll have to build that army even with kids and old people if necessary, I—"

"Rob, stop there. It won't work. It doesn't matter how many people join the army. It won't be big enough."

"I'm sure we can get millions of people. The army has millions of members between active duty and reserve personnel."

"How many millions, Rob? Two, three, maybe five or six? The next wave is going to involve tens of millions of people." Her eyes filled with tears. "Even if you can assemble a big enough group, how are you going to deploy them across the country in such a short time? The test showed that coordination at that level is practically impossible."

It became clear to me. This was the end. This was it. Everything we could do we'd already done. Everything we could say had been said. We remained silent, staring at the perfectly white walls, sealed in and safe.

"You know, maybe we're not taking the right approach," Ely said.

241

"What do you mean?"

"Assembling an army to defend the population."

"Who else? We have soldiers to protect our country, police to protect citizens, firemen to protect our homes. That's how society works. We need to assemble the group of people who can stop this, give them some training and organization, then get them into place. No matter what name you give it, it's an army."

"But what if the people were already in place? Maybe the time has come for each individual to take responsibility for the future of everyone else."

"You mean . . ."

"Alert all citizens to look after one another."

"But—"

"Colleague to colleague, neighbor to neighbor, friend to friend, black to white, young to old, rich to poor, stranger to stranger. Nobody in this country should go unprotected. Everyone has to look after and be looked after by someone. It's the only way this can work."

"Ely, set aside human selfishness and fear for a second. Do you know the scale of what you're asking?"

"You just said you were willing to do the impossible. It looks like that's what it will take."

"I take it you have no clue how we're going to do it."

She shook her head.

"Come on, Ely, there must be something you can tell me. We have to send the message to every corner of the country, convincing every person to put aside his or her own individual survival instinct and look after someone else that might not even know. People aren't ants or bees used to blindly following orders and sacrificing themselves to save the queen."

She remained silent.

"Right now, we have panic and chaos throughout the country. People are taking their families and running away, leaving everything and everyone behind. There's looting. Armed gangs are forming. Society is coming apart at the seams. It's not a moment for selfless, collective action."

"And yet we have to believe it's possible."

"Belief isn't enough."

"It has to be. When a person faces the possibility of losing everything, his or her last hope, no matter how impossible it might be, becomes that person's battle flag."

"Ely, please. You're asking us to change human nature on a grand scale!"

"Don't look at it as moving a mountain. Just start with one rock at the time. If I were you, I'd leave the ant/bee issue to the military and the government and concentrate my efforts on finding a way to send the message across the nation. You need to be able to get the message to every single person."

"But that won't do any good."

"It's all I can say, Rob. Go back and get the help of anyone willing to believe you. I'll see if there's something we can do from our side."

She stood up. I took her hand to try to stop her from leaving. Her eyes betrayed a deep, unbearable sorrow.

"Me too," I said.

She disappeared, leaving me alone in my safe, sterile room.

How could she ask me something like that? She left me with only one option, an impossible one. If she was right, the meeting would be a disaster, followed by a catastrophe. Had my dream gone too far?

However, I had an immediate problem to deal with. How I was going to leave this white prison? I tried to push the walls, but they were like solid rock. It seemed I would have to wait until I woke up. I sat in the chair and began thinking about the meeting . . .

When I woke up, the plane was still on route. The cabin lights were off, and everything was quiet. Most of the other passengers were sleeping. I didn't want to make any noise, so I stayed in my seat.

I couldn't help thinking why everything had gone so wrong. What else could I have done? Now I had all my cards on the table. But without a good outcome from the test, and impossible logistical problems on the horizon, everything was pointing to only one thing: just sit back and wait for the end. Would my efforts make any difference with such a certain and inevitable final destination?

After a while the lights came on, and the captain announced we were beginning to descend. As soon as we landed in a private sector of the airport, a fleet of black cars approached the airplane. We left without wasting any time. Two police motorcycles led the way, in a cordoned off area so no traffic lights stopped us. Definitely head-of-state treatment. I'd have enjoyed it under any other circumstances.

We approached a building that I recognized immediately: the Pentagon. For the first time I was shaking. What was the Department of Defense expecting from me? Whatever it was, this was the highest I could reach.

Two soldiers escorted me inside the building. David and Peter were taken to a different section. I was led into a lift, then down a corridor on the second floor. Four men were standing on either side of a set of double doors. One of them asked me to wait while he entered the room. He left the door slightly open, so I managed to overhear the conversation taking place inside.

"Doctor, is that the best you can do?"

"Sir, we have the country's top scientists working on it. We hope to have an antidote soon."

"Our people are dying out there. More than a quarter of our population is already gone."

Then I heard a woman's voice. "Sir, I'd strongly suggest you consider the other options."

"Don't tell me that you believe that stupid theory. Come on, Jessica."

"With all due respect, sir, this has behaved largely as he predicted. I think we should listen to what he has to say. Let him in."

The doors opened, and an agent waved me in. I stepped into a room full of people, at least twenty. Some sat on leather chairs around a large oval table. Others were seated against the wall. At the head of the table was him, the president of the United States.

"What is this person doing here?"

"Mr. President, this is Robert Kline. I asked him to come here."

It was her! The FBI woman.

"Why, Jessica? This meeting isn't open to the public. We're talking about issues of national security. Take him out."

A soldier moved toward me. I knew this was the decisive moment. If Jessica wanted me there, I needed to do something.

"Mr. President," I said, "with all due respect, I think a quarter of the population already dead makes this meeting relevant to every citizen."

The soldier took my arm, but I dug in my heels. "Sir, I only want the chance to explain what I've seen and what I believe. Then I'll go. Please."

The president made a signal, and the soldier released me. I looked at Jessica. Finally, I knew her name. She nodded. That gave me the confidence to go ahead.

"I'm neither a doctor nor a scientist, as you know. I can't ask you to believe me because of my credentials. But by sheer chance I experienced something that I believe can stop this nightmare." The most powerful people in the country had their eyes on me, but somehow, I found the words to continue. "I don't know what's causing the deaths; I'll freely admit that. But whatever it is, it has a weakness: time. If we can keep the victims alive long enough, its effect gets weaker until it disappears. Basically, it kills itself."

"Mr. President," one of the others said, "this man isn't a scientist. There is no organism, no mechanism known to humanity that behaves the way he's describing. And he's asking us to risk everything on this theory. Can anybody in this room tell me why we're listening to him? Have we lost our mind"?

"Because nobody has a better answer to what's going on," I said.

That silenced the man—probably a scientist—for a moment.

"It's true," I admitted. "I don't know what this mechanism is, but I do know that if we wait until we understand it before we act, we will waste our last chance of survival."

"Mr. President," the scientist who had objected earlier said, "we're working on the antidote. We hope it's going to be ready soon. As a doctor I can assure you that we will find the cure."

He clearly had the president's confidence. It was obvious that I wouldn't be able to convince the president with such a strong opponent. Then someone entered the room with some papers. That gave me a valuable couple of seconds to structure my thoughts.

"Hope?" I said. "What's the difference between your hope and my belief?"

"Your belief has already been tested," the scientist said. "Your experiment from the one hundred locations didn't provide any conclusive results."

It felt like a stab in the back. I wasn't aware that they had seen and discussed the outcome of the test. What could I say to change their opinion? Clearly, their minds were made up.

As the silence stretched on and hope drained away, a voice broke through. "Actually, that's not entirely true," Jessica said.

The president turned to her. "Do you have something you want to share with us?"

"Mr. President, by the time we were preparing for this test, we'd received reports of mass suicides in towns close to our borders with Canada and Mexico. With the disease spreading outside our borders, and without any conclusive results from the other options, I thought this test could be our only chance to identify a cure. So, I decided to perform an independent double check of Mr. Kline's theory. We ran two more tests in parallel with what we originally planned, applying the approach to two hundred additional locations with the help of all FBI and CIA agents plus some private security contractors. We've just gotten the results. We managed to save the lives of 97.3 percent of the people with the symptoms."

"Then why did we get such a low result on the first test?"

"It was a timing issue, sir. In most of the cases, soldiers reached the victims too late. We saved many more when we ordered people out of their buildings and into the street. If we gather people together ahead of time, we can keep them alive."

"What if the locations you picked were not actually infected?" the scientist asked. "You don't know that for sure, do you?"

"We selected two hundred locations within a ratio of one hundred miles around the first hundred test locations. They were close enough to ensure they were also contaminated."

"Jessica, you're telling us that by doing nothing but keeping people alive, the whole pandemic will go away? Don't you think this leap of faith is too risky?"

"Not if it's our only choice. Let's look at the facts, Mr. President. There's no solid evidence that this is being caused by a terrorist attack. We haven't found any sign of gas or chemical poisoning in the victims' bodies. Also, no trace of a virus or bacteria so far, so how do you prepare an antidote if you haven't isolated the virus? But even if we do have a vaccine, it will take months to bring it into production and distribute it to millions of people. If deaths continue at this rate, soon there'll be nobody to administer the vaccine, much less receive it."

I couldn't believe what was happening right in front of my eyes. That cold, arrogant, insensible woman was defending me. Perhaps miracles did happen after all.

The president closed his eyes, trying to concentrate, and the room fell silent. The decision was difficult, and I was afraid he might go for the safest option.

But ... wait a second. They could do whatever they wanted as long as they also helped me.

"Mr. President, if you'll allow me," I said. "I don't think things need to be black or white. As . . . Jessica said, there's no clear understanding of the cause; therefore, there's no clear reason to choose my theory above the others. But why do we have to choose at all? The more options we work on simultaneously, the better our chances of success. The doctor can continue his work on the antidote, the terrorist option can also be studied, and at the same time we can work on how to take the test to a national level. By the way, it's not a matter of doing nothing and hoping for the best. At the very least, we may keep the country's population alive long enough for something else to work."

The president turned toward the group of military brass across the table from the civilians. "What's your recommendation?"

"Mr. President," an army general said, "any of the options we have on the table could work. At this point, pursuing all of them makes a certain amount of sense."

"Gambling that one of them works."

"The more lottery tickets you buy, the better your odds."

"I agree." The president pointed at the scientist. "Doctor Lansky, do the impossible, and find a cure." He turned to Jessica. "Do whatever is necessary to replicate across the country what you did with the CIA and the FBI. We need that 97.3 percent statistic to hold."

He stood up. Everybody else followed. "I want an action plan on my desk by 14:00 hours tomorrow." Without another word, he left the room, escorted by two soldiers.

We all stared at each other in silence. There wasn't much to say.

Jessica stood up and gathered a few papers. I caught her before she reached the door.

"Um . . . thank you," I said.

"For what?"

"For what you did for me."

"I didn't do anything for you."

"I know."

"Then why the thanks?"

"For believing me. Trusting me."

"I didn't. Why do you think I ran my own test?"

"But if you had the results, why did you ask me to be here? You could've managed the meeting without me."

"I needed him to listen to you. It's an impossible decision to make, and I knew numbers wouldn't be enough. You believe so passionately and uncompromisingly that only you could have convinced the president."

I had never met anyone quite as emotionless as her. Everything was deliberately calculated. Being beside her made me feel . . . used. But maybe this was exactly the kind of person the situation needed.

"Let's not waste time, Mr. Kline. We have work to do. I suggest you take a rest. I need you here with your friends in one hour. We have an action plan to deliver for 14:00 tomorrow." Then she left the room.

At that point I realized I was not alone anymore. I had an ally—one I could meet with outside my dreams.

CHAPTER 42

ROB

A soldier took me to a section of the Pentagon that looked like a mid-priced hotel. It had equally spaced doors, numbered and with swipe card locks, carpets, and, from time to time, a painting on the wall. We stopped at room 3B321.

The room was bigger than I expected—a studio apartment with a kitchenette. I was exhausted, so as soon as the soldier left, I lay down on the sofa. I was still shocked by Jessica's about-face. And her discovery—97.3%. Wow! That was the first tangible proof that we might have a chance.

I heard some voices just outside my door, then someone knocked.

"Who is it?"

"Sir, they're waiting for you."

Already? I must have fallen asleep without noticing. The time went by like a blink of an eye. I opened the door.

"Peter! David!"

"Hi, Rob," Peter said. "They said you needed us. Where are they taking us?" That was the Peter I knew, nervous as a bird.

"We have a meeting. They want us to put together a plan for what to do next."

"A plan?" David asked cautiously.

"They're going to scale up what they did in Chicago to a national level."

Peter broke into a huge smile. "Then the test was a success?"

"Kind of. It's a long story." As we walked to the meeting room, I explained what had happened with Jessica and the other tests.

We arrived at a big, empty, open-concept room. One section was closed with glass walls. Dark vertical blinds kept us from seeing inside. However, the voices were so loud that we could still listen to the discussion going on inside. The soldier knocked on the door. Someone from inside opened it. A tense silence fell upon the room.

It was packed with at least fifteen people. Only one person was in uniform. The rest were in civilian clothes. Some were standing, and others were seated around a rectangular table in the center of the room illuminated with a strange-looking lamp hanging from the ceiling. Before we could say hello, someone broke the silence.

"Well, maybe the expert can shed some light on this discussion," a man with a large beard said. I guessed he was an academic of some sort.

I didn't understand why I had faced so much hostility since I arrived. I didn't know any of these people, and yet they all seemed to hate me. Maybe it was just a feeling of helplessness. Maybe the simplicity of my solution seemed like arrogance.

"Sit down, Anton," Jessica said from the head of the table. "The enemy is not inside this room. Robert, please take a seat. We're talking about the available options. We need to find a way to replicate what we did during the test with the resources we have."

I sat in the only free chair left at the table. Peter and David found two chairs at the back of the room.

"How can I help?" I asked politely.

"Well, some people are in favor of using only the military. Others want to call all the country's security services—the FBI, the CIA, and the TSA."

After my tense discussion with the president, I was a little hesitant to impose my ideas on the rest of the group. "Do you know how many people we need?"

"At least a million."

She was below what we really needed. Not a good start.

"But how many died in the last wave?"

"Well, the chaos makes it hard to collect the information, but at least a few millions. Why?"

Millions gone, and she wondered why I had asked that question. I kept my mind focused on those we could save instead of thinking about the ones who were already gone.

"Because I think you're underestimating what we need. Even if the next wave is the same size as the last—and they have been growing exponentially—how can a million soldiers protect several million people?"

"We're assuming that, with the proper training, a soldier can look after up to ten people at the same time."

"How do you gather the ten potential victims in one place?"

"We believe it can be done."

"And what if the soldier is one of the victims?"

"Can people who have already suffered from it be identified and employed?" Anton asked.

"But how do we know if they have immunity?" I asked

The room fell silent once again.

"I don't know if you remember the results of Peter and David's calculations," I said, turning to my friends. "Guys, how many people do we need to keep an eye on?"

"It depends on how many were killed in the last wave," David said. "But it's on the order of tens of millions."

"And what's worse," I said, "is it has spread across the country already. There may be people infected in every corner of the US."

Jessica was silent, just listening. This new Jessica was taking some time getting used to.

"We're talking about training an army of millions and deploying them across the country in days or maybe hours," I said.

"Which is why we need the help of all security services of the country," Jessica said.

"But—"

"No, listen everyone," Jessica said, overruling Anton. "I want to match all security forces in the country with the expected outbreak locations. Diana, I need you and your team to get the GPS coordinates of all military, police, firefighters, FBI, CIA, every institution involved in the security of this country. John, Anton, get the number of people assigned to each one of these locations. Peter, David, I need you guys to download your fractal model into the DARPA network."

Everybody split into teams and left the room, their tasks clearly defined. Although I knew I couldn't help much, I joined Peter and David.

Two hours later we were all back. Everything was downloaded, and presumably everyone else had gotten their information together. As I entered the room, I saw Jessica putting on a pair of gloves. She touched something on the table's surface. The glass table illuminated like a computer touch screen. The lamp on the ceiling turned on. Then things went sci-fi. A three-dimensional map of the country formed above the table. She started manipulating the image with her hands. Moving the model around, zooming in and out, adding layers of color, and so on.

"The red dots represent the locations of the four million people who belong to our security forces," she said. "If we consider the health sector—doctors, nurses, paramedics—we can add another four million. Here's how they're distributed."

New blue points appeared on the image. "We have a higher concentration here, here, and here," she said. "Let's see what we have when we superimpose the expected outbreak locations of the fractal model."

That was the last word I heard from Jessica. Everybody stared at the 3D image. When the dots of the model were added, the entire image turned white. Now it was clear to everyone; Jessica's army of helpers wasn't enough.

After a minute that seemed like hours, Jessica broke the silence. "Does anyone have a better idea?"

"You know this isn't the first time we're discussing this matter," Anton said. "We've been looking for a solution to this puzzle since the first deaths were detected. We've run out of fresh ideas."

Jessica shook her head. "That doesn't help us, Anton. We have to find an answer."

A woman at the back stood up. "Sorry, but I have a family to look after." She took her things and left the room.

"Wait, Alice, I'll go with you," another woman said.

Then everyone started talking, all of it with an edge of panic.

I couldn't take my eyes off the 3D image. The white dots were spread so widely across the country that it seemed like the next wave would appear everywhere, touching everyone. Everyone? That was exactly what Ely was worried about. She kept telling me that we would not be enough unless everyone took responsibility. Well, if there was ever a time for impossible ideas, this was it.

"Maybe our approach is wrong," I said.

The room went silent. Everyone looked at me.

"Look, the idea of gathering an army, a group of saviors, heroes who will save us, maybe that's not the way to go."

"Don't be sarcastic," Anton said.

"I'm not. The situation has gotten out of hand. These whites show that every person in this country may already be infected, but they also tell us that everyone can help someone else."

"You mean train the population to take care of itself," Jessica said.

"Exactly! We have to go directly to every American and explain the situation as we understand it and what needs to be done. We have to tell them the truth." That was ironic. I was giving them an idea created in a dream and telling them to be honest.

Everyone started talking at the same time.

"Nonsense! How can we expect civilians to do this?"

"No way! Just think of the panic on the streets."

"Hey, hey, hey!" Jessica banged on the table. "We can cut down the panic if we make them understand that everything isn't over, that there's hope. They may—"

"And tell them what?" Anton asked. "That everybody is infected? That if they just go to bed and fall asleep, they'll wake up fine? That's not a hope they can believe in. Hell, I don't even believe it."

"They'll think we're hiding the truth, that they're all going to die," someone else said.

Everyone was worried more about the difficulties than the possibility of hope. Maybe that was what they needed, a moment of catharsis. In any case, it was frustrating to know the reason behind it and yet not be able to say it aloud.

I checked the time; it was already past midnight. There was no sign that the discussion would wind up soon. I had planted the seed, so now I had to wait and see. I exchanged a glance with Jessica, who nodded, then asked one of the soldiers outside the door to take me to my room.

I walked away wondering whether there was any chance of survival, given that the decision rested with a room full of closed-minded people. I felt like every part of my body weighed a ton.

As soon as I got to my room, I walked straight to the bedroom and fell onto the bed. I kicked off my shoes and closed my eyes.

What if they weren't able to draw up a plan? Maybe it would take too long to reach an agreement, so by the time they started to act, it would be too late. And how would it work? I guessed big cities would be easy. People lived close to one other, sort of. But it was possible to live in a building with dozens of apartments and still not know one's neighbors. Were people ready to help each other in order to help themselves?

Small towns were much more likely to cooperate, but then there was the problem of distance. There were little towns in every corner of the country. We could use the Emergency Alert System to send the message, but how could we gather them together before it was too late? We had so many problems with only a few hundred locations.

My body was so tired that I felt I could sleep for days, but my mind was in overdrive. At a certain point of the night, I realized that just staying in bed was stressful enough to keep me awake.

If I wanted to rest, I had to regain control of my thoughts. Fresh air, that's what I needed.

I checked the time: 2:27 a.m. I put my shoes on, walked to the door, and turned the handle without making any noise. I leaned out the door. Nobody was outside.

I didn't know the building, so I figured any direction was as good as any other. I went right, expecting to find an elevator. I figured I could be in one of the Pentagon's ring corridors, so I had to look carefully for an exit, or I might come back to my room without noticing. Finally, I found a staircase.

Up or down? Betting that the building had a terrace, I decided to go up. After three floors, the staircase ended at a metal door. Wanting to breathe fresh air, I opened it.

Amazing! There was a garden on the roof. Exactly what I needed.

It was a carefully designed rooftop garden. Plants were placed in big pots, and the floor was covered by synthetic grass. Water fountains and stone paths with benches were scattered under trees. It was a serene and tranquil retreat.

I walked to the edge of the building and took in the astonishing view of the Potomac River and the Washington Monument. The sky was so clear that the tiny stars stood out from the dark background. The moon was waxing in its crescent phase. Its soft reflection on the river was stunning.

I heard a sound. "Who's there?" I asked. Then I saw not far the silhouette of a man standing close to the edge. "What're you doing?" He moved closer. "Stop!" I shouted, then took hold of his arm. He quickly pulled away, but I managed to hold him from behind. I dragged him down to prevent him from slipping over the edge. Then the same pattern happened; he started shaking violently. I knew what to do. I held him tightly until he came back to himself.

"Mr. Kline."

"Mr. President. Are you OK?"

He tried to stand up but with difficulty. I helped him over to the nearest bench.

"It was so bizarre," he said. "I got to my office when suddenly

I felt overwhelmed by the situation, then powerless, depressed. How did you find me?"

"I didn't know you were here. What's happening is too disturbing to leave aside and just go to bed, even if only for a few minutes"

"That's a good sign, you know."

"Of what?"

"Of your soul. You care about what really matters."

He held his head with both hands. "Have you ever wished to be somewhere outside the glass bubble that we live in?"

"What do you mean, sir?"

"Most of us devote our entire lives to improving our society. I've spent so much time dealing with things that everybody considers important—economic stimulus, social equality, foreign policy. We've built a self-consistent, self-sufficient world, isolated from its surroundings, a world where nature isn't invited in. But the fact is, we're deeply connected to this planet, and when we push the boundaries a bit further, a storm or an earthquake reminds us of that."

"You think the pandemic is the result of us crossing a line somewhere?

"It would be foolish to think that it just fell from the sky."

The conversation had an intimate, almost mystical, feel. Maybe this was the moment to test how far I could go with the truth.

"What if it did?"

He gave me a quizzical look. "Are you trying to say this pandemic, what happened to me, has extraterrestrial origins?"

"Not exactly from outer space but in some way alien to our world."

"Well, in that case I wonder what we've done to piss someone off so badly."

"I'm sorry, Mr. President."

"During our lives we do many things—some conscious, others unconscious. But whatever actions we take, they're always met by a reaction. It's like a boomerang; sooner or later it comes back to us. This pandemic . . . well . . . it's the first time nature has threatened the entire human race with the possibility of extinction."

"What makes you think nature is behind it?"

256

"Only humans are infected. It's targeted to eradicate us specifically."

I remained silent. I couldn't argue against that, not without losing all credibility.

"If this pandemic is the boomerang coming back," he said, "how much have we pushed nature's limits? And for how long? Just imagine the scope of our collective actions that created a reaction of this magnitude."

"We've also done good things, sir."

He nodded. "I know. I've seen a lot of them in just the last few weeks. We're good people, so our good actions should outnumber our bad ones, shouldn't they? In any case, it makes me wonder if maybe it's not a matter of being good or bad but being able to turn bad into good."

"Learn from our mistakes, is that your point?"

He stood up. "Mr. President . . ." I tried to help him.

"I'm fine." We walked to the edge, and then he looked at the sky. "Don't you think it's ironic?"

"What's that, sir?"

"In our society, we reward individualism, and we take pride in our control over nature. Now that we're facing extinction, our knowledge, technology . . . everything is useless. Our only hope of survival depends on our collective willingness to look after one other and, most importantly, let nature take its course without our interference. Two things we haven't practiced much."

"Could that be why this is happening, sir? To teach us a lesson?"

"I don't know. But whether something's trying to teach us or not, we need to learn that lesson. And fast."

With that he turned. On his way to the door, he stopped. "What happened tonight, keep it to yourself. And, Mr. Kline . . . Robert, thank you." Then he left the garden.

I remained a bit longer, reflecting on what had happened. Now he knew. After a while, I could barely keep my eyes open, which was good considering how late it was. I found my way back to my room with no problem. A soldier was outside my door.

Walking to the room revived me some. I picked up an IT

257

magazine from the bedside table, but I fell asleep a few pages into it.

I woke up at dawn with no memories of any dream, but I felt different. I got up knowing exactly what we needed to do. I got dressed and then grabbed the IT magazine on my way out. My escort was waiting for me outside.

As I approached the meeting room, I heard people arguing. I hoped it hadn't been going on all night.

"Good morning, Robert." Jessica said when I entered. "We've been talking over what you said last night about making people part of the solution. We think that if we explain what's happening, they'll cooperate, and it will be easier to gather them into groups of thirty. Meanwhile, we can assemble an army of ten million. We can cover the entire population with this approach."

"Are you going to tell them the truth?" I asked.

"Part of it. That this is a government exercise to reduce the effects of the pandemic."

It was depressing. One night of discussion, and they were still stuck on the same idea.

"And what about the consequences if they don't cooperate?" I asked. "There are going to be holdouts."

She shrugged. "If people refuse to come in, maybe they deserve to die."

I was armed with the clarity of mind from a good night's sleep, and this was just too much. "Do you realize what you're saying?" I asked. "You have to convince a population of terrified people to gather in places that you have yet to identify without telling them why. At the same time, you have to build an army of five—sorry, ten million people—train them, and send them across the country, with many of them being already infected. I can spend hours describing in detail what you'd need to execute this plan. The truth is, we can't implement an effort of this magnitude. We don't have time. Big Brother can't watch over every one of us. We have to watch over ourselves."

"This is the best we can do," she said as David and Peter entered the room.

I shook my head. "I'm not sure it's enough. As I said yesterday,

258

it doesn't matter how big it is. We can't rely on a group of people. The entire population has to look after itself. We have to tell them the whole truth. Responsibility comes with understanding."

"How would you suggest we do that?" a woman down the table asked. "We need to coordinate the actions of each citizen across the country."

I took a deep breath. "First, we need to be able to reach each citizen, no matter where they are, and this is how we're going to do it."

I put the IT magazine on the table. The cover had a big headline: "Finally, 100% Wireless Penetration in the US."

Anton read the headline and then looked at me. "Do you suggest we call every single American and explain what they need to do?"

I glared at him. I didn't need to say anything.

"As you said," I continued, turning back to the woman. "We need to be able to talk in real time not only with every single citizen but also to have two-way communication with everyone at the same time."

"I don't really understand why we would need two-way communication," she said. "Why not simply give them a training video on how to deal with someone being affected? We could send out instructions via the Emergency Alert System. By the way, has anyone seen Jacob? He works for FEMA. He's the perfect person to tell us about the EAS."

"It's not a problem of communication," I said. "We can't guarantee there will be enough unaffected people in each group to save the rest. They need to be able to ask for support."

"A real-time social network!" somebody said.

"Twitter?"

"Exactly," I said. "If we put together these two elements, cell and Twitter, we have a way to establish contact with virtually every person in this country, wherever they are."

"But we can get the same coverage with TV. Isn't it more reliable and far better to make announcements on all the news outlets than send out instructions via the Emergency Broadcasting System?"

"Yes, but it would be only one way. By combining them, we

can put in place a two-way, real-time, person-to-person communication network through which we can contact and be contacted by every citizen in this country."

"Even assuming this can be done," Jessica said, "the problem remains: how do we know they'll be ready to listen? What are we going to tell them that they're likely to believe? Who's going to do it?"

After my encounter the previous night, I had no doubts. "Our president. He's the only person with the values, moral weight, and credibility to tell people the truth and still hold the country together."

I didn't know if I had convinced them, but when I mentioned the president, everybody's expression changed.

"But how are we going to create this network?" Anton asked. It was encouraging that this was his first "how" rather than "why" question.

"We have to create a Twitter account assigned to each mobile number," I said. "These accounts are set up to follow a master account. Every tweet created in this master account will be viewed in real time by everybody in the country. The same way we create regional accounts for each state. They will be set up to follow those accounts with a mobile number registered in the state. If someone has a problem, all they have to do is send a tweet, and it'll be seen by the regional team." I looked at David. "This is all doable, right?"

He nodded. "I think so."

I turned to Jessica, who also nodded. "Yes, Robert. We can assign these Twitter accounts to regional commands located in our FBI centers across the country. From each center, we can coordinate a quick response to those in trouble. In fact, using a combination of the cells and the nation's GPS system, we'll be able to pinpoint to the exact location and send help."

"We can use all our websites to set up pages describing what people have to do," someone at the back of the room said. "The president's speech can be broadcast continuously online, on TV, and on the radio."

"We'll transform the country into a single social network!"

260

someone else said.

Everybody started talking again, but unlike the previous night, it was a brainstorming session rather than an argument.

"We need to contact the five biggest mobile operators. They cover more than ninety-five percent of subscribers."

"Twitter already has more than three hundred million active users. They can add three hundred million mobile accounts to their network just by mirroring the duplication of their system. Difficult but feasible."

"The accounts can be assigned an ID and password equal to the mobile number. We can skip the registration process. Nothing easier to remember than your own mobile number."

Everybody was participating in the discussion except Peter. He was silent, watching what was happening. But when he looked at me, he gave me a big smile and a thumbs-up. The snowball was already rolling down the hill.

CHAPTER 43

ELY

I left Rob's dream wondering if I had revealed too much of my true feelings. I was afraid that the pressure of dealing with so much might make him vulnerable to an Antiscians attack. The conscious dreams, the killing waves . . . me. Everything was unbelievable and almost impossible to assimilate. I couldn't imagine how difficult it was for him.

During our time together, he had been the one protecting me, making me feel secure by just being at my side. Now that I had left, I was the one trying to be always at his side. But he was still the source of my strength. I knew it was supposed to be different. I should have been worrying about the fact that humanity might be destroyed. But my main concern was still Rob and how to protect him from falling into the hands of the Antiscians. I could lose him forever.

Fortunately, I did not have to worry about that for the moment. I knew he didn't like the white room that he had created in his dream, but for me it was comforting. The way his subconscious reacted to protect him was amazing. A sealed space with no entry or exit. White inside, so there was nothing to remind him of what he'd seen. It was sealed against memory, and it was the perfect caring, secure, and relaxing shield. It was so comforting that I was lucky to be able to leave it.

I still wasn't sure how I'd been able to leave. Maybe because I was not part of his dream or because his subconscious recognized I was not a threat. In any case, I was sure he was going to be OK for the time being.

It was time to return to the computer room in Chicago. I was expecting to see Michael and Gabriel, but when I got there, it surprised me to find only one person.

"Mom!" I was so happy to see her. I hadn't been with her since Grandma took me for mentoring.

"Sweetheart, I've been waiting for you. Come, give me a hug."

I threw myself into Mom's arms as I used to do when I was a kid. I had forgotten how things worked in my new world. My body merged with hers. It was amazing. I felt her feelings like they were mine. For a moment, thoughts were not necessary; we were just profoundly connected.

"Mom . . ."

"I know . . . me too."

"Grandpa showed me everything you've done," she said when we separated. "I'm very proud of you, my little girl."

"Don't say so, Mom. We still have tough times ahead."

"Yes, but we're a lot more prepared now, thanks to you"

"So why have I never been so scared in my entire life? Either of them?"

"Ely, you've grown as no other person has done in this world. Look at you; you move in time and space as if you've been here for ages."

Her words made me realize I hadn't had the time to properly assimilate my own death. I hadn't thought much about my new situation. It had just become . . . natural.

"You're right, Mom, but does it matter when we're about to

lose our loved ones?"

"No, darling, we still have one more chance, and I tell you, your loved one is going to need all your strength and courage. You've never needed each other as much as now."

"And at the same time, we've never been so far apart."

"You still look at things with the eyes of a person from a world where most things have a beginning and an end. When you have eternity in front of you, there's no more waiting or wasted time. Such things have no meaning anymore. Maybe this is an area we should work on with Grandpa and Grandma when all of this is over."

Her words were like oxygen to my soul. I wished one day I would be able to have her serenity and wisdom. I was very lucky to have her close to me.

"Sweetheart, things are about to get bad. Your will is going to be put to the test. You'll be faced with the choice between what you want do and what you should do. But no matter what it's at stake, look to your heart. Only your strong beliefs and your deep love for Rob can show you the right thing to do."

Choice? She knew how much I loved Rob. He was and would always be the center of my world. So what was she saying? And why did it sound like a premonition? She didn't give me time to respond.

"Just remember. Now we have to go. Grandpa and the others are waiting for you."

"Where are we going?"

"Where they're assembling the army."

"Mom . . . wait." I extended my right hand to her. She smiled softly and took it, and we moved out of the room together.

A moment later we were in a location that I recognized, having seen it on the TV. It was a huge, arid plain with high mountains far on the horizon. It was deserted; not a single green plant was in the area.

"Mom, I know this place. It's . . . it's . . ."

"The Black Rock Desert Playa, darling. They use it for high-speed car tests."

"Of course. I've seen them on the National Geographic channel. But why are we here? There's nobody here."

"There's nobody here now. They're waiting for us in 1945."

"1945? Mom, that's not a year we're proud of."

"The Hiroshima bomb is one of those events known by every human generation. Even people who lived thousands of years ago know that day. A sad date. Nevertheless, that's exactly why we're heading there. Every warrior called to join our army knows how to find November 6, 1945."

What could I say to something so logically depressing? We moved back in time. A small group of people was congregated around Michael, including Grandpa and Gabriel.

"Good, you're finally here," Grandpa said.

"Sorry," I said.

"It's OK. We're waiting for the rest to arrive."

Michael was silent, concentrating on himself. Then I saw people arriving. Then more. And more. They were appearing from every direction. I recognized some of them by the way they were dressed—Roman legionnaires, Greek hoplites, Samurai warriors, medieval longbowmen, Mongols, Doughboys, La Gran Armada, crusaders, Turks . . . It was the moment we were waiting for. After a few seconds, the playa was packed with sixty-four million warriors.

Silent, no thoughts. A profound stillness even though we were surrounded by millions of people. Everybody was looking at Michael. At the center of the army, he was the source of the stillness—calm and concentrated in his thoughts. I couldn't see inside his mind; he was closed to everyone. A yellowish aura surrounded him, a pure, shining yellow that I'd never seen before. He looked like he was in harmony with something far away.

I saw Grandpa kneeling down. Mom had already left. They closed their eyes as if they were meditating. Then everybody else kneeled as well. It was obvious that I was missing something. Why? I walked around the little circle formed between us and the army.

"Why are you so worried?" Gabriel asked. Nobody else seemed to hear him. Was he talking only to me?

265

"Why? Look around. I'm not part of what's happening."

"Ely, you still don't get it, do you? You and your husband are the key people in this war. Neither world can face the situation alone. We need to work together, and that's only possible thanks to the unique connection that you two have. This is our most valuable secret weapon, and it must be protected no matter what."

"Do you mean these people don't know . . ."

"Exactly. They've been told that the living world is dealing with this situation as if it were a disease of pandemic proportions. They have been told that only we know the real cause of what is happening, and we're only taking advantage of what people are doing to fight what they think is a virus."

I took a moment to reflect. So far, I had been in contact with only a handful of people—my grandparents, my parents, and a few Gli Custodi. But if only a few knew it, what was the problem with me talking to these people?

"Because you're still not good at protecting your thoughts," Gabriel said.

I was about to object until I noticed his slight smile. He was right again. My mind was open to him.

"All we would need is for one of these people, one out of sixty-four million, to leave his mind or her mind open to the Antiscians. They would go after Robert, and if that happened . . ."

"OK, I get it now." I wasn't a superstitious person, but I also didn't like to push that belief too far.

Michael, who had remained silent, stood up and turned to us. Gabriel moved beside him. The army stopped meditating, and everybody stood up.

"My friends, you all saw it." The voice was in my head, presumably from Michael, though it was hard to tell. "As we speak, the Antiscians are preparing a massive attack on the material world. This is not our first clash. We have been in constant battle since the beginning of time, and we still stand victorious. Not because we're stronger or because we outnumber them but because we believe so deeply in good that we're prepared to do whatever is necessary to prevail."

The army cheered.

"This time the threat of eternal darkness is closer than ever before. They're trying to wipe out the human race to create an army big enough to take us on right here, in our own world. And we don't yet fully understand how they're doing it. Our world and the material world have always co-existed in parallel, harmoniously and independently. They have bridged that gap and manipulated peoples' fragile equilibrium between good and evil, using their own fear, pain, and hatred to break down the most primary feeling of all: self-preservation. When a soul reaches that point, nothing else can be done."

A tense silence filled the space around us as he continued. "But I stand in front of you fearless and convinced that we will prevail again. Not because we're destined to victory but because I know you are all people of faith. You have lived and died for your beloved families, inspiring kings, promising lands, and divine kingdoms. Now prepare to sacrifice yourselves for the noblest cause of all—the right to exist. Take your righteous blades, merciful bows, fair rifles, just hammers, and faithful shields. We have only one chance. Let's make it their judgment day."

Everybody opened their minds in a collective tsunami of hope and goodwill, reaching every direction.

Then, one by one, each warrior disappeared. Even Grandpa went away.

I remained behind with Michael. "Where are they going?" I asked.

"They're taking their positions. Everyone was instructed to go to a specific location where we expect the shadows will appear."

"But they'll notice that we're waiting for them."

"You know how easy it is to hide in this world. Everyone is moving to a particular time known only by them. They will stay there until the attack begins."

"Have they been told what to do?"

"When everyone knelt and you felt left out, I was giving instructions. What to do, where to go . . . everything was shown and communicated."

It was clear that everything was already planned out. No detail had been left unattended. Maybe because I was unfamiliar with this mode of communication, I still didn't feel like I was part of it.

"Don't, Ely. As I said, you're part of everything."

"I appreciate your sympathy Michael, but I'm tired of being called the key person just before I'm shut out. And by the way, it's not polite to root through someone's mind."

Maybe I had been too harsh on him, but he took my comment easily.

"Come, Ely, we still have work to do. Follow me."

We moved to another place that I knew well: Monument Valley, one of my parents' favorite vacation spots. We stopped at the top of a big mesa. Then we moved back to June 3, 838. Gabriel was there together with a dozen people forming a circle at the center of the flat surface. Judging by their appearance, they seemed to be people from different times.

"Why here?" I asked.

"This is one of the few places in the world where no human being has ever set foot," Michael replied. "And the date, well, it's a date lost in time. The perfect time and place to have a secret meeting. This is our headquarters."

As we approached the circle, it opened, allowing us through. Everyone looked at me, then bowed their heads in welcome. It was obvious they already knew me. It wasn't a fair situation to be in, particularly when I didn't know anyone—well, almost no one.

"Ely, these are the leaders of the most important groups participating in the army." Michael said. Once again, he had been looking into my mind.

"Emperor Augustus Caesar, King Felipe the Second, Grandmaster of the Knights Templar Jacques de Molay, Marshal Ferdinand Foch, Alexander the Great, George Washington, Sun Tzu, Napoleon Bonaparte, Salahuddin, Hannibal Barca . . ."

That was unbelievable. In front of me were the greatest military leaders who had existed over the last 3,000 years, and they were bowing to me!

"It's my privilege to be here," I said.

"El honor es nuestro, Doña Elizabeth," King Felipe II said.

That was sublime. I didn't understand how they knew me. I turned to Michael.

"They know all about Robert and you," he said. "They had to in order to strategize."

"I see."

"Now that we all know each other, we can get down to business," Michael said. "Gabriel, please."

Like a holographic image, a 3D map of the country appeared in the center of the circle. Gabriel shared his thoughts and mental images with us. I couldn't help thinking how cool it was.

"As you all know, our success depends on concentrating all our efforts on the next wave," Michael said. "The locations highlighted in shining white are where we expect the Antiscians to attack. We have let them think they have a clear superiority over us. Our planned inferiority during the last wave was so obvious that we expect we've given them the confidence to go ahead without looking in detail at what we're doing."

"We have all our people in position." Emperor Augustus said.

"Good," Michael replied. "The tactical maneuver requires a great deal of coordination and timing. We'll wait until they get connected to their hosts before revealing our true forces. If we arrive early, they can leave. If we're late, they'll kill the host."

"How will we know when the attack begins if we can't be beside the victims?" I asked.

He turned to me. "Here is where the two of you are so critical. Our first movement must be coordinated with Robert's people. They will show us when the attack begins. From that moment, the clock will tick down for us to get there when the shadows are still attached to the victim." Then he addressed the group. "Gabriel has already shared with each one of you the details of the plan. We will gather again ten minutes after the wave begins. We have to validate that the Antiscians' attack is developing as expected. Now go, my friends."

Everyone turned back, prepared to leave.

"How do we know if the people under Elizabeth's consort are prepared?" George Washington asked.

Everybody looked at me again. Now it was my turn. "They're

preparing the entire population for the next wave," I said. "They'll be ready."

They'd have to be.

CHAPTER 44

ROB

O nce I got the ball rolling, there wasn't much I could do. The proposal evolved like a chain reaction, with one idea sparking the next. At the end of the discussion, everyone's idea had been heard, debated, and added to the overall plan, with an action plan for everyone but me.

I didn't make a big deal about that. With everybody engaged in the plan, my absence would pass unnoticed. Things were happening fast. Just a few weeks earlier, I had been an ordinary citizen, completely anonymous. Now I was at the Pentagon meeting the country's top military and security chiefs. Even having late-night bull sessions with the president. It was surreal. I needed to spend some time in a quiet place, calm . . . alone. There was so much to think about.

I left the room before the meeting was finished. There were several empty meeting rooms in the corridor. I told my bodyguard not to follow me and walked into the first empty one I found. No one needed to know where I was.

Luckily, there was a window. I had spent so much time in closed rooms that I had lost all sense of time. Apparently, it was late in the afternoon. The sun was near the horizon, and the sky was brushed with so many colors that it was absolutely beautiful.

Was I witnessing the sunset of our civilization? Thousands of years, hundreds of generations, billions of people, all reduced to ashes, a final end without a purpose or a legacy. The hopes, plans, expectations, and the future of billions of living souls just gone . . . I didn't want to die like this.

Was there going to be a tomorrow? A seed so the human race could start over again? Would we have the same luck that we had had in the past? Was I part of that seed?

Please Ely, I don't want to die like this . . .

A voice whispered my name, louder and louder.

"Robert, Robert . . . wake up!"

When I opened my eyes, I saw David touching my shoulder. Two soldiers were at the door.

"David, what's going on?"

"The president, he's ready to give the speech."

I didn't know how long I had been asleep, but it was dark outside. I got up and followed David. We took the elevator three floors down. Then he led me into a large room.

"Where are we?" I asked.

"The control center," David replied.

Everyone was waiting for the broadcast. The image of the empty corridor with the podium and the presidential seal was on every screen. Nobody acknowledged my arrival apart from Jessica.

"Where is he?" I asked the person beside me.

"He's in the Oval Office. He'll be out in a minute."

The president stepped into the corridor and made the long walk to the podium. He seemed resignedly calm as he took his place at the podium.

"My fellow Americans, it is true what most of you have heard. A pandemic is wiping out our country. I know most of you are hoping I'll announce that we have found the cure for this deadly virus. I'm afraid we have not. We have the country's top scientists working nonstop, and yet we haven't gotten any positive results. We haven't been able to isolate the virus, much less find a vaccine.

"Where does this virus come from? Where does it hide? How does it affect our minds? The answers to those questions are still unknown, but that doesn't mean we're without hope. While we haven't isolated this virus, we know how it spreads. And that means we're not totally at its mercy.

"At its peak of strength, the virus causes victims to go through a period of extreme depression in which they can't bear to live anymore and attempt to commit suicide. We've discovered that this symptom has a limited duration. If the person remains alive long enough, the virus loses its strength until it simply dies. That simple fact gives us a way to defeat it.

"Can a person remain alive on his or her own? No. The victim's depression is so deep that no one can fight it alone. But it can be prevented with the help of a healthy person. The difficulty is that we don't know how to tell an infected person from a healthy one. We estimate that half of the population already has the virus. Any one of us could already be infected, but it's also true that any one of us can be healthy. Therefore, to stop the virus from spreading, we have to make sure that no citizen, not even one, is left alone.

"For the first time in humankind's history, we must unify behind a single goal: our survival. We're used to looking after our families, friends, and colleagues. Now we must drop all differences that separate us and open our hearts to those in need. Differences in religion, skin color, language, and wealth simply do not matter. We shall care for the elderly, we shall care for the homeless, we shall care for the poor, we shall care for the sick, and we shall care for our enemies. We shall care for friends and strangers alike. Our willingness to open ourselves to others will define our chances of survival as a nation and as a race.

"As I speak, we're building the networking infrastructure needed to communicate with every citizen in this country. Everyone will be able to receive information as well as send a request if he or she is in trouble. Regional centers with trained personnel will be ready to support those in need of help. TV, radio, websites, social media, and call centers will explain what to do. I promise, no one will be left alone.

"We may be at risk of becoming another extinct species in the history of this planet, but all is far from lost. The power to stop this rests in the hands of every one of us. So, as your president, I ask you—I implore you—care for one another. And we will come through this together."

For a long time, nobody moved or said a word. None of us was expecting to hear so clearly and directly the proclamation of a death sentence with the option of a reprieve.

Finally, Jessica broke the silence. "OK, people we have work to do. We have to deliver what the president has just said. I want the content up and running within the hour."

She approached me. "Robert, we have a review meeting in five minutes. I want you to be there. I need everyone's help to make sure we're covering all the bases."

"Of course." I followed her to a door at the end of the mezzanine. It was an internal meeting room with a big window overlooking the control center. The control room's big screens were impressive. People were walking from one side to the other, talking to one another. I could see what was happening inside like I was watching a silent movie.

"Robert, please." Jessica's voice brought me back. I turned around. The room was full of people.

"I want to go through every point of the plan. Let's start with the civil force. Have the police in all states been notified? What about medical services and hospitals?"

"The police have been contacted," someone said. "We have roughly seventy-three percent of the hospitals covered so far, one hundred percent by meeting's end."

"Good, and what about . . ."

We went through every item in the plan. I didn't say much because I was not involved in any of the teams. When the review finished, Jessica looked at me. "Any comment?"

"Just a question. What's plan B?"

"What?"

"If something goes wrong, or at least not as planned, we should have a backup."

"Robert, everybody here knows that there is no room for error. This is our only chance. If we fail, there won't be any tomorrow." I think that, for the first time, I had managed to annoy her.

"All right, people," she said, "next review in two hours. Meeting dismissed."

I was the last person to leave the room. No Plan B was all the proof I needed. They were committed to making this work.

CHAPTER 45
ROB

W e had the meeting two hours later, as planned. Everything was ready—sites, pages, accounts—and everyone was in place.

It was impressive to watch these people work. Everything was planned to the smallest detail. Each person was delivering what he or she had been asked to do. All tasks were on schedule. That night the campaign would roll out across the country.

That level of organization and planning was worrying. What if something didn't go as planned? No doubt Jessica was so resourceful that she could improvise on the run if something went wrong. But was it enough? Was everyone else as flexible as her? Maybe it was common sense, but it wouldn't have been a bad idea to leave some room for error.

At a certain point in the night, I found myself with nothing to do. Everyone was focused on their assigned tasks. Even Peter and David were doing some final checks to make sure the forces were sent to the regions where there would be the highest level of victims.

I thought it was the right moment to leave. I needed to talk to Ely.

I told Jessica and Peter that I would be in my room in case they needed me. Then I asked my bodyguard to show me the way to my room.

I turned the TV on as soon as I got there. I wanted to see what the news channels were saying about the president's speech.

I sat on the sofa with some crackers and a Coke and flipped through the main channels. Interviews with government figures, public question-and-answer sessions, and information programs explained what to do. All the channels were sending the same ancient message: care for your neighbor as yourself. But now it had much more urgency.

After being on the sofa for a while, I managed to calm down, letting my accumulated tiredness take over.

"Rob! Wake up."

A fading voice brought me awake, and I found I was in my room with the TV on and the bag of crackers and the Coke beside me. Ely was cuddled under my arm.

"Ely? How did you get here? This is—"

"A dream. You must be very tired. Your subconscious didn't even bother creating something new."

I stood up and hugged her with intensity.

"It's alright, sweetheart," she said.

I knew everything was happening in my dreams, that when I woke up, it would all be only a memory, but it didn't matter in the slightest.

"I see you've been busy," she said.

"I guess you already saw the control room. I just made a suggestion. Then people smarter than me took over."

"They did well. Twitter, smart idea."

"You inspired me."

"Did I?"

"Don't you remember? Get the message to every single person?"

I noticed some tension in her look. I hoped I hadn't missed anything. We sat on the sofa.

"Is something wrong? I've done exactly what you told me."

"I know . . . it's nothing."

"Come on, Ely, you really think you can hide your feelings from me?"

"It's just . . . I have a feeling that something isn't right. I can't explain it."

"What are you worried about?"

"I don't know. Everything seems to be in place. Your people are prepared, and mine are ready. We know where they're going to appear. Everything seems perfect. Too perfect."

"It hasn't been so perfect. They've already taken millions."

"Come on, Rob, you know what I mean. I can't help thinking that they realize this is our last chance. They've got some smart people on their side too. They must be taking some steps. I'd have expected to encounter some obstacles."

"That's . . . I just realized I've been feeling the same way. I was with Jessica moments ago, looking at the plan, and she was very happy with how perfectly organized and flawlessly deployed everything was. I recognized that she was right, but I—"

"You two are getting close, aren't you?"

"Sorry?"

"You and the FBI woman, Jessica."

I knew Ely very well, and I knew what that comment meant. "We've been working together on the plan. That's all."

"You're on a first-name basis, and you've been—"

"Stop right there, Ely. You're right. We've been getting closer but not in the way that you think. She's been my only ally in this. Without her, we wouldn't be where we are today. She's trying to make it work, and I admire her for it. There's nothing more than that, really."

She narrowed her eyes, clearly unconvinced. It never occurred to me that I was going to have a jealousy scene with her.

"Can we go back to where we were?" I said. She nodded.

"I asked Jessica, the FBI woman, if we have a plan B. We don't. What about you?"

"We don't have one either."

"Do you think we should?"

"Maybe."

"What should we do?"

"We have to prepare ourselves for the unforeseen. If we both have the same feeling, that's not a good sign. If neither side is concerned, then we're alone on this."

We started talking about different scenarios, what to do if we didn't have enough troops, if the time needed to save the victims was longer than expected, and so on. We spent the entire dream discussing worst-case scenarios.

When we were on our seventh one, she stood up. "This is nonsense," she said. "We can't be prepared for everything. Too many things could go wrong."

"But at least we're considering the possibility that something can go wrong. They aren't."

"Yes, you're right. We've done our exercise. It's not worth continuing."

She stared at the wall as if she was looking far away. "Sorry, Rob, I think the time has come. I have to go now." She stood up. "I love you."

I couldn't say goodbye. I guessed she left a bit mad at me. A sudden noise of dropping bombs and shooting guns woke me up.

It was the TV. A film about WWII was on the screen. I turned it off, but it didn't matter. I wasn't going to get back to sleep again that night.

I couldn't stop thinking about how we both felt the same. I wondered if our hunch was the product of us being scared and inexperienced or if it was grounded in reality. Too perfect? Maybe. Maybe our capacity to reach every corner of the country was the weakest point of the plan. Maybe it was about people. How could we be sure that the population would look after itself? Maybe this was why things were so quiet.

I knew I had to keep focused but I wasn't able to get those

thoughts out of my head.

I got up and prepared to take on the day. Even though I'd been awake most of the night, I felt good, full of energy.

I spent the morning in the control center going through all the information posted on the social media sites. Jessica wanted Peter and me to review all instructions given to the public. David was updating the model with real-time data. Despite the field experience that the trials brought to the team, she still wanted us to check that precise details on what infected people were expected to feel and what healthy people were expected to do were included on the sites.

Although several dozen people were in the control room, not a sound could be heard. Only people's startled reaction to a phone ringing revealed the true stress beneath the silence.

So far, no change had been detected in the population. One team in the room was responsible for analyzing the trends of incoming calls and tweets. Since the mobile accounts were opened, a constant stream of calls had been flowing in to the different regional centers. Most people were calling to ask how to use Twitter. Others were calling 911 to ask for company, others simply because they were scared. A controlled, but steady panic was building.

I sat beside Peter to review a web page. "Do you still believe it'll work?" he asked.

"Why do you ask that?"

"We still don't have a solid idea of what we're up against. We still don't know if what was tested by the FBI will work again. Even if it does, we don't know if our strategy will work on a national scale."

"All true. What do you believe?"

"That's not the point, Rob. We've all put our hope in your words. You're the one they all believe in."

"What are you trying to say?"

"Look around. Nobody is completely convinced by the pandemic theory, and yet they're doing things as if it'll work, following you on pure trust. Everyone's hope is in you. You represent literally the last chance."

"Do you think it's important?"

"What?"

"To be right? Sometimes the need to believe in something can be much stronger and more inspiring than the belief itself. The despair that comes from feeling hopeless is so devastating to the human soul that believing in something, even if it's a false hope, can make the impossible possible."

These words were not meant just for him. My memories of Ely were still with me.

When Peter saw my tears, he turned back to his document.

"It'll work, Peter," I said. "It has to."

CHAPTER 46
ROB

The last twenty-four hours had been calm, given the situation. Most people in the control center were checking that the communication infrastructure was in place, that police, hospitals, private clinics, firefighters, FBI, CIA, military forces, and many more organizations were properly synchronized across all states. It was an impressive coordination job, all under Jessica's command.

Still no sign of the expected wave. We were just waiting, feeding our uncertainty, powerless, silently questioning if all our preparations made sense. I was worse off because I hadn't dreamed of Ely the previous night. It felt like something was wrong.

It began innocuously enough.

"The average number of tweets is climbing," someone said.

"What about phone calls?" Jessica asked.

"Same trend."

In the next hour, we received more than half a million tweets. The volume of people contacting us was increasing at an explosive rate.

"What's happening?" I asked Jessica.

"The pandemic is more extensive than we anticipated. A lot of people are asking for help from areas where we don't have much infrastructure. We're trying to mobilize some forces to the new affected areas, but it takes time."

"That leaves the main areas unprotected."

"You have a better option?"

If our theory was right, the model should have predicted the areas with a high concentration of cases. Everything was based on the model. Holy shit! If the model was off, our people were in the wrong place.

I ran to Peter's desk. He and David were working frantically on the computer.

"Guys, can you check the locations from where people are contacting us? I need to compare them with the predictions of the fractal model."

"We're already updating the model." Peter said.

A minute later, David had everything on the screen. It was clear that most of the messages and calls were coming from new locations. The model was wrong!

"How is that possible?" I asked.

"It worked with the last waves," Peter said. "It should be working now."

"But it isn't."

"I don't know what's going on!" Peter said. "The math hasn't changed. We calibrated the model with the previous waves. Something else must have changed."

"Something? Like what? Come on, Peter, we have people dying right now."

"Stop yelling at each other," David said. "We know the virus follows a pattern, right? The messages show that the virus has changed its normal pattern, but it must still have one. Let's find it, shall we?"

"Can you do it?"

283

"We did it once."

"Then stop listening to me, and get at it."

They started working immediately. I stayed beside them in case they needed something. Ely was right; the plan had been too perfect to be true. In just ten minutes, the control room turned into chaos. People were rushing from one corner to the other, papers from one desk to another, all phones ringing.

I noticed two people with tears in their eyes hurrying toward the exit.

"Stop them!" I shouted to the soldiers outside the room. They grabbed them immediately. "Hold them and, whatever happens, don't let them go."

I looked for Jessica. She was on the other side of the room, giving instructions to three people at once. I decided to go and talk to her. She needed to know what we were doing.

"Jessica—"

"Bad time, Robert."

"The virus had changed its pattern. We're trying to identify the new one. It's going to take a while."

"Look around you. We're on overload. Phone lines, 911, Twitter—it's too big to handle. The previous pattern didn't work. How do you know this one will?"

"That model was based—"

"Don't give me details. If there's a new pattern, find it. Now!"

Now it was all in Peter and David's hands.

After the longest half an hour of my life, we heard Peter's voice.

"Got it! Incredible! It's also a fractal pattern."

I ran to where he was. "Great job, guys! Get the new coordinates to Jessica's team. I also need a printed copy. Can you do that?"

"Sure, but why?" David asked.

"Just do it."

The printer was right next to us. I took the printed papers and spread them on the table close to a wall, not far from where we were. I hoped Ely could see them.

"What are you doing?" David asked.

I said the first thing that came to mind. "I need a global

picture of the new pattern. There must be some connection between the new locations that can explain the way it spreads. We need to understand why it changed its previous pattern. It could change again."

I stared at the papers as if I were analyzing them. Then I heard Jessica's voice. "Robert, we're having an emergency meeting in the main room downstairs. I need you there."

"OK. Give me a couple of minutes."

"I'll wait for you downstairs." She left the room with some members of her team.

I was afraid that if I left immediately, Ely wouldn't be able to identify the new coordinates. I needed to leave a mark, something to show her where the papers were. It had to be something that no one but Ely would recognize.

Of course!

I took a pen and drew Ely's signature on the board hanging beside the table. Then I left for the meeting. On my way out, I saw Peter looking at the board. I hoped he wouldn't make a big deal out of it.

I ran to the main reception area, where there were a couple of elevators. I pushed the "down" button. One lift stayed on the ground floor, and the other went straight to the upper floor. I was already late for the meeting, so I took the emergency stairs two at a time.

Suddenly, I felt a deep, sharp, short pain in my head. I couldn't maintain my balance, and I stumbled, falling down.

Then everything went black.

CHAPTER 47

ELY

I kicked myself as I left Rob's dream. What a stupid thing to do! But I couldn't help myself. For the first time in my life, I was jealous. How could I feel that way given that I was the one who had left him? Dreaming with him was revealing the real me. My mind could find ways to justify, even to enjoy this new life, but my heart was a different matter and beyond my control.

I couldn't handle it even when I was in Monument Valley. I had assured the top military leaders that Rob would be ready. How could I have thought that? Of course Rob could do the impossible, but what about the other people?

When I left the mesa, I was more concerned about hiding my doubts from Michael and the others than the killings of the next wave. That was one of those moments when I wished I knew how to shield my thoughts. They probably thought I was too weak, too scared for this battle and that the pressure of it all was starting to affect me.

I needed to step away for a moment. I needed a place where I could be by myself, somewhere I could feel like I was at home.

Home.

A few moments later, I was at our house. It was so relaxing being there again. I understood why some people found it so hard to leave their homes after they died. Everything there made me feel like I was still alive.

I sat on the sofa and looked at the blank TV screen. We had spent many nights together on that sofa. Although I was not touching it physically, I could still sense the smooth texture of its fabric. Memories, memories, memories . . . always playing tricks on us.

I stood up and went outside to the back garden. I knew where those memories would lead me, but I wasn't ready to let them seduce me. It was late in the afternoon. The sunlight passing through the trees played hide and seek with the leaves.

I tried to review the scenarios that Rob and I had gone through in his dream. I might have been stubborn, but I had always trusted my feelings. I didn't know if I still could, but I had to hope they would help me prepare—or at least not be surprised—if something went wrong.

The sunset began its daily show. I knew I should leave, but I didn't want to. I moved inside the house to the main bedroom and lay down on the bed. This time I gave up and let my memories take me to the past.

"Ely! Where have you been? We've been looking for you."

It was Grandma. How much time had I spent in bed? I didn't know. The sun was up again.

"What's going on, Grandma?"

"The wave has started! Come, Michael wants to see you."

I followed her back to the mesa in Monument Valley in 1945. Some of the Gli Custodi were there when we arrived. Michael and Gabriel were surrounded by a reddish aura. They weren't even bothering to hide their stress and worry anymore.

"What's wrong?" I asked Grandma.

287

"They knew we were waiting for them," Gabriel said.

"What? A leak?"

"Not precisely, at least not intentionally, or so we think. Maybe one of the warriors didn't protect his thoughts well enough. We don't know exactly."

"Are we taking them on?"

"We're fighting in a few locations only to convince them we're still interested. Most of our army's still hidden."

"But they're attacking, threatening people's lives. We need to send them now."

"So far, Robert's people have done a good job keeping most of the hosts alive."

"But what are we waiting for? We don't know how long they'll hold out."

"It's not that simple," Michael said. "They've changed their pattern of attack. We don't know their current target locations, and if we try to search for them in the present, they'll see us before we even get to the first one. We need to wait."

"For what?"

"Robert's feedback."

"Have the people at the control center shown any change of pattern?"

"We have a dozen of our best Gli Custodi there watching what they're doing. So far they've reported no change."

Of all the situations that Rob and I had run through, we had never considered a change in the pattern behind their attacks. We might have gotten to it if I hadn't decided to bail out of the dream. I should have listened to him. Maybe he'd already detected this change and found a way to counter it.

"I can't just wait and do nothing. I have to go."

Without sparing any time, I went to the control center. When I arrived, the room was buzzing with activity. People were running in every direction, talking to one another. I searched for Rob but couldn't find him anywhere. That was strange. If there was a problem, I would have expected everybody to be there trying to solve it, including Rob. So, where was he?

I approached David. He was talking on the phone about a

new pattern that was being sent to someone. Ah! The FBI woman. It was clear they'd found something. If there were new results, the information would be there. I knew my Rob; he would have left a clue somewhere.

There were papers everywhere and computer screens covered with graphics and numbers. I couldn't understand any of them. I was getting nervous when I saw Peter at the back of the room standing in front of a board—a board with my signature on it!

That was my love, a clever man. The new model was on the table with a copy of the map with the new locations. We were back!

I called two members of the Gli Custodi. They memorized the new information in seconds, and a blink of an eye later, we were with Michael and the rest at headquarters.

"We have the new locations!" I shouted.

"How?" Gabriel asked.

The two warriors opened their minds to Michael and Gabriel. They didn't need to read mine. They saw in my face how proud I was of Rob.

"Great work, Elizabeth," Michael said. "We still have a chance."

At that moment, the battle for our future began.

CHAPTER 48

ELY

Michael communicated the new plan of attack to the generals and the other members of the Gli Custodi gathered on the mesa.

"Remember," he said, "all warriors must take their positions before we attack. It must be coordinated simultaneously across the country. That's where the element of surprise lies. It's now or never!"

Everyone left for different parts of the country to prepare for the new plan. Soon, only Gabriel remained.

"Gabriel, you have the Southwest Division. I'm counting on you to stop the Antiscians from spreading beyond the Mexican border. Align your tactics with Augustus and Tzu's in the West Mountain and Pacific Divisions. They're some of our best."

"I'll do it," Gabriel replied and then left.

"We're in charge of the New England Division," Michael said, turning to me. "You'll fight beside us. We're facing the moment of truth. If we fail, there's no tomorrow. Every person counts."

Finally, he was talking to me like I was one of them. I knew him well enough to expect conditions, but it didn't matter. I was no longer the same shy person I was when I arrived. I was a grown-up who didn't require any protection.

"Shy or brave isn't the point," he said. "Of course you still need protection. That's why you're coming with me."

Once again, I realized I needed to learn how to hide my thoughts.

"However, two waves ago I saw you fighting an Antiscian. You defended yourself quite well. Martial arts? Maybe one day you can teach me."

How mistaken I was. I left that wave thinking I hadn't received the deserved recognition. Apparently, I was wrong.

"Enough talking. Ready to go?"

I nodded.

We went back to June 17, 1775, then moved to Boston. I knew the place from my high school American history class. Bunker Hill was surrounded by our warriors—maybe a few hundred thousand—and they were all expecting us. Immediately after our arrival, Michael shared the map and coordinates with them. We didn't need to say a word. After a few seconds, each warrior left to take his new position. Three Gli Custodi warriors remained with us. Forget about Google maps or GPS; this was real-time analogue communication expanding across the time-space continuum.

"Stop thinking nonsense, Elizabeth. Focus."

Shit! When was this mind-reading thing going to stop?

"It will end when you stop fooling around. Now take this; it will help you."

"A sword?" That was what I would call nonsense.

"Warriors use projections of weapons in battle. Since you can't produce one for yourself, I brought one for you."

I hefted it. It was a straight, double-edged, single-handed sword, short enough for me to handle.

"It's a Roman gladius," he said, "a perfect slashing weapon."

I admired the sword. No high-tech weapons, just a sword and a robe. Something was written on its hilt.

"Stultum est timere quod vitare non potes. It is foolish to fear that which you can't avoid," he said.

"With an inscription like that, it should belong to someone important."

"Publilius Syrus. A good friend of mine. He's a writer, not a warrior, or at least he was in his last life. He wanted you to have it. Is there a problem?"

"Sorry. It's just I don't know how to use it."

"It's meant to cut the link between the shadows and the hosts. Just use it like a kitchen knife." He paused for a moment. "Are you ready?"

"Yes, I am."

Michael, the three Gli Custodi warriors, and I moved to an office building in Boston town center. We stopped at the top floor where a big, open-concept office occupied most of the space.

"Be prepared," he said, "and remember, no matter what we find, it's not expecting us."

Each of us took our place at a corner of the room with Michael in the center. Then we moved to the present.

A dozen people wearing suits appeared. Five of them were being attacked by black shadows. Two of them were trying to jump out the windows. The other seven people were trying to hold them back.

Immediately, each of us chose one.

From my last encounters with the Antiscians, I already had a good idea about how shadows reacted to our presence. They couldn't fight us freely while the host was still alive—the attachment restricted much of their movement. So, the advantage of taking them by surprise was useful if we moved fast.

As I rushed the one closest to me, the shadow turned around at an amazing speed and hit me first. I was thrown back a few meters.

It caught me completely off guard, the shadow moving like it knew I was coming. I turned to Michael; he was struggling as well. Something was different this time.

We were fighting fast . . . really fast. When moving at light speed, even a microsecond of hesitation could make a huge difference. Thinking what to do while fighting was not an option. They were more aggressive and definitely ready to fight back. But having lost the element of surprise, I had to start thinking several moves ahead.

I tried several tactics—frontal attack, thrust and retreat. None of them worked. For some reason, the shadow was always one step ahead of me. I needed to try a different approach, to trick it so that I could get closer to the host.

I feinted to its right, then moved fast to the left and grabbed it from behind while it was focused on my sword. It worked! When I had it in my grasp, I pulled the sword out and cut the link. The shadow's scream was terrifying. Then I checked for Michael and the Gli Custodi, but they already had their shadows already tied up. Still, not bad for a beginner.

We grouped the five shadows together. While we were tying them up, the five people started to recover. Hugs and tears. That moment was everything I needed. Once finished, one of the Gli Custodi took them away.

We looked outside the windows. The street below was a battlefield. People were trying to prevent victims from killing themselves, and warriors from every era were fighting shadows. It was like watching two movies superposed over each other.

We jumped out the window, landing smoothly on the street.

"Ely, go with them." Michael said. "John and Paul, watch her at all times. Never leave her alone. She needs to be protected."

They nodded. Then he made his way through the street to the entrance of a building where a person was trying to help two people simultaneously.

We moved in the opposite direction, toward the back of the street, to an area with no warriors at all. We were outnumbered, so it wasn't hard to find a victim. Even though we split up, Paul and John kept an eye on me.

The shadow I was facing was another tough one. Even the trick I used a couple of minutes earlier didn't work with this one. It hit me several times. With a move so fast that I didn't see it, it grabbed my arms from behind. I tried to get free, but it was strong . . . and fast. How was this possible if it was in symbiosis? I was totally confused when, out of nowhere, a second shadow appeared in front of us. It held my legs, so I couldn't move. Then they pulled me toward the host.

That's when I understood. The link between the first shadow and its host was far larger than any I'd seen. The shadow was detaching from the host.

I was completely immobilized when the two Gli Custodi, John and Paul, took on the shadows from behind. Immediately, the shadows released me. Without much thought, John and Paul drew their swords, cut the link, and quickly tied them up.

"Are you alright?" John asked.

"Yes, thank you. You got me just in time. The second shadow was holding me while the first shadow tried to detach from the host."

He shook his head. "Two shadows attacking the same person? First time I've seen it."

"They wanted to take you with them," Paul said. "They must know who you are."

Kidnap? Maybe they were right. The first shadow had been waiting for me when I arrived. The second shadow appeared only after the first managed to get hold of me. They wanted to take me somewhere, away from Paul and John. How did they know about me? We had been so cautious—

Wait a moment. If they knew about me, then they also knew about the dreams. And Rob.

I hadn't seen him since I went to the control center. The Gli Custodi warriors had left the room with me when we identified the new locations. Oh no! Nobody was protecting Rob.

I didn't take time to explain to John and Paul. I just moved to the control center. There was a bit less confusion there than the last time. I searched desperately for him. I saw David with Peter but no sign of Rob.

I moved through the different rooms on that floor. Nothing. How could I have forgotten him? How could I have left him unguarded?

I moved through the floor to the level below. I ended up in a meeting room full of people. Rob was not there either, but I spotted the FBI woman. I stopped for a moment to listen to her, thinking she had to know where Rob was.

"It looks like we're making progress," she said. "The trend of tweets is stabilizing, and the number of 911 calls is also decreasing. We used the new model to send our forces where they're needed most. Thanks to Robert and his friends, we're controlling the pandemic. By the way, can someone go upstairs and bring Robert here? I told him we needed him urgently."

A soldier left the room.

So, they were expecting him to be upstairs too. But if he was neither there nor in the control center, where was he? I figured I'd better search for him again but this time more carefully. I searched each room on that floor. Nothing.

Walking slowly through the corridor I saw the emergency exit door slightly open. A soldier came out and ran down to the end of the corridor looking for . . . the stairs! That was the only place I hadn't checked.

Rob was laid out on the stairs.

I moved beside him. He was alive!

I looked for any sign of a shadow, but there was none. He was just sleeping. Dreaming.

But this time it was different.

He was hermetically sealed. I couldn't enter his dream. He was inside a black box with . . . something happening.

I hoped it wasn't too late.

CHAPTER 49

ROB

I woke up with my head pounding. I must have hit it when I fell. Where was I? I managed to open my eyes and . . .

I was lying on a bed in an open space. The sky was filled with galaxies, so close that I could even see the stars and planets inside. I had never imagined such perfection could exist.

I felt sheets covering my body. They were perfectly smooth and pure white, like snow. I tried to get up. I felt dizzy for a moment, but I managed to swing my legs off the bed and sit up. Incredible! The floor was made of pink marble, absolutely uniform and shining with the most amazing pink veins I had ever seen.

But it wasn't perfect. There were undulations on the surface, like little waves. My eyes followed them to the horizon, growing fainter as they propagated away. Distant mountains surrounded me in all directions, far away, high white peaks in every direction.

More waves appeared on the marble surface, bigger ones. I looked under the bed. Its legs were half submerged in the marble. I realized I was the source of the waves. Fascinating! The floor looked like solid marble, but it behaved like a liquid.

I looked around again. The bed was maybe five yards from the shore of a tiny island in the middle of the liquid marble lake. The island couldn't have been larger than a few hundred yards long, but my eyes kept drifting back to the sky. A huge planet floated just above the horizon. Then I realized the galaxies were not fixed in place but were orbiting around me.

I spotted the Orion nebula, my favorite cosmic body. I extended my right hand to touch it. Its gas and dust slipped right through my fingers.

Absolutely beautiful.

Wait! What was that? A haze was rising from the island. That was weird. I tried to see it again, but it disappeared. Then I noticed a subtle distortion of the background. It was a straight line, then a shape . . . a high, narrow object. It was the silhouette of a . . . column? I looked up. The same distortion appeared overhead. A roof? Whatever it was, the object was a building made of a transparent material capable of refracting light.

As spectacular as it was, it didn't take away the fact that I was stuck there. I needed to find a way to reach the island. I had to walk on that unique marble floor, but I didn't know how it would react to my weight. I put my left foot down. It felt cold . . . hard.

That was crazy, a liquid substance on which I could walk as if it were solid, well sort of. It felt solid at the beginning then it turned muddy.

I stood up carefully, still holding onto the bed with my hands. So far, so good. Little undulations formed around my feet. I didn't want to test the marble floor for too long, so I walked quickly.

As I got closer to the sandy shore, the light distortions became more specific, better defined. The vertical objects looked like ancient fluted columns. Then I identified a few white statues of humans half buried in the marble floor. I was inside something like an ancient temple, maybe Greek, made of perfectly transparent crystal. It was beautiful beyond imagination.

I touched one of the columns. It felt cold and smooth.

As I walked, the temple turned into a hall of mirrors. I saw different angles of the island through the light reflected on the temple walls. In one of the multiple images, a boat was floating on the marble lake, a small boat docked at the back of the temple. That was my way off the island.

I found a pair of oars inside the boat. I looked in all directions and spotted what looked like a small beach on the opposite side of the lake. It seemed to be a perfect place to go. I began to row toward it.

It was strange to see that, although the boat was floating, and I was rowing, there were no waves on the lake's marble surface. It was even stranger that I didn't care about that much. I simply wanted to leave the island ASAP.

After rowing for a while, I stopped to rest. I was about halfway to the shore. There was no movement on the surface—no wind and no sound. It was like being inside a surreal fantasy poster, like the ones I used to draw so often. Although it was almost painfully beautiful, the loneliness made me uncomfortable. I started rowing again, faster now

I kept my eyes focused on the shore. However, after a few minutes, the shore was no closer. The faster I rowed, the less I moved. I shuddered at the possibility of being stranded forever in the middle of that lake. I began rowing even faster.

On some level, I was aware that this was only a dream, but I couldn't help feeling scared. I pictured myself as the man in Munch's The Scream.

I was rowing desperately fast when I noticed that, for the first time, waves began to form on the lake's surface. Scared, I continued to row even harder.

Suddenly, a shadow appeared beside the boat. It looked like a big fish. I was still far from shore and not getting any closer. I stopped rowing for a moment. My mind became foggy. I looked around, searching for the fish. It had to be somewhere. Holy shit! I shouldn't have stopped.

The waves got bigger as I moved from one side of the boat to the other looking for the fish. Instead of fading away, the intensity of the undulations increased the farther they got from me. Bubbles appeared not far from the boat. Something was boiling out of the lake.

The figure of a naked woman rose from under the water. It was huge, maybe fifteen or twenty feet high, and made of the same liquid marble. As it looked at me, it screamed, an almost unbearable noise.

I was paralyzed.

The figure bent, submerging its hands into the liquid marble and shaping it as if it were snow. It made a perfect sphere, a perfect marble ball. Then it threw it at me!

The ball fell a few yards from the boat. The impact was like a meteorite falling into the sea. I held on tight as the waves it created almost flipped the boat.

None of this made any sense. A liquid ball with the strength of a rock. I was swinging between awe and terror. Why was that thing attacking me? Was it trying to drown me?

It began forming another ball.

I rowed away as fast as I could. The next ball landed even closer, practically lifting the boat off the lake. I barely hung on. Although I was a good swimmer, the only image in my mind was being trapped and sinking in a quicksand-like liquid marble. Every part of my body was invaded with the fear of death.

The next ball was close enough that the impact tore the oars from my hands. I knew I couldn't fight the creature. Even so, I lunged for the oars to continue rowing. As I did, my body hung half outside the boat, my cheek a few inches from the lake's surface. My face was reflected on the surface as if it were a mirror.

How could that be? I was in the middle of turbulent waves. The boat was bouncing from side to side, yet the surface around the oars was quiet. Why was that?

I managed to stand up and look around. Everywhere was calm except for right around the boat and that thing. The boat was moving so much that I was thrown to the deck, but not before I saw the thing preparing the next ball, perhaps its last.

"Stop panicking and think!" I shouted. There had to be a rational explanation.

Instead of creating waves that expanded in circles like a stone falling into water, the boat was creating waves that moved only toward the thing. There were no undulations in any other direction. The closer the waves got to her, the bigger they became. Somehow that thing was feeding on the waves. How? Why?

I tried to remember the first time I saw a few waves forming on the surface. It was after I stopped in the middle of the lake. I was scared—actually, I was beginning to get scared. The more frightened I became, the bigger the waves grew. Then that thing appeared after I had the panic attack. Waves ... fear ... Could the waves be caused by my fear? Was it possible that the thing was feeding on my fear? There was only one way to find out ...

I stood up again, this time I faced the thing with my eyes closed. I tried to stay calm, to remain still, and most importantly, not to be afraid. I knew the next ball would hit the boat, and if it sank, I would drown. All my instincts were pushing me to row away as fast as possible, but instead I concentrated, focused my mind.

A few seconds passed. I was expecting to hear the deafening impact of the ball breaking the boat, but nothing happened. The boat stopped moving. I heard the sound of falling rocks but no more waves. I slowly opened my eyes.

The thing was breaking into pieces. No more waves were leaving the boat, and all movement had stopped. As the broken thing sank to the bottom, the lake's surface became calm again.

And I was no longer afraid.

Wasting no time, I grabbed the oars and started rowing toward the shore, this time relaxed. Dense fog invaded the lake, reducing the visibility to almost nothing, but I was confident that I would reach the shore soon.

What kind of dream was this? I had never had violent dreams before. That . . . thing had to be the materialization of my fear, the fear of being left alone . . . a fear that I had developed once Ely died.

I had never imagined how deeply rooted that feeling could be. I had missed Ely all this time, and with every passing day, that loneliness was becoming more unbearable. But why did it attack me if it represented my own loneliness? And why did it feed on my fear?

I was still trying to figure it out when I thought I saw something in the thick fog. Slowly, a row of partially submerged, perfectly rectangular white granite columns emerged from the fog. They were in two lines, comprising a runway to the shore. It was clear that the columns would guide me to a particular location on the beach.

I rowed slowly through the columns, making no undulations on the lake's surface. As I got closer, a red sandy beach became clearer. I got out of the boat as soon as it touched bottom. It was good to feel solid ground under my feet again. Everything on the beach had the same reddish color—sand, rocks, even small plants. What an interesting landscape.

Which direction should I go? It was my dream, so there probably weren't any wrong answers. I turned right and walked along the beach with my eyes fixed on the lake. No more surprises.

After a while I stopped to rest. Looking for a place to sit down, I noticed small white spots just beneath the sand. I knelt for a closer look, brushing away a bit of red sand. Spots of white sand! Like the white granite columns, they marked my path forward. I began to follow them. Everything in the dream was pushing me in the same direction.

After a few minutes of walking, small rocks started to appear. Then the sand disappeared, and I entered a large forest—well, not exactly. It was more like the remains of a forest. Dead trees, petrified over time, were everywhere. Everything was grey, dry, and lifeless. The cold emptiness inside me made the landscape so appealing, so comfortable, so seductive.

The road turned away from the coast, heading through the forest. I had no choice but to follow it.

I stayed alert, paying attention to any hint that something strange lay ahead. But above all, I was trying not to be afraid. That thing in the lake was terrifying, and I didn't want to create something similar.

As I walked deeper into the forest, the trees, rocks, and everything else became even stranger. The branches looked like they had been torn apart long ago. Their shapes resembled arms, hands seeking desperately for help. Rocks were fractured like bodies mutilated by an unimaginable force. Even the sky was frightening—cloud shapes painted it with diabolical dark-grey figures.

I kept walking. The road took me to a small hill from where I could see the horizon. It was an endless, sterile landscape. Then, far away, I saw a plume of dust as if a car were approaching. I stared at it, but it was too far to see what was creating it. I walked a bit faster, not taking my eyes off it. As the object got closer, a human shape started to form. However, the way it was moving was unnatural, artificial, mechanical.

When it was close enough, I couldn't believe my eyes. It was a robot. What on earth was a robot doing there?

I stopped to look directly at it. I wouldn't make the same mistake of running away, even though it didn't look friendly and was approaching fast.

The robot stopped about three hundred yards from me. I guessed it was studying me the way I was studying it. It was big, maybe ten feet tall, and roughly human shaped but with a small waist and wide shoulders. It had a rotating head with some kind of photo cells pointing in all four directions. The cells' surface was so shiny that they reflected light like four mirrors. The rest of the robot's body was made of silver, shining as if it had been recently polished.

Unlike the thing on the lake, the robot had no face, so I couldn't guess what was going on in its brain. Unable to anticipate what it was going to do, I decided to wait and see.

For a couple of minutes or so, we both remained completely still. Was it waiting for me to make the first move, or was it waiting for something to happen, someone to show up? In any case, I thought the best option was to stay calm and keep waiting.

What did this mean? That thing in the lake was the manifestation of my fears. So what kind of feeling did this robot represent? Another fear? If so, fear of what? I wasn't prepared to stay there forever, so I decided it was time to get a closer look at its intentions.

As soon as I started walking, the robot ran toward me and punched me hard enough to throw me against a nearby tree.

Before I could react, the robot came at me again and lifted me as if I weighed nothing and tossed me away.

Under normal circumstances I should have already broken nearly all my bones, but this was a dream. My dream. Whatever this robot represented, I had to face it with the conviction that it wouldn't harm me. So I closed my eyes and concentrated on staying calm, as I had at the lake.

Before I could stand up, the robot attacked me again. This time the blow was harder, so much that I was sent more than ten yards away. OK, staying calm wasn't working. I was living my own, private, made-to-measure nightmare, and I was afraid it was being directed by someone else.

I couldn't think of what to do except run.

It didn't work. The robot caught me and punched me again, sending me against a rock. At that point I was beginning to feel pain. I needed to find a way out soon.

After a few more punches, it was clear that everything I tried was taking me nowhere. And the pain was getting worse. I had to be missing something, but what?

The thing in the lake only appeared when I began to get scared. The robot was already running when I saw it for the first time. So, what triggered its presence? I didn't have any recollection of anything particular happening. No, I must have been doing something just before it appeared. I kept replaying what had happened between one punch and the next. The only strange behavior the robot had was when we stood still before each other for a few minutes. It didn't move at all, and then it attacked me when I moved.

Exactly! When I moved! Motion detectors. The four cells probably gave it a 360-view at any moment.

Again, there was only one way to know if the theory was true. The robot hit me again, but this time I didn't get up and run afterwards. I lay on the ground where I fell.

It stopped! Its head was turning around, looking for me, but it couldn't detect me. Good. At least I had managed to buy some time to think.

I quietly considered my options. I could move slowly, so slowly that the robot couldn't detect my movement. I could throw rocks in different directions to create a random disturbance, so it would get confused. But I suspected the only clear way out was to confront it, to fight it.

The only fact that I was sure of so far was that the robot represented something about me. It was able to detect and mimic my movements almost instantaneously, like an image in a mirror. It was like I was trying to defeat my own reflection. Was it possible to fool my own image? Hardly. If I was in front of a mirror, the only way to get rid of my reflection was to break the mirror itself.

The robot's cells!

The robot had four cells on its head. Could I destroy them all? I would have to attack it simultaneously from four directions, which was impossible. I needed to deactivate one cell at a time. But how? If I destroyed one, the robot could still use the other three cells. He might learn what I was trying to do and then defend itself. The only way to do that was to attack and then almost immediately retreat to where it couldn't see me. That could be the solution.

Deception and ambush. I remembered the book about military strategy I had read when I was in that military center—on guerrilla warfare in the Vietnam War. Attack and hide, then attack and hide again. I would have to be able to disappear in the death forest. But how could I do that?

What kind of motion sensors did it have? Infrared? No, the robot stood still for minutes in front of me without seeing me. Microwave sensors? Some sort of echolocation? Bats used such a mechanism to hunt for food.

Hiding from soundwaves. How could I "look" like the background if I was being tracked by sound? I looked around and I saw nothing but rocks and broken dead trees . . . that happened to resemble human bodies or parts of them! That's it. If I could adopt the same posture as the trees, it would be relatively easy to be confused as one of them. I had seen photos of people dressed in clothes with the same design as the wall behind them. It was almost impossible to spot them. The perfect camouflage.

If I could use the same principle, I would go unnoticed. I could do quick attacks without being detected. I didn't know if it was going to work. I didn't have any other choice either.

I planned several moves in advance, selecting the rocks and trees I was going to use to hide behind after each offensive. The attacks had to be precise and quick. If the robot had a learning capability, I couldn't give it time to use it.

I grabbed a small stone off the ground. In a fraction of a second, the robot turned one of its cells toward the movement and started running. I threw the stone at its head, hitting one of the cells. It broke into two pieces.

For a second the robot stopped. He modified the original square-shaped cell configuration into a triangle. It was enough time for me to stand beside a nearby small tree. Perfect! It was working. The robot was looking around, trying to locate me.

I scooped up a second rock. By the time the robot turned to find me, the rock was already in flight, and I was hiding elsewhere.

Twice more I threw a rock, and twice more I smashed a cell. I was impressed by my aim, but then again, it was my dream.

My movements were not the only thing perfectly executed. My thoughts were much more focused. My reasoning had never been so clear. In fact, I'd never felt so in control of a situation.

After the last cell broke, I walked away. The robot stood in place, its head spinning helplessly, literally blind.

Meanwhile, I felt just as blind with no way to know where to go, unable to see what was happening around me and apparently with no control whatsoever over the dream.

Most people didn't remember their dreams, and if they did, they didn't know the reasons behind them. They were used to experiencing them as spectators, but I was conscious of everything happening to me. I could interact with things around me and, even more, I could change the course of actions. Could it be possible that, after my dreams with Ely, my mind had detached so much from my body that my conscious and unconscious minds could interact with each other as if they were completely independent?

No. As much sense as that made, it didn't feel like that.

This was my dream, so the aggression shown by the robot and the thing in the lake could only have been caused by me. Did I want to hurt myself? Why would I do something like that? There had to be something else. The lake thing fed on my fear. Could it be that the robot only wanted to scare me? Maybe that was the common factor between the robot and the thing from the lake.

The robot hit me many times, but it didn't cause me a single wound. The thing in the lake also tried to hit me with the marble balls, but they only got close. Both had scared me, but neither one had hurt me. So, who was benefiting from my being afraid? It was like I was living someone else's dream.

The conspiracy theory. Easy, appealing, and seductive. The perfect excuse to blame someone else for our own sins. "Come on, think straight! There's no such thing. Don't forget what Ely told you."

Wait a minute . . . Ely had gotten into my dreams, so why couldn't someone else? Yes, someone from Ely's world—

Peter, the woman, they had experienced similar feelings . . . afraid . . . scared to death . . . the pandemic! Was this what it had been like for Peter? For the woman? Was it my turn now?

Now that there was something genuine to be afraid of, was I trying to kill myself? Was someone helping me? Holy shit! I had been alone in the compound, and that meant only one thing—if I wanted to survive, I had to keep myself alive in this dream.

Now it was clear to me; whatever was creating this dream, I had to face it, and quickly. So, with no fear, and with a determination to end this nightmare once and for all, I started walking again.

I went to the point where the robot attacked me the first time. After looking around for a few seconds, I found the white track a few yards away. I walked along the marks until they started disappearing. Soon the road turned into a small trail through the forest. I continued walking until the path ended at the bottom of a hill. I walked up to the top. To my surprise, the hill wasn't small, as I thought. The other side overlooked a huge complex of mountains surrounding a deep valley. In the center of the valley was a city. I didn't know how, but I had a feeling that the city held the reason for my dream.

I looked around for a way to get down into the valley. To my right, a narrow stairway was carved into the rocks. It didn't look safe, but it was the only way down. Without any hesitation, I started descending. With every step, the details of the city became clearer.

The stairs ended at a wide, empty road which, on one side, ran straight into the mountain as if it continued through a tunnel that wasn't there. The other direction led to the city, cutting through a wall of three-story rowhouses that defined the city's border. An empty tollbooth stood to one side.

The buildings along the street reminded me of European cities with nineteenth-century town centers—London or Paris. The buildings were made of perfectly cut stones of white limestone. Big, ancient columns made their entrances opulent.

The street was otherwise empty, quiet, and desolate. I was walking down the sidewalk when a car parked on the opposite side drew my attention. It looked strange. The tires were placed horizontally, like life preservers. Instead of driving on the road, the car was floating over the road. How was that possible?

I kneeled for a better look. The asphalt was liquid! The streets were more like canals, like Venice.

I reached the corner of the block. There was no apparent way to cross the street, but there was a pedestrian signal. What was it for? No traffic, liquid streets. I pushed the button anyway. The traffic light turned yellow, then red. An effervescent bubbling appeared on the street, then white stones like the ones in the buildings rose to the surface. They were the size and shape of the white stripes of a pedestrian crossing. I began jumping between the stones, but when I reached the middle of the road, the light turned yellow. I ran before the stones submerged again. It was the funniest way to cross a street that I had ever seen.

I kept walking until I reached what seemed like an important junction. I noticed a few undulations on the surface in the middle of the road. Then I heard the sound of footsteps. Big footsteps. I turned around, looking for the next test. This time I was prepared.

On the wall of one of the buildings, the streetlights projected the shadow of something approaching. I hid inside a garage entrance in one of the buildings. I didn't want to have another fight. I was tired. As the steps got closer. I moved farther inside the garage to find a car to hide behind. As I walked down the entrance ramp, I realized I was falling victim to the same attitude that had started the last two encounters. If I wanted to stop the continuous stream of creatures once and for all, I had to change my attitude right then and there.

I turned around and went back out onto the street, ready to face whatever monster was coming after me. I heard its steps, felt the vibrations; it was close. Then it turned the corner. An ogre? A troll? Whatever it was, it was a damned ugly monster.

It walked toward me growling and showing its strength. It stopped right in front of me and bent down until its face was inches from mine. Its head was immense, and its eyes burned into me. It roared with such intensity that I struggled not to fall back, but I still stared at it, unblinking.

This time the encounter was short. The monster just stepped back and then left. It was a relief that it ended without a fight. Most importantly though, the message had been sent. I hoped it was clear to whoever was controlling my dream that things had changed.

Now I was after him.

CHAPTER 50

ROB

The street was empty with no trace of the troll. I felt a sense of relief that this could be the end. However, after a few yards, I noticed something different. There was a small hill at the end of the street with a strange building on top; something I hadn't seen before. I didn't pay much attention to it since I was already used to changing conditions within my dreams.

I turned onto the intersecting road to see if my next test was around the corner. I saw the same hill at the end of that road.

I looked in the other direction, and there it was again. It didn't matter which direction I looked—right, left, front, or back—the hill with the house on top was everywhere at once. Well, it was obvious where whoever was controlling my dream wanted me to go.

I walked along the main street, crossing each corner using the pedestrian stepping stones. I had a strange combination of fear and curiosity. I was intrigued about who I was going to find in that house and what he or she wanted from me. I knew it would not be easy, whoever or whatever was. The aggressive behavior of the last three encounters spoke for itself.

Thinking back, I realized something always allowed me to get out of the situation. With the thing in the lake, I was scared to death, but I still managed to conquer my fear. With the robot, I ran at first, then found the courage to face it and defeat it. The troll was the easiest one. I understood from the beginning how to be above my emotions and stand firmly for what I believed. I wondered what creature was waiting for me in the house and if these lessons would be enough to face it.

I stopped at the bottom of the hill. Two big metal gates opened as soon as I approached. An invitation.

Stone stairs led to the top of the hill. The day had become cloudy, gray, and windy. I walked all the way to the top. There was no living plant on the entire hill, only the remains of a dead tree with all its branches reaching away from the house. The exterior of the house reminded me of an old church, with a big tower at the back. The center of the house was set between two wings that almost formed a corridor leading to the main entrance. Stones were all over the place. The walls were falling apart as if a huge fight had taken place there.

I walked between the looming wings and opened the double doors. There was no sound of a haunted house or rusted hinges creaking, as I was expecting. The inside was impressive. A massive room with glass mosaics three stories high. Two windows with curtains undulating with the wind, a wind so smooth that I could hardly feel it. The gray light entering the room created gloomy shapes that appeared and disappeared in time with the curtains.

Everything inside was broken, definitely not a good sign. I kept walking, stepping around the rubble. At the end of the room was a big staircase. Strangely, I couldn't tell if it led up or down. There was no way I was going to try it. On my left was a long corridor with a door at the end. As I approached the door, I heard the soft sound of a piano. Satie's "Gymnopédie No. 1." I had always loved that song.

I slowly opened the door. There was another big room, which was empty except for a grand piano in the center. A person wearing a hooded cloak was sitting at it. The person continued playing without noticing me. I walked around, intrigued by who might be.

It was a woman. Her hood partially covered her face, but I could tell she was beautiful. Light and shadows played slightly to define her flawless cheekbones and gorgeous profile. Her nose, lips, and skin . . . she was perfect.

The piano fell silent on an unresolved chord. "You're hard to crack, my dear Robert," she said. "I never thought it would be so hard to get to you."

I didn't move or say a word. Her voice . . . her voice was a melody. I was surprised to hear her speak my name, but what else could I expect?

She stood up and walked toward me, removing her hood. With each step her figure was revealed before my eyes. I couldn't believe such a beautiful creature could exist. The way she glided toward me, looked at me, said my name . . . it was addictive, obsessive.

This couldn't be happening. She must have altered something inside me, something basic to my sense of self.

"Surprised that I know your name?" she asked. "Don't be."

I couldn't take my eyes off her. I was hypnotized.

"I'm sorry, is my image making you uncomfortable? I can change it if you wish. Perhaps someone more familiar?"

In a flash, she became Michael Jordan.

"Or maybe a businessman?" Now "she" was Bill Gates!

"No, you prefer to see what you were expecting, a villain," she said, transforming into Hitler.

"As you can see," she said, returning to her original form, "appearances can deceive. They don't define who we are. In any case, beautiful women also have the right to be bad girls, don't you agree?"

"Maybe," I replied, only able to articulate a single word.

"Did you enjoy my little creatures?"

"Why did you put me through those tests?"

"Oh, they weren't tests. They were intended to break you."

"They didn't."

"I can see that. Unfortunately, your subconscious doesn't have a proper repertory of options to play with beyond your love of sci-fi and the surreal. In any case, I underestimated your resilience. Definitely a good opponent, with a touch of brilliance."

"What do you want from me?"

"Your soul, of course."

"What?"

"You know the old saying, the devil is in the details. It's a shame that in this case it's not completely true. I always thought we planned for the unexpected, with all possible outcomes accounted for, but honestly, I was not prepared for an anomaly like this one."

"What are you talking about?"

"A mutation . . . a soul mutation, something with a probability of one in a trillion. Absolutely nobody would have considered it a real option. That was really clever of Michael."

Michael? None of this made any sense, and at the same time she seemed to know so much about me.

"Confused? Too narrow a vision to appreciate the whole picture, my dear Robert? My apologies. I should've noticed that you weren't following me. But don't worry; soon you'll see things with your own eyes. As I said, there's only one way this will end. Our way."

"Why wait? Why don't give me a glimpse right now? You can start by telling me who you are. You're one of the Antiscians, aren't you?"

"Oh yes, that's what they like to call us. They think it describes us. But I've told them many times that we're not on opposite sides. Extremes are closer than we imagine. In any case, the question is not who I am but what I represent."

She looked me up and down, probably deciding if it was worth giving me an explanation.

"Since the first human gatherings, there have been special individuals who have been rejected by their equals. Just a few at the beginning, they grew and thrived through time to become one of the most powerful forces for change in humanity. Through the centuries, the basic human emotions of hatred, rancor, jealousy, and revenge, mixed with the blind desire for power, provided the common link among those who share this repudiation of convention. Helped by the trends in injustice and inequality, they created the foundations of the oldest organization that has ever existed, the Eaternum Fraternitatem."

"The everlasting satanic sect," I said.

"Come on, Robert, you're a modern man. Don't cling to outdated superstitions. We're more a fraternity of souls that share, let's say, the same feelings about humankind."

"You mean against humankind."

She shrugged. "Technicalities."

"Why? Why are you doing this?"

"You know how important it is for an organization to grow."

"Don't take me for an idiot. You don't kill people just so they can join your club."

"That's good, Robert. Club? I like it. We might consider changing our name. 'The Latin' is getting old."

"You're destroying humanity, and you're being sarcastic?"

"I'm not. I'm just trying to put things more according to modern times. In any case, I'm sorry. I didn't mean to make you feel that way. So, back to our conversation. Since the beginning of the . . . brotherhood, we've been trying to reach a certain size to deal with some issues—which, by the way, do not concern you and your world. For thousands of years we've been seeking to communicate with the material world to bring new souls directly into our organization. In the beginning, we managed to unconsciously influence some people through dreams. Later, we developed ways to make them feel our presence in the form of hunches. Their superstition and ignorance were weaknesses that fed nicely into our plans, and I can tell you, after centuries, we became very efficient in bringing them into our organization.

"But no matter how hard we tried, it was always impossible to extend the influence beyond a few people at one time. Granted, some of those people had . . . outsized influence—Attila the Hun, Genghis Khan, Caligula, Ivan the Fourth. But it wasn't until the Renaissance of the inspiring Italians, the Industrial Revolution of the ever-proud English, and the technological advances of the almighty Americans that we discovered what we needed to succeed—a rational thinking and scientific approach. Hitler was wonderfully systematic in what he did. Definitely my favorite. He and others paved the way to what we're doing today."

"You're the most evil person I've ever known."

"Thank you for using the word 'person.' It makes me feel like I'm still one of them. But there's no need to be so aggressive. Remember, symmetry is part of everything in the universe, so goodness can't exist alone—which brings me back to why we're here. I'm afraid I have to take you with me, Robert. I'm sure we'll learn a lot from each other."

"Why me?"

"We were ready to take control of all living people. Then we found out about you and Elizabeth, your precious wife. A mutation of your souls has made the unthinkable possible—spontaneous communication between a dead person and a living person. But this little detail can jeopardize all our plans. So, as you can see, I have no other option."

"It seems your last three attempts have failed. What makes you think this time will be different?"

She nodded. "True enough, they didn't work out as expected. But every person has a weakness, a point of fracture from which we can derive what we want. To make sure it will work this time, I asked for help from someone you'll appreciate."

She turned around and walked toward a set of French doors located at the end of the room. "Come with me, Robert." With her harmonious hand, she beckoned me to follow.

The door led outside. A sudden coldness invaded my body.

"Ely!"

I ran to her but almost fell into a huge hole. A chasm separated us. I peered over the edge, but I couldn't see the bottom. On the other side, Ely hung from several bright, incandescent strings, as if electricity was heating them up. She was unconscious.

"What have you done to her?" I said.

"Nothing . . . yet. She's . . . call it asleep. But don't worry; she'll be fine."

It was too much to cope with. I was living through her loss once again. I broke into tears. "I beg you. Please don't hurt her."

"Come on, no more scenes." She helped me stand up. "As I said, she'll be fine. I just need you to do something for me—well, for us."

"Say it!"

"You see this chasm? If you throw yourself into it, I promise I'll let her go."

"What's down there?"

"Nothing, literally. It's a bottomless pit. You'll keep falling until we finish our business out there. Then I'll come back for you."

I was scared for Ely. I would never forgive myself if something happened to her, but I didn't trust the woman to keep her word. I had to wake up from the dream quickly.

"My dear Robert," she said with a distant smile, "at the moment, your body is in a deep coma, not a dream. You can't wake up, and no one can help you."

For the first time in that dream, I was ready to throw the first punch. I stepped up, ready to take her on when a fireball fell close by, throwing me against the wall.

"That won't help," she said. Let's be civilized. You jump in, and I'll free your wife.

"And why should I trust you? How do I know you won't push her into the abyss too?"

"You've got a point." She put her right hand on her chest. "I promise I'll let you both go. If you don't believe me, ask her."

Ely opened her eyes and looked at me.

"Ely—"

"You and your lovely wife will live the rest of eternity together. Isn't it what you both want?"

"And what about you? You'll get what you want."

"Which makes this a win-win situation."

With Ely and me under her control, she would cut the connection between the two worlds, and the pandemic of suicides would probably spread throughout my world.

315

"I don't think most people would consider it a win."

"Does it matter? Are you willing to trade your eternal happiness for a hollow moment of silent glory? Even those who you are trying to save wouldn't reject it."

"And live forever in an empty world? Sorry, try again."

"If you insist."

Something unfolded from her back. Wings! Huge, leathery wings! Then her beautiful appearance changed into an ugly, scary figure.

Something punched my face, knocking me back. What was that? She was still standing a few yards away. I tried to stand when something threw me toward one of the walls. I knew this was a dream, so she couldn't kill me. Still, if I fell into the chasm, I would probably never wake up. I would be in a coma for the rest of my life.

I tried to run to the house but suddenly could not move. I started rising into the air as if something was holding me by my neck.

She walked over and stopped in front of me. "So, Robert, you think you can protect everyone or, even better, change my mind? I think you can see now that you're not the one in charge. And who are you risking everything for? A race that has no shame over enslaving and killing their own? If you don't take responsibility for your actions, I'm not going to accept any blame for mine."

"I know you'd like to think the killer's knife is on our side, but you should look beneath the distorted, twisted footsteps left behind by the actions of your people. When your hoards gather and pray for salvation, they kneel on sand soaked with the blood of centuries of injustice. Last-minute repentance is futile, as your martyrs know. Now Robert, accept your destiny, as everyone must and prepare to unveil your soul for the new beginning."

With a movement of her hands, she threw me toward the abyss. I sank my fingers as deep as I could into the ground and managed to stop on the precipice. It was like having a boulder on top of me, pinning me there. I struggled to get free, but she was too strong, too powerful.

With one leg over the edge, I turned to Ely to look at her for the last time. Her eyes were fixed on me. Then, with clear difficulty, she managed to say one word.

"Architect."

Architect? Of what? This was not the moment to decipher puzzles. I couldn't just give up and let her go. I made a last effort to grab a stone and threw it at the woman, but it was too far away. Unexpectedly, the stone moved closer. Odd, isn't it?

She twitched one finger, and another stone flew and hit mine, breaking both of them into pieces.

The sky became frighteningly dark, and lightning struck nearby.

"Come on, Robert, let's be reasonable." She bent down to look me in the face. "You can't fight me, and you can't outrun me. I built this world. Don't give up everything that matters to you for people you don't even know."

Had she said "build"? Architect? The sky . . . the city. Could that woman have built this world using concepts, images, and rules designed in my subconscious? If she was the builder, was I the architect of this world? That explains the stone. If there were rules in my dreams, was this woman bound by them? Was that what Ely meant?

"You're quite right," I said. "This world might be created by you, but this is my dream, a dream governed by my rules and laws."

I concentrated on removing gravity. The heavy force that kept me almost immobilized disappeared, and I began to float. In fact, everything around me was floating. It was working!

I looked at the sky, and all I had to do was think about it. A lightning bolt hit close to her, and she was thrown against a rock.

Amazing! At that moment I understood Ely's message.

"You may have built this world," I said, "but I control the physical laws governing this dream."

Surprised, she stood up and attacked me again. This time nothing worked. Fireballs, shockwaves, moving statues, I stopped every attack.

Then it was my turn.

Spotting some huge stones from a wrecked wall, I threw them at her with a flick of my hand. They drove her to the floor. I took her in my hands and threw her toward the house. The impact brought part of the roof down on top of her.

At that moment I saw Ely's string break into pieces. She fell down and rolled toward the edge of the abyss. I moved a few rocks in her path.

As long as that bottomless hole existed, so would the threat of falling into a permanent coma. I looked at the abyss and concentrated my thoughts on a simple image. A moment later, the sides of the pit moved toward one another. The vibration and the noise were almost unbearable.

When it closed, Ely was lying a few yards from me. Before I could move toward her, I heard a loud sound behind me.

"Do you think a handful of stones can make any difference?"

I turned back and spoke with a courage that I didn't know I had. "That's enough of this nonsense! You know we can't hurt each other. And you know you can't justify this genocide by the victims' lack of integrity. We are as we are; it's in our nature. It's not our choice, but you, you're far beyond anything we've done. You have chosen destruction as your path. You said before that we should be reasonable. Well, yes, let's."

"Mercy to the innocent? That's not my style, Robert. Pulling back now is a meaningless choice that will only delay the inevitable assimilation of humankind. If you don't have choice, you can't evolve, and no species with such a limited future should exist."

"I won't let you destroy my people, the people I love."

"You say that as if you have a choice. No, Robert, it's I who will stop you. I can simply keep us here forever."

"I don't think so."

Before she had a chance to react, vines burst from the ground, wrapping her body as if they were chains. She struggled to move, but she was finally trapped. The curious thing was, I had nothing to do with those vines.

I ran to Ely and took her in my arms. "My love."

She looked at me with fragile eyes. "You did it."

"*We* did it."

Then the incredible happened.

Close to the house, space itself started to crack. It was like watching a mirror breaking into pieces before my eyes. Light emanated from the cracks until a shining sphere hovered in front of us. Four people with strange uniforms and blades were standing inside it.

The roots wrapped around her body and carried the woman to the glowing ball. She was calm and gave me a last look and a slight smile. Then the four figures cut the roots with their blades and took her away.

As she entered the lighting ball, an earthquake shook the house. Everything started falling apart. Fractures appeared in the ground.

"Rob, listen." Ely's voice was weak but clear.

"Shh . . . everything's going to be fine." I created a shield to protect us from the falling bricks and rocks.

"No, it isn't," she said. "You're dying."

"What? How could that be possible? The woman is gone."

"Look at the light. Who do you see?"

I looked again. This time I recognized a fifth person.

"Your grandfather . . ."

"He's not part of your dream," Ely said. "None of them are. They're real . . . like I am. You have to leave and go back to the city. This house and this hill are her creation. She opened a mind gap in your dream to create it. Now that she's gone, your subconscious is trying to reclaim the lost space. Everything on the hill will be destroyed, including you. Go now. You don't have much time."

"I don't want to lose you again. I'll stay with you, whatever happens."

"My love, there's a time for everyone, and this isn't yours. We'll be together, I promise, but not now."

My eyes filled with tears. "I can't lose you again."

"You never lost me. I'll always be with you."

I held her with passion, I didn't want to let her go.

"Please, you don't have much time."

I stood up, Ely in my arms. I removed the shield and walked toward the bright sphere. Grandpa stepped forward but remained on the other side of the sphere. He extended his arms.

I passed Ely to him.

For a moment we were all touching each other. A peaceful joy invaded me. I felt the kindness and the gratitude of . . . well, apparently, of everyone. For an instant I knew what it felt like to be with them. That was the most enlightening feeling I had ever experienced.

"Go!" she said.

I stepped back and ran as fast as I could. Back through the house and down the long stone staircase to the two main steel gates. As I walked through the entrance, the hill and the house imploded and disappeared, together with the two steel gates at my sides.

CHAPTER 51

ELY

I was too weak to move. I almost lost consciousness after Rob put me in Grandpa's arms. It felt like when I was in Genève.

"Grandpa?"

I didn't see his lips move, and yet I heard his voice, "Keep calm, Ely."

I saw Rob on a bed surrounded by medical equipment. Where was he?

Grandpa took me quickly to a different time, away from the present. He laid me down on the floor of the room. Gabriel, Michael, and five other Gli Custodi warriors appeared and formed a circle around me. They knelt and extended their hands toward me. I couldn't comprehend what was going on, but I tried to be brave. "I'm fine. You don't have to—"

"Ely, listen carefully," Michael said. "You've lost too much soul energy. We don't have much time. We need to bring it back to your normal level. I need you to stop thinking about what happened. Clear your mind of all thoughts. Remove all barriers, and open it to us. Now."

He was ordering me to do something that I didn't want to do. Everyone would be able to see inside me.

"Do it now!"

I felt too fragile to oppose such pressure. As soon as I let my thoughts fade, the Gli Custodi started to emit an aura so intense that I could hardly look at it. Each aura had a different tone. Michael had the whitest and brightest light of all. Grandpa and Grandma were a milky white. Their auras grew, extending more than a foot around them.

Then something amazing happened: the light bent toward me. Their auras melted into a single light ray that penetrated my body. It felt like a strong static-electric shock.

Images of young and old faces, memories of ancient events, flashbacks of intense emotions. For a moment I felt transported across millennia. I experienced the human spiritual evolution through thousands of generations. We all were one, and I became part of the collective of humanity. The shock was so profound that my body started blurring.

Then the aura of each Gli Custodi faded.

"How do you feel?" Grandpa asked.

It was incredible—pins and needles of the soul. I slowly lifted my head and looked at everyone. "Thank you all. I feel much better."

"Don't thank us," Michael said. "It's good to have you back."

"What happened to me?"

Grandpa helped me stand up. "Do you remember Rob's dream?"

"I was trying to find a way into Rob's black box dream when something dragged me in. I don't remember much until I woke up tied up."

"Your bonds drained your soul energy somehow. We don't know what they were, but they were conducting it out of you like a lightning rod."

"So, what did you just do?"

322

"We helped you to stabilize your internal soul energy equilibrium," Michael said.

"I thought soul energy was irreplaceable."

"In most cases, yes. We had to perform an ancient ritual to reestablish your soul level, a ceremony so old that it goes back to the beginning of life on Earth."

Incredible. They had literally fed me with their soul energy. I knew they cared about me, but that sounded like something that wasn't done for an ordinary person.

"Why me?" I asked.

"Because we can't afford to lose you," Michael said.

That was pretty much a non-answer, but I could worry about that later. "Does anyone know what happened to Rob?" I asked. "Is he well?"

"I'm afraid he didn't have time to leave the house," Grandma said. "The doctors are fighting for his life."

I knew it. I had been worried, but he wouldn't listen to me.

Wait, he would only die, something that would happen someday anyway. And that meant we would be together sooner than expected. So why did Grandma look so worried?

"What's going on, Grandma?"

"Rob might remain trapped in his subconscious."

"So?"

"He might not be able to leave his body."

"Grandma, please, what are you trying to say?"

"If he was still on the hill by the time his subconscious regained control of his dream, he probably didn't make it out before the mind gap created by the woman collapsed. In that case, he might still be trapped, unable to make the transition. He will die alongside his body. I'm so sorry, Ely."

That was not fair. After all we had gone through, to end like this, he was about to die without having any chance to fight for his life. It was enough that one of us had to give up everything. This time I was not going to let him go, no matter what.

I wasn't feeling completely recovered, but I managed to move to the present. Grandma followed me without saying a word. Luckily, Michael and the other Gli Custodi understood that I didn't want any other company.

When we arrived, two doctors and two nurses were bringing CPR equipment into Rob's room. I had told him to leave the house. Why didn't he listen to me?

They administered the first electric shock . . . nothing.

Then the second CPR shock. Still nothing. No heartbeat. Losing him was not an option.

Then the impossible occurred to me. Michael and the others had given me a shot of their soul energy to bring me back. What if I gave him part of mine? If it worked with me, maybe it would work with him. I didn't know what that would do to me, but it didn't matter.

"Grandma, I have to do it. It's his last chance." I was counting on her to be listening to my mind.

"We can't do it. It's forbidden."

"You don't have to. I'll do it alone."

"Elizabeth, only certain people are capable of performing the ritual. People with a unique level of spiritual evolution, the old ones."

"Like Michael?"

"Exactly. Grandpa and I only provided backup to him. A resurrection of this kind has only been used a few times in history for special people and under unique circumstances. The last time it was performed was about two thousand years ago."

I understood what she was saying, but I was ready to break any rule as long as Rob survived.

"He needs another chance. He can't be left without a choice, like me."

"Ely, please, it could be very dangerous. And Rob—we don't know how the ritual could affect someone who's still alive. It could have devastating consequences."

"Grandma, if he dies, I'll lose everything. Eternity means nothing without him. I'm prepared to do whatever's necessary no matter the risk."

The doctor was ready to give him a third and probably last CPR shock. I could only hope Grandma was willing to help me.

Without saying a word, she opened her mind and allowed

me to see how the ritual was performed. I needed just a fraction of a second to learn the theory. I just hoped it wasn't the sort of thing that a person had to practice.

I concentrated with all my strength, following the ritual step by step. An instant later, my hands started getting bright, and my aura expanded. It wasn't as bright as the others. I didn't know what that meant, but I didn't have time to ask.

I waited until the doctor applied the third electrical shock. If both shocks hit at the same time, the effect would be stronger, or so I hoped. I was about to test the strength of our connection. If what everybody said was true, I would be able to help him. As the doctor said "clear" for the last time, I touched Rob's heart with my hands, letting my aurora blend with his. The combination of shocks threw me across the room. Then I heard a voice.

"He's back!" a nurse said.

I pulled myself upright and looked at the monitor. Sure enough, the green line was tracing the path of a regular heart-beat. Rob was back.

"Ely, are you alright?" Grandma was standing over me.

"I'm fine." Actually, I was over the moon. "That was—"

"Incredible, wasn't it?"

We stayed silent beside him, watching the monitors until his vital signs stabilized.

In the meantime, Grandpa arrived. Grandma showed him what I had just done.

"How'd you manage that?" he asked. "It's supposed to work only with special people. Only a dozen are known to have this gift."

"I'm not sure, Grandpa, but it didn't seem too difficult."

"The temporary connection that living organisms establish between the Soul and Space dimensions is very weak," Grandpa said. "It works at an extremely short range within the DNA helix at scales below the quark level. In a normal situation, the ritual would have broken the connection without allowing the transition to happen. In other words, you could have killed Robert. Forever."

"But I didn't."

"I can see that. Maybe both shocks compensated each other,

producing a net-zero effect, I don't know. Something between the two of you . . . what a foolish girl."

Grandpa and Grandma moved to a corner of the room to converse. To my surprise, I couldn't penetrate their mental barriers. Grandpa was definitely fed up with me. If it really was forbidden, I would be in trouble.

"Am I missing anything?" I asked.

"Of course not," Grandma said. "I'm just so happy for Rob."

Rob? Why not us? Her silence told me more than her words. I stared at her, waiting for a better answer, but it was Grandpa who spoke.

"I don't know how else to say it, Ely. It's going to be hard for you, but from now on you can no longer intervene in his life. What you did today is against all rules. He has to live his own life, and you have to respect that."

"But if—"

"You both have a gift that should not be abused. He has to move on, making his own decisions, whether they're good ones or not. Sweetheart, don't make it more difficult. That's the way it has to be."

Unconsciously I knew this moment would arrive sooner or later. This beautiful, perfect, bucolic situation where we could still be together was not normal. "How much time do I have?"

"The quicker, the better," he said.

"Do I have the chance to say goodbye?"

"Of course, my darling." Grandma said. "Don't feel any pressure, but could you do it tonight?"

I nodded.

Everyone left. At least they were considerate enough to leave me alone with him.

I spent the afternoon on the sofa. I wanted simply to be at his side. For the first time I saw him calm and serene, with a different light in his eyes. I waited in the room until night, when he fell asleep.

It was a busy road full of shops and cafes. It reminded me of our trip to Paris when we spent days walking the city's many

326

pretty petit streets. The area was dynamic, people walking in all directions, cafés full of couples having engaging conversations. It was the perfect setting except for one thing: Rob. I couldn't find him anywhere.

I walked along the road looking for him. It was his dream, so he had to be there somewhere. I stopped in front of a traditional café on a corner and looked inside through a big glass wall. He was there on one of two chairs around a small, round table. A couple of glasses were in front of him, one with red wine, the other empty. He was concentrated on his thoughts. He seemed to be unaware of where he was, totally disconnected, even though it was his dream.

How would he react? Was I going to cause him even more pain? Wouldn't it be better to leave his dream without talking to him anymore? Of course, that would be the simplest and easiest way.

No. This time I wanted to say goodbye, and no matter how hard it was, I had to keep my emotions under control. I didn't want to break his heart again. I needed to face it, the quicker the better.

"Here's my hero," I said, approaching the table.

He stood up and gave me a loving embrace. It was going to be as hard as I'd guessed.

"You're alright," he said.

"Of course I am. I was protected by my personal bodyguard."

"You know it wasn't like that. I was worried that something could've happened to you."

"Don't be. As you can see, I'm fine. We were the ones who were worried about you. There was a point when I thought you were going to die."

"Because I saw what I wasn't supposed to see."

He recognized that there was something strange about that vision, but he didn't know how threatening the destruction of the house was. Going into detail would be pointless. It was over, and it had ended well.

"You saw those people because, for just a moment, you crossed over to my world."

"I wasn't afraid."

"That's good. That'll come in handy someday. But leave it to destiny to decide how and when that will be. We don't need to hurry things."

"So you know when it's going to happen?"

That was the only thing I wasn't sure about.

"No. But I know I'll be beside you when the time comes." Now was the moment; I had to say it. "Until then, you have to think about your life and how you're going to live it."

"Are you trying to say goodbye?"

Suddenly, I had no more words. I was struggling to find the strength to carry on conversation. I knew I would not be able to keep myself together for much longer.

"Ely, you can't go away like this. You left me once. I won't let you leave me a second time."

Was he right? After all we'd gone through, should we follow the rules? Should I let them put our relationship at risk? Separate us again?

He looked at me with sad eyes. I wished I could take my words back. "Rob—"

"Sorry. I'm not making this easy, am I?"

He was the one most affected by my departure, and yet he was ready to give up on me. Once again, his courage was the source of mine.

"It's hard for both of us," I said, "but that's the way it should be. Having you close to me again was a gift that showed me how precious every moment we spent together was. But above all, it taught me never to give up. I'm counting the days until we'll be together again."

"A lifetime without you," he said.

"No, waiting for eternity."

That was it. I knew it was the last time I would be in his dreams. Maybe the last time I would ever be with him. But I knew what my last words had to be.

"I love you."

CHAPTER 52
ROB

A shiver went through my body.

"We have him. He's back."

I opened my eyes. Everything was blurry. Too much light to focus. Silhouettes surrounded me and voices that I didn't recognize.

"Robert, can you hear me?" someone asked.

"Where . . .?"

"Don't worry. Everything's fine."

Nothing was making sense. I couldn't move my body. I kept hearing voices in the background. Everything was confusing.

"Blood pressure 110 over 65, heartbeat stabilizing, doctor."

"Good. I want a nurse to be with him twenty-four seven. We have to monitor him closely until we're sure he's out of danger."

"Yes, Doctor."

"Take it slowly, Robert." a female voice said. "You'll have time to talk later. Now stay calm. A nurse will be here in case you need something."

I didn't have the strength to reply. I guessed I didn't have to.

After a while, I could feel my hands and legs again, and my vision cleared. The nurse was looking at me with more kindness than most people would ever show to a stranger.

"Where am I?" I asked as she checked the saline solution.

"In the hospital."

"What hospital?"

"The University of Virginia Medical Center."

"Why am I here? What happened to me?"

"You went into cardiac arrest."

I wasn't very good at talking yet, but she was even worse. I stared at her, waiting for more details.

"The doctor performed CPR and, well, here you are."

I looked around. I was alone in the room. After a cardiac arrest, I would have expected Peter to be at my side, or at least a guard from the FBI. Of course, they must have been asked to remain outside.

"Could you ask them to come in, please?" I said.

"Sorry?"

"The people outside. I'd like to see them."

"There's nobody outside the room."

I couldn't keep it in anymore. "OK, you've got to give me more details. What do you mean there's nobody outside?"

"Well, nobody apart from a soldier. There were some people here at the beginning, but after a few days, they left and haven't come back."

"Wait, a few days? How long have I been here?"

"Ten days since you were brought here from ER."

Ten days? It felt like moments ago that I left Ely in my dream. If nobody was there, they had to be at the Pentagon. The pandemic was probably still spreading. Ten days! It was time for another wave.

As I spun apocalyptic scenarios, the doctor entered the room. "So, how's the hibernating bear? You scared some important people."

"Sorry, Doctor."

"You've been in a coma for ten days."

Coma? The woman, the abyss . . .

"Do you remember the last thing that happened to you?"

My silence answered her question.

"I see. It seems you collapsed on the emergency stairs at the Pentagon. You lost consciousness as a result of hitting your head on one of the steps. You've been lucky to recover so quickly."

I remembered the stairs, I was supposed to attend a meeting when . . . Jessica! They were probably still trying to stop the pandemic.

"Sorry, Doctor, but I can't stay here any longer. I have to go." I tried to get up.

She put her hand on my shoulder. "You're not going anywhere. We have to run some tests to make sure you're alright."

"Don't you see? Every minute can make the difference."

"The kind of brain trauma you've had can have serious consequences in terms of the way you walk, speak, and think."

I didn't care about my condition. "Doctor, the pandemic, they need my help. We need to stop it."

She looked straight into my eyes, surprised at first, and then she smiled.

"Calm down. It's under control. We haven't had a new case since last week. It's over."

I let myself fall back onto the bed. No more suicides! Finally, we had been able to stop it completely. I had been hoping to hear that for so long.

"We're going to run some tests today. For now, you must rest. Don't worry if you experience some disorientation and confusion. Your mind needs to recover from the trauma."

She left the room, relatively satisfied with my condition. To be honest, I hadn't listened to much of what she said.

The strategy worked.

That woman in my dream, she must have been one of the leaders of the Antiscians . . . no, the Everlasting Brotherhood. In any case, I hoped Ely's people had taken care of her.

An hour later, the nurse took me to a lower floor, where I spent the rest of the afternoon getting poked and prodded in various ways. The last one was an MRI scan. The doctor was there.

"Well, the scan still shows signs of contusions. Are you sure you don't remember anything?"

"Not a thing. Do I have anything to worry about?"

"Not at all. Your brain is functioning perfectly, which surprises me, to be honest. We placed you in the Intensive Care Unit immediately after your arrival to the ER. You were initially diagnosed in coma level seven GCS. We monitored your brain activity for days, during which we unexpectedly detected moments where your brain was producing only delta waves."

"Which means . . ."

"You moved back and forth between a coma and deep sleep. We thought you might recall some of these transitions, something that could give us a clue to explain this bizarre behavior."

"As I said before, no recollection whatsoever. Sorry, Doctor."

"Never mind. The important thing is that you're back. We'll keep you overnight to monitor your progress. If there are no complications, tomorrow morning you'll be free to go home."

"Thanks, Doctor." At least there was evidence. It was not my imagination; I really had been dreaming.

After she left the scanner room, a couple of nurses took me back to my room. I was feeling much better by then.

The medical team kept coming and going for the rest of the afternoon. I wasn't really interested in the results of the tests. I knew I was fine and that what had happened wasn't going to show up on an MRI. But I wished I knew Ely's condition. Strangely, despite all that had happened, I was not worried about her. I was calm and serene, and that was a good sign.

I turned the TV on during dinner. The news was all about the end of the pandemic, with unending specials about the aftermath. It was heartbreaking. Memorials to the victims were being held across the country as symbols for the millions that had to be mass cremated or buried in mass graves. Too many had died too quickly. It was going to be a very difficult period for people to move past. As I surfed through the channels, something didn't make sense to me. I was expecting to see a general grief among the people interviewed, but instead they were sharing joy and gratitude.

I thought maybe it had to do with coming to terms with the relief that the danger was over and that the sadness for their losses was still under the surface. Maybe the sense of well-being that I felt was happening elsewhere too. It was difficult to explain; I just felt it.

The night passed without much to do. I fell asleep quickly, hoping to see Ely. Dreaming with her had become the oxygen of my life.

I was sitting in a café, alone. The tables around me were occupied by couples in animated conversation. Usually, it was Ely who let me know I was dreaming. This time I was already aware of it, and she was nowhere to be seen. I needed desperately to find her, to be sure she was alright.

Worried about the well-being of my dead wife, what a magnificent feeling. I had an uncontrollable need to go to sleep and wake up in this dream world of mine. Maybe this was why many people never returned from insanity.

The wine tasted familiar. I checked the label—a Barolo vintage 1988. Could I tell the difference between that bottle and a real one? I had trespassed the line a long time ago, and now I was surrendered to her wishes.

"Here's my hero."

I turned around, and there she was. I didn't say anything, just embraced her with all my heart.

"You're alright." I whispered.

"Of course I am. I was protected by my personal bodyguard."

"You know it wasn't like that. I was worried that something could've happened to you."

"Don't be. As you can see, I'm fine. It was us who were worried about you. There was a point where I thought you were going to die."

"Because I saw what I wasn't supposed to see."

She nodded. "You saw those people because, for just a moment, you crossed over to my world."

"I wasn't afraid."

"That's good. That'll come in handy someday. But leave it to destiny to decide when that will be. We don't need to hurry things."

"So you know when it's going to happen?"

"No, but I know I'll be beside you when the time comes. Until then, you have to think about your life and how you're going to live it."

I didn't like the sound of my life. It was too cold. "Are you trying to say goodbye?"

Her silence was all I needed.

"Ely, you can't go away like this. You left me once. I won't let you leave me a second time."

I looked at her as the sound of my own words echoed in my mind. Leaving me again? Nonsense. I was with her. She had never left me.

"Rob . . ."

"Sorry, I'm not making this easy, am I?"

"It's hard for both of us," she said, "but, that's the way it should be. Having you close to me again was a gift that showed me how precious every moment we spent together was. But above all, it taught me never to give up. I'm counting the days until we'll be together again."

"A lifetime without you"

"No," she smiled softly, "waiting for eternity."

I knew it was the last time I was going to see her. I clutched her hands.

"I love you." Those were her last words, and then she just disappeared.

"I love you too," I said to the emptiness.

A noise woke me up.

"Good morning, Mr. Kline." It was the nurse opening the door to my room. "How do you feel today?" She opened the blinds. The sunshine warmed every corner of the room. It was a gorgeous day. Strangely, I felt calm and serene.

"I feel like I've been resurrected, like a new man," I said.

"That's appropriate for someone who just came back from the dead." She continued looking outside the window. "It's a perfect day, isn't it? I hope our new man is ready for his new life. If you feel well enough, you can leave the hospital after the doctor sees you."

That was superb. I was so anxious to see the sky again, to breathe fresh air. The nurse suggested I should eat breakfast while I waited for the doctor. I agreed. She had been very kind to me. A person of few words but very supportive.

As I expected, the doctor found no reason to keep me in the hospital. An hour later, I was ready to leave. I asked the nurse to call for a taxi. I wanted to spend some time alone before calling Peter.

Everybody I came across on my way out of the hospital was very kind to me. I wondered what was special about that hospital. Definitely the human resources department had an eye for good people.

I took the elevator to the ground floor. When the doors opened, two men were waiting for me.

"Mr. Kline, would you mind coming with us?" one of them said.

After what had happened over the last few weeks, I had learned to spot special agents. "Is there a problem?"

"Not at all, sir. This won't take long."

They accompanied me outside the hospital. A black SUV was parked in front. As we approached, the back door opened.

"Can I talk to you?" a familiar female voice asked.

"Jessica." I couldn't help but be a bit cautious. The military facility was not a place to which I wanted to return. "I'm guessing you haven't come here to arrest me again."

She didn't reply, so I got in.

"What about the pandemic?" I asked as the vehicle began to move. "Did we really stop it?"

"Yes, it's under control. Thanks to you and your friends, we managed to stop it from spreading across the country. And the world."

"I was heading to meet you at the conference room," I said. "I remember I was in a hurry, so I took the emergency staircase. I don't remember anything after that."

"It happened quickly. After Peter and David identified the

new pattern, we broadcast the information to all control points across the country. Support teams were mobilized immediately to the new locations. For locations where no support was available, we tweeted a message of help to the residents of the area. It was impressive how fast people stopped calling 911. The number of calls started reducing slowly until about one hour later when it dropped by half in a few minutes. We're all shocked and gloriously happy. The way the population behaved was simply amazing. It was as if the number of people helping each other reached a critical mass that triggered a collective reaction across the country. A few hours later, we knew the pandemic was under control. It happened exactly as you said." It was evident that she had harbored doubts she hadn't mentioned.

"I suspect there are a lot of people to thank."

"Don't be humble. You know what I mean. Everyone knows we were lost until you arrived with your crazy idea of a self-cure."

"Crazy, but it worked. Maybe it was inspiration."

"Or divine intervention gave us a second chance."

I didn't know how to respond. Her comment took me by surprise. She was so close to the truth.

"Anyway," she said, "talking about divine things, there's something I want to ask you."

"Shoot."

"When we returned to the control room, searching for you, I found Peter looking at a board. There was a sign, a sign you drew before you disappeared, just above the papers with the new locations, unfolded as if left there on purpose for someone to read. Peter said it was your wife's secret signature, and—"

"It was just a sign," I said, though I didn't know how long I could keep hiding the truth. "A desperate reaction. I thought it might bring us luck. Nothing more."

"Luck? There will be an investigation, and we'll do whatever is necessary to understand what happened."

I knew I hadn't convinced her, but I was not going to say anything else. Apparently, she realized that.

"The president wants to talk to you, privately."

I should have felt overwhelmed by the invitation, but meeting the president was not one of my priorities at that moment. "It's an honor that I would prefer to postpone."

"Of course. Would you like me to take you somewhere?"

"Just stop here. I need to feel people around me again."

The SUV stopped on a street full of shops, most of them empty. Not to be surprised as people would be pulling their lives back together. Before I got out, she touched my hand kindly. "Robert, the country is in your debt. Whatever you need, and I mean anything, call me." She gave me her business card. There was a handwritten phone number at the back.

Her tender smile showed me what I had always suspected. Behind the image of a tough, cold woman was a person who, in her own way, believed in me. I smiled back.

As I walked away from the SUV, she lowered her window. "Robert, don't be surprised by what you're about to see. It's a new world out there."

Then she left.

I didn't know the city, so I just kept walking without a specific location in mind. After an hour or so, I ended up in a circular junction with a farmers' market. The same kindness that I saw in the hospital was evident in the behavior of the few people around. Kindhearted people were talking to everyone, looking after one another.

I stopped in front of a news kiosk near the market. Every newspaper headline had the same message: "A New Era Upon Us." Not even one incident in the last week. Business leaders were rethinking labor policies. Wall Street was redefining stock market rules. Democrats and Republicans were working together to approve social laws . . . Something had definitely changed.

While I was reading the newspapers, a stranger approached me. "It's different, isn't it?

"Sorry?" I said. I had no idea who he was, and judging by the way he was dressed, he was homeless.

"How people behave."

"What do you mean?"

"I was one of those infected by the virus. When I was about to cut my veins, a red Ferrari stopped beside me. I don't remember much, but after a while I found myself in the car beside the driver. He was holding my arms. I was saved by a passing Wall Street hedge fund manager. Can you explain that?"

I shook my head.

"Neither can I, but I can tell you, I've never seen a look like his. It was pure compassion."

"Why are you telling me this?"

"I saw you from the other side of the road. It felt like you needed some help." Then, as quickly as he appeared, he walked away, but before he disappeared into the crowd, he turned around and gestured with his arms. "It's all around you."

Everything was so peaceful, and yet I was surrounded by so many people. The hospital, the TV news . . . could it be possible that the extreme pain and hopeless desperation that we all experienced brought out the best qualities inside every one of us? We were so close to being wiped out, and the only thing that saved us was our collective willingness to set aside self-interest and care about our fellows. Was that man right? Was a new Renaissance at our doorstep? Had we finally changed our nature and overcome the ultimate human weakness: our lack of compassion for our fellows? Only time would tell if it was a long-lasting lesson. The only change I was sure would last forever was the one that had happened inside me.

I kept walking, wishing I could shout out the real cause behind what had happened, but I couldn't. How could I spin a story like that without evidence? How could I show the world that the pandemic was not a pandemic and that Jessica's statement about divine intervention was true? It might have been the biggest stroke of luck in human history. A man with paranoid schizophrenia hallucinated that he was dreaming of his dead wife and just happened to stop Armageddon.

Did it matter? After all, however it happened, it happened for a reason. I was left with the feeling that I had been the instrument of something much bigger, something beyond my comprehension.

At the moment, I had a long journey ahead, and I was ready to walk it to the end. I had learned one lesson from all of this: never to be afraid of what was before me. I was going to live a life of plenty, treasuring every moment, every encounter, knowing they would remain with me forever.

I had never been a believer, but for the first time in my life, I truly understood what it meant to be a man of faith.

"Wait for me, my love."

CHAPTER 53
ELY

I left Rob's dream feeling frustrated, running away from a reality that I was not prepared to face. I headed south. I stopped when I found ice everywhere. I moved up above the clouds and saw only white, all the way to the horizon. I moved back in time to maybe 1243 or so; I wasn't sure. I didn't care as long as it was far from everything, everyone.

I knew I had been lucky, but I didn't feel that way. I had been given the chance to be with Rob after I left, a gift that I was now forced to give away and with it perhaps the last chance to keep him. I left open the door for him to build a new life, a possibility that I was unprepared to accept. How could I let him go if I loved him so much?

Was I denying what was in front of my eyes? Maybe I should have been honest and asked myself if Rob was prepared to live the rest of his life alone.

I had friends who had gotten remarried and rebuilt their lives with another person. If this was a real possibility for some people, was it also an option for Rob? Could he find someone else to cure the pain that I had inflicted on him? How could I accept that?

"It was never my decision!" I shouted. I was being driven crazy by the uncontrollable fear of being left out of Rob's life. "It's our destiny! We're meant to be together!"

Was destiny my last hope? Why not? After all, we were born the same day. Our families lived all their lives together next door to each other. We grew up sharing every moment. In fact, I could not recall any part of my life that he wasn't in. It was like we had lived a single life between us.

Now, after my departure, our union was supposed to be stronger than ever. A unique union between two souls with a level of connection that extended across worlds, a once-in-a-lifetime event, they said. With this background, could I think of any alternative other than being together? Actually, did any other option for our future exist? Was that what I could call destiny?

But no matter how much I wanted it to be true, I couldn't believe in destiny. I was a scientist, and as such I was trained to think in terms of facts. I could calculate the probability that two independent events could happen at the same time and place. I could calculate it for three, four, five, or ten events. But a lifetime of events shared by two supposedly independent people? The probability of that happening was effectively zero. And yet, looking back on it, it seemed clear we were born to fight the final wave of killings, as if everything was laid out in advance, following a predefined order, a fixed plan, a single purpose. I couldn't make any sense of that. There was no explanation, at least not a scientific one.

"Why, why, why?" I asked.

"That's always the question," a female voice replied.

"Mom! Dad!"

They appeared at my side. I hugged them with all my strength. I was so happy to see them.

"I'm sorry. It's just . . . how did you find me?"

"Everyone is worried about you. We've been watching you."

"Don't tell me it's going to be like that from now on," I said.

"No, my darling." Dad replied. "Nobody will be looking over your shoulder anymore. You're free to do whatever you wish with your life." Freedom of choice; for the first time I was so afraid of that gift.

"But before that," Mom said, "there's still something left to do."

"More problems?" I asked.

She smiled kindly. She was calm, serene. I wished I could have that peace someday.

"Sometimes, sweetheart, climbing the mountain teaches more than the view from on top," my father said. "That battle going on inside you between what you think is possible but unlikely and what you believe is impossible but apparently happened . . . well, it's not which side finally turns out to be right that matters. Reaching the point of confronting and doubting your fundamental dogmas has opened your heart and made you ready to embrace the truth."

I looked at him. Now more than ever I needed his guidance, his words of wisdom.

"You're a scientist; you believe in facts. So let me give you some. One of the amazing things about the universe is its perfection, right?"

I nodded. From where we were above the clouds, we could look at a horizon where earth and space blended smoothly together with an undetectable harmony. It was pure perfection.

"Everything moves and interacts with such incredible coordination and synchronization. Some people think it's just the way it is, the result of self-ordering mechanisms within the natural state of chaos. But you agree with me that, even though it may look like that, everything has its place, its role . . . its purpose. If everything has a reason to exist in this universal order, some kind of a master plan must define who does what, where, and when."

Dad paused for a moment. "Ely, you're right about you and Robert. You were meant to be together. You've been prepared from the beginning, so you both could play the role you have

342

just played. It was not the product of order within chaos or coincidence or a soul mutation. You've been part of a plan carefully crafted by someone who works in mysterious ways. He reveals himself in the lives of people in the same way he did with both of you. You have performed your duties to perfection. Now you're ready to meet him."

My Mom took my hand. "Come with us, Ely, we have to pay a visit."

I remained static, silent. Only one thought echoed inside me: *Oh my God!*

Printed in Great Britain
by Amazon

65982756R00206